lastnight

STEPHEN LEATHER

lastnight

HODDER &
STOUGHTON

First published in Great Britain in 2014 by Hodder & Stoughton
An Hachette UK company

2

Copyright © Stephen Leather 2014

A CIP catalogue record for this title is available from the British Library

Hardback ISBN 978 1 444 74265 7
Trade Paperback ISBN 978 1 444 74266 4
Ebook ISBN 978 1 444 74267 1

Typeset in Plantin Light by Palimpsest Book Production Limited,
Falkirk, Stirlingshire

Printed and bound by Clays Ltd, St Ives plc

Hodder & Stoughton policy is to use papers that are natural, renewable
and recyclable products and made from wood grown in sustainable forests.
The logging and manufacturing processes are expected to conform
to the environmental regulations of the country of origin.

lastnight

Superintendent Ronald Chalmers slotted a piece of chewing gum into his mouth and studied the burned corpse laid out on the stainless-steel table. He had been a police officer for more than twenty-five years and had seen more than his fair share of dead bodies over that time but this one was definitely in the top five when it came to making him nauseous. Chalmers had put a dab of Vicks VapoRub under his nose before entering the room but even so the stench of barbecued meat was strong enough to make his stomach churn.

A deep Y-shaped incision had been made from the top of each shoulder down to the sternum and then the cut had continued to the pubic bone deviating to the left of the navel. The cut always went to the left. Chalmers didn't know why, but it was always done that way. The internal organs had been removed and preserved. Then the top of the skull had been sawn off and the brain had been placed in a solution of formalin.

The superintendent looked over at the coroner who had performed the post-mortem. She was a heavy-set woman with short permed hair and thick-framed spectacles. Her name was Lesley MacDiarmid and Chalmers had known her for the best part of ten years. 'So what do you think?' asked Chalmers.

'Definitely dead,' growled MacDiarmid.

Chalmers sighed. MacDiarmid was known for her dour Scottish sense of humour but she was also the best coroner in London, by far. 'So tell me what I need to know,' said Chalmers patiently. 'Is this the body of Jack Nightingale?'

MacDiarmid flicked a sheet of paper over and stared at the sheet under it. 'No question,' she said. 'We fast-tracked the DNA analysis and compared it with the sample you gave us. There's no doubt.'

'And cause of death?'

MacDiarmid opened her mouth to say something sarcastic but she saw from the look on the superintendent's face that he wasn't in the mood so she studied her report instead. 'The fire was the actual cause. There was smoke and fire damage to his lungs so he was alive when the fire started. But he was in no state to get out. Someone had clubbed him over the back of the head with the proverbial blunt instrument.'

'Any thoughts as to what that might have been?' asked Chalmers.

'A hammer, possibly. Something circular and metallic. Three distinctive blows. Two at the back of the head and one more on the top.'

'So someone hit him twice and then again on the top of his head as he went down?'

'I would say so, yes,' said MacDiarmid. 'The fire was presumably started in an attempt to dispose of the body.'

'That sounds about right,' said Chalmers. 'The body was found in a burned building and the arson investigator thinks that the fire started in the room where the body was found.'

'And they found the accelerator, of course?'

'Petrol, they said.'

MacDiarmid nodded. 'It was poured over him, no doubt about that. Someone wanted to make sure he burned. They probably assumed that he was dead already.'

'But there's no doubt about the ID?'

'There's no mistake with DNA,' said MacDiarmid. 'Back in the day when we needed fingerprints and dental records then a good fire might well have made identification impossible, but these days you'd have to reduce a body to ash and a petrol-based fire isn't going to do that. You'd need a crematorium furnace.' She looked over at him and raised her eyebrows. 'Was he one of yours?'

'Used to be,' said Chalmers. 'He left the force a few years ago. He's a private detective now.' He forced a smile and corrected himself. 'Was a private detective.'

'I'm sorry,' said MacDiarmid. 'Do you have any suspects?'

Chalmers shook his head. 'Place was burnt to the ground pretty much so there's not much evidence to go on. He had more than his fair share of enemies and we're working through his client list.'

The doors to the post-mortem room opened and a young man in a blue suit mimed holding a phone to his ear. 'Call for you, Leslie,' he said.

MacDiarmid patted Chalmers on the shoulder. 'I have to take this, it's about a suicide we had last night.'

As she left, Chalmers stared down at the burned corpse chewing thoughtfully. Eventually he sighed and shook his head, almost sadly. 'Well, Jack, I always said you'd burn in Hell. Looks like I wasn't far off the mark.'

I

TWO WEEKS EARLIER

The church service had been straightforward enough. A few hymns, a couple of prayers, and three readings. Jenny McLean had given the third reading, brushing away her tears with a lace handkerchief as she spouted some nonsense about death being a beginning and not an end. Twice she looked down from the lectern and caught Nightingale's eye and he had smiled encouragingly. Nightingale sat towards the back of the church. The irony wasn't lost on him that the man being lauded in the picturesque sixteenth-century church with its steepled bell tower and religious stained-glass windows was a confirmed Satanist who Nightingale was fairly sure had long ago sold his soul to a demon from Hell.

There were more than two hundred mourners crammed into the church. Plenty of famous faces were dotted around including three Members of Parliament, two newspaper editors, and writers, actors and television personalities who regularly appeared in the glossy Sunday supplements. Marcus Fairchild had been a truly evil man but he'd had a lot of friends.

Several times during the service Nightingale had noticed

a group of men in the front pews turning around to look in his direction. There were half a dozen of them, big men in black suits, with greying hair and hard eyes. They were sitting together but barely spoke to each other and didn't appear to be singing or praying.

Jenny was sitting on the right-hand side of the church, in between her mother and father. Nightingale didn't know if Fairchild had any family, as far as he knew he wasn't married and didn't have children. It looked as if Jenny was the only mourner still in her twenties, the majority seemed to be aged fifty and older. Grey hair, parchment skin and watery eyes were the norm.

Once the ceremony was over, the six men who had been sitting close to the front acted as pallbearers and carried the coffin outside. As they walked by, two of them turned to stare blankly at Nightingale. The mourners filed after the coffin, starting from the front pews and working backwards. By the time it was Nightingale's turn to join the procession, the coffin was at the graveside and the vicar was preparing to speak again, the wind ruffling the pages of the Bible in his hands.

Nightingale stood at the entrance to the church and watched as the pallbearers used thick green ropes to gently lower the coffin into the ground. Jenny was standing to the right of the vicar. She'd obtained a yellow flower from somewhere and was holding it to her chest. Standing behind her was her father, James, a big man with an expensive tan and short curly hair. He had his arm around his wife, Jenny's mother. Melissa McLean was in her early forties, a decade or so younger than her husband and had the look of a former model – soft, glossy blonde hair and high cheekbones. Her eyes were red from crying and she kept resting her head on her husband's shoulder. They were standing close to two other people that Nightingale recognised – Marc Allen, overweight with several chins and drooping eyelids, and his much younger and prettier wife, Sally. Also among the mourners Nightingale saw Lesley Smith, a Channel Four newsreader who had just had her first novel published, and Wendy Bushell, a sixty-something woman with shoulder-length grey hair who worked for the billionaire George Soros. He had met them once at a dinner with Jenny's parents. Marcus Fairchild had been at the same dinner. Standing some way behind them was a white-bearded man with red veins threaded through his bulbous nose. Lachie Kennedy was the gamekeeper on the estate owned by Jenny's parents. Kennedy was with a white-haired woman who was clutching a black handbag to her chest. Nightingale had never met her but he assumed it was Kennedy's wife.

The vicar was in full flow now. The wind helped carry his voice over to where Nightingale was standing but the words were unintelligible. Jenny held the flower up to her lips and kissed it softly. Nightingale knew she was going to toss it into the grave and he had a sudden urge to run over to her, grab the flower and tell her the truth about her godfather, that Marcus Fairchild had been a member of a Satanic group that believed that sacrificing children was the way to amass power and money and to guarantee a place at Satan's side in the fires of Hell. She wouldn't believe him, of course. Who in their right mind would? Marcus Fairchild had been a family friend from before she was born, and his death had hit her hard. Her parents wouldn't believe him, either. The only people who would believe Nightingale would be those mourners who were also in the Order of Nine Angles and they were all sworn to secrecy.

As Nightingale stood watching Jenny toss the flower into the grave he was aware of two men moving up behind him. He turned to find them looming over him. One was close to six and half feet tall, the other only a couple of inches shorter. They both had close-cropped hair and were wearing black raincoats.

'Jack Nightingale?' growled the taller of the two men in an Essex accent.

'Who wants to know?' asked Nightingale, trying to sound more confident than he felt.

'Don't fuck around,' said the man. 'Are you Nightingale or not?'

'Of course it's him,' said his companion. His accent was Essex too, but smoother and more polished, as if he'd gone to a halfway decent university before joining the police.

'What do you want?' asked Nightingale.

The shorter of the two men reached inside his raincoat and Nightingale stepped back, half expecting a gun to appear in the man's hand.

The man smiled. 'Nervous type, huh?' He took a Metropolitan Police warrant card holder from his coat and held it out. His companion did the same and they flicked them open at the same time to reveal two warrant cards. Detective Inspector Jon Cooper and Detective Constable Andy Peters. Peters was the taller of the two.

'Superintendent Chalmers wants to see you,' said Cooper.

'I'm in the middle of something here,' said Nightingale. He gestured over at the grave. 'In case you hadn't noticed.'

'Body's in the ground, looks like it's all over to me,' said Cooper. 'And it's not as if you're family, is it?'

'What's this about?'

'Superintendent Chalmers will tell you himself,' said Cooper. 'Please don't give me a hard time, I've had a really shitty week.'

Nightingale looked at his watch, then over at the grave where Jenny was standing looking tearfully down at the coffin. Her mother and father moved to stand either side of her, offering moral and physical support. The inspector was right: Nightingale wasn't family. He was only at the funeral because Jenny had asked him to be there. And there was definitely something hypocritical about his attendance, considering that he was the reason Marcus Fairchild was dead. 'Okay,' said Nightingale. 'Let's go.'

The black Vauxhall Vectra came to a halt outside Bethnal Green police station, a nondescript brick building with the traditional blue light over the main entrance. 'I'll walk him in,' said Cooper. 'You can park the car and meet up in the incident room.'

Cooper climbed out and waited until Nightingale joined him on the pavement. 'You used to be in the job, right?' said Cooper as the car drove away.

'Yeah. CO19, and I was a negotiator.'

'Wish they'd give me a gun,' said Cooper. 'These days that's just about the only way a copper is going to get any respect.'

'Have I got time for a cigarette?'

Cooper looked at his watch. 'Yeah, go on.'

Nightingale took out his pack of Marlboro, lit one and offered the pack to the inspector. 'I'm a Rothmans man myself, but beggars can't be choosers I suppose,' said the detective, helping himself to a cigarette and then bending down so that Nightingale could light it for him. The two men blew smoke up at the leaden sky. 'When did you leave?'

'Three years ago.'

'And you're a private eye now?'

'Yeah, for my sins.'

'How's that working out for you?'

Nightingale shrugged. 'Pays the bills, pretty much.'

'What sort of jobs do you get?'

'Insurance work, checking that people are as injured as they say they are. Divorce, following unfaithful spouses. Tracing people. The usual stuff.' He gestured at the main entrance. 'What does Chalmers want?'

'He didn't say, just said he wanted you in his office ASAP.'

'Anything happen to have caused his sudden desire to see me?' Nightingale held smoke deep in his lungs.

'We just do as we're told,' said Cooper.

'What, are you like his Number Two?'

'Nah, I only met him two days ago. He's been brought on to our Murder Investigation Team. I'm based here, he's just visiting.'

'You got a murder?'

'Five murders. Goths. You know the type. Dress in black and listen to gloomy music. We've got a serial killer who likes to butcher them.'

Nightingale nodded. 'I read about it in the papers. How's it going?'

Cooper scowled. 'Not great,' he said. He flicked away what was left of his cigarette. 'We'd better get a move on.'

Nightingale took a last drag on his cigarette and followed the detective inside. They went through a door and along a corridor to the lifts. 'Do you mind if we walk up?' asked Nightingale.

'Are you on a fitness kick?'

'I just don't like lifts,' said Nightingale. 'Never have done.'

'Are you serious?'

'I can walk up and you can take the lift. It's no big deal.'

The detective chuckled. 'No sweat, I could probably do with the exercise.' He pushed open a fire door and took Nightingale up the stairs to the third floor. They headed down a corridor and Cooper stopped at an office on the left and knocked on the door before opening it. Chalmers was sitting behind a desk looking at a computer terminal. As Nightingale walked into the office, Chalmers gestured with his chin at Cooper and the detective left, closing the door behind him.

'I was at a funeral, Chalmers.'

'Anyone close?' said Chalmers, his eyes fixed on the screen in front of him.

'Not really. Marcus Fairchild, as it happens.' He dropped down on to a chair facing the superintendent.

'He was your lawyer, wasn't he?'

Nightingale shook his head. 'I only knew him through Jenny. He was her godfather.'

Chalmers took his eyes off the screen and sat back in his chair. 'Funny the way he died, wasn't it?'

Nightingale frowned. 'Funny? He was shot in the back of his car by a hit man on a motorbike. Where's the humour in that?'

'I meant funny peculiar, not funny ha-ha,' said the superintendent. 'Lawyers usually settle their differences in court. I can't remember the last time a lawyer was murdered like that. And with a MAC-10 and all. Anyway, what was the turnout like?'

'Pretty good,' said Nightingale. 'He had a lot of friends.'

'But you weren't one, right?'

'Why do you say that?'

'Just a feeling, Nightingale.' The superintendent smiled. 'I have to say you wouldn't find me shedding a tear over a dead lawyer.'

'Can we get the small talk out of the way, Chalmers? Why did you bring me here?'

Chalmers pushed his chair away from his desk. 'As crazy as it might sound, I need your help.'

'The Goths?'

Chalmers wagged a finger at Nightingale. 'You're a sharp one, Nightingale, and that's the truth. Just be careful you don't cut yourself. I'm not happy about having to ask you for help, but I don't seem to have a choice.'

Nightingale's eyebrows headed skyward. 'I'm not a cop any more, remember?'

'I'm not over the moon about this either, but conventional investigating is getting us nowhere,' said the superintendent.

'I'm not a cop,' Nightingale repeated.

'At least hear me out,' said Chalmers, pushing himself up out of his seat and walking around the desk. 'You're not a cop but last time I checked you were still a citizen and that comes with responsibilities.'

'I pay my council tax,' said Nightingale. 'And my television licence.'

'Well done you,' said the superintendent. 'Come and have a look at what I'm dealing with.'

He opened the door and headed out. Nightingale sighed and followed him. They walked down a corridor to a set of double doors. There were meshed windows on each door and over one of the windows someone had stuck a sheet of paper on which the letters MIT were printed. Murder Investigation Team.

The room was about fifty feet long and twelve feet
wide. A dozen tables had been set up in the middle of
the room, each with its own computer terminal. There
were half a dozen civilian workers sitting at terminals.
Nightingale assumed they were inputting information
into the HOLMES system, a vital part of any murder
investigation. Strictly speaking it was HOLMES 2 as
the first Home Office Large Major Enquiry System had
been substantially improved. By inputting every single
piece of information into HOLMES, the detectives
could spot patterns and links that they would otherwise
miss.

Another four tables had been pushed against the wall
furthest from the door and four detectives in suits were
on the phone. There were files and stacks of paper everywhere and a row of metal filing cabinets on top of which
were tea- and coffee-making equipment. It was, like most
incident rooms, organised chaos.

Five whiteboards had been fixed to one wall and even
before they walked up to them Nightingale knew there
was one per victim. 'Five Goths all killed in the past two
weeks,' said Chalmers. 'Three male, two female. Ages
between eighteen and thirty-nine. Two from North
London, one from West London, two from South London.
Two were gay and three were straight, so far as we
know. Two students, one long-term unemployed, one
website designer, one shop assistant. The one thing that
they have in common is that they were Goths. Strike
that – it's the *only* thing they have in common.'

'So they're hate crimes?' said Nightingale.

'That's the theory we're working on,' said Chalmers.
'But that's our problem. If the victims are being singled

out because they're Goths, that doesn't give us a profile of the killers.'

'Killers, plural?'

Nightingale walked over to the first of the boards. Written across the top, in felt tip capital letters, was the name of the victim – STELLA WALSH. To the left of the name was a head-and-shoulders shot of a pretty teenage girl with spiky black hair and heavy mascara. Below the head-and-shoulders photograph were five crime-scene pictures. Stella had been stripped naked and her flesh cut to ribbons. Nightingale grimaced as he looked from photograph to photograph.

'The nature of the crime scenes suggests that there are more than one,' said Chalmers. 'But the only thing we know is that they hate Goths. That's not enough to go on. The Senior Investigating Officer is Detective Chief Inspector Rawlings but he's getting nowhere. Not from want of trying, it has to be said, he's done everything by the book but with zero results. Now we've got a tweeting campaign saying that if two of the victims hadn't been gay, we'd be doing more to solve the case.'

'Are you serious?' asked Nightingale, turning to look at him.

Chalmers nodded. 'The Met is now being described as institutionally homophobic and the commissioner is looking for heads to roll.'

'The powers that be care that much about Twitter?'

'About public perception, sure. We've now got celebs tweeting about the investigation, everyone from Stephen Fry to One Direction. I had my own daughter asking me yesterday why we hadn't solved the case. That's all down to her favourite One Direction singer tweeting about it.'

'Seems to me that it's the tail wagging the dog these days.'

'Doesn't matter what's wagging what, what matters is that the commissioner wants this case breaking and he's dumped it on my desk like a huge steaming turd.'

'And you think you can dump it on me?' Nightingale laughed. 'I know in the job shit rolls downhill, but I'm not even on the hill any more.'

'Rawlings hasn't put a foot wrong,' said Chalmers. 'It's not his first murder enquiry and he hasn't done anything differently to the way I'd've handled it. There's no link between the victims other than they're Goths. We're looking at it as a hate crime but there are no obvious suspects. They've been trawling through social media and anti-Goth and anti-gay websites but there's no one who stands out.'

Nightingale looked back at the crime scene photographs. 'And you're sure it's not a lone psychopath?'

Chalmers shrugged. 'These aren't simple killings,' he said. 'What's being done to them takes time. It seems a lot of work for one person.'

'And what's the cause of death? Please don't tell me she was alive when they cut her up?'

'The coroner says that she was alive but almost certainly unconscious; she'd been hit on the back of her head. But the cause of death was blood loss.'

Nightingale shuddered. 'Were they all killed the same way?'

'Rendered unconscious and then mutilated,' said Chalmers.

'When was the last killing?'

'Four days ago, at least that was when the body was found.' Chalmers walked over to the whiteboard furthest

to the right. He pointed at a head-and-shoulders photograph of a man with a double chin and thinning hair that
had been dyed black and gelled. He had mascara and
eyeliner and what looked like black lipstick. 'Daryl Heaton,
thirty-nine and unemployed. He was found in his flat in
Kilburn after the neighbours had complained about the
smell. His was the last body found but the coroner puts
the TOD at about a week earlier.'

Chalmers moved to the next whiteboard along.
'Assuming she's right about the time of death, that would
make Abbie Greene the last victim. She was found six
days ago.'

Nightingale looked at the head-and-shoulders photograph at the top of the whiteboard. Abbie Greene was
barely out of her teens. She was blonde and blue-eyed
and had a cute smile that suggested either good genes or
expensive orthodontics.

'That was taken from her university application,' said
Chalmers. 'She went Goth about six months ago. Dyed
her hair black.'

Below the photograph were half a dozen gory crime
scene pictures. Abbie was lying across a blood-soaked
bed with barely an intact scrap of flesh on her, except
for her face. 'He doesn't slash the face,' said Nightingale.
'Just the bodies.'

'Maybe it's sexual,' said Chalmers. 'The face turns him
on, he can look at them as he butchers them.'

'It's not butchering though, is it?' said Nightingale.
'He doesn't sever the hands or the feet, or rip out organs
or cut off their ears. It's not Jack The Ripper stuff, is
it? More like he's skinning them. Skinning them bit
by bit.'

Below the crime scene photographs was a handwritten timeline that showed everything Abbie had done and everyone she'd met in the twenty-four hours before she died. According to the timeline, the last person who had seen Abbie alive, apart from her killers, was her girlfriend, Zoe. According to Zoe, Abbie had gone to see a film with a friend and had never returned. Her body was found the next day in a bedsit in North London, more than five miles away from where she lived. 'The friend?' asked Nightingale.

'We don't know,' said Chalmers. 'We checked all the numbers on her mobile and they're all accounted for. If it was a friend, they didn't talk on the phone.'

Nightingale walked from whiteboard to whiteboard, scratching his neck. 'Two of them were found on Hampstead Heath?'

'Luke Aitken. He lived in Hampstead with his parents. And Stella Walsh. She lived with her parents in Islington. Very little blood at the dump sites so they were killed elsewhere.'

'Any attempt made to hide the bodies?'

Chalmers shook his head. 'Dumped not far from the road in both cases. Wrapped in polythene. No forensics at all. The bodies were probably dumped at night and were discovered the next day. Gabriel Patterson was also wrapped in plastic and dumped on a railway embankment. Also no attempt at concealment.'

Nightingale waved a hand at the five boards. 'And all these took place over a two-week period?'

Chalmers nodded. He took out a pack of chewing gum and slid a piece between his lips. 'You're wondering why so many, so fast?'

'I'm wondering how a killer like this comes from nowhere. Serial killers generally work their way up to it. They start with rape and assault and then they move on to killing. This guy seems to have hit the ground running, don't you think?'

'There have been no other killings of Goths in the UK since Sophie Lancaster in 2007 and Greater Manchester Police caught the gang responsible.' He nodded at the whiteboards. 'This is totally different to the Lancaster case. This is organised and well planned and whoever is responsible leaves no evidence behind. No hairs, no fibres, no nothing. We're working on the theory that the killers use forensic suits and foot coverings and probably hair nets.' He pointed at the Abbie Greene crime scene photographs. 'There was a lot of blood on the floor and signs that someone had stood in it, but no prints. Just smudges.'

Nightingale frowned and scratched his head. 'So they know about forensics.'

'So does anyone with a TV set these days,' said Chalmers. 'But the point isn't that they know about forensics, it's the fact that they go to all that trouble not to leave any evidence behind. There's a lot of planning and forethought going into these killings and that's not normally associated with hate crimes. With hate crimes you tend to get unplanned violence, someone gets angry and lashes out.' He flashed Nightingale a tight smile. 'Someone out there hates Goths enough to go to a great deal of trouble – we've tried to find them and drawn a blank. I'm hoping you might have more luck.'

Nightingale walked over to the single window in the room and looked down at the street below. 'Why are you asking me, Chalmers? You cut me off your Christmas card list a long time ago.'

'This is your area of expertise, Nightingale. At least that's what it says on your website.'

'My assistant looks after my web presence,' said Nightingale. He turned his back on the window and folded his arms.

'Yeah, well, according to her you're a world authority on supernatural matters.'

'And that's what you think these killings are? Supernatural?'

'I think that whoever is killing these Goths is part of that crazy, mixed-up world that you move in and out of. Rawlings has been sending his people in and the shutters come down. But you.' He shrugged. 'You they might talk to.'

'If you hadn't noticed, I don't wear mascara and tight black jeans.'

'No, but you talk their language.'

'And you've got a budget for this?'

The superintendent frowned. 'Budget?'

'Payment. Money. I'm not a cop, Chalmers. Haven't been for a while. I work for a living these days.'

Chalmers shook his head. 'There's no budget. You can do it pro bono.'

'I was never a fan of U2, to be honest. Mind you that "Sunday Bloody Sunday" was a good tune.'

'What the hell are you talking about, Nightingale?'

'If you're going to start talking Latin, how about quid pro quo. As in you give me quids and I work like a pro.'

'I don't have money to pay private investigators, Nightingale.' He walked over to a table on which he'd placed photographs of the five victims. 'Look at them. Five innocent people, killed and butchered. You're a citizen, right? Time to do your civic duty. Find out what the freaks are saying.'

'The freaks?'

'The devil worshippers, the Wicca mob, the people who think that things go bump in the night.'

'You're asking me to solve your case, is that it?'

'Not solve. Just get me some leads. Someone out there is butchering Goths and somebody must know who and why. Conventional profiling gives us the usual serial killer crap – a middle-aged white male who wet his bed and tortured his pets. But you and I know, despite what you see on TV, profiles don't lead to convictions. It's police work that gets convictions, plain and simple.'

Nightingale stared down at the five photographs. 'And if I get you leads, what does that get me? What's the quid pro quo?'

'What do you want?'

'A bit of help now and then, maybe? Access to the odd database.'

'Let you go prowling through the PNC whenever you feel like it?' He shook his head. 'That's not going to happen. How about this? You help me with this case and I'll make sure you don't fall foul of the Private Security Industry Act of 2001.'

'And why would that be a problem for me?'

Chalmers flashed him a tight smile. 'You can use your imagination, I'm sure. The word of a high-ranking police officer could smooth the way or . . .' He shrugged. 'Like I said, I'm sure you can use your imagination.'

'That sounds like a threat.'

Chalmers shrugged but didn't say anything.

'Fine,' said Nightingale. He gathered up the photographs. 'I'll see what I can do.'

'I need to know why,' said Chalmers. 'Give me the why and I'll probably be able to nail down the who.'

'I said I'll look into it,' said Nightingale. He slid the photographs into his raincoat pocket. 'I can't promise anything.'

'Well, I can make a promise, Nightingale. If you don't help us crack this case I'll make your life unbearable.'

Nightingale smiled thinly. 'Good to know you've got my back,' he said. 'I feel so much safer knowing that.'

3

Nightingale jumped as the office door opened but he smiled when he saw it was Jenny. He was making himself a coffee so he reached for a second mug. 'You're early,' he said. She was wearing a long Gucci coat with a large floppy collar and carrying a mustard-coloured Dior handbag. She dropped the handbag on her desk and hung the coat by the door. 'I've got to get our VAT returns done today,' she said. 'And knowing the state your receipts are in I figured I'd need an early start. What happened to you yesterday? I looked for you at the reception but you'd gone.'

'I went after they'd done the grave thing,' said Nightingale. 'I saw you drop the flower in.'

'You should have stayed.'

'I wasn't close and it's not as if I knew a lot of people there. Though it was a hell of a turnout, wasn't it?'

'Uncle Marcus was well loved, that's true,' said Jenny. Nightingale handed her one of the coffee mugs. 'You should get in early more often,' she said.

'You're welcome,' said Nightingale. He took his coffee through into his own office where he'd set up a whiteboard on an easel. Nightingale had used Blu-tack to stick up the photographs that Chalmers had given him around the edge of the whiteboard. In the centre he'd fixed a map of London and he'd used a red felt marker to link the photographs to the locations where the bodies had been found.

Jenny frowned at the whiteboard as she sipped her coffee.

'Chalmers needs help with a case,' Nightingale explained. 'Someone's been butchering Goths.'

'He's paying you?'

'He wants us to do it pro bono.'

'See now, I think Bono's a pretentious turd and U2's music is very over-rated.'

Nightingale grinned. 'That's what I said but Chalmers has no sense of humour.' He sat down at his desk and swung his feet up.

Jenny pulled up a chair and grimaced as she stared at the photographs

'They were all hacked up pretty badly,' said Nightingale. 'Virtually skinned. I can get crime-scene pictures but trust me, you don't want to see them. Three men, two women, so probably not sexual, despite what the gay activists are saying. But he leaves the faces alone, just mutilates the bodies. I say "he", but we're probably talking about multiple assailants.'

'So it's a hate crime. Someone who hates Goths or what they stand for.'

'What do Goths stand for?' asked Nightingale. 'All I see is the black clothing and vampire make-up.'

'It's more about the music and the lifestyle than anything else,' said Jenny. 'Why would Chalmers want you involved?'

'I've got you to thank for that,' said Nightingale. 'The

new corporate website mentions the supernatural cases I've worked on.'

'He thinks there's a supernatural element to this?'

'He thinks that Goths are freaks and that I'm more at home dealing with freaks than his men are.'

Jenny shook her head in dismay. 'He's a moron.'

'No argument from me. But the quickest way of getting him off my back is to give him a lead he can work on.'

'A lead?'

'His murder investigation team is clueless. He thinks if I go and talk to the Goths, I'll pick up on something.'

'Well, good luck with that,' she said, and sipped her coffee.

'To be honest, I'm not sure where to start,' said Nightingale. 'Any idea where Goths hang out? I'm guessing graveyards and abandoned churches, right?'

Jenny laughed. 'You're such an idiot sometimes,' she said. 'Jack, Goths are just kids who like to hang out together and listen to the Cure and Depeche Mode or whatever the latest Goth band is. They wear black and eyeliner and generally just keep to themselves.'

'How come you know so much about them?'

'I used to hang out with a Goth couple when I was at university. They were a couple of softies but one night the boy got beaten up really badly. A group of skinheads just decided to give him a kicking. He was in hospital for two weeks. Almost lost his spleen.'

'Bastards.'

'Yes. Bastards. There are some sick people out there who like to hurt people who are different. Because of their colour, or their clothes, or their sexuality.' She gestured at the photographs with her hand. 'But this is more than a kicking, Jack. That's not just anger, is it? That's something much much worse.'

'You're telling me,' said Nightingale. 'Chalmers thinks the killings are ritualistic and that according to that wonderful website you set up, I'm a world authority on the subject.'

'So you're blaming my programming skills, is that it?'

Nightingale grinned and shook his head. 'Nah, he would have given this to me anyway,' he said. 'He can't get his own people to go knocking on Satanic doors, but he knows that I can talk their language.'

'Jack, are you listening to yourself? You're going to be on the trail of a psychopathic killer. How's that going to end well?'

'Like I said, it's probably going to be killers, not killer. There's too much going on for it to be the work of one man.'

Jenny folded her arms and pouted. 'That doesn't actually make me feel any better.'

'Look, I'll ask a few questions, come up with a motive and he'll do the rest.'

'And what if the killers find out that you're on the case? You're not thinking this through.'

Nightingale waved at the photographs. 'They kill Goths. I'm not a Goth.'

'You don't know what they might do if they find out you're trying to track them down.' She sighed. 'Just be careful, Jack.'

'Always,' he said.

She shook her head. 'It goes in one ear and out of the other with you, doesn't it?'

'I'm listening, kid. Really.' He nodded at the whiteboard.

'So now here's the thing. Five Goths, different ages and living in different parts of the city, all killed in the same way.'

'No connections between them?'

'Not that the cops can find and they're usually good at things like that. The way murder investigations work these days involves getting as many cops to ask as many questions of as many people as they can, shove it all into the HOLMES computer and get it to highlight anything significant.'

'And HOLMES has come up with nothing?'

'That's what Chalmers says. But here's the thing I don't understand. If it's someone who hates Goths, why travel around the city? Why not just go to one place where Goths hang out.'

Jenny nodded. 'That would seem logical. Why do you think they haven't?'

'Maybe they think it'll mean they've less chance of being spotted if they move around.' He shrugged. 'It just seems to me that there might be a connection that HOLMES has missed. That they all met the killer, or killers, in the same place.'

Jenny looked at the map. 'Well, they're all within the M25,' she said.

'And all within Zone 2 on the Tube network. I don't think that helps. Two were teenagers, two were in their twenties, and one was in his late thirties. Three were straight and two were gay. So Chalmers is working on the theory that they were killed because they were Goths.'

'So they were just unlucky, they were in the wrong place at the wrong time when the killers were looking for a victim.'

Nightingale shook his head. 'The way the killings were carried out it had to have been planned. They had equipment, and in three of the killings they did it at the victim's home. So they must have cased the area first. They might have been targeted randomly, but once in their sights the killers did their research.'

Jenny waved her coffee mug at the whiteboard. 'So what's your plan?'

'I need you to take a look at their social media pages. Facebook and Tumblr and whatever else people are using these days. Build up a profile for each of the five of them.'

'Hasn't Chalmers already done that?'

'For sure, but now they'll be at the not being able to see the woods for the trees stage. A fresh pair of eyes might see something that they've missed.'

'I'll give it a go,' said Jenny. 'What will you be doing while I'm chained to the keyboard?'

'I need to talk to Goths. Where's a good place to meet them?'

'Are you serious?'

'Chalmers is right, they won't talk to cops, but they might talk to me.'

Jenny chuckled. 'I'd love to be a fly on the wall when you start chatting to a teenage Goth,' she said. 'I'll ask around. But I know the best place is on a Saturday, a club called The Crypt. It's been running for almost thirty years. Every Saturday night from 10 p.m. until dawn. But you're going to have a problem – I think there's a dress code.'

'I'll manage,' said Nightingale.

'I don't mean you need to wear a tie. There's a Goth dress code.'

'Yeah, well, maybe I'll hang about outside and talk to them on the way in.'

Jenny laughed. 'Yeah, and I can't see that ending badly,' she said. 'I'll get the details for you.' She sipped her coffee. 'So what'll you be doing between now and Saturday?'

'Thought I'd visit the relatives, flatmates, anyone who could shed some light on the sort of people they were and why anyone would single them out.'

'The cops would have done that, surely?'

Nightingale nodded. 'Yeah, but again fresh eyes might come up with something. I figured I'd do the two South London victims today. That's Abbie Greene, the last to be killed, and Gabriel Patterson, the second victim. The rest are North London and I'll do them tomorrow.'

'Sounds like a plan. But what about the rest of our cases?'

'We've nothing urgent,' said Nightingale. 'Everything can certainly hold fire until Monday by which time we'll have a better idea of what's going on.'

'Does Chalmers think that the killers will strike again?'

'I guess so. There hasn't been an attack for over a week, though. So maybe they've stopped. The five murders took place over ten days, so it was rush rush rush. It could be that the police activity has persuaded them to go to ground.' He sipped his coffee.

'You're loving this, aren't you?' said Jenny.

'What?'

'Being a detective again. Come on, admit it. You're as pleased as Punch that Chalmers has brought you in on this case.'

'To be fair, Jenny, five people have been murdered. It's not about me, it's about them.'

'I get that, of course I get that, but let's not forget that we've got a business to run.'

Nightingale held up a hand. 'Speaking as CEO and MD and VIP of Nightingale Investigations, I can assure you that I'm very well aware of that.' He grinned. 'Seriously, kid, just a few days and then we'll see where we stand. And let's not forget that if we do crack this case, the publicity will mean we'll have clients lined up down the street.'

'Assuming that Chalmers allows you to take the credit.'

Nightingale looked at her over the top of his coffee mug. 'You think he won't?'

'I think you can trust him about as far as you can throw him,' said Jenny. 'And the state you're in, that's not too far.'

'I'm offended,' said Nightingale. He patted his stomach. 'It might not be a six-pack but I'm not fat.'

'It's not about fat, Jack. You don't eat enough to get fat. It's about smoking and drinking and your complete lack of interest in sport.'

'I watch football,' said Nightingale. 'And rugby. And I was cheering with everyone else at the Olympics.'

'You know what I mean. The only exercise you get is a bit of walking.'

'And you do what? Hunting, shooting and fishing on your parents' estate?'

'I could outrun you, any day of the week.'

He grinned. 'Are you challenging me to a race?'

She laughed. 'Any time, anywhere.'

Nightingale looked her up and down. There wasn't an ounce of fat on Jenny McLean; she was as fit as the proverbial butcher's dog. She stood waiting for his answer, her hands on her hips and an amused smile on her face. 'There'd have to be some sort of handicap, you being younger,' he said.

'You're taller. But okay, I'll give you a ten per cent start over whatever distance you want.'

He stood up and swung his arms around. 'Ten per cent?' He jogged on the spot.

'Sure.'

'And the winner gets what?'

'How about the loser agrees to get the coffee for the next six months?'

He jogged around his desk and stood in front of her. He held out his hand. 'It's a bet,' he said.

She shook his hand. 'It's a bet,' she repeated. 'When do we do it?'

'Now,' he said, turning and running through to her office. 'First one to your desk wins!' He reached her desk, slapped his hands down on it and then raised his arms in a Usain Bolt victory pose.

Jenny glared at him in disgust. 'What are you, twelve?'

'Milk and one sugar, please,' he laughed, in between gasping for breath. 'Then I'll go and talk to Mrs Patterson.'

4

Lisa Patterson was in her early twenties, her face pale and drawn, her hair dry and lifeless, frizzy at the ends and flecked with dandruff. She held a baby boy in her arms, less than a year old and oblivious to the fact that his father had been skinned alive. She sat on the sofa and did her best to stop the tears from trickling down her cheeks. Nightingale had refused her offer of a cup of tea but had accepted a glass of water and it sat untouched on the coffee table next to his armchair. 'What did you say your name was?' she said. She ran a hand through her hair and tried unsuccessfully to tuck it behind her ears.

'Jack,' he said. 'Jack Nightingale.'

'Have they found them? Have they found the animals who killed my Gabe?'

'I'm sorry, Mrs Patterson. Not yet. That's why I'm here, just to add to the information we have on our files.' He looked around the cramped flat. It was above an off-licence in Clapham on a busy street. Trucks and buses roared by at regular intervals and each time the windows rattled. There were half a dozen half-drunk cups of tea on the table, several with thick brown scum on the surface, and an open pack of Pampers. The television was on with the sound muted and there was a towelling dressing gown on the floor by the door. Mrs Patterson was wearing a long denim dress, the front of which was spotted with dried milk and spittle. 'Is there anyone here to help you?'

'My mum pops around but she has to take care of Dad, he had a stroke last year.'

'I'm sorry.'

She forced a smile. 'They say bad things come in threes. My dad had his stroke, my sister crashed her car and was in a coma for two weeks – and then Gabe . . .' She put her hand up to her face and shuddered, then shook herself and took a deep breath. She looked down at the sleeping baby and bit her lower lip. Nightingale knew what she was thinking, that the baby was all she had left.

'Should I call your mother, ask her to come back?'

Mrs Patterson shook her head. 'She'll be back once she's checked up on my dad.' She looked up at him and forced a smile. 'I'll be all right, Mr Nightingale. Is it mister? Or sergeant?'

'Call me Jack,' said Nightingale.

'It comes and goes,' she said. 'I go to bed and cry myself to sleep and when I wake up I forget that he's dead and then it's worse. There was a woman here from Victim Support who said every day the pain will get a little less but that's not happening.'

'I'm sorry, Mrs Patterson, I can't imagine what you're going through.'

She looked up from her baby. 'You know, you're the first person who's said that,' she said. 'Everyone else says they understand, they know how difficult it is, how they know how I must feel, but they don't. No one does.'

Nightingale smiled sympathetically. His time as a police

negotiator had taught him that sometimes when you were dealing with a person in crisis it was best to remain silent.

'It's not just that I miss him, Jack. It's that I wasn't there when he died. He must have been so frightened, so scared. They hurt him so much and I know he must have been thinking about me and I wasn't there to help him.' She looked up at the ceiling and blinked away tears. 'Sometimes I can hear him screaming my name and it's like a knife in my stomach.'

'Mrs Patterson, I've seen the post-mortem report and I can tell you with my hand on my heart that Gabe was unconscious when it happened,' Nightingale said, his voice little more than a whisper. 'He wouldn't have known what was happening.'

She took a deep breath and then nodded slowly. 'Sometimes I wish I was dead, too,' she said. She moaned and the sound sent a shudder down Nightingale's spine. He got up and sat down next to her. He knew he was breaking every rule in the book but he wasn't a cop any more so he figured the rules no longer applied to him. He put his arm around her and she buried her head in his shoulder and cried, hugging the baby to her chest. She sobbed for several minutes and he felt his shirt grow damp with her tears. He said nothing, knowing that there was nothing he could say that would make her feel better.

Popular wisdom said that there were five stages of grief when a loved one died: denial, anger, bargaining, depression and acceptance. But Nightingale knew the five stages didn't always apply. Sometimes grief just hit you like a train and there were no stages to go through. There was just pain and loneliness and an empty black hole where the loved one had been. He held her and waited for her to stop crying. The tears would stop eventually, he knew, not because her sadness had gone, simply because her tear ducts would be empty.

It was only when the baby began to cry that she moved away from Nightingale. She fussed over the baby, making shushing sounds as she groped for his bottle. The baby sucked greedily and she smiled down at him, her cheeks glistening wet. 'I'm sorry,' she said, her eyes on her child, but the words were meant for him.

'You've nothing to be sorry about,' said Nightingale. His mouth had gone dry so he picked up his glass of water and sipped it.

'What is it you need from me, Jack?' she said. 'I told the detectives everything I knew.'

'I'm asking the same questions that you've been asking yourself,' he said. 'I want to know why anyone would want to hurt Gabe.'

'Because they're sick,' she said. 'There's no logic to it.'

'That's what the police seem to think,' said Nightingale. 'Gabe was in the wrong place at the wrong time.'

'What's the alternative?' she said as she watched her baby feed. 'Somebody hated him so much they'd do that to him?' She shook her head. 'Gabe would never hurt anybody. He was a kind soul.' She looked up at Nightingale. 'The police say it was a hate crime. They killed him because he was a Goth.'

'Did he dress like a Goth at home?'

She chuckled to herself. 'He never dressed like a Goth, Jack. He was a Goth. It wasn't a costume that he put on whenever it suited him. That's what he wore. He never went out without make-up. Even if he was just popping down to the shops he'd make sure his mascara and lipstick was right. And he did his nails every few days, they always had to be perfect.'

'But you're not a Goth?'

She looked down at her denim dress and smiled. 'Not always,' she said. 'For me it was about dressing up. I've got black wigs and all the gear. But Gabe was a Goth twenty-four seven.'

'They didn't mind him dressing like that at the office?'

'They were fine. They were good about his ink, too.'

'His ink?'

'His tattoos. Most of them were on his back but he had a few on his arms and a lot of places won't hire you if you've got tattoos. But his firm were totally cool. They design video games so they're all a bit . . . creative, I suppose you'd say. There's a pool table and all sorts of games and stuff for them to play around with.' She shrugged. 'Gabe always said it was the only place he wanted to work.'

'Had he always been a Goth? I mean, since you knew him?'

She nodded and forced a smile. 'We met at college. He was studying computer programming and even in the first year he wore make-up to classes and his hair was all spiky and he had these amazing boots with high heels.'

'Did he have any problems at college?'

'Haters, you mean?' She shook her head. 'Students are cool, mostly. Live and let live, right? Outside the college it was hit and miss. If he was in a pub then maybe someone would want to have their picture taken with him or they'd want to thump him.'

'Did he get hit a lot?'

She laughed and shook her head. 'He was too smart for that. He had the knack of knowing who was trouble and who was just having a laugh. If he sensed trouble he'd either defuse it with a joke or he'd just move away. He never got into a fight, not all the time I knew him.' She shrugged. 'But then he was careful about where he went. If you're a Goth there are places that you wouldn't want to go at night. And other places where you'd have a great time.' She ran a hand down her face. 'That's why I don't understand what happened. I don't see how he could have got himself into a situation where he would have been hurt.' She pulled tissues from a box and dabbed at her eyes. 'We'd be in a pub and everything would be cool and then he'd see a group at the bar and he'd know, he'd just know, that they were trouble and we'd leave. It was like a sixth sense. So how did he let those animals get so close to him that they could do that?'

'I don't know,' whispered Nightingale.

'And if he knew he was in trouble, why didn't he fight back?'

'Maybe they surprised him. Maybe they caught him while he was busy doing something else.'

'Gabe always knew what was going on around him,' she said. 'You never saw Gabe playing with his phone or wearing headphones while he was out. He was always aware, you know what I mean? He always knew what was going on around him. He loved people-watching, and listening to what they were saying. He wanted to be a writer.'

'Yeah?'

She nodded quickly, as if she feared that he didn't

believe her. 'Oh yes, he was really talented. He was writing short stories. Horror, mainly. Like Dean Koontz, the American writer. But Gabe was better.' She smiled. 'That's what I thought anyway. He painted pictures with his words. And a lot of what he wrote about came from what he saw and heard.'

'So I'm guessing he was always happy to talk to strangers?'

'All the time. He was so interested in people, you know? What made them tick, why they said the things that they did.'

'Did you get out much, once the baby was born?'

She laughed, though there was a brittle quality to the sound as if she was close to crying again. 'You don't have children, do you, Jack?'

Nightingale shook his head.

'They tell you that kids change you for ever, but you don't really understand what they mean until you have one for yourself. You stop being your own person. It's all about them, about satisfying their needs. You have to clean them, feed them, keep them warm, amuse them, get them to sleep. There isn't a waking minute when they're not the centre of your universe.' The baby shifted in her lap and she looked down at it and made soft shushing sounds. 'So the short answer is no, we didn't get out much once Robert was born.' She smiled down at the baby. 'We called him Robert Smith, after the lead singer of the Cure. Gabe's a huge fan. Had his picture taken with him a few years ago. He'd travel across the country to get to one of their gigs. We both would. Now we'll have to wait . . .' She shuddered and closed her eyes as she realised there was no more 'we' any more. There was just her and the child.

'Where would you go for a Goth night out?' he asked, keen to keep her talking.

'North of the river, usually,' she said. 'There isn't much here in Clapham. Soho, usually. We liked Garlic and Shots in Frith Street and the Royal George in Charing Cross Road. He used to go every second Thursday because that was when the London Vampire Group meets.'

'Vampires?'

'Not real vampires, obviously,' she said. 'Just Goths who like to go that bit further. They have sharp teeth and drink blood. Or tomato juice, anyway.' She smiled. 'I always thought they were a bit silly, but harmless enough. If it was a vampire night Gabe would go on his own, usually, and I'd have a girls' night out. And our big thing was the Crypt. You've heard of the Crypt, right?'

Nightingale nodded. 'Torrens Street, near the Angel Tube station.'

'Yeah, we used to go there a lot.'

'Did he go alone?'

'After Robert was born, you mean? Sometimes. Not so much, though. He shared the feeds and nappy-changing with me. He loved being a dad.'

'The night he was killed, he'd gone out on his own, right?'

'Yes, but not to the Crypt. The Crypt is only open on Saturdays. He was at a work thing, in Vauxhall, not far from the office. He left the pub at ten and that was the last anyone ever saw of him. He didn't come home, there's no CCTV footage of him getting on a train, he wasn't picked up by a taxi. He just vanished. Until . . .' She closed her eyes, unable to finish the sentence.

'I know you'll have already been asked this, but did you ever see any of these people with Gabe?' Nightingale asked. He reached into his jacket pocket and took out photographs of Luke Aitken, Daryl Heaton, Stella Walsh and Abbie Greene.

Mrs Patterson looked at the four photographs and shuddered again. 'They were the other four victims, weren't they?'

Nightingale nodded. 'Yes. I'm sorry.'

She shook her head sadly. 'Why would anyone kill people just because of what they look like?' She looked as if she was about to cry again but the baby lost its grip on the bottle and she concentrated on getting him to feed again.

'There are some very sick people in the world, Mrs Patterson,' said Nightingale quietly. 'Did you ever see Gabe with any of them?' he pressed gently.

She shook her head. 'The detectives asked me that already. I'm positive that Gabe didn't know any of them. I know all his friends.' She wiped her eyes again. 'You see, that's what I don't understand. Why would anyone do that to someone just because they were different? Why does being different inspire such hatred?'

'Sometimes it's jealousy,' said Nightingale.

'Do you think they'll catch them?'

'Yes,' said Nightingale emphatically. 'I do.'

'How can you be so sure?' she asked.

Nightingale forced a smile as he wondered how he should answer that question. The simple fact was that most serial killers carried on killing until they got caught. Eventually they made a mistake or, more likely, they were unlucky. If the killers were skilled and careful, then regular police work wouldn't catch them. It wasn't like it was portrayed on television and in the movies. Dogged detectives didn't use intuition to solve crimes, they asked questions, filled out forms and fed information into computers. Sometimes it paid off, but more often than not they were going through the motions. Forensic evidence could prove guilt, but outside of television drama scientists and technicians didn't solve crimes. The true answer to her question was that at some point the killers would be spotted near a body, or walk by a CCTV camera, or more likely would be interviewed by the police about something totally unrelated. Peter Sutcliffe, the serial killer they called the Yorkshire Ripper, was interviewed nine times by murder squad detectives but he was only caught after being pulled over by police who spotted he had false plates on his car. But that wasn't what Mrs Patterson wanted to hear so Nightingale smiled and lied. 'The police will do whatever it takes to arrest the people responsible,' he said. 'They won't rest until they're behind bars.'

'They should hang them,' said Mrs Patterson. 'Scum like that, they should hang.'

Nightingale nodded but didn't say anything. Her eyes were blazing and the colour had returned to her cheek. In a way the hatred and anger would help her because at least they were emotions that were aimed externally, rather than the sadness that was eating her up from the inside.

Mrs Patterson took a deep breath, then nodded at her baby. 'I'm going to have to put him in his cot,' she said.

'I understand,' said Nightingale, standing up. 'I've taken up enough of your time.'

'Just find them, that's all I ask,' she said, looking down at the baby. 'And when you find them, ask them why. Ask them why they killed my Gabe.'

5

Nightingale lit a cigarette as he walked back to his MGB. He'd managed to find a parking space down a side street but when he got back to the car he found that the vehicles he'd parked in between had moved and he was now hemmed in front and back. He stood at the front of his car and stared at the non-existent gap between his front bumper and the rear of the Honda CRV. He blew smoke as he considered his options, which seemed to be two-fold: wait for one of the drivers to come back and move their cars, or head off to his next interview by public transport. He looked at his watch. It was just after eleven o'clock in the morning. There was a traffic warden down the street, checking residents' parking permits and heading his way.

He peered through the windows of the SUV, looking for clues as to who the owner might be. There were two car seats in the rear and an iPad on the front passenger seat. If he were lucky it'd be a housewife who had just popped off to do some shopping

The vehicle at the other end was a nearly new blue Ford Fiesta. Its nose was an inch away from his rear bumper, but there was almost three feet of space at the rear. He shaded his eyes and looked through the windscreen of the Fiesta but the car was empty. Nightingale cursed under his breath. As he straightened up he saw the traffic warden looking at the MGB.

'Yours?' asked the man. He was in his twenties, fresh-faced and gawky with shoulder-length hair that didn't seem to have been washed in a while.

'Yeah,' said Nightingale.

'Nice.'

'Thanks.'

'Owned by the Chinese now, MGB?'

'Yeah. Wouldn't touch a new one.'

'Why would you when you get to drive a classic.' He looked at the gap between the MGB and the Honda. 'You did well to get it in there,' he said.

'They came after me . . .' began Nightingale, then shook his head as he realised the traffic warden was joking. 'You got me.'

The man grinned. 'Now you're thinking a traffic warden with a sense of humour, that has to be a first,' he said. 'You could try bouncing it out.'

'Bouncing it out?'

'Did it with a group at mates at uni once. We had a Mini and it got hemmed in. You all stand around the car and bounce it up and down and then you move it as it bounces.'

Nightingale's eyebrows shot skyward. 'You went to university?'

'Newcastle,' he said. 'Upper second in Media, Communication and Cultural Studies.' He laughed when he saw the look on Nightingale's face. 'I know, I know, it's not the career I'd planned for myself but what can you do? I've got a student loan and a young kid and this is better than walking the streets.' He grinned. 'Oh, wait . . .'

Nightingale laughed. 'Nice one.' He saw the traffic warden looking at the cigarette in his hand so he took out his pack of Marlboro and offered it. The traffic warden looked around as if he feared being seen, then took one and smiled his thanks. Nightingale lit it for him.

'Name's Harry,' he said. 'So what do you for a living?'

'I'm Jack. I used to be in law enforcement, like you,' said Nightingale.

Harry frowned, and then chuckled. 'Yeah. Law enforcement. Nice one.'

'I was a cop. I was in CO19, a firearms officer, and I was a negotiator.'

'Yeah? Talking down suicides?'

Nightingale nodded. 'That and domestics, most of the time.'

'I could do with a negotiator in this job,' said Harry. 'Can't be easy.'

'I've been hit three times.' He shrugged. 'It goes with the turf. So what brings you to sunny Clapham?'

Nightingale blew smoke at his trapped MGB. 'I'm asking around about that Goth killers case.'

Harry pulled a face. 'That's some evil shit going on. But what's the Clapham connection?'

Nightingale pointed down the street. 'One of the victims lived down there.'

'You don't say? They were chopped up, right? Into little pieces?'

Nightingale shook his head. 'They were skinned.'

Harry shuddered. 'Who would do something like that? A psycho?'

Nightingale smiled. 'Well, it's not normal behaviour, that's for sure. But there has to be some reason for it. It's not random. They're targeting a particular sort of person and doing something very specific to them.'

'They? There's more than one?'

'Has to be,' said Nightingale. 'There's too much going on for one person to do. Some of the bodies were dumped from a vehicle and it's hard for one person to do that.' He took a long pull on his cigarette. 'Are there any pubs around here where Goths hang out?'

'Not that I know of. Plenty of Goths around, though. There's a few take their dogs on the common.'

'Yeah?'

Harry nodded. 'Near Eagle Pond, not far from the Windmill pub. There's a bench there and you'll usually see two or three of them there this time of day.'

Nightingale looked up and down the street. There was no sign of anyone coming to move the cars either side of him. 'I'll give it a go,' he said. He flicked his cigarette butt into the gutter and it disappeared into a grid in a shower of sparks.

'Be lucky,' said Harry.

'Lucky would be good,' said Nightingale.

'Tell you what, give me your mobile number and I'll send you a text if your motor gets released.'

'You're sure?'

'I'm in the area for the next hour or so. It's no problem.'

Nightingale gave him a business card. 'How long have you been a traffic warden?' he asked.

Harry shrugged. 'A month. Why?'

'No reason,' said Nightingale. He thanked him and

started walking towards the common. He looked back over his shoulder, half expecting to see Harry printing out a ticket, but the traffic warden just smiled and flashed him a thumbs up.

6

Nightingale walked slowly across the grass. There were grey clouds threatening rain overhead and a stiff breeze was blowing in from the north, ruffling his hair and sending a shiver down his spine. He stopped short when he saw the figure sitting on a bench ahead of him. She was wearing a black leather bomber jacket with chains hanging along the back of it. Sitting on the ground next to her was a black and white collie. He was about a hundred feet away from the girl and the dog but his heart was pounding as if it was about to leap out of his chest. He took a deep breath. The last time he'd seen Proserpine he had been standing in a protective circle in his garage and he'd summoned her from the bowels of Hell. That was how it was supposed to be done – confronting a demon from Hell under any other circumstances could easily end in tears – if not eternal damnation.

He took another deep breath, his mind racing. If it was Proserpine, what did she want? There was a time when Proserpine had a claim on his soul, but no longer. He'd won his soul back and he intended to keep it that way. The only time she appeared was when she wanted something from him, but at that moment he was in no mood to be doing any favours for one of Satan's nearest and dearest.

He started walking again, his hands deep in the pockets of his raincoat. Was she connected to the dead Goths in some way? Was she there to warn him off? Or to help him?

As he got to within fifty feet of the bench she turned to the side and he realised it wasn't her. She had the same black lipstick, thick mascara and pale white skin, but her face was rounder and her nose more upturned. Nightingale exhaled and he realised he had been holding his breath.

He decided not to come up behind her so he headed off to the left, joined the path and then walked back towards the bench. From the side she looked even less like Proserpine, she was a few pounds heavier and a fair bit curvier and her eyes didn't look as if they belonged to something that had been dead for a long time.

He slowed as he reached the bench. 'Nice dog,' he said. He squatted down in front of the collie. 'What's your name, then?'

'His name is I Don't Talk To Strangers,' said the girl.

Nightingale grinned and straightened up. 'That's a mouthful,' he said. 'Must be fun calling him in at night.'

'He's a she,' said the girl. 'And I don't talk to strangers either. Especially old men in raincoats.'

'That's a bit harsh,' said Nightingale. 'I'm early thirties, that's not even middle-aged.'

'You look older,' said the girl, squinting up at him.

'My name's Jack.'

'Still don't care.' She looked at the dog. 'Do we care?'

The dog woofed softly. She looked up at Nightingale again. 'No, we don't care.'

Nightingale took out his cigarettes and lit one. 'Jack Nightingale.'

'Like the bird?'

'I don't know. Is Jack a bird's name?'

The girl laughed and held out her hand for a cigarette.

'How old are you?'

'Half your age, now give me a fag or piss off.'

Nightingale held out the pack. She took out a cigarette and he lit it for her. 'Mind if I sit down?'

'Providing you stay at your end of the bench,' she said.

'I'm not a child molester,' he said, putting the cigarettes away.

'That's what all the child molesters say.'

Nightingale laughed as he sat down.

'I'm serious,' said the girl. 'When was the last time a child molester sat down next to a kid and said, "Hello, little girl, I'm a child molester." It doesn't happen.'

'Your parents taught you well,' said Nightingale.

'Mum did. Dad ran off when I was three.'

'Ouch.'

'Yeah. Ouch. What about your parents?'

'I was brought up by foster parents. My father was a Satanist who sold my soul to the devil and my genetic mother killed herself in a lunatic asylum.'

She looked over at him with narrowed eyes, blew smoke up at the sky, and nodded. 'Respect,' she said.

Her dog jumped to its feet, startling them both, and seconds later another dog joined them and the two animals stood nose to nose, their tails thrashing about. The new arrival was a brown and white Jack Russell with a black leather collar. 'Mojo, behave!' shouted a girl who was walking over the grass towards them. She was wearing a long black leather coat that brushed the grass as she walked, and had jet-black hair that had been cut with a severe fringe that gave it the look of a glossy motorcycle helmet. In her right hand she was swinging a black leather lead. She stopped by the bench and looked at Nightingale with an amused smile. Like the girl on the bench she had thick mascara and black lipstick and there were half a dozen small silver rings piercing her left ear. 'Is this the new boyfriend, then?' she asked.

'Ew,' said the girl. 'As if. I mean, seriously. His name's Jack, he's a child molester.' She unclipped her lead from her dog's collar and the two dogs ran off, barking excitedly.

'See, that's not funny,' said Nightingale. 'If someone hears that they could get the wrong end of the stick.' He smiled at the girl who had just arrived. 'The name's Jack. I used to be a policeman but now I'm a private detective.'

'He tells great stories,' said the first girl. 'His father's the devil.'

'That's not actually what I said,' protested Nightingale.

'Becky was never very bright,' said the girl. 'My name's Hannah. You've got cigarettes?'

Nightingale took out his pack and offered her one. She motioned with her hand for him to scoot over so he shuffled next to Becky while she sat down on the edge of the bench.

'No funny business,' said Becky.

'Scout's honour,' said Nightingale. 'Now, forgive me for asking, but how old are you girls.'

'I'm eighteen,' said Hannah. 'Becky's seventeen.'

'Eighteen in two weeks,' said Becky.

'Are you at school?'

'Do we look like we're at school?' scowled Becky.

'We're sort of on a gap year,' said Hannah.

'Yeah, but all we've got to go on is Jobseeker's Allowance,' said Becky. 'And that doesn't go far.'

'Ever been to the Crypt?'

'Loads of times,' said Becky.

'I thought you had to be eighteen to get in?'

'I'm almost eighteen.'

'We're going on Saturday, probably,' said Hannah. 'Why do you ask?'

'Thought I might try it. There's a dress code, right?'

Hannah shrugged carelessly. 'You might want to lose the raincoat, but not everyone there is Goth or Emo.'

Nightingale blew smoke down at the ground. 'What's the difference between a Goth and an Emo?'

'That's a good question,' said Hannah.

'Any chance of an answer?'

The girl sighed. 'I'm not one for labels. But I guess when you're a Goth, you hate the world. When you're an Emo, the world hates you.'

'So you hate the world? Seriously?'

Becky smiled thinly. 'What's not to hate?' she asked.

'But doesn't being different make it worse?'

'Everyone's different,' she said scornfully. She nodded down at his shoes. 'What are they, Hush Puppies?'

'Yeah. I hear they're coming back into fashion.'

She laughed. 'They're not,' she said. 'But you choose to wear them, they're your style.'

'I do a lot of walking and they're comfortable,' he said.

Becky gestured at the chains hanging from her jeans. 'And I feel comfortable like this,' she said.

'Why are you so interested in Goths?' asked Hannah.

'I'm working with the cops, trying to find out who's behind the killings.'

Becky looked across at him, her eyes narrowed. 'Seriously?'

He nodded. 'Yeah. Seriously. I was just talking to the wife of one of the guys who died. Gabe Patterson. And I'm heading over to Battersea to talk to Abbie Green's flatmate.'

'I met her once,' said Hannah.

'Who?'

'Abbie Green.'

'Really?' said Nightingale.

'Yeah, in the Crypt. She was with her girlfriend. What was her name?'

'Zoe?'

'Yeah, that's it. Zoe.' Hannah leaned over to look at Becky. 'You remember Zoe? The blonde with the tits? She kept hitting on you?'

Becky wrinkled her nose and shook her head.

Hannah laughed at Nightingale. 'She was out of her head, she usually is at the Crypt. Zoe was a bit older than Abbie.' She grinned mischievously. 'Not as old as you, obviously. Late twenties. Thirty, maybe, hard to tell with all the make-up. Seriously, she kept hitting on Becky even if she doesn't remember. Wanted to take her back to the flat with her and Abbie.'

'When was this?'

'A few months ago. It was no big deal.'

'She thought I was a lezza?' asked Becky.

'I don't think she cared,' said Hannah. She took a long pull on her cigarette and smiled at Nightingale as she blew a tight plume of smoke up into the air. 'So why are you helping the cops? You some sort of Sheer-luck Holmes?'

'All hands to the pumps,' said Nightingale.

'You need to catch the bastard, and quick,' said Becky.

'The cops are working on it,' said Nightingale.

'By bringing in a private dick?' said Hannah scornfully. 'What about DNA? CCTV? I mean, they listen in on all our phone calls and read all our emails, don't they? How hard can it be to catch someone who's killed, what, five people?'

Nightingale nodded. 'Yeah, five.'

'You know what I don't understand?' asked Hannah. 'How does the killer get them to go with him? I mean, we've just met you, right? If you said you wanted us to go with you so that you could show us some puppies we'd tell you what to do with yourself, right?'

'I hope so,' said Nightingale.

'So how does the killer get five adults to go off with him so that he can cut them up into little pieces?'

'Is that what he does?' said Becky.

'He uses a knife to mutilate them,' said Nightingale. 'He doesn't cut them up, he just slices their skin.'

'What sort of sick bastard does that?' asked Becky.

Nightingale shrugged. 'We'll know when we catch him. But we don't think it's just one guy. Two, maybe more.'

'But that's what makes it even more strange,' said Hannah. 'I'm not going to go off with two guys I don't know, am I?'

'Are you sure?'

'What do you mean?' She took a final drag on her cigarette and flicked it on to the grass. In the distance the two dogs had ganged up on a German Shepherd and were chasing it back and forth.

'Puppies wouldn't work, but what if I said I could get you into a concert you wanted to see? You'd get into my car then?'

'Depends on the band.'

'But you see what I mean? If I dangle the right carrot in front of you, you'll bite. Do you take drugs?'

'Now that is a cop question. I'll take the fifth, officer.'

Nightingale laughed. 'What I mean is, suppose you're partial to ecstasy. Suppose I gave you a couple of tablets every time I saw you. Then one day I say we have to go out to my car because the tablets were there.'

'Have you got some E then?' asked Becky.

'I'm talking hypothetically,' said Nightingale.

Becky frowned at Hannah. 'Does he or not?'

Hannah smiled at her friend. 'No,' she said.

'But you see what I mean?' said Nightingale. 'Serial killers generally don't snatch people off the streets. They charm. They wheedle. They persuade. They find out what it is the victim wants and then they offer them that. Suppose I was the killer, and I pick on you. I might sit here and offer you ecstasy. Or offer to take you to a concert. But if I was being really devious, I'd turn up with a dog. A small, cute dog. Maybe a Jack Russell like Mojo. You'd trust a guy with a dog. And once I've gained your trust, I've got you.'

The two girls looked at each other. 'Have you got a Jack Russell?' asked Becky.

Nightingale smiled. 'I live on my own, I can't have

pets.' He finished his cigarette and ground it out with his heel. 'What do the people you talk to think is going on?' he asked Hannah.

'It's a hate crime, innit?' said Becky.

Hannah nodded. 'That's what everyone thinks, right? Someone who hates Goths. It's not the first time that Goths have been killed because of the way they look. It's no different to attacking people because they're gay or they're black.'

'Except that you choose to be a Goth,' said Nightingale.

Hannah frowned. 'What are you saying? That it's our fault?' She shook her head fiercely. 'I can't believe you said that.'

'No, of course not,' said Nightingale hurriedly. 'That's not what I meant. But there is a difference. You don't choose to be black. You don't choose to be gay. But you could stop being a Goth.' He sighed. 'I don't know where I'm going with this.'

'It's a hate crime, end of,' said Hannah. 'People are being killed because they're different.'

'So what sort of person would hate Goths?'

'Everyone hates us,' said Becky, sourly.

'Not everyone,' said Hannah. 'But yeah, we get spat on in the streets. We get looks. We get a lot of looks.'

'From who?'

Hannah shrugged. 'Like Becky says, everyone. Old people who say that we should get a job. People in suits who say that we look ridiculous. Kids saying that we're vampires. There are a lot of haters out there.'

Nightingale nodded. 'But you'd know that, wouldn't you? You'd know if someone hated you and you'd keep away from them.'

'Sometimes you can't move away,' said Hannah. 'We were sitting in a pub once and group of guys threw tomato juice over us. I mean, how do you deal with that?'

'I don't know,' said Nightingale. 'What did you do?'

'Cleaned ourselves up and went to another pub.'

'The landlord didn't do anything?'

'He didn't want us in there in the first place. He was laughing along with the rest of them.'

'Bastards,' hissed Becky.

'But bastards like that you wouldn't go near, right?' said Nightingale. 'That's what I can't work out. You can spot a hater. So how did the five who died end up letting the haters get so close?'

'Maybe they overpowered them?'

'When they were on their own? How often are you alone out in the open, Hannah? So alone that strangers could grab you without anyone seeing.'

Hannah wrinkled her nose but didn't say anything.

Nightingale waved a hand at the common. 'How many people can you see, right here? A dozen? Fifteen?'

Hannah solemnly counted. 'Nineteen,' she said. 'And six dogs.'

Nightingale pointed at the line of houses overlooking the common. 'And see all those windows. If you were to start screaming now, people would look out to see what's going on. They might not dial nine nine nine, but they'd remember. And no one, absolutely no one, remembers seeing any of those five people being abducted. That's what I finds so curious. This is London, there are more CCTV cameras per head of population than anywhere else in the world. And there are, what, eight million people living in the city. You're never alone. But no one saw anything.'

'Which means what?' asked Hannah.

'It means that whoever is doing it doesn't look like a hater, and doesn't act like a hater. It's planned, it's organised, and it's carried out so efficiently that no one sees it happening. And that's not what normally happens with hate crime.'

Nightingale's phone buzzed in his pocket to let him know he'd received a text message. He looked at his watch. 'Okay, girls, I'm going to have to love you and leave you. He took out his wallet and gave them business cards. 'If either of you do come across anything, you know, weird, give me a call.'

'Weird?' said Hannah. 'How would we know?'

The two girls laughed and in the distance their dogs pricked up their ears.

'That's a good question,' said Nightingale. 'That's the thing about serial killers. Everyone expects them to look strange or menacing, like they do in the movies. They don't. They look completely normal. They can be charming, that's how they get up close.' He took his phone out. He didn't recognise the number but the message made him smile. 'YOUR CAR IS FREE NOW' followed by a smiley face. Nightingale wasn't sure how long Harry would carry on working as a traffic warden but he hoped the job wouldn't change him.

'So how do you know?' asked Becky. 'How do you know if someone is a psychopath?'

Nightingale shrugged. It was a good question. 'You need to step back and take a look at the situation,' he said. 'Look at what's happening to you and ask yourself if what's happening is logical. If a stranger starts chatting you up, is he doing it because he fancies you, or because he wants to get you on your own? Generally if you're in a crowd, you're safe. So never get into a car or go into a house with someone you don't know.'

Becky laughed. 'Come on now, Jack, we're not kids. We're adults, remember.'

Nightingale stood up. 'And all five victims were adults, too. Remember that.' He turned up the collar of his raincoat and walked away.

7

There was no sign of Harry the traffic warden when Nightingale got back to his MGB, but there was no sign of the CRV either and the car that had replaced it, a white VW Golf, had been considerate enough to leave him with more than enough room to get out. It was starting to rain, which was never a good thing because the MGB's windscreen wipers were less than efficient. The rain stayed light during his drive from Clapham to Battersea and by the time he'd found a parking space close to Abbie Greene's apartment it had pretty much stopped.

The apartment block was by the river. There was an automated entry system with CCTV. Nightingale pressed the number of the apartment followed by the hash key. There was a strident beeping sound that went on for a few seconds, then a woman's voice. 'Yes?'

Nightingale introduced himself and explained why he was there, looking up at the CCTV camera and smiling.

'I've already spoken to the police at length, Mr Nightingale.'

'I understand that, Miss Anderson, but I've been asked to get a few more details from you.'

The intercom went quiet for a few seconds and then the door buzzed and Nightingale pushed it open. There were three lifts but once again Nightingale took the stairs. He was breathing heavily when he reached the ninth floor and stood for a minute in the lobby to get his breath back. There were four doors leading off the lift lobby, two to the left and two to the right. Zoe Anderson's was to the left. He pressed the doorbell and a few seconds later she opened it. She was blonde, her hair piled up and held in place with a black clip, and she was wearing a baggy pink pullover over denim shorts. Nightingale figured that after a good night's sleep and a touch of make-up she'd look good but there were dark patches under her bloodshot eyes, her skin was white and pasty and there were flecks of dandruff on her shoulders.

She flashed him a weak smile and held the door open without saying anything. He walked through a white hallway into a double-height room with stunning views over the River Thames, east and west. Nightingale didn't know much about interior design but even he could tell that a lot of money had been spent furnishing the flat. There was a lot of black leather and crystal and on the walls were unframed canvases that looked as if the artist had simply thrown paint at them.

The floors were varnished oak and his shoes squeaked as he walked. He pointed at his Hush Puppies. 'Should I take them off?'

She shook her head.

'This is a lovely flat,' said Nightingale. 'The view is—'

'Breath-taking?'

'Yes. Breath-taking.'

'Well, that's what four million quid gets you,' she said. 'You're wondering how I can afford it.' She sniffed and rubbed her nose with the back of her hand. When she'd opened the door he'd figured that she was in her late twenties but now close up and with the sunlight streaming through the windows, the crow's feet around her eyes suggested she was in her thirties.

'No, not really.'

'I can see it on your face, Mr Nightingale. I've seen it on the face of every police officer who's been up here, and there's been a few over the last week or so. I'm a trust-fund kid, my parents paid for it.'

'I was just thinking that it's a bit high up for me,' he said.

She snorted softly. 'With a name like Nightingale, I thought you'd be good with heights.'

He laughed. 'Please, call me Jack. And no, I prefer my feet on the ground.'

She waved a hand at one of three low beige fabric sofas, angled so that they were all pointing towards the windows. 'Please, sit down. Do you want a coffee or a tea?'

'I'm fine, Miss Anderson.' He took off his raincoat, draped it on the back of the sofa, and sat down.

'If I'm calling you Jack, the least you can do is call me Zoe. But I'm not sure what else I can tell you that I haven't already said at least three times. Abbie was a random victim. She went out and she never came back.' There was a box of tissues on the coffee table and she leaned over and grabbed one.

'Abbie was your partner, right?'

Zoe nodded and dabbed her eyes with the tissue. 'We'd been together for the best part of two years.'

'She's not from London?'

'Sheffield.'

'She came to London to study?'

'I wish. She ran away when she was sixteen. Her mum had remarried and her stepfather couldn't keep his hands to himself. She was on the streets for a while, then found herself a boyfriend who slapped her around, got involved with drugs, then the boyfriend put her on the game to pay for the drugs.' She wiped her nose again. 'Life, huh? Some people have it so easy and others . . .' She shrugged. 'She never had a chance.'

'And then you met her?'

Zoe nodded. 'Two years ago. Sat next to her in a Starbucks and just got talking.' She smiled. 'Do you believe in love at first sight?'

'It's never happened to me,' said Nightingale.

'If you're lucky, one day it will,' she said. 'It's like hitting a wall. Everything stops. You realise that everything up to that point doesn't matter and the one thing you want to do is to spend the rest of your life with that person.'

'And Abbie felt the same?'

Zoe's eyes narrowed. 'What do you mean?'

'She moved in with you?'

'I was a better choice than an abusive boyfriend, is that what you mean? She loved me, Jack.'

'And she started studying?'

'On and off,' said Zoe. 'She was at art school.' She waved at the paintings on the wall. 'Abbie did these. She's very talented.'

'You're not a Goth, obviously.'

'I am sometimes,' said Zoe. 'But it's not a lifestyle thing for me.'

'But it was for Abbie?'

She nodded. 'Totally. But it looked good on her. Sexy

as hell. She got into it about six months ago.' She smiled, but her eyes were tearful. 'I was sorry to see her blonde hair go, though. She had wonderful hair. But she wanted it black, so black it went.'

'And you went with her to Goth bars?'

'Sure. It made her happy. She went with me to galleries and museums, and even tried the opera. I went with her to Goth bars and concerts. I could never really enjoy the music, but I got such a kick out of seeing her enjoying herself. And the dressing up was fun, I suppose.'

'Did you know any of her Goth friends?'

'I'm not sure if I'd call them friends. More like acquaintances.'

Nightingale leaned over and took the photographs of the four other victims from his raincoat pocket. He spread then out on the coffee table. Zoe's lips tightened and the blood drained from her face. 'I can't bear looking at them,' she said, turning away.

'You've been shown them before?'

She nodded. 'And they're all over the papers and TV whenever they mention Abbie. I hate the way they all get lumped together, as if they stop being individuals.'

'You never saw Abbie with any of them?'

Zoe sighed. 'I don't think so, but I can't be sure. We went to so many places. Abbie was pretty and fun, she always had lots of admirers around her. I'd buy them drinks but most of what they said went in one ear and out the other.'

'Did any of them ever come around here?'

'Sometimes. Abbie would get bored sometimes, so she'd get a few people around to drink and watch TV. Horror movies, mostly.'

'Can you do me a favour and just have a close look at the photographs, just to make sure.'

Zoe nodded and wiped her eyes, then slowly went through the photographs. She held the picture of Stella Walsh close to her face and squinted at it. Nightingale realised she probably needed glasses. 'This one, maybe,' said Zoe. 'Pretty little thing. How old is she?'

'Eighteen,' said Nightingale. 'That's Stella Walsh. She was the first one to be killed.'

Zoe nodded thoughtfully. 'Maybe I saw her in the Crypt,' she said. 'A few months ago, perhaps. But it's hard to say, with the make-up they tend to look alike. That's the point, isn't it?'

'The point?'

'The whole Goth thing. They say they're expressing their individuality but actually they all end up looking the same. Black hair, white make-up, black lipstick, black clothes.' She handed back the photographs. 'But maybe I saw her. I can't swear on it.'

Nightingale put the photographs back in his raincoat pocket. 'The night that Abbie died, she went out alone?'

'She said she was meeting a friend. She wanted to see a film, some stupid sci-fi nonsense. I didn't want to go.' She took a deep breath. 'Biggest mistake of my life.'

'And you don't know who the friend was?'

'Either she didn't say or she said and I forgot. I wasn't feeling great.'

'And she didn't say where she was going to see the film?'

Zoe shook her head.

'Because she was found in North West London. Five miles from here.'

'In a stinking bedsit, that's right.' She blinked away tears. 'I keep thinking how scared she was, how she was probably calling out for me, and I wasn't there. When she needed me, I wasn't there.' She stood up and walked over to the window and stared over the river as she dabbed at her eyes.

'The police checked her mobile and none of the people she called went to see a film with her. And they checked CCTV footage of all the cinemas within ten miles and there was no sign of her.'

Zoe whirled around. 'She lied to me, is that what you're saying?'

'No, of course not. Maybe there was a change of plan. Maybe she was intercepted before she got to the cinema.'

'Or maybe she lied to me and was off screwing some guy, that's what you're thinking, isn't it?'

Nightingale shook his head. 'No, of course not.' He shifted uncomfortably on the sofa. 'It's just that no one seems to know how she ended up in a bedsit in Shepherd's Bush.'

'The police say that the bedsit was empty, no one was living there.'

'That's right. It had been empty for two months or so. Which is why it doesn't make sense that Abbie would go there.'

'Presumably someone forced her to go.' Zoe dabbed her eyes again.

'That's what it looks like.'

'Except that Abbie would never have gone with strangers. She was street smart. And I mean that literally, Jack. She was homeless for a long time and it's as dangerous as hell out there, specially for a young girl. Her bastard of a boyfriend had her on the game. She was getting into cars with strangers so she had to weigh men up in seconds. She was a good judge of character; she had to be. Her life depended on it.'

'But she made a bad choice when it came to a boyfriend.'

'She needed protection.'

'He used her, Zoe. She made a bad choice right there.'

Zoe shook her head. 'He was a bastard and he used her, but he didn't kill her. Abbie could take care of herself.' She forced a smile. 'She always had a knife, can you believe that?'

'A knife?'

'A flick-knife. You know, you press a button and the blade flicks out. I told her, if the cops were to catch her with it, she'd go to prison, but she didn't care. She always had it in her bag.'

'You think she would have used it if she was attacked?'

'I'm sure of it,' said Zoe. 'She pulled it out a few times when she was on the street.' She tilted her head on one side. 'You're wondering why she didn't use it when she was attacked.'

'I'm assuming she didn't get the chance,' said Nightingale.

'The police said she was stunned. Whoever killed her, hit her on the head.' She took a deep breath and wiped her eyes again. 'They said she was alive when she was skinned.' She shuddered.

'She wouldn't have felt anything,' said Nightingale, hoping that was the truth.

'That's what the police said, but they don't really know, do they? She might have felt every cut.' She shuddered.

'It's a sick world. I can't understand why the police haven't arrested anybody.'

'It takes time,' said Nightingale. 'If the police are lucky then the killers get caught in the act, but if not it comes down to police work. Asking questions, drawing up time-lines and then checking and cross-checking.'

'But they've killed five people. How can they do that in this day and age?' She wiped her eyes and then blew her nose on the tissue before crumpling it up and throwing it in a bin by the side of her sofa. She looked up at Nightingale. 'It had to be someone she knew. Someone she trusted. She wouldn't let a stranger get close to her.'

'But you've no idea who she was going to go to the film with?'

'Like I said, I don't think I even asked,' said Zoe. 'She left here about six and said she'd be back at eleven. When it got to two o'clock in the morning I called the police but they said she was an adult and had to be missing for twenty-four hours before they could do anything. The woman I spoke to said she'd probably turn up, that most missing people did. By the time the twenty-four hours was up, she was dead.'

Nightingale said nothing. He wanted a cigarette badly but he didn't see any ashtrays around.

'Do you know how they found her?' Zoe asked.

Nightingale shook his head. He did, but he wasn't sure what the police had told her.

'Her blood,' said Zoe. 'Her blood dripped down off the bed and through the floorboards and then it trickled down the light fitting of the bedsit below. Her blood, Jack.' She shuddered again.

Nightingale sat in silence. The desire for a cigarette

was almost overwhelming but he knew enough about psychology to know it wasn't a nicotine craving that was kicking in, he wanted to do something to cover his embarrassment. He could see how upset Zoe was but there was nothing he could do or say to ease her pain. Whoever had given her that information deserved a serious dressing down. There were some things that didn't need to be said, and the condition of Abbie Greene's body was definitely on that list.

'I had to identify the body,' she continued. 'I think they tried to contact her parents but they either couldn't find them or they didn't give a damn.' She reached for another tissue and dabbed at her eyes. 'They'd covered her body up but her face was . . .' She sighed. 'It was like she was asleep. Her eyes were closed and I sort of thought if I just brushed her cheek she'd wake up and smile at me.' She took a deep breath and then let it out in a slow moan, then her whole body was racked with sobs. She folded her arms and bent over as she moaned. Nightingale watched her, helplessly. She wailed for several minutes as she rocked back and forth, then she slowly sat up and tried to smile at him. 'I'm sorry,' she said.

'You've got nothing to apologise for,' he said.

'I just miss her so much.' She looked up at the ceiling and sighed. 'I used to love this flat,' she said. 'Now I hate it. Everything in it reminds me of her. I look at the paintings and I remember when she did them. Her cosmetics and perfume are in the bathroom. I haven't changed the sheets because I can still smell her.' She wiped her eyes and took a deep breath. 'I don't think I want to stay in this world without her,' she whispered.

Nightingale leaned forward. 'Zoe, is there anyone who can come and stay with you?'

'Victim Support, you mean? They sent someone around but I sent them packing. Some stupid woman who just wanted to talk about house prices. I don't need support from a stranger. I need Abbie back, that's what I need.'

'I meant family. What about your parents?'

'They're in the Bahamas.'

'Do they know what's happened?'

'I don't think they care.' She sniffed and blew her nose. 'I'm an only child and they were, let's say, a bit disappointed when I turned out to be gay. All their plans to get me married off to minor royalty fell to bits and they've never forgiven me.' She waved her hand around the apartment. 'I think they'd have taken this back if they could but the money came from my grandfather and the trust fund he set up is pretty much impregnable. So no, Mummy and Daddy won't be around anytime soon.'

'No family at all?'

'My uncle. Uncle Murray.'

'Is he in London?'

She nodded. 'He works in the City. But he's always busy, I haven't seen him in months.'

'You fell out with him?'

'No, I always got on really well with him. He's my godfather, too. But he's never out of the office.'

'You need to call him,' said Nightingale flatly.

'He won't come.'

'Then I'll call him,' said Nightingale. He held out his hand. 'Let me have your phone.'

She shook her head and wiped her eyes. 'I'll be fine,' she said.

'No you won't,' he said.

'What, you're an expert on grief now, are you?'

Nightingale smiled but didn't reply. More often than not, men lashed out when they were in crisis, women tended to strike inwards. Nightingale could see that Zoe wasn't far off hurting herself. And the fact that she had articulated her desire to end her life didn't make it less likely that it would happen. It was a fallacy that people who talked about suicide didn't carry it out. Nightingale knew from experience that the opposite was true. Those serious about killing themselves often tried several times before they succeeded and they would often tell those around them what they intended to do.

'I'm fine, Jack. Really.' She held a tissue to her face and her hand trembled.

'Just let me talk to your uncle,' he said quietly.

Zoe sighed theatrically, then picked up her iPhone off the coffee table. She scrolled through her numbers and then passed the phone to Nightingale.

'You know what, I could do with a cup of tea,' he said. 'Do you mind?'

She smiled and stood up. 'Of course,' she said. 'I could do with tea myself. Milk? Sugar?'

'Milk and one sugar,' he said. He waited until she had disappeared into the kitchen before calling the uncle. He answered quickly. 'Zoe, love, I'm up to my eyes,' he snapped.

'This isn't Zoe, this is Jack Nightingale, I'm with the Metropolitan Police,' said Nightingale, which wasn't strictly speaking a lie because Superintendent Chalmers had authorised him to help with the investigation. Nightingale quickly explained where he was, and why, and that he needed Murray to come over immediately.

'That's not going to happen,' said the man brusquely. 'I've got back-to-back meetings, then I'm due at a marketing lunch, then I'm involved in a major presentation that is potentially worth eight figures to my firm. I could perhaps get there later tonight, but it would be late.'

Nightingale stood up and walked over to the window. The balcony ran the length of the apartment. There were sun-loungers and a barbecue and large ceramic pots filled with plants. There was a metal railing that ran above waist-high panels of tempered glass that surrounded the balcony, but other than that there was nothing to stop anyone going over. 'Now listen to me, Murray. I'm with your niece in her flat, which I'm sure you know is on the ninth floor. She keeps looking out at the balcony and telling me that she wishes she was with Abbie. I've seen people like this before and I can tell you that it doesn't end well. What she needs right now is for someone to hold her and to tell her that she's loved, and with the best will in the world I can't do that. You're her uncle and her godfather. That has got to count for something. From what she tells me you're the only person left that she cares about so you're going to have to decide right now which is more important to you: your job or your niece. And I'd think long and hard about that if I were you because if I leave her on her own and something happens, it'll be on your conscience for the rest of your life.'

Murray said nothing for several seconds and neither did Nightingale. Nightingale had said all that he had to say. There were times when it was best to stay quiet and wait for the other person to fill the silence.

'I'll leave now,' Murray said eventually. 'Can you stay with her until I get there?'

'Sure,' said Nightingale.

'Thank you,' said Murray, and it was clear from his voice that he meant it.

Nightingale ended the call and went through to the kitchen. It was about the same size as his entire flat, with a marble floor, a massive two-door stainless steel fridge and a range of equipment that wouldn't have been out of place in a Michelin-starred restaurant. Zoe was sitting on a stool next to a square marble-topped island below which were wine racks holding hundreds of bottles. Above her head dozens of cast iron pots and pans were hanging from a metal rack. He slid on to a stool next to her and slid the phone across to her. 'He's on his way,' he said.

'That's a first.'

'He's your godfather, that comes with responsibilities.'

'Murray doesn't believe in God, and neither do I. How could God, any God, have allowed that to happen to Abbie?'

Nightingale didn't have an answer and he doubted that anyone did. She kept looking at him, waiting for him to say something, and he said a silent prayer of thanks when the kettle came to the boil, switched itself off and she went over to pour water into an old-fashioned brown earthenware teapot. She had already set out two cups and saucers. 'One sugar?' she said.

'Terrific,' he said. 'You should have sugar, too.'

'I don't have a sweet tooth.'

'It's good for shock.'

She turned to look at him. 'I'm not in shock.'

Nightingale nodded. 'Yes, you are. Not the sharp, jolting kind. The numbing, pressing kind, the sort that makes your chest feel tight. Sugar can help. Seriously.'

Zoe sighed. 'I'm too tired to argue with you,' she said. She reached for a sugar bowl and put one teaspoonful in each of the mugs.

'Two would be better,' said Nightingale.

Zoe laughed. 'Fine, I'll have two if you do.' She added another spoonful to each of the cups, and took them over to the island. 'You've done this before,' she said.

'Suggested sugar? We're taught to do that.'

Zoe opened the left hand side of the fridge and took out a blue and white striped milk jug. She put it down in front of Nightingale and then fetched the teapot. 'Taught?' she said as she sat down and poured tea into the two cups.

'I used to be a police negotiator,' he said.

She frowned. 'What, talking to armed robbers with hostages and stuff?'

Nightingale laughed. In fact he had undergone hundreds of hours of training to deal with people in crisis. He'd spent two years as a police negotiator and while in the movies that meant talking armed robbers out of hostage situations, in the real world more often than not it involved talking to people who wanted to hurt themselves or their nearest and dearest. 'More often than not the person in crisis doesn't have a weapon,' he said.

'Is that what you think I am, a person in crisis?'

Nightingale shook his head. 'Well, if you threatened to kill yourself, then you are, yes.'

Her eyes narrowed. 'Because of what I said, before? About not wanting to live without Abbie?'

'You sounded as if you meant it.'

She sipped her tea before answering. 'I think I probably did, yes. But it's a big step between thinking that and killing myself. I'm not suicidal, Jack.'

'No, but you're in shock and you're vulnerable. And I could see why you didn't want Victim Support, but they do help a lot of people.'

'There's nothing anyone can do to help,' she said. 'No one can bring Abbie back.' She took another sip of tea. 'You don't do it any more then? Negotiating?'

Nightingale shook his head. 'No. Not any more.'

'I'm guessing it's very stressful.'

'Yeah, and it doesn't get any easier. You have to empathise, and that takes its toll. Empathy is a two-way street. You have to open yourself up to the other person and their unhappiness can spill over.' He forced a smile. 'Sorry, that sounds a bit crazy.'

'No, it makes perfect sense. I can see that you genuinely care about me. Unless you're faking it.'

Nightingale laughed. 'I'm not that good an actor. But I was a good negotiator because I could empathise. I could feel what they were going through so I was usually able to help them through it. But every time it was over, I felt a bit more . . . sad, I guess you'd call it. As if I'd taken some of their grief from them.'

'A problem shared is a problem halved, they say.'

Nightingale nodded. 'More often than not they just wanted someone to talk to. Or, more importantly, someone to listen to them.'

'You're good at that, listening.'

'Thanks.'

'No, I'm serious. Most men when they listen to a woman, they're just waiting for a chance to speak. They nod and they pretend to be interested but really they just want to tell you what's on their mind. But you really listen, don't you?'

'I try.' He smiled. 'But yes, I do want to hear what you have to say.'

'You see, if they'd sent you instead of that silly Victim Support woman, you might have helped.'

'Well, I hope I've helped now.'

She nodded and smiled over the top of her cup. 'You have. And the sweet tea was a good idea.'

'Now I was taught to always offer a person in crisis a cup of sweet tea and ideally a biscuit,' he said.

'Would you like a biscuit?'

Nightingale laughed. 'I thought you'd never ask.'

8

Nightingale sat with Zoe for thirty minutes until her uncle arrived. Murray was in his fifties with greying hair and wire-rimmed spectacles and wearing a Savile Row suit that had almost certainly cost more than Nightingale's entire wardrobe. He hugged Zoe and nodded at Nightingale over her shoulder. Zoe began to cry almost immediately and Nightingale slipped out, knowing that there was nothing left for him to do.

He took the stairs down to the ground floor, retrieved his MGB and drove back to South Kensington. Jenny was at her computer when he walked into the office and she smiled up at him. 'How did it go?' she asked.

'So far so good, I guess,' he said, hanging his coat up by the door. 'You?'

'I've spent the day Facebooking and checking Twitter accounts but I don't see any direct connections.'

'That's a pity.'

'There are some indirect connections. Oh, I should say that Daryl Heaton didn't have a Facebook account or a Twitter account.'

'Maybe he had a real life,' said Nightingale. 'He was almost forty, he probably couldn't be bothered. I don't see the point in all that social media stuff.'

'You know you have a Facebook page?'

'I do not.'

'I set it up for you. It's linked to your blog.'

Nightingale's jaw dropped. 'My blog?'

Jenny grinned. 'You've got just over two hundred likes.'

'Likes?'

'People who like your page.'

'When did all this happen?'

'Over the last couple of months. It's all about bringing in new business, Jack, and social media and blogs can do that. I've just put you on LinkedIn, too.'

'I'm not going to bother asking what that is.'

'You don't have to, I'll handle it all for you.' She nodded at her monitor. 'There are some connections that I've found. For instance, Gabe and Luke followed each other on Twitter. But Gabe has fifteen thousand followers and pretty much follows anyone who follows him. I can't find any conversations between the two of them.'

'Fifteen thousand?'

'That's nothing in the Twitter world,' said Jenny. 'Justin Bieber has more than forty million.'

'How does anyone have forty million friends?'

'They're not friends, Jack. They're the people following his tweets. Gabe had fifteen thousand and I guess it's because he tweeted a lot about music and video games.' She sat back and stretched her arms above her head. 'I've been working my way through their Twitter feeds and I can't see them being at the same place at the same time. But I've only been back about a month. Luke was a compulsive tweeter and so was Stella. Fifteen or twenty times a day.'

'Did they tweet on the days they died?'

Jenny nodded. 'Stella tweeted from a pub called the Hobgoblin. It's a Goth place in Camden. Six tweets in all, mainly saying how all the guys she saw were less than attractive.' She grinned. 'She said there were only two-baggers there.'

'Two-baggers?'

'I think the idea is that they're so ugly that you have to put a bag over their head. And one for your own head so that no one recognises you.' She shrugged. 'She had just turned eighteen, Jack. A kid.'

'But then nothing?'

'The last tweet was at ten fifteen. She said she couldn't decide between lemon Bacardi Breezer or orange. She was asking for advice.'

'Anyone reply?'

Jenny shook her head. 'Luke was also tweeting throughout the day that he disappeared. He was having some problems with his father. Half a dozen tweets about not being on the same wavelength, asking why don't fathers listen instead of lecture, regular teenage angst. Then there was a tweet at just after eight o'clock saying that he was waiting for his date, then nothing.'

'He didn't say who the date was or where he was going?'

'That was his last tweet.'

Nightingale wrinkled his nose. 'All these tweets and nothing that's any use.'

'That's the twitterverse for you,' said Jenny. 'Generally it's just people shouting and no one listening. Anyway, I'm pretty sure the police will have gone through all the stuff on Twitter.'

'You can't assume that,' said Nightingale. 'These days

they probably give the job to some Community Support Officer and they're as much use as a chocolate teapot. But yeah, once the information is in HOLMES, the computer should throw up any links.'

'I had a bit more luck on Facebook, but unfortunately again no direct links,' said Jenny. 'For instance Stella Walsh and Abbie Greene both liked the page Gothic And Amazing, and they both posted pictures on it. But there are more than 15,000 likes for that page so it's not necessarily significant. And four of them liked the Cure's page, but that page has about six million likes.'

'Which four?'

'The only one who didn't was Daryl, and he doesn't have a Facebook page.'

'And there was no direct communication between the other four?'

'Not that I can see. Between the four of them there are twelve pages in common, mainly music-related. But the only other page that all four liked was the Crypt. What I'm doing at the moment is working through all the photographs they've posted and checking faces. But so far I can't see any indication that the five ever met each other or spoke to each other.'

'But they all went to the Crypt?'

'Four of them liked the Crypt page. That doesn't mean that they went to the club. And we don't know about Daryl Heaton.'

'I'm going around to his place tomorrow.'

'Has he got family?'

Nightingale shook his head. 'There's an ex-wife somewhere. But the cops couldn't find his parents.'

'So who identified the body?'

'His dentist.' Nightingale shrugged. 'That's sad, right. The only person they could find who could identify him was the guy who worked on his teeth. I'm going to talk to his neighbours, see if they know where he hung out.'

'Tomorrow?'

'Yeah, I'll do all three. Heaton lived in Kilburn, Stella Walsh in Islington and Luke Aitken was staying with his parents in Hampstead.'

'And how did it go today?'

'Make me a coffee and I'll tell you.' Jenny opened her mouth to argue but Nightingale showed her the palm of his hand. 'You lost the race, remember.'

9

Nightingale had his feet up on his desk and he was staring at the whiteboard when Jenny walked in with two coffee mugs. She put one of them on his desk, by his feet. 'Cheats never prosper,' she said.

'Says the girl who'll be making the coffee for the foreseeable future.' He picked up his mug and put it to his lips but stopped when he saw her smile. 'What?' he said.

'What, what?'

'You're smiling.'

'I'm a very happy person.'

Nightingale sniffed his coffee. 'Did you put something in this?'

'Coffee. Milk. Sugar.' She grinned. 'What, do you think I put something else in?'

'Well, did you?'

She snorted dismissively. 'What sort of person would play a childish trick like that, Jack?' she said. Her face went suddenly serious. 'I suppose the sort of person who thinks cheating is acceptable, I suppose that sort of person might think it funny to put something disgusting in another person's coffee.'

He narrowed his eyes and looked at her for several seconds, then he slowly smiled. 'Nah, you're too nice a person.'

'I am,' agreed Jenny. 'I'm as nice as pie.' She smiled brightly but Nightingale didn't like the twinkle in her eyes.

He sipped his coffee and then smacked his lips. 'Tastes good.'

'Glad to hear it.'

He narrowed his eyes again. 'Did you put something in it?'

'Of course not.' She smiled angelically and put her finger cutely against her cheek.

'Maybe I'll make the coffee next time.'

'That would be nice,' she said. She turned to look at the whiteboard. 'Now how did it go today?'

Nightingale took another sip of his coffee. 'I didn't get much, to be honest,' he said. 'But neither of the Goths seemed to be the victim type.'

She turned to look at him, a look of confusion on her face. 'What do you mean?'

He shrugged. 'If I was looking for Goths to kill, neither of them would be my first choice. Gabe Patterson was very outgoing, his wife said he'd talk to anybody and was always well aware of what was going on around him. Abbie Greene was suspicious of strangers and carried a flick-knife.'

'You think that's important?'

'It comes down to motive,' said Nightingale. 'There has to be a reason why the person or persons doing the killing chose them.'

'If it's a hate crime then the fact that they were Goths would be enough to set them off.'

'Yes, but if you want to kill Goths, wouldn't you choose the easy option? Like lions when they hunt? They don't go after the biggest and fastest antelopes, they take down the old and the sick. The easy targets.'

'That's based on research, or your gut feeling?'

'It's the way of the world, kid,' said Nightingale. 'You hear a lot of the cops doing profiling. They look at the way the victims are killed and from that they deduce the profile of the killer. More often than not they come up with something like a white middle-aged male who wet his bed and tortured animals when he was a child. But in fact it's the serial killers who are the best profilers. They can look at a group of people and work out who will go without a struggle, who they can overpower, who they can talk into going off with them. They're skilled at spotting people's weaknesses. Paedophiles are the same. They can look at a group of kids and know which are the vulnerable ones.'

'So you're saying that neither of them were defenceless?'

Nightingale nodded. 'Gabe was quite a big guy and looks like he could take care of himself. Abbie had a knife. But both ended up dead so it seems to me that they weren't confronted.' He swung his feet off the desk and went over to join her at the whiteboard. 'They had to have been caught by surprise.'

'Both of them were hit on the head, right?'

Nightingale nodded again. 'From behind. But I can't see that could have happened out in the open, in the street or in a public place. I can't see that either of them could have been snatched off the street.'

'So they knew their attackers?'

'Either that or they didn't see them as a threat.' He sipped his coffee. 'Somehow the killers got close to all five of them,' said Nightingale.

'Serial killers are charming, right?'

'Charming or at least give off a non-threatening vibe,' said Nightingale. 'But that doesn't square with these being hate crimes. People who carry out hate crimes aren't usually in the least bit charming or non-threatening.'

'Which means that these killers hide their hatred, until it's too late.'

Nightingale stared at the photograph of Abbie Greene. 'Yes, but I don't see that someone like Abbie would be fooled. She was on the game for a while, and hookers tend to be good judges of character.'

Jenny frowned. 'The Yorkshire Ripper killed prostitutes. How many was it?'

'Thirteen. But that was over a five-year period. He'd go for months without killing. And a lot of potential victims turned him down.'

'What I'm saying is that if prostitutes were good at reading people, wouldn't they have seen him for what he was?'

Nightingale wrinkled his nose. 'Maybe they did, but then the need for cash overruled their misgivings, at least long enough for him to get them on their own.' He gestured at the whiteboard. 'This is different from the Yorkshire Ripper in so many ways. The Ripper targeted women. In particular, prostitutes. What we've got here is two men, three women, two gays, three straight, and none of them prostitutes.'

'Abbie hadn't gone back on the streets?'

'There was no need,' said Nightingale. 'Her girlfriend was paying all her bills.'

'But you said she was carrying a knife?'

Nightingale shrugged. 'Old habits die hard.' He went

back to his desk and sprawled in his chair. 'I was trying to explain something to a couple of Goths today, about hate crimes. It didn't come out right.'

'In what way?'

He pointed at the whiteboard. 'Well, these are hate crimes, right? That's the assumption Chalmers and his team are working on.'

'They don't come much more hateful than skinning people alive.'

'And Goths are being targeted. Because they're Goths.'

'That seems to be what's happening, yes.'

'And these Goths I was talking to said it was a hate crime the same as if gays or blacks were being killed.'

'Sounds right.'

Nightingale grimaced. 'Okay, so what I said was that it wasn't the same because Goths choose to be Goth. No one forces them to wear the make-up and dark clothes.'

'And I'm guessing they didn't take it well?'

'I backpedalled pretty quickly, but I could see that I'd touched a nerve.'

'Do you think?' She threw up her hands. 'Sometimes I despair of you, Jack.'

'It's a valid point though, isn't it?'

Jenny frowned. 'You still don't get it, do you? It's a hate crime if someone lashes out at somebody because they're different. It doesn't matter what that difference is.'

'I get that, Jenny. I'm not stupid.'

'What about religion? People choose their religion. But if you attack someone because of their religion, then it's a hate crime.'

'But Goth isn't a religion. It's a cultural thing. Look, I'm not trying to excuse what's happening, I'm trying to understand it. I can see why straight people might be offended by gays. I can understand why white people might hate non-whites. But I don't understand why being a Goth can inspire this level of hatred and violence.'

'I still don't get what you're saying, Jack.'

Nightingale took a deep breath. 'I don't fully understand it myself,' he said. 'It's just that what's happening seems out of all proportion to the provocation.'

'Now you're saying that the Goths are being provocative?'

Nightingale sighed. 'Jenny, they choose the gear, they choose the make-up, they choose to hang out with each other. Everything they do is by choice.'

'And like I keep saying: that's what makes it a hate crime.'

'But what's happening is planned. Very well planned. And carefully carried out. And that's not what happens with hate crimes. Hate crimes come from hatred. From emotion. What's happening to these Goths doesn't seem to involve emotion.'

'The bodies were mutilated, that seems to me to be fairly emotional.'

Nightingale shook his head. 'Actually no. The mutilations were cold and clinical. And done in such a way that there was no evidence that could identify the perpetrators. Then most of the bodies were dumped, and dumped carefully. Where's the hatred, Jenny? I see the crime, but I don't see the hatred.'

She nodded slowly. 'I'm listening.'

'These Goths – a couple of girls – were telling me about the time some guys threw tomato juice over them in a pub.'

'Tomato juice?'

'I guess it was a vampire thing. But when they were telling me that I thought, yeah, I see the hatred. Guys in a pub get pissed off at Goths, for whatever reason, and they react by throwing a drink over them. It's a heat of the moment thing, right. Hatred followed by rage.'

Jenny frowned. 'Spur of the moment?'

'Exactly. And gay-bashing, when it happens. How does that work? Usually in the street, a gay couple walk by hand in hand or kiss and a group of Neanderthals kick off. The gays get bashed and the Neanderthals run away. Hatred followed by rage.'

Jenny brushed a stray lock of hair behind her ear. 'No planning. No forethought.' She nodded. 'They just lash out, right?'

'Because the attacks are inspired by hatred. By emotion. But what's happening with these Goths shows zero emotion.' He held up his hand. 'I know, the mutilation looks like emotion, but even that is carried out clinically. I've seen the crime-scene photographs and there was no obvious emotion involved.'

'So you're saying they're not hate crimes?'

'I don't think they were inspired by hatred. Not the sort of hatred that led to them having a drink thrown over them in the pub. These five murders have been well planned and carefully carried out. That's why the cops have zero evidence to go on. So we're not going to get anywhere thinking of them as simple hate crimes. There has to be a motive, Jenny. There has to be a logical reason for these killings.'

'The killers could just be sociopaths, Jack. Have you thought about that?'

'Sociopaths aren't usually motivated by hate,' said Nightingale. 'And they tend to attack one sex or the other. That's what's so strange about these cases. We've got male and female, gay and straight, young and middle-aged. Sociopathic serial killers tend to be much more selective about their victims.'

'So we're looking for some other connection, other than the fact that they're Goths?' said Jenny. She pulled a face as if she had a bad taste in her mouth.

'You don't agree?'

'I think you might be overthinking it,' said Jenny. 'You might be giving too much credit to psychopaths who just want to hurt people.'

'Okay, but look at what they do to the victims. They slash their bodies to ribbons, right? But then they do nothing to the faces. If it was really about hatred, isn't the face what they'd go for? The face makes it personal. That's how it works with shooters. If you want to shoot someone you shoot them in the chest because that's the biggest target. But if there's hatred involved, if it's personal, you shoot them in the face.'

'That's a fair point,' said Jenny, looking back at the whiteboard. 'None of the faces were touched.'

'Exactly. Dozens of cuts and slashes, but only to the body. And they were all naked.' He closed his eyes as he tried to remember what he'd seen in the incident room.

'Are you okay, Jack?' asked Jenny.

He held up his hand to silence her as he tried to recall the crime scene photographs he'd seen on the five white-boards. 'The clothes were cut off,' he said. He opened his eyes. 'Three of them were dumped outside, and they were naked when they were dumped. And the two who were found indoors – Daryl Heaton and Abbie Greene – were also naked.'

Jenny frowned. 'So?'

'So where's the hatred in that? If you're angry at someone and want to slash them to death, surely you'd just hack away? Knives go through clothes just as easily as they cut through flesh. But they cut the clothes off. They were tossed aside and there was no blood on them.'

'Are you sure?'

Nightingale closed his eyes again and tried to picture the crime scene photographs. Abbie Greene had been found in a bedsit in Shepherd's Bush, and while the bed she was on was covered in blood her clothes had been cut off and tossed on a chair. Daryl Heaton's naked and mutilated corpse was also found on the bed, his clothes strewn around the room. He opened his eyes. 'I'm sure,' he said. 'There was no blood on the clothing so it was definitely cut off before cuts were made.'

'That doesn't make sense, does it? Why cut the clothes off and then cut the bodies?'

'Getting rid of the clothes makes sense, because they'd harbour forensic evidence. But again, it does suggest that there was no rage, no hatred. It was cold and deliberate. And very carefully planned.' He sighed. 'I don't know. Maybe you're right and I'm overthinking it. I'll know better tomorrow.'

'What about your other cases?' she asked.

'We don't have much on at the moment.'

She raised her eyebrows. 'Have you forgotten Mrs Hetherington's husband? It's Thursday and Thursday night is his so-called poker night.'

'Bloody hell,' said Nightingale, looking at his watch. 'What time does he finish work?'

'Six, that's what he tells his wife, anyway.'

Bruce Hetherington was a North London estate agent who may or may not have been having an affair with his personal assistant, a very pretty redhead about half his age. Mrs Hetherington had found a few incriminating text messages on her husband's phone and rather than confronting him with the evidence had set about protecting herself. She had consulted a solicitor and set about identifying all their assets and savings, including Mr Hetherington's substantial pension. Now that she had all her financial ducks in a row she needed hard evidence of the affair. Once she had the proof she needed the hapless Mr Hetherington was going to be turfed out of their five-bedroom detached house in Fulham and discover that he had lost all access to the joint bank accounts. According to Mr Hetherington, Thursday night was poker night, when he got together with other estate agents and didn't get home until the early hours. But having seen the text messages between her husband and the personal assistant, Mrs Hetherington was convinced that it wasn't card playing that was keeping him out late. 'Poker? More like bloody poker-her,' is what she'd said in his office, and to his credit Nightingale had just about managed to keep a straight face.

'Bugger,' said Nightingale. 'The MGB's playing up. And it's not the best car to be tailing anyone in.'

'Because it's a pile of crap?'

Nightingale glared at her. 'Because it's a racing green classic car,' he said. 'It sticks out. How about we use your Audi?'

'How about you sit pillion on Mark McKay's Ducati?'

'Have you called him?'

'Called him and booked him and he'll be here at five.'

Nightingale had used McKay several times on surveillance jobs. He worked part-time as a motorcycle courier and knew the streets of London as well as any taxi driver. Nightingale's surveillance jobs paid better than delivering parcels so McKay was always happy to work for him, no matter the short notice. 'You're good,' he said.

'But unappreciated.'

'I appreciate the hell out of you.'

'Pity that's not reflected in my pay packet.'

Nightingale frowned. 'How much do I pay you?'

'You see, the fact that you don't know worries me.'

'When did you last get a pay rise?'

'Last Christmas.'

'Do you think you should have another?'

'Do you?'

'Kid, I just want you to be happy. This business, such as it is, would fall apart without you. If that's not appreciation, then I don't know what is. Have a look at the books and let me know what you think you should be paid.'

She smiled. 'Thank you.'

'You're welcome.'

'I mean thank you for what you just said. For the extra money as well, of course. But more so for what you said.'

'I mean it.'

'I could see that. That's why I'm thanking you. And just to show you how lucky you are to have me, I came up with something very interesting while I was trawling through Facebook, though it's not Goth-related.'

'Not porn, I hope.'

Jenny ignored his attempt at humour. 'Remember Nicholas Drummond? The guy who got hit in the rear at the traffic lights by a double-decker bus?'

'Yeah, he gets his cheque next week, right?'

The bus company had hired Nightingale to check that Mr Drummond's injuries were genuine. He had a doctor's report claiming that he had five bulging discs in his neck and spine and that walking caused him almost unbearable pain. Which meant that he was unable to work. Nightingale had staked the man out on three occasions over the past six months and had never seen anything untoward. Most of the time he stayed indoors and when he did appear he always had a neck brace on. He used a crutch to get to and from his car and seemed to have difficulty getting in and out. His wife drove and she was always on hand to help him. Nightingale had filed three reports, each saying that the man's injuries appeared to be genuine.

'The cheque was supposed to be sent out to him this afternoon,' said Jenny. 'But this morning I discovered that he's set up a sponsorship page for running the half marathon in Brighton on Sunday. He's raised three hundred pounds for Cancer Research.'

Nightingale's jaw dropped. 'How the hell did that happen? I was on his doorstep three times and I never saw him training. How does a guy in a neck brace and using a crutch suddenly go to running a half marathon?'

'That's what I thought,' said Jenny. 'So I called our guy in the claims department and had a quiet lunch with him. Seems they've had a few claimants using the same doctor as Mr Drummond. All with bulging discs and all backed up by convincing MRIs. Except on closer examination, they're the same MRI.'

Nightingale grinned. 'That's interesting.'

'It gets better,' she said. 'There are four claims in all, at various stages of being processed, all of them being handled by the same woman in the claims office. And she's only been there a year.'

'So she's the mastermind behind this little scam, is she?'

'Not so little, Jack. The four claims total almost three million quid.'

'But Drummond hasn't got his money?'

Jenny shook her head. 'That's the thing. The cheque was supposed to go out this afternoon, by courier. But now Mr Drummond has been told that the cheque has been delayed until Monday.'

'You are an absolute star.'

'It gets better,' said Jenny. 'They're not just paying us a fee; we're getting a percentage of the money that Mr Drummond would have got. Five per cent.'

Nightingale tried to do the sum in his head. Mr Drummond had been due to receive a little over one million pounds. Five per cent of a million pounds was a lot.

'Fifty grand, Jack,' she said.

'Wow. Who's a clever girl, then?'

'That would be me.' She grinned. 'So the long and the short of it is that you need to get yourself down to Brighton on Sunday with a video camera. They need a video of Drummond starting and finishing, along with a record of his time.'

'No problem,' said Nightingale.

'I did good, didn't I?'

'You did brilliant, kid.'

'So I was thinking, maybe I should get a chunk of the finder's fee.'

'A chunk?'

'Twenty per cent.'

'God, you're good.'

Jenny grinned. 'I'll take that as a yes.'

10

Nightingale didn't get home until two o'clock in the morning. McKay had dropped him off and helped him strip out of his motorcycle leathers. Nightingale was exhausted but it had been a productive nine hours. They had been outside Hetherington's office when he had left with the pretty redhead in tow. McKay had fixed up a small video camera on the top of Nightingale's full-face helmet that was connected to a portable hard drive in his inside pocket. There was an on-off switch connected to the camera but there was more than enough space on the hard drive to store ten hours of video. They had filmed the couple walking towards Mr Hetherington's Bentley soft-top, and caught a very incriminating hug and kiss before she went over to her white VW Golf. For a moment Nightingale thought they had been wasting their time but then the VW drove off and Mr Hetherington had followed in his Bentley.

McKay had kept a decent distance between the bike and the car, closing the gap only when they got close to traffic lights. The girl kept the VW at just under the speed limit and Mr Hetherington stuck close to her. They drove to a Spanish restaurant in Muswell Hill and parked outside. Nightingale got more video of the two kissing and hugging before they went inside, arm in arm. McKay drove down a side street where Nightingale stripped off his leathers and helmet before heading into the restaurant. There was a bar to the right and a dozen tables with red tablecloths and candles in old Rioja bottles. Nightingale sat at the bar and ordered a Corona and some tapas – anchovies in vinegar and oil, chorizo in hard cider and patatas bravas.

Mr Hetherington was sitting at a corner table, splitting his time between sipping red wine and kissing his PA on the lips as they waited for their food to arrive. Nightingale was alone at the bar and he managed to record several minutes of video on his smartphone. The loving couple shared a large dish of paella and then took it in turns to feed each other crema catalana. Nightingale managed to video the dessert sharing and when their coffees arrived he paid his bill and went outside to join McKay.

He was back on his bike in his leathers and with his helmet on when Mr Hetherington and his PA emerged arm-in-arm from the restaurant. Nightingale snatched more video of the two kissing on the pavement before getting into their respective vehicles. Again the VW led the way, this time to a terraced house a short distance from Alexandra Palace. Mr Hetherington parked his Bentley first but it took his companion several attempts before she managed to squeeze in between a black cab and a people carrier. Nightingale and McKay watched from a side street as Mr Hetherington made fun of the woman's attempts to parallel park, and Nightingale managed to get footage of them kissing in the road and walking together to the front door of the woman's house where they kissed again before she took her keys out of her bag and let them in.

The lights had gone on downstairs, and then the light had gone on in the upstairs bedroom. McKay had driven slowly by the house and as luck would have it the woman was drawing the curtains just as the bike was level with the house. Nightingale was fairly sure he'd managed a shot of the woman in the window with Mr Hetherington standing behind her, cupping her breasts.

They had parked up in a side street and Nightingale had videoed Mr Hetherington leaving the house at one o'clock in the morning. They hadn't bothered following him home as Nightingale had all the footage he needed.

Nightingale let himself into his flat, had a quick shower and fell into bed. He was woken up eight hours later by his mobile ringing on the bedside table. He groped for it. 'Yeah?'

'Are you coming in today?' It was Jenny.

Nightingale groaned. 'What time is it?'

'Ten. I wasn't sure if you were coming in or going straight to the Goth interviews.'

'The latter,' he said, sitting up and running his hand through his hair.

'You're in bed, aren't you?'

'Please don't tell me that you've got CCTV rigged up in my bedroom.'

'You sound like you've just woken up.'

'Guilty as charged. But on a more positive note we have Mr Hetherington bang to rights. Loads of video of them canoodling and him going into her house with her and leaving in the small hours.'

'Brilliant, Mrs Hetherington will be thrilled. When can I have it?'

Nightingale swung his feet off the bed. 'I'll do the three interviews first, I should be back this afternoon.'

He ended the call then shaved and showered and put on a dark blue suit, a white shirt that he'd only worn once and a green tie with yellow MGB logos on it. He had scheduled three visits on the Goth case, all north of the river. He needed to talk to the neighbours of Daryl Heaton, who lived alone in Kilburn. He had to talk to the parents of Stella Walsh, the first victim, in Islington, and the parents of Luke Aitken, who lived in Hampstead. Geographically they were only a few miles from each other but the quirks of the London transport system meant that the easiest and quickest way of getting to all three was to drive. His stomach was growling but he figured he didn't have time to make his regular bacon sandwich breakfast so he picked up a coffee and muffin from Starbucks on his way to his car.

His first stop was Kilburn. Daryl Heaton lived in a three-storey terraced house that in Edwardian times had probably been home to a family and servants but which had long ago been converted into studio flats. It was a short walk from Kilburn High Street and Nightingale managed to find a parking space between a skip piled high with wood and plaster and a British Gas van. To the left of the front door was an intercom with six buttons, six at the top and one on the bottom. According to the police file, Heaton lived in Flat 3. Nightingale pressed the button for Flat 4 and waited. After a minute he pressed it again but when there was still no answer he pressed Flat 1. Again there was no answer. Nightingale sighed and stabbed the button for Flat 5. This time a man answered and it sounded as if he had just woken up. 'What?'

'I'm with the police,' said Nightingale, which he figured was an approximation of the truth. 'I need to talk to you about Mr Heaton.'

'Again? This is the third time.'

'I won't take long, a few minutes at most,' said Nightingale. The door lock buzzed and Nightingale pushed it open. There was a pile of junk mail and fast food leaflets on the floor and a pushchair at the bottom of the stairs. The stair carpet was threadbare and had worn completely through in places. The walls were streaked with dirt and the single light bulb hanging from the ceiling was covered in dust and there was a cobweb running from the flex to the wall. Nightingale picked up the mail and flicked through it. There were several bills among the junk including a mobile phone bill addressed to Joe Lumley. He tossed the envelopes to the side and went upstairs.

There was police tape across the door to Flat 3 and a letter had been stapled to it saying that no one was to gain entrance and that any queries could be dealt with by calling one of three phone numbers. The wood around the lock had splintered, presumably from when the police had broken it down, and it had been roughly repaired with a few pieces of cheap timber.

Flat 5 was directly above Heaton's flat. Nightingale knocked on the door and it was opened by a man in his late twenties wearing Mickey Mouse boxer shorts. He looked at Nightingale blearily and yawned, showing perfect white teeth. 'Yeah?' he said, then yawned again.

'Joe Lumley?'

The man nodded and ran a hand through his unkempt hair as he tried to focus on Nightingale's face. 'Yeah.'

'I'm sorry to have woken you up,' said Nightingale.

'I haven't been to bed yet,' said Lumley. Nightingale looked at his watch. It was ten o'clock. 'I work nights,' the man growled. 'I only just got in.'

'Sorry,' said Nightingale.

Lumley opened the door wider. 'No sweat. You want tea?'

'Yeah, thanks,' said Nightingale. The man padded over to a table on which there was a microwave and a kettle. He switched on the kettle, then grabbed a pair of jeans and a black pullover and disappeared into the bathroom. He reappeared a couple of minutes later wearing the jeans and pullover and having attempted to run a comb through his hair.

'Like I said, I've spoken to the cops already. There's not much I can add. I must have been out when he was killed. I never heard anything.' He smiled ruefully. 'That was the point, actually. For the first time in over a year he was quiet. I should have realised something was wrong when he wasn't playing his stereo full blast in the afternoon.'

'Noisy neighbour?' said Nightingale.

'You don't know the half of it,' said Lumley. The kettle switched itself off and Lumley dropped teabags into the mugs and poured in hot water. 'I know I shouldn't speak ill of the dead but Daryl was a nasty piece of work. He really didn't give a toss about anyone other than himself. He was up late at night but that was okay because I worked nights. I know the girl in Flat 1 was always complaining and even got the council environmental people around once, but you couldn't reason with him. I think he had two ASBOs from his last place. That was council-owned so they got him out eventually but this is private so there was no way to get him out.'

'He's out now,' said Nightingale.

Lumley looked over his shoulder. 'Yeah, but skinning him alive was a bit drastic, don't you think?'

'I suppose they looked at the woman in Flat 1?'

Lumley laughed. 'She's five foot nothing. Daryl was a big lad.' He bent down to open a small fridge tucked away under the table. He sloshed milk into both mugs. 'Sugar?'

'Sweet enough,' said Nightingale.

Lumley handed him one of the mugs, a tea bag still floating in the brew. 'So they're no nearer catching the guys that did it?'

'What makes you say that?'

'What I read in the papers. Plus the fact that you're here.' He waved Nightingale to the one chair in the room, a wood one with a high back. Lumley sat down on the bed.

'I was hoping to talk to whoever was in Flat 4. I wanted to know if they saw Daryl with any visitors.' Nightingale took photographs of the four other victims and gave them to Lumley.

'They're the others that were killed, right?'

Nightingale nodded. 'Did you ever see any of them here?'

'I didn't see much of him or his visitors, truth be told,' said Lumley. He flicked through the pictures and then handed them back. 'We were in different time zones. Once I got into the habit of sleeping with earplugs I rarely had any dealings with him.' He sipped his tea. 'You know what he was like, right?'

'A thirty-nine-year-old Goth, unemployed. That pretty much says it all.'

Lumley chuckled. 'Yeah, he wasn't a great one for nine to five, that's for sure. He wasn't a Goth though. I think they just said that to make it a better story. The first four were Goths, right? Two young guys and two young girls. Then they found Daryl all cut to bits and they wanted to label it the Goth Killers so that's how they described him. But I heard the music he played and he wasn't into the Goth stuff. More heavy metal. The heavier the better.'

'Goth stuff would be what, then?'

'Pierce The Veil, Sleeping With Sirens, My Chemical Romance. The Cure if you're old school. Not Aerosmith and AC-DC.'

'So you're saying he wasn't a Goth?'

'He wore black, sure. But none of that make-up nonsense. Black jeans, black shirts, black motorcycle boots. He was more of a biker.'

'Did he have a bike?'

Lumley laughed. 'No, he was a biker without a bike. But he did have biker mates. Not Hells Angels exactly, but serous bikers. I saw the picture they used in the papers, and it was him, sure, but it showed his face and his hair was spiky and gelled but usually he just wore it natural. And you didn't see the tattoos in the picture, his arms were covered in them. All sorts of stuff. Fish. Animals. Flowers. A pirate. A sword. The times I saw him he was wearing a denim jacket with the sleeves hacked off.'

'So you saw bikers around but never Goths?'

'Like I said, he wasn't a Goth. I think the papers just wanted to say that he was to make it a better story. I mean, it's not a great headline to say that cops are hunting a Goth and biker killer, is it?'

'I guess not,' said Nightingale. 'You said Daryl was the fifth to be killed. Actually he was the fourth. But his was the last body to be found.'

'Yeah, it was me that reported it. You could tell that something was wrong from the smell in the hallway. At first I thought a rat had died under the floorboards but it got worse. I knocked on the door a few times and eventually I called the landlord.'

'Not the cops?'

Lumley shook his head. 'I'm not a big fan of the cops,' he said. 'If I'd called it in then I'd be in the system. You know what it's like, some bright spark would wonder if I'd done it and would start giving me the third degree. So I called the landlord and let him handle it.'

'The cops don't think you did it, I can tell you that much,' said Nightingale. 'Anyway, most of the killings took place late at night when you'd have an alibi.' He sipped his tea. 'So what do you work at?'

'I'm a night porter at a hotel in Covent Garden,' he said. 'Well, I'm a student but that's what I do to pay my bills. They're pretty cool about me reading textbooks while I'm there, so it's all good.'

'But Daryl, he was just on the dole?'

'He must have been getting cash from somewhere,' said Lumley. 'The amount he spent on booze and dope.'

'Dope?'

'Used to smell that in the hallway, too.' He grinned and tapped his nose. 'Sensitive nose, me,' he laughed. 'Plus I'm not impartial to a bit of . . .' He grimaced. 'Whoops, probably shouldn't say that.'

'It's practically legal these days,' said Nightingale. 'And all I'm interested in is who killed Daryl.'

'Has to be a psycho, right?' said Lumley. 'Cutting him up the way they did. Must have taken an hour or so, to kill him and chop him up.'

Nightingale nodded. 'There are some sick people around.'

'When I heard he'd been killed I thought maybe it was a drug thing. Maybe he'd been dealing and he'd pissed somebody off. But then this whole Goth Killers thing blew up. I mean that's really sick, right? Killing someone because of what they look like.'

'But you said Daryl wasn't a Goth.'

'Yeah, but he wore black. Maybe they made a mistake.'

Nightingale stared down at the tea bag in his mug. 'Maybe.' He drank his tea and stood up. 'Well, I'll let you get to bed,' he said.

'Sorry I wasn't more help. But I do hope you catch them, whoever's doing it.'

'You and me both,' said Nightingale.

11

The Aitken home was in Hampstead, close to the village. It was detached and there were two cars parked outside, a white Lexus and a green Mini Cooper. The house looked Edwardian, the red bricks were weathered and the slate roof was dotted with patches of moss. It was Luke's mother who answered the door, a stick-thin woman with dark patches under her eyes that suggested she wasn't getting much sleep. She wore a pale blue cardigan with a string of pearls around her neck. She was in her mid-forties but the death of her son had hit her hard and she looked a good ten years older. She led Nightingale down a hallway to a sitting room with a large cast-iron Victorian fireplace either side of which were book-shelves lined with leather-bound books. There were two green leather Chesterfield sofas either side of an oak coffee table piled high with books and she waved Nightingale to one. 'My husband has gone to work,' she said. 'He didn't want to but if he's not there, the place falls apart.' She shrugged and forced a smile. 'Can I offer you a tea or a coffee?'

'I'm fine, Mrs Aitken, thank you,' said Nightingale.

She walked over to a drinks cabinet in the corner of

the room. 'I'm going to have a sherry,' she said. 'Would you like one?'

'I'm driving, but thank you,' he said. He saw her hand pull away from the decanter and the look of disappointment etched on to her face. 'Go on then,' he said. 'Just a small one.'

She beamed, poured two glasses of sherry, gave him one and sat down on the sofa opposite him. 'You had some questions, you said?'

'I'm trying to get a feel for who your son met during the days before he died,' said Nightingale.

'The investigation has stalled, hasn't it?' she said. She was sitting with her back ramrod straight, the glass of sherry in her lap.

'Not stalled exactly,' said Nightingale. 'There are as many officers on it as there was when the investigation began. And witnesses are still being canvassed and CCTV is being looked at. But we're keen to open up more lines of enquiry.'

'I don't follow you,' she said. She was watching him intently and he had could see that she was weighing him up. He had her marked down as a housewife when she'd opened the door but it was clear that she was used to dealing with people from a position of authority. He looked over at the mantelpiece. There were framed photographs there, mainly of Mrs Aitken, her much older husband, and Luke, the son. There was also a photograph of Mrs Aitken in the robes and wig of a barrister.

He looked back at her and smiled. 'We're trying to work out why Luke was targeted.'

'Wrong place, wrong time,' she said. 'I've been trying

not to play the "what if" game. What happened, happened, and we have to deal with it.'

Nightingale nodded. 'We're looking for a possible connection between those who died,' he said. He deliberately avoided the word 'victim' and 'killed', though he could see that Mrs Aitken didn't need to have her feelings spared.

'If you can find that connection, it will help identify the killers,' she said. 'That makes sense.' She sipped her sherry.

'I'm sure you've already been asked this, but have you ever seen Luke with any of these people?' Nightingale took the five photographs from his pocket, took out Luke's and handed the remaining four to Mrs Aitken.

She looked at them carefully, then shook her head emphatically. 'I have seen the pictures before and no, I don't recall ever seeing any of them with my son.' She handed them back and took a longer sip of her sherry.

'Luke was a student?'

'He was, at Exeter University.'

'But it was term time, right?'

'Luke was having problems at university and we felt that it would be better for him to spend some time at home.'

'Problems?'

Mrs Aitken sipped her sherry again. Her glass was already half empty. 'Luke was always . . .' She looked pained. 'A little confused. He always went into things with enthusiasm, but that enthusiasm never lasted for long. He just wasn't enjoying being at Exeter. At first he said it was the course that he didn't like, but it soon became clear it was the place. We were looking at the possibility of him transferring to London.'

'He had a lot of friends here?'

She nodded. 'I think that was part of the problem. He had so many friends here that he didn't give Exeter a chance.'

'His friends were mainly Goths?'

'I hate that label,' said Mrs Aitken. 'The Gay Goth the tabloids called him. And the gay community has been using him as the poster boy for their campaign to criticise the police. As if his sexual orientation had anything to do with it.' She finished her sherry and walked over to the drinks cabinet and poured herself another. 'Luke was a gentle soul. He never had a girlfriend and I don't think he had a boyfriend. He went to gay clubs but I think that was just him experimenting. It was the same with the Goth thing. He only got into that before he left for Exeter. He said he liked the music.' She shuddered. 'My husband and I hated it. He has his own apartment in the basement but we could still hear it if he played it loud. Horrible lyrics.' She shuddered again and then went to sit back on the sofa.

'Do you know what clubs he went to?'

'Soho mainly,' she said. 'He never said which ones. Just Soho.'

'Did he go alone or with friends?'

'He'd meet up with friends when he was there.'

'So it is possible that he might have known one of the other four?'

'I suppose so.' She took another sip of sherry. 'My husband is taking it very badly.'

'It must be a nightmare,' said Nightingale.

'Do you have children?' Nightingale shook his head. 'We only had the one. And we nearly lost Luke when he was born. He was premature so he was straight into the neonatal babies unit. The first few days were touch and go.' She forced a smile. 'But he was a fighter. There was a strength about him, under the surface. He was soft and gentle but deep down, he could be like steel.'

Nightingale took a drink of sherry as he listened. He wanted her to talk because anything that she said might be helpful. But at the end of the day, maybe she was right – her son had simply been in the wrong place at the wrong time.

'Luke and his father had a big argument, two days before he died,' said Mrs Aitken. 'Luke had been to get a tattoo. He hadn't told us. I don't even know when he got it. I just noticed it one day. On his shoulder. I told him it wasn't a smart thing to do, that these days a lot of firms won't hire anyone with a tattoo but he said I was being silly and that any shirt would cover it.' She sighed and sipped her sherry again. 'I made the mistake of mentioning it to Gerald, my husband.' She raised her eyes to the ceiling and sighed out loud. 'It was a huge mistake, but then hindsight is always twenty-twenty, isn't it?'

'I suppose so,' said Nightingale.

She lowered her head and fixed him with steel-grey eyes. 'There's no suppose so about it, Mr Nightingale. I just wish there was some way of undoing what's been done.' She smiled sadly. 'And there was me saying that I've been trying not to play the "what if" game. But yes, I should have just kept my big mouth shut.' She took a long drink of sherry and then licked her lips. 'I told Gerald about the tattoo and he let rip with Luke, told him he was an idiot, then it escalated and Gerald started on about the Goth thing, and about him running away from university, before I knew what had happened Gerald was spouting this litany of accusations and Luke just stood there and took it. That was his way, he could soak up anger like a sponge. He just kept looking at Gerald until he ran out of steam and then he just smiled and asked him if he'd finished.' She raised her eyes to the ceiling again. 'Gerald hit the roof then.' She sipped her sherry then stared at the glass as if surprised to see that it was almost empty. 'He screamed at Luke to get out of the house. And that's what Luke did.' She stood up, walked stiffly over to the drinks cabinet and refilled her glass.

'When was that?' asked Nightingale.

'Three days before Luke . . . died.' She closed her eyes and sipped her sherry but the sip turned into a swallow and then she drained the glass. She refilled it and carried it carefully back to the sofa where she sat down and pressed her legs together. 'Gerald never got the chance to apologise to Luke. He was working hard and Luke was either asleep or out. I talked to Luke and he was okay, he said he understood why his father was angry and that he'd sit down with Gerald and smooth things over. But he never got the chance. Gerald wasn't even here when the police came around to tell me what happened. He was at work, I had to phone him.' Her lower lip began to tremble and she bit down on it. Nightingale could see that she was fighting back tears.

'The day that Luke died. He went to Soho, right?'

'He said he was going to meet a friend.'

'But he didn't say who?'

She shook her head. 'To be honest, we never really met any of his friends. Sometimes they would come to pick him up but they would just beep their horn and he would go out. He never invited them in.'

'You think he was ashamed of his friends?'

She forced a smile. 'Quite the reverse,' she said. 'I think he was ashamed of us.'

'The car outside. The Mini. That was his?'

'We bought it last year as a present to say well done for getting into university.'

'But he didn't drive to Soho?'

'He was very good about not drinking and driving. Someone came to pick him up.'

'And you don't remember who?'

She shook her head. 'I was in the kitchen. I heard a horn sound and Luke rushed out.' She sighed. 'He didn't even say goodbye.' She put a hand up to her face and took a deep breath. 'He didn't even say goodbye,' she repeated to herself. She jerked as if she had only just realised Nightingale was there. 'Is there anything else?' she asked.

'No, I think that's enough,' said Nightingale.

She fixed him with her tear-filled eyes. 'You need to find them, Mr Nightingale. I can't go on like this. I need to know who did this to my son and why.'

Nightingale stood up. He wanted to say something to reassure Mrs Aitken but he didn't want to lie to her. There were no guarantees. He would do everything within his power to move the investigation forward and he knew Chalmers would give it one hundred per cent, but the police didn't solve every case. So far the murderers of her son hadn't made any slips that would lead to their early arrest, and dogged police work hadn't produced results. What they needed now was a break – which was another way of saying that they needed luck. 'As soon as we find anything, I'll be sure to let you know,' he said.

Her eyes narrowed, just a fraction, and then she smiled, letting him know she respected his honesty.

'Thank you, Mr Nightingale,' she said quietly. 'You're a good man.' She lifted the sherry glass to her lips. 'Do you think you could be a dear and show yourself out?'

'Of course,' said Nightingale. He headed for the door. He didn't look back but he knew tears were running down her cheeks.

12

The Walsh family lived in a three-bedroom council flat on a tower block named Noll House on the sprawling Andover estate in North London, not far from Arsenal Tube station. It wasn't the most salubrious of areas and the graffiti-covered walls and unswept streets suggested that Nightingale's MGB would be better off in a car park some distance away. He lit a Marlboro as he walked to the estate. Parts of it had been built in the fifties, and it was added to in the sixties and seventies, but it had always had a bad reputation for crime and drug use. The three main triangular blocks were named after the local architects who had designed them but who would never in a million years have wanted to live there. Nightingale doubted that anyone would choose to live there, unless they were a particular sort of masochist.

A group of teenagers in hoodies were standing in front of the barred windows of an off-licence. One of them muttered something and they all laughed. Nightingale had an urge to cross the road away from them but knew that would be showing weakness so he just smiled brightly. 'How's it going?' he asked as he walked by.

'Give us a smoke, will ya?' asked the tallest of the group. He was a few inches shorter than Nightingale and one on one Nightingale knew he wouldn't have a problem but there were five of them and there was a good chance that most, if not all, were carrying knives. He could ignore them and carry on walking but then they'd be behind him. Images of a pack of hyenas bringing down a lion sprang to mind. He took out his pack of Marlboro and offered them around. Five hands sprang out and grabbed cigarettes like shoplifters on a deadline. One of the hoodies had a disposable lighter and he lit them one by one.

Nightingale could see they were weighing him up, probably wondering what sort of phone he had and how much cash there was in his wallet. 'Can I ask you guys a question?' he said, figuring that he ought to take their minds off mugging him and perhaps get him something in return for his smokes.

'Not history, is it?' said one of the hoodies. 'I was always crap at history.'

'You were crap at everything,' said another hoodie and he punched the first hoodie on the shoulder.

'About Goths,' said Nightingale.

'Goths?' repeated the punching hoodie.

'He means the vampires,' said the tallest hoodie, the one who had asked for a cigarette.

'There are some on the estate, aren't there?'

'A couple,' said the punching hoodie.

'Do they get a hard time?'

'From us?'

'From anyone?'

'One of them got killed, a while back,' said the tall hoodie.

'You a cop?' asked the punching hoodie.

'Used to be,' said Nightingale. 'What I'm asking is, would you ever give them a hard time? The Goths?'

'Like what?' asked the tall hoodie.

'He thinks we're the ones that killed her,' said the punching hoodie. 'He's probably wired.'

'I'm not wired, I'm just interested,' said Nightingale, trying to sound more relaxed than he felt. 'Do they get much abuse?'

'Sure, we take the piss,' said the tall hoodie. 'Why wouldn't we? They walk around like vampires and shit, why wouldn't you take the piss?'

'Because they're different?'

'Come on, bro. You've seen the gear they wear and that stupid make-up. If you dress like a vampire you've gotta expect to have the piss taken, right?'

Nightingale shrugged. 'I was thinking maybe live and let live?'

'They're asking for it, bro,' said the punching hoodie.

'Asking for what?' said Nightingale. He blew smoke up at the leaden sky.

'For a bit of piss-taking,' said punching hoodie.

'Does it ever go further than that?' said Nightingale. 'Does it get physical?'

'Of course not, bro. What'd be the point? They couldn't fight their way out of a paper bag.'

'They might scratch your eyes out,' said tall hoodie. 'Nails like claws, right.' He laughed harshly and shook his head. 'Nah, we take the piss, end of.'

'That's good to hear,' said Nightingale.

'You don't beat someone for the fun of it, bro,' said the tall hoodie. 'You need a reason. And walking around like a vampire ain't no good reason.' He grinned. 'Now beatin' on a man to get his watch and his wallet and his phone, now there'd be a point in that.' Nightingale couldn't tell if he was joking or not.

'I'll bear that in mind,' said Nightingale. He winked. 'Be lucky.' He walked away, taking a last drag on his cigarette and flicking the butt into the street. The laughter of the hoodies faded behind him but it was only when he turned the corner that his heart stopped pounding.

There was an intercom system at the main entrance to Noll House but it wasn't working and the door wasn't locked. There were lifts but Nightingale ignored them and headed up a flight of concrete stairs, wrinkling his nose at the stench of stale urine and vomit.

The Walshes lived on the fifth floor. It looked as if there had once been a fire in the flat next to theirs. There were soot streaks on the ceiling and the front door had been replaced. The door to the Walsh flat was older, the paintwork was chipped around the Yale lock and there were kick marks all along the bottom. There was a thick mat with WELCOME on it and a smiling puppy with a heart hanging from its collar.

There was a doorbell in the middle of the door and Nightingale pushed it. He heard a buzzing sound akin to a chain saw at full throttle and a few seconds later the door opened on a security chain. A woman peered from behind the door. She was in her late thirties, pale and with dark patches under her eyes. Her hair was dyed blonde and the dark roots were showing through. 'Mrs Walsh?'

She nodded.

'Who is it?' shouted a man from inside the flat.

'My name is Jack Nightingale, I'm with the police. I have some follow up questions for you?'

'Who is it?' shouted the man again.

'It's the police.'

'Is it that woman from Victim Support? Tell her we need bread. And we're out of cereal.'

'It's a man.' Mrs Walsh closed the door, took off the security chain, and opened it again. She was wearing a Nike sweatshirt that was several sizes too big for her over a pair of black leggings. There were large hooped earrings dangling from her ears and a silver crucifix around her neck. 'Down there,' she said, nodding down the hallway.

Mr Walsh was sprawled on a sofa with his feet on a pine coffee table. He was playing football on an Xbox and his eyes stayed on the screen as Nightingale walked into the room. He was wearing an England football shirt and blue Adidas tracksuit bottom but the beer belly and jowls under his chin suggested that his sporting activity was confined to the flatscreen TV. There was a tattoo of a bulldog waving an English flag on one forearm and the words ENGLISH AND PROUD emblazoned on a shield on the other.

Mrs Walsh came up behind Nightingale and he turned to give her a reassuring smile. Her husband roared as he scored a goal and he punched a fist in the air. There was a can of lager by his feet.

'Do you want tea, Mr Nightingale?'

'I'm fine, Mrs Walsh,' said Nightingale. 'Do you mind if I sit down?'

Mrs Walsh shrugged as if she didn't care either way.

There was a pizza box on the armchair by the door,

and a black and white cat on a second armchair by the television. There was a dining table by the window with four wooden chairs around it so Nightingale pulled out one and sat down. He took out his notebook and pen, figuring that would make him look a bit more official. Mrs Walsh sat down next to her husband and folded her arms.

'Can I just say that I'm so sorry for your loss,' said Nightingale.

Mrs Walsh nodded but her husband kept his eyes on the TV. From his skill at passing the ball from player to player it was clear that he'd invested a lot of time in the game.

'I'm trying to get a sense of who she hung around with, who her friends were.'

'From school, mainly,' said Mrs Walsh. 'And she spent a lot of time on the Internet, like kids do. Facebook and Twitter and all those websites. I've never understood it, why don't they talk to real friends? Why does it all have to be online these days?'

'Waste of bloody time, the Internet,' muttered Mr Walsh as his thumbs clicked away on the controller.

'Did she go out much, to Goth pubs and the like?' asked Nightingale.

The father's eyes narrowed but he continued to stare at the TV. 'She was still at school.'

'I know, but she was eighteen.'

'She was eighteen a month ago, and I told her, no pubs, no bars.' An opposition player whisked the ball away from his player and headed towards the goal. Mr Walsh cursed.

Nightingale smiled at Mrs Walsh. 'And she did as she was told?'

For the first time, Mr Walsh turned to look at Nightingale. He hadn't shaved in a few days and his receding hair was lank and dull. 'What are you saying? Are you saying that I didn't take care of my little girl?' There was a roar from the crowd as the opposition scored, but Mr Walsh didn't notice. He was glaring at Nightingale and his hands had tensed on the controller.

'Mr Walsh, of course not,' said Nightingale hurriedly. 'Absolutely not. I'm just trying to work out where Stella went and who she met. For instance, a lot of the Goths go to pubs in Soho. They hang out and listen to their music. That's all I meant. Eighteen-year-olds can go into pubs, there's nothing wrong with that.'

'And stop saying she was a Goth,' said Mr Walsh. 'She wasn't a Goth. She was a teenager, she wore black, she wasn't one of those freaks.'

'Goths aren't freaks, Mr Walsh. They're just kids having fun.'

'You're as bad as she is!'' shouted Mr Walsh. 'She wasn't a Goth. She didn't go to pubs. She was a good girl.' He stood up and tossed the controller on to the sofa. 'You know one of the papers said she was a hooker?' The cat quietly slipped off the chair and crawled under it.

'That was a mistake, they printed a correction,' said Mrs Walsh.

'They said she was a hooker, someone had seen her walking along the street in a black miniskirt so that paper called her a hooker.' He glared at his wife. 'You should never have let her go out like that.'

Mrs Walsh flinched as if she expected to be hit. 'Chris, please . . .'

Mr Walsh opened his mouth to say something else but

then seemed to have second thoughts and stormed out. A short while later they heard the front door open and slam shut.

'He blames me for everything that's happened,' whispered Mrs Walsh, close to tears.

'He's angry and he's lashing out,' said Nightingale. 'You're the one who is closest so he lashes out at you. He'll get over it.'

She shook her head. 'He's going to the pub and when he comes back . . .' She shuddered and didn't finish the sentence.

'I'm sorry, Mrs Walsh,' said Nightingale, though he knew sorry wouldn't be any help when her husband came back full of drink and keen to take out his frustration on her.

'He says I encouraged her, but what was I supposed to do? Do you have kids, Mr Nightingale?'

Nightingale shook his head.

'The thing about teenagers is that if you try to stop them doing something they'll just go and do it behind your back. When she was fourteen she wanted her ears pierced. Her dad said no but she went and did it anyway.' She shrugged. 'That's what they do. They test boundaries. Chris doesn't understand that.' She sighed. 'I've always said to her that if she wants to try something she should try it but I want to know. Like sex, right? Teenagers are going to have sex. That's what they do. I was at it like a rabbit when I was sixteen.' She jerked a thumb at the door. 'Don't bloody well tell him that I said that.'

Nightingale smiled. 'Your secret's safe with me, Mrs Walsh.'

'Emma, for God's sake. You make me feel a hundred years old calling me Mrs Walsh. I'm only thirty-five.'

'You had Stella young?'

'I was eighteen when she was born, nearly nineteen. Chris doesn't get it, he was sleeping with me when I was the same age as Stella is.' She winced. 'Was. I can't get used to thinking of her in the past tense.'

'Did Stella have a boyfriend?'

'She had boys who were friends, but she wasn't sleeping with anyone if that's what you're asking. She wasn't on the Pill. I always told her that if she wanted to have sex to make sure she was on the Pill. She didn't have to tell me, just go to the Family Planning Clinic and get it from them. They hand them out like sweeties these days.' She smiled and drew her legs up underneath her. 'She didn't have a lot of confidence.'

'With boys?'

Mrs Walsh smiled. 'With anything. At school, around the house. She wouldn't say boo to a goose. That's why she liked the Goth thing. All she needed to be accepted by them was to wear the clothes and the make-up. She was at ease with them.'

'So she was a Goth, despite what your husband says?'

'Of course. She toned it down at school and she knew better than to have the full make-up in the house so if she was going out she'd take her Goth stuff with her and change at a friend's.'

'So she did go to Goth pubs?'

'She always told me where and she had her phone with her all the time. I checked with the parents of the kids she went with and she always had a curfew.' She bit down on her lower lip. 'I'm not a bad mother.'

Nightingale smiled. 'I can see that.'

'Stella was the oldest but I have two more, both girls, and I can see they're just the same.' She took a deep breath to steady herself. 'I'll tell you this much, though. I won't be letting them out of my sight.'

Nightingale took out the photographs of the other four victims and put them down on the table in front of her. 'Did you ever see her with any of these people?'

Mrs Walsh looked at the photographs and shook her head. 'The police already showed them to me. She didn't know those others. I'm sure of it. They were all older, right? Stella was just eighteen.'

Nightingale tapped the photograph of Luke Aitken. 'He was eighteen. And he didn't live too far away. Hampstead.'

'I never saw him,' said Mrs Walsh. 'But yeah, she could have met him away from the house. But like I said, she wasn't keen on boys, not really.'

Nightingale gathered up the photographs and put them back in his coat pocket. 'The night she went missing. She was with friends?'

'They'd gone to the Hobgoblin in Camden. Kentish Town Road. I said two Bacardi Breezers but no more and definitely no drugs. There were three of them. She left early and said she was walking to the Tube station.' She moaned and put her hand over her mouth. 'And that was that. Next day they found her body . . .' She trembled and put both hands over her face. 'Chris didn't know. I said she was studying at a friend's house. When she didn't come back, I had to tell him . . .'

'It wasn't your fault,' said Nightingale.

Mrs Walsh nodded and wiped her eyes. 'I know. But

if I hadn't let her go out that night then maybe they would have chosen someone else and our little girl would be upstairs doing her homework.' She shook her head. 'I'm sorry.'

'You've absolutely nothing to apologise for,' he said. 'Do you know if she ever went to a place called the Crypt? It's not far from here. Near the Angel Tube.'

Mrs Walsh nodded. 'I'm fed up hearing about that place,' she said. 'Stella was always asking if she could go but it's a club and it doesn't open until ten or eleven. I know she was eighteen but I didn't want her out until the early hours. Her curfew was midnight so there'd be no point in going somewhere that opened late. On that one I put my foot down.' She forced a smile. 'She wasn't happy, I can tell you that. But I'm sure she didn't go behind my back.'

'Usually she got her own way?'

Mrs Walsh smiled and wiped a tear from her eye with the back of her hand. 'With me, sure. Not so much with her dad. Funny that because it's usually the dad that daughters twist around their little fingers. But it was me that she always came to when she wanted something.' She wiped her eye again. 'Like with the tattoo.'

'Tattoo?'

'She nagged and nagged last year. Said that all her friends had them. You can't have a tattoo unless you're sixteen but if you're between sixteen and eighteen you need a letter from a parent saying it's okay.' She sighed and shook her head. 'It took her weeks to wear me down but eventually I agreed. But only if it was somewhere that would be covered by a T-shirt and shorts. A lot of people won't give a job to anyone with a tattoo.'

Nightingale nodded. 'I've heard.'

'That's Chris's problem, I think. He hasn't worked for getting on five years and I think it's his tattoos that are to blame. He had them done when he was a kid and I'm always telling him his tattoos have held him back.'

Nightingale nodded sympathetically, though he figured that Mr Walsh's lack of employment was probably more to do with the fact that he preferred to sit on the sofa all day playing video games and drinking lager than going out and doing an honest day's work.

'And no tramp stamps, either,' continued Mrs Walsh. 'Those tattoos across your arse. I said that was a definite no. She looked at me like butter wouldn't melt in her mouth and said she was going to have a dolphin or a butterfly or some cute animal. So eventually I signed the letter and she went off and got one.' She grinned and shook her head. 'Turns out I needn't have worried because the law says you have to be eighteen, letter or not.'

'So she didn't get one?'

'Oh no, she was more devious than that. She did it on her eighteenth birthday. Went into the shop with her birth certificate. Came back with some horrible goat thing, but at least it was on her shoulder.'

'A goat thing?'

'With curly horns. I don't know what it was supposed to be. I said she'd promised me it was going to be a dolphin or a butterfly and she said she'd only promised that it would be an animal.' She threw her hands up in the air. 'Managed to keep it hidden from Chris because he would have hit the roof. Silly girl.'

'Where did she get it done?'

'Some place in Camden.'

'Did she say why she'd chosen that particular tattoo?'

'Said the tattooist had talked her into it. Said all the Goths were getting it.' She looked back at Nightingale. 'She was easily led, sometimes.'

'Can you remember the name of the shop?'

Mrs Walsh screwed up her face and scratched her chin. 'The Ink Spot,' she said. 'Something like that.'

13

Nightingale pulled up at a set of red lights just as his mobile began to ring. He was on the way back to South Kensington and the traffic had reduced his MGB to a slow crawl that wasn't much faster than walking pace. Nightingale had read somewhere that traffic in central London moved at an average speed of ten miles an hour – about the same as horse-drawn carriages had managed a hundred years earlier, and equivalent to the top speed of a running chicken. But the Friday traffic he was caught up in would have allowed any hen to lay a couple of eggs and still get back to his office before him. He glanced at the screen of his phone. It was Superintendent Chalmers. He took the call on hands-free. 'What are you playing at, Nightingale?' growled the superintendent.

'Driving back to the office, getting ready for the weekend,' said Nightingale. 'You?'

'Don't mess me around, Nightingale. Who told you to go around talking to relatives of the victims?'

'The way I remember it, you asked me to help on the case. Correction, you pretty much railroaded me into it.'

'I didn't tell you to start bothering grieving relatives. I wanted background on the Goth world. I wanted alternative lines of enquiry. What I didn't want was grieving fathers ringing me up asking why a lone detective is going around upsetting his family.'

'Mr Walsh?'

'It doesn't matter who it was, you shouldn't be pestering the relatives. We have professionals who've been trained to do that.'

'That's as maybe, but it's fair to say they haven't been much help so far.'

'And have you done any better?'

'I've a question,' said Nightingale.

'You're trying my patience, Nightingale.'

'All five were unconscious before they were mutilated, right?'

'Yes, thankfully.'

'I got the impression they'd all been hit, but I didn't have time to read all the details when I was in the incident room. Can you enlighten me?'

'Stella Walsh was hit on the back of the head. So was Abbie Greene. And Luke Aitken. Daryl Heaton had traces of Gamma-hydroxybutyrate in his system, but there was also alcohol, ecstasy and cannabis.'

'GHB? The date rape drug?'

'It's also used recreationally. There's no way of knowing if he took it himself or if it was given to him.'

'But he was alive when they mutilated him?'

'We're assuming he was so doped up he didn't feel anything. There was no sign of him fighting back, no defence wounds. But yes, the cause of death was blood loss.'

'And Gabe Patterson?'

'Why this sudden interest in cause of death, Nightingale? I wanted you to go out and talk to the crazies and see what the word is out there.'

'That's what I'm doing. But I need to know whether they were overpowered physically. What was the story with Patterson?'

'He had GHB in his system but he was hit as well. Blunt object, back of the head.'

'And you didn't think it was worth telling me two of the guys had been drugged?'

'Again, as I said, GHB is taken recreationally.'

'True, but it would explain how two physically fit men could be overpowered without anyone hearing a thing. There were no defence wounds which means they went down without a fight.'

'Nightingale, I'm telling you one last time to stop pretending you're a detective. I gave you very specific instructions. I want you to talk to the Goths, and find out who has been giving them grief. That's all I want from you. Understood?'

'Understood.' The line went dead in his ear. The traffic lights turned green and a horn sounded behind Nightingale, telling him to get a move on. 'All right, all right,' muttered Nightingale. He put the MGB in gear, eased back on the clutch and swore as the car stalled.

14

Jenny was pulling on her coat when Nightingale arrived back at the office. 'I didn't think you were coming back,' she said.

'Clearly,' said Nightingale. 'But I said I would, remember?'

Jenny looked at her watch. 'It is five o'clock.'

'Traffic was bad,' said Nightingale. 'You heading off for a weekend of hunting, shooting and fishing?'

'I am, actually, yes.'

'Love to Mummy and Daddy.' He saw a hurt look flash across her face so he raised his hands. 'I'm joking, seriously, say hi to them.'

'You should come. There's always a room for you. We've got a big shoot planned for tomorrow.'

'I've got to hit the Crypt tomorrow night,' said Nightingale. 'Look, can you give me fifteen minutes?'

Jenny took off her coat. 'Sure. Traffic's going to be bad for the next couple of hours anyway. What's up?'

He took the portable hard disc from his raincoat pocket. 'Here's the video of Mr Hetherington.' He gave it to her and then fished out his mobile phone. 'I got some video of the two lovebirds in a restaurant on this. Can you download it on to your computer so we have a backup copy?'

Jenny sat down at her desk and connected the phone to it. Nightingale put his coat on the hook by the door and turned to look at her. 'Tattoos,' he said.

'Tattoos?'

'Stella Walsh had one, had it done a couple of weeks before she died. Daryl Heaton was covered with them. Gabe had tattoos but kept them covered. Luke Aitken was killed just two days after he had his done. That's four out of the five.'

Jenny looked up from the computer. 'Abbie Greene had one on her shoulder.'

'How do you know?'

'Her Facebook page. She had her girlfriend's name on her shoulder, at the back. Zoe. With a red rose. The girlfriend had Abbie's name on her shoulder and the same rose. They posted selfies.'

'Selfies?'

'It's when you take a photograph of yourself.'

'Of course it is. Okay, so they all had tattoos. What do you think? Is that significant? You're the Goth expert.'

She disconnected the phone and handed it back to him. 'I'm hardly an expert, Jack. But I have to say that Goths tend to go more for piercings than tattoos.'

'So what I'm thinking is that the place where they got tattooed is the common factor.'

'The shoulder, you mean?'

Nightingale looked at the ceiling and sighed. 'The tattoo parlour,' he said. 'I meant they went to the same place, maybe.'

'You know I was joking, right?'

'Sometimes I wonder,' said Nightingale. 'I couldn't find a common factor other than the tattoos. They didn't know each other and we can't find any common point of contact. So it looks to me like the tattoo parlour is the best bet. I can take the photographs, see if anyone recognises them. Stella Walsh's mum said she went to some place in Camden called the Ink Spot or something.' He held up his hand. 'Give me a minute.' He tapped out Zoe's number as he walked through to his own office. She answered on the fourth ring and it sounded as if she had been crying. 'Zoe, it's me, Jack Nightingale. Sorry to bother you again but I just wanted to check something with you.'

'Okay,' she said.

'You and Abbie had tattoos, right?'

'Tattoos?'

'Yeah, I was wondering where you went to have them done?'

'Me? I went with Abbie to a place in Wardour Street. You know, in Soho.'

'Ah.'

'Something wrong?'

'No, I was hoping you'd gone to Camden, that's all.'

'I think Abbie did. A few weeks ago. She went on her own.'

'Why?'

'She liked tattoos.'

'How many did she have?'

'Six,' said Abbie. 'All on her back. Plus my name on her shoulder.'

'I don't suppose you know the name of the one in Camden do you?'

'I'm sorry, no. She wanted me to go with her but I can't stand the needles. She nagged me into getting her name tattooed on my shoulder and I was okay with that, but I told her I didn't want any more.'

Nightingale thanked her and ended the call. He went through to Jenny's office. 'Any joy?'

'There's an Ink Pit in Camden,' she said.

'Abbie had half a dozen tattoos, according to Zoe.'

'The only one on show on her Facebook page is the name one,' said Jenny.

'They were on her back. I guess you'd only see them if she was naked. So there's no Ink Spot?'

'None that I can find anyway. And the only one with Ink in the name in Camden is the Ink Pit.'

'That's probably it, then,' said Nightingale. 'Let me just give Mrs Patterson a call.' He walked back into his office and tapped out Mrs Patterson's number. When she answered her voice was a dull, flat monotone. 'I forgot to ask you about Gabe's tattoos,' he said. 'Do you remember where he had them done?'

'Lots of places,' she said. 'He had some on his shoulders done when we were on holiday in Thailand. And he had his first one in Birmingham, before he came down to college.'

'What about in London? Where did he go?'

'His favourite was New Wave in Muswell Hill. He used to hang out there sometimes. And Jolie Rouge in the Caledonian Road. He went somewhere else for his last one. It was only a few weeks ago. Where was it now? Somewhere in Camden, I think.'

Nightingale's heart began to pound but he kept quiet, resisting the urge to prompt her.'

'The Ink Pit,' she said. 'That's it. A friend had recommended them and he went and had one done on his hip.'

'That's brilliant, Mrs Patterson.'

'Is that a help?'

'I think so,' said Nightingale. He ended the call and beamed at Jenny. 'Gabe Patterson had a tattoo done at the Ink Pit too.'

'That's it then,' said Jenny. 'You can tell Chalmers that you've found the connection and pass it back to him. The answer's probably in their client list. They might even have CCTV.' She smiled brightly. 'Case closed, as good as.'

'Think I might pop around there tomorrow,' said Nightingale. 'Ask a few questions myself.'

'Why, Jack? All Chalmers wanted was a lead and you have that.'

'I'll call it in on Monday,' said Nightingale. 'Besides I'm going to go to the Crypt tomorrow night.'

'Hoping to pick up Goth girls?'

'Yeah, that's exactly what I had in mind.' He smiled sarcastically. 'I'm planning on showing the photographs around, see if anyone remembers them.'

'The police will already have done that, surely?'

'If I know anything about cops it's that they generally take the easy way out. They probably just had a few council cops on the door handing out flyers.'

'Whereas your plan is?'

'To walk around, see what's what, and talk to people.'

'In a Goth club playing music at full blast? Well, good luck with that.'

'I can look for Goths with tattoos. That seems to be the link.'

'If it was me, I'd just pass it back to Chalmers and get on with my life.'

'I will, on Monday, I promise.'

Jenny's printer whirred and she handed him a printed sheet. 'There's the details of the Ink Pit, and a map, just so you can find it.'

'You're a star,' he said.

Jenny stood up, retrieved her coat, and blew him a kiss. 'See you Monday.'

He blew her a kiss back. 'Not if I see you first.'

Nightingale woke up early on Saturday morning, ate a bacon sandwich in his boxer shorts, then shaved and showered and went for a walk around Hyde Park to clear his thoughts and smoke a couple of cigarettes. The park seemed to be full of joggers and skateboarders and women in Lycra on rollerblades. Nightingale sat on a bench and wondered whether rollerblades would be a smart way of getting around town, what with traffic now reduced to the pace of a running chicken, but he decided that the downside of looking ridiculous in a helmet, kneepads and figure-hugging Lycra probably wasn't worth the extra speed.

As he sat on the bench, two Goth teenagers walked by, both male, tall and spindly with spiky hair, chains hanging down from their black leather jackets. One had tight black jeans, the other was wearing baggy black combat pants. They were both carrying cloth bags with the logos of bands, the Cure and the Ramones. Nightingale stood up and spent a few minutes following them as they walked across the park in the direction of Harrods. Nightingale wasn't so much interested in the two men as he was in the way that other people reacted to them. And the short answer to that was they provoked no reaction at all. Nobody gave them a second look as they strolled through the park. They were ignored. There were no taunts, no sneers, no comments. No one cared. The Goths were different from the average park user, but no more ridiculous than the Lycra-clad rollerbladers or the middle-aged men in sports gear and trainers who hadn't broken into a run for decades. Pretty much everyone was wrapped up in themselves – or their smartphones or MP3 players – to pay the Goths any attention at all. The only person who gave them a second look was a pretty blonde girl and it was clear she was admiring the backside of the guy in the tight jeans. Nightingale stopped following them and blew smoke up at the clouds as he watched them walk away. The simple fact was Goths didn't inspire hatred or contempt, not in the same way that people tended to look down on skinheads or punks. Goths were quiet and easy-going and kept to themselves. They didn't shout racist comments or swear or try to intimidate others in the way that skinheads tended to do. And they didn't dress to shock or offend in the way that punks often did. Nightingale finished his cigarette and walked back to Bayswater, deep in thought. Goths were non-threatening and Nightingale couldn't understand why anyone would be so fired up by them that they would want to mutilate and kill them. When there were so many other people who went out of their way to be provocative and hateful, why single out a group who seemed to want nothing more than to listen to their own music and hang out with their own kind? It didn't make any sense at all.

Nightingale collected his car from his lock-up. It took three turns of the key to get the engine turning, which suggested that the battery was on its last legs.

Battery-changing was one of the many jobs that Nightingale was capable of carrying out himself, he just needed to find the time to pick up a new one. He drove to Camden with the print-out that Jenny had given him on the passenger seat and managed to find a parking space a short walk from the Ink Pit.

The tattoo parlour was sandwiched between a shop that sold leather bondage gear and another that sold vintage dresses. There were various tattoo designs around the edge of the window and by the door was a printed note saying that only those above eighteen would be tattooed and another that promised a twenty-five per cent discount for serving soldiers. Through the window Nightingale could see three leather reclining seats, only one of which was occupied. A young girl was lying face down while a bearded man with round-lensed glasses bent over her. He was wearing blue latex gloves similar to the ones used by SOCO and he alternated between using a tattoo gun on her shoulder and dabbing her skin with a tissue. From where Nightingale was standing it looked like an eagle. Or an angel. There was a young woman standing behind a cramped reception desk

There were framed photographs of tattoos all over the walls and a few signed photographs of what Nightingale assumed were famous people who had been tattooed on the premises. The tattoo artist looked up from his work, blinked a few times, and then bent over the girl again. Two more girls – presumably her friends – were sitting on chairs against the far well, peering over at the work in progress.

A bell dinged as Nightingale pushed open the door and the receptionist looked up. She had dyed blonde hair that was dark brown at the roots and more than a dozen bits of shiny metal hanging off her face and ears. She had three rings in each ear, connected by fine chains, a curved chrome pin through her lip, studs either side of her nostrils and three rings in each of her eyebrows. There was another stud in her chin, just under her lip.

'Do you set off metal detectors at airports?' Nightingale asked.

She grinned and stuck out her tongue to reveal another bulky silver stud. 'These don't,' she said. She patted her groin. 'But the one here definitely does. Is that what you want? Penis piercings are very very sexy.'

Nightingale winced. 'I think I'll pass on that.'

'Trust me, you give your girlfriend a good seeing to with a penis piercing and she'll never stray.'

'Sounds like you're speaking from experience.'

She winked. 'That would be telling,' she said.

'I'm actually here to talk to the owner,' said Nightingale.

'There are two,' said the girl. 'Rusty and Jezza.' She nodded at the man doing the rose tattoo. 'That's Jezza.'

'What about Ricky? Ricky Nail?' Jenny had told him that Ricky Nail was one of the owners.

'No one calls him Ricky,' said the girl. 'He's Rusty. Rusty Nail. Geddit?'

'Okay, is Rusty around? Seeing as how Jezza's busy?'

'We haven't seen him for a few days. We think he's off sick.'

'You think?'

'You're not from trading standards, are you?'

'Nah,' said Nightingale. 'I'm with the police, I just need some information on some clients.'

'Not underage?' she said. 'We're really tight on that,

we don't do kids. We insist on a photo ID and if we've any doubts we call their parents, too. Kids can be really devious.'

Nightingale smiled. 'No, it's not about underage kids.' He took the five photographs from his pocket and turned them over to show her the names. 'I want to confirm that these five people had tattoos done here. What about your computer? Do you have a database you could check?'

The girl shook her head. 'We had a break-in last week. They took the register, the computers, pretty much everything that wasn't nailed down.'

'Bugger,' said Nightingale.

'You're telling me,' said the girl. 'We lost all our appointments, all our phone numbers, this week has been a disaster.'

'Did you call the police?'

'They weren't interested,' said the girl. 'You know what they're like. They never get out of their cars these days.' Her eyes widened. 'Oh, sorry, no offence.'

'None taken,' said Nightingale.

'I mean, they came around eventually but they didn't take fingerprints or anything. They just gave us a crime number and the phone number of some victim support thing and then they went. Suggested we get a burglar alarm, they did.'

'Probably good advice,' said Nightingale. 'Best I talk to Jezza then,' said Nightingale. 'How long until he's done?'

The girl looked over at the work in progress. 'Twenty minutes,' she said.

'I'll wait,' he said.

'I could do you a penis piercing while you wait,' said the girl. 'I could give you the forces discount.'

'I'd love to but I'm gasping for a cigarette,' said Nightingale. 'I'll wait outside.' He went out and lit a Marlboro and paced slowly up and down as he smoked it. There was a Costa Coffee outlet across the road and he was just about to walk over and get himself a coffee when the door opened and Jezza came out. The girl he had been working on was at the reception desk, talking to the receptionist.

'Joyce said you wanted a word,' said the tattoo artist. 'And seeing as how you're a smoker we might as well do it here.'

Nightingale took the hint and offered his pack to the man and then lit it for him. He drew the smoke into his lungs and then held the cigarette up and nodded at it appreciatively before exhaling a cloud of smoke. 'Used to smoke these at school,' he said.

Nightingale grinned. 'Behind the bike sheds?'

'With a couple of teachers. I think it was the cowboy thing. Marlboro Man.' He shrugged. 'He died, didn't he? Cancer?'

'I think the jury's out on that,' said Nightingale.

Jezza looked at him sideways. 'What do you mean?'

'The anti-smoking lobby likes to say that the Marlboro Man died of lung cancer but there were a number of Marlboro Men and they didn't all die that way. Plenty of smokers die of old age and plenty of non-smokers die of lung cancer.' He shrugged. 'Everyone dies, Jezza. There's no getting away from that.'

'Are you always as cheerful as this?' asked Jezza. He laughed and took a long pull on his cigarette. 'Joyce said you were asking about clients.'

'Yeah, she said you had a break-in?'

Jezza nodded. 'Yeah, bastards. Took our computer and the cash float, our stereo system and a DVD player.'

'Joyce said you called the cops but they weren't much help.'

Jezza smiled. 'Break-ins are pretty low priority these days,' he said. 'They're too busy hunting down DJs from the sixties and racists on Twitter.' He shrugged. 'The insurance will cover it but our premium will shoot up. Who'd expect anyone to break into a tattoo parlour?'

They both blew smoke and then Nightingale took the five photographs out of his pocket. 'Do you recognise any of these people?'

Jezza went through the pictures one by one, taking a good long look at each one. He smiled when he got to the picture of Stella Walsh. 'This one, for sure,' he said. 'She was in here about six months ago claiming to be eighteen. We said she needed photo ID and she said she had her birth certificate. That showed she was nineteen but it wasn't her. We asked her for her address and we got her home number and called it and she hit the roof. Turned out she was seventeen.'

'That happens a lot?'

Jezza nodded. 'Fifteen, sixteen, seventeen. A lot of people think that if you have the permission of a parent we can do it at sixteen, but that's not true. If you're not eighteen, it's against the law. We told her she'd be okay for a piercing, but she wanted a tattoo.' He grinned. 'She got really upset and threatened to sue us, which was funny.' His face suddenly hardened. 'Oh my God,' he said quietly. He flicked through all of the pictures. 'They're the ones that got skinned, right?'

Nightingale nodded.

'Shit, I never realised. I've seen the story in the papers and on TV but it didn't click.'

'Yeah. Stella Walsh. She was the first.'

'That wasn't the name she used.' He shook his head sadly. 'She was so funny, shouting and stamping her feet like not having a tattoo was the worst thing that had ever happened to her. She was almost eighteen anyway, just a few months off, I think. We told her to spend the time planning it. I offered to work with her on the design. But she wasn't having any of it. She wanted it then and there.' He took a drag on his cigarette. 'Kids,' he said, after he'd blown smoke. 'They don't seem to realise that a tattoo is for life. It's not something you rush into. It has to say something about you, something personal.' He pointed at a seashell on his right arm. 'When I was a kid my dad took me walking on the beach at Blackpool. We found a shell, just like this. He told me this long story about a mermaid who used a shell as a mirror. Every time I look at that tattoo, I think of my dad, God bless him.' He held up his left arm and rotated it slowly so that Nightingale could see all the tattoos on it, more than a dozen. 'Every one means something to me, every one has a story. That's how it should be.'

'And what did Stella want?'

'Words. I love Justin Bieber or something. In some fancy typeface. That's why I reckon the law's right – kids shouldn't be allowed to have tattoos.'

'Did she come back?'

'I don't remember seeing her.' He went through the pictures again. 'None of these others ring a bell.'

'And you're there all the time?'

'I'm there during our regular opening hours,' he said.

'Ten until seven. We run an appointment system, we have to because otherwise people would phone up to book a time and then not turn up. We insist that they come in and talk to an artist, plan their design and then book a time. And put down a deposit, of course.'

He gave him the photograph of Gabe Patterson. 'You're sure about this guy? His wife said he'd had a tattoo done here.'

Jezza looked at the photograph carefully, then shook his head. 'Definitely not.' He handed the photograph back and took a long last pull on his cigarette and flicked away the butt. 'He could have done a walk-in with Rusty, I suppose.'

'A walk-in? How does that work?'

'Like I said, we have a strict appointment system during working hours. But Rusty kept the place open at night and would take anyone.' He shrugged. 'He said he did his best work at night. Experimental stuff.'

Nightingale finished his cigarette. 'What do you mean by experimental?'

Jezza looked uncomfortable. He scratched his chin and swayed from side to side. 'It was his style. Freestyle, I guess you'd call it. See, my way is to let the client decide what they want. It's their body and their tattoo. And with the appointment system, that's how it works. We show them designs, we talk it through, there's a lot of thought and planning goes into it. That way there are no surprises. But Rusty would open late at night, usually Friday and Saturday, and he'd do anything on anyone. Not underage, that was a rule we never broke, but he'd do drunks, crackheads, whatever. I told him he was playing with fire and that he'd end up being sued but it's his shop so I couldn't argue.'

'I thought you were joint owners?' said Nightingale.

'He put in most of the money when we started, so he always has the last word,' said Jezza.

'These late-night sessions, Rusty was here alone?'

'Yeah, more often than not. I wasn't happy about it. Clients need to have a clear head when they plan a tattoo, and the tattoo artist has to have a clear head when he's doing the work. What you don't want is a couple of kids deciding they want matching tattoos when they're drunk at three o'clock in the morning and then regretting it next day.'

'And Rusty didn't care?'

'He cared, but he cared about the art. He wanted to push the envelope and he tended to do that at night.' He gestured at the photographs in Nightingale's hand. 'Any one of them could have come in during the late-night sessions.'

'Did Rusty keep records?'

'Sure, it would all have been on the computer. We're VAT registered so everything had to go through the till.'

'But the computer's gone?'

Jezza nodded.

Nightingale put the photographs away. 'Where is Rusty?'

'He's gone walkabout.'

'Walkabout?'

'He goes AWOL from time to time. Sometimes he's on a bender and sometimes there's a girl involved. This time he's not been in for four or five days. What day is it today?'

'Saturday.'

'Then it was last week when he was last in. We've

phoned a few times but it goes straight through to voicemail.'

'And no one's worried?'

Jezza laughed. 'You don't know Rusty. It's like he has an on-off switch. He's either working every hour of the day or he's just . . . AWOL. One time he disappeared and then called us from Vietnam. He'd gone to Heathrow and got on the first long-haul flight he could.'

'I'd really like to talk to him,' said Nightingale.

'I'll get Joyce to give you his details,' said Jezza, pushing open the door. 'If you do track him down, tell him he needs to call. We've got to do our VAT filing and without the computer we need all hands to the pumps.'

'I'll tell him,' said Nightingale, following him inside.

Jezza told the receptionist what he wanted and she wrote down an address and a phone number for Nightingale. Jezza went back to his workstation. The girl he had tattooed was admiring her inked angel in a mirror while one of her companions had slipped off her shirt and was lying face down on the reclining seat.

'You might try his present girlfriend. Suw. With a double-u.'

'Does he live with her?'

She scribbled down the name and address and gave him the piece of paper. 'Sometimes. He's lived with half a dozen over the last few years. I think sometimes he stays with Suw and sometimes she stays with him. They do a lot of music festivals and stuff. Rusty was talking about the Warped Tour in the States and I thought he might have gone there.'

'He wouldn't tell anyone? He's just up and go to America?'

Joyce laughed. 'Rusty? He's a free spirit. Which basic-ally means he doesn't give a shit about anyone else.' She leaned forward and lowered her voice. 'I don't know what Jezza said to you, but Rusty has seriously screwed us over by going walkabout. We're backed up with appointments and our other tattooist is down with the flu. Jezza's working non-stop and we're still behind. If you do find Rusty, give him a kick up the arse and tell him to get back here.'

Nightingale slipped the piece of paper into his back pocket. 'I will do.'

He opened the door and the bell dinged. She grinned and waggled her fingers at him. 'And if you change your mind about the penis piercing, you know where to come.'

'You'll be the first person I call,' he said.

16

Nightingale decided against driving to the Crypt and took the Tube instead, getting on at Queensway and changing to the Northern Line at Bank. It took him a little more than half an hour, which was probably quicker than using his car, especially considering the way the battery had become so temperamental lately. He had left his raincoat behind and was wearing black jeans, a black polo shirt and a black linen jacket. He had drawn the line at make-up, figuring that at least he'd made an effort. He got off at the Angel station and took the escalator up to street level. There was nothing biblical about the name chosen for the station, it was named after a local pub.

The Crypt was a short walk from the Tube station. In a previous life it had been a cinema and where once the films had been advertised were the words THE CRYPT in capital letters and SATURDAY FROM 10 P.M. in smaller letters. It was eleven o'clock at night and Nightingale had assumed the club wouldn't get going until the early hours but there were dozens of Goths heading that way and when he got there he saw a long line waiting to get in. Most of those in the queue were teenage Goths but there was a sprinkling of girls wearing Victorian dresses and he saw one young man in a top hat and tails. At the head of the queue were two large men in black suits and shades, with the impassive bored faces cultivated by bouncers the world over. One had a shaved head, the other shoulder-length grey hair tied back in a ponytail. Both looked as if they worked out a lot and had their blue plastic Security Industry Authority licences on display on their left arms.

Nightingale walked up to them and smiled. They looked back at him, their faces set in stone. Nightingale suddenly felt as if he was ten years old and about to be told it was his bedtime. 'Hi, guys,' he said. The two men didn't react. Nightingale could feel a dozen or so pairs of mascara-laden eyes watching him and he turned so that his back was to the queue. 'I'm with the cops, getting information about the Goths that were killed.'

'So you'll have a warrant card, then?' said Ponytail.

'I said I was with the cops. I'm a private detective. I used to be a cop, though.'

'Yeah, well, I used to be a male model but you won't see me on the cover of *Vogue*.' Ponytail grinned at his colleague but the smile vanished when he turned to look back at Nightingale.

Nightingale frowned. 'What?'

'I'm saying, what's past is past. You're not a cop so that makes you a civilian so if you want to get inside you're going to have to join the queue. Unless you're a member. But you don't look like a member.' Ponytail looked across at Shaven Head. 'Does he look like a member?'

Shaven Head took a deep breath and let it out slowly. 'No,' he said eventually. 'He doesn't look like a member.'

He unclipped a thick black rope and allowed half a dozen Goths inside before replacing the rope.

'Okay, how about not letting me in but having a look at these instead?' Jenny had given him a print-out with pictures of the five Goths on it. He took it from his pocket, unfolded it and handed it to Ponytail.

The doorman frowned as he studied the five faces. 'The cops already showed me these,' he said. 'A couple of times.'

He gave the sheet of paper to Shaven Head who stared at it for several seconds, pulled a face, and handed it back to Ponytail who then gave it to Nightingale. 'And you don't remember seeing any of them?' asked Nightingale.

Ponytail jerked a thumb at the long line of Goths. 'I'll tell you what I told the cops. They all look the same to me.'

'You must know some of them though. The regulars. The ones that stand out. The members.'

'Of course,' said Ponytail. 'But they checked with management and none of them was a member. No details on file.' Nightingale squinted at the ID card on the man's left upper arm but couldn't get a good look at it. The doorman lifted his arm closer to Nightingale's face. 'More than happy for you to have my name,' he said. 'John Brown.'

'Cheers, John,' said Nightingale. He took out his wallet and gave him one of his business cards. 'Happy to return the favour.'

Ponytail squinted at the card. 'Nightingale?'

'Yeah.'

'Like the bird.'

'Very much so.' He gave a card to Shaven Head who put it in his top pocket without looking at it.

'So can I go inside?' asked Nightingale. 'I just want to show those pictures around, see if anyone remembers them.'

'Sure,' said Ponytail. 'Just join the queue and we'll make a decision when you reach the front.'

'Decision?'

'We have a dress code.'

'Seriously?' Nightingale held out his arms to the side. 'Is this not Goth enough for you?'

Nightingale could see that Ponytail was trying not to smile.

'End of the line,' said Shaven Head. He unhitched the black rope and allowed another group of a dozen Goths to go inside. Since Nightingale had started talking to the doormen, another forty or so Goths had joined the queue. He smiled hopefully at Ponytail but could see that he was wasting his time.

'Jellybean, are you giving Mr Nightingale a hard time?' said a voice behind him.

Nightingale turned around. For a second he didn't recognise the two young Goths then he realised they were the dog-owners from Clapham Common.

'You know him?' said Ponytail, surprised.

Hannah and Becky slipped their arms through Nightingale's. 'He's our new best friend,' said Hannah.

'You know he's a private dick?' said Becky.

'And they're the best kind, Jellybean,' said Hannah, and for the first time the doorman's face broke into a smile.

'And his soul was sold to the Devil, so you'd better be nice to him,' said Becky.

Ponytail unhitched the black rope. 'If he's with you, he can go in. But make sure he behaves himself.'

'He'll be on his best behaviour,' said Becky, and she blew the doorman a kiss. Hannah hugged Shaven Head and then kissed Ponytail on the cheek.

'Thanks,' Nightingale said to Hannah. 'How come you get the VIP treatment?'

'I'm a member,' she said. 'And I dated his boss for a few weeks.'

Nightingale followed the two girls down a corridor and into the main ground floor bar area. 'Why do you call him Jellybean?' asked Nightingale.

'Because that's his name,' said Becky, scornfully.

'His name's John Brown.'

'That's right. John Brown. JB. Jellybean. It's not rocket science.'

'And he knows how old you are?'

'He thinks I'm eighteen. Which I am in a few weeks. Now are you going to get us drinks or what?'

'A Coke?'

'Yeah, with a Jack Daniels in it.' She looked at him and laughed. 'Hey, if you get it it'll be a Jack with a Jack and Coke.'

'You're a hoot,' said Nightingale. He looked across at Hannah. 'Least I can do is to buy you a drink.'

'A Bloody Mary,' she said.

'Are you serious?'

'My favourite tipple,' she said.

Nightingale headed for the bar. Above his head was a massive chandelier and around the walls were flickering candles. The walls were lined with red velvet curtains and there were black sofas and armchairs around the edge of the room. When he returned, the two girls were deep in conversation with two lanky Goths, guys in their twenties who were both well over six feet tall and stick thin, their height emphasised by spiky hair and high-heeled boots. They both grinned when they saw Nightingale and he realised that in the club, even with his black clothing, he was the one who looked strange.

'I'll catch you girls later,' he said, handing them their drinks. 'And thanks again for getting me in.'

He weaved his way through the clubbers, his bottle of Corona in front of him, and headed upstairs. Most of the clubbers were in their teens or twenties, and the vast majority were in Goth gear. The doorman had been right, after a while it became difficult to tell them apart. The black clothing and the black make-up made them all blend together, though the clubbers in Victorian gear did show more originality in their choice of dress. The club was spread over three floors. The ground floor and a mezzanine level above it had music on at full blast, so loud that conversation was pretty much impossible. There was a lot of dancing going on, and a fair amount of drinking, but the atmosphere was good-natured despite the frequently gloomy nature of the music being played. A lot of the songs seemed to be screamed at the top of the singer's voice and what lyrics Nightingale could make out appeared to involve death, loneliness, pain and despair.

It was quieter in the basement. There were leather armchairs and more sofas and dummies dressed in Victorian gear and gilt-framed portraits of unhappy-looking people on the walls. Nightingale moved from group to group, explaining who he was and showing them the photographs. There was a bouncer in a black suit standing by the stairs that led up to the ground floor, his head swivelling professionally from side to side as if it was on castors. Nightingale wandered over and showed him the photographs. 'Jellybean said he didn't recognise any of these people, what about you?'

The bouncer didn't look at the sheet but stared at Nightingale. 'You a cop?'

'I'm working with them. Just trying to find a connection between them.'

'Jellybean said it was okay?'

'Sure.'

Nightingale looked at the man's ID, fastened to his left forearm. Billy Moore.

'You know we've had cops here before, showing the same photographs?'

'I think the idea is that they'll get different people at different times.'

'Yeah, well, look around. It's the same faces every week.'

'And these five? Do you remember them?'

'It's hard, mate,' said Moore. 'If I talk to them or there's a problem, then sure I'll remember. But most of the time they're just bodies.' He pointed at the picture of Daryl Heaton. 'I can tell you what I told the cops before. If I'd seen him I'd probably remember him. He looks like trouble, you know. He's the type to start throwing punches after he'd had a few drinks. So him I'd have been keeping an eye out for.' He pursed his lips as he studied the print-out. He tapped the photograph of Abbie Greene. 'The cops didn't show me this picture.'

'Yeah, for some reason they had her as a blonde. She dyed her hair about six months ago.'

The man nodded. 'Yeah, I think I do remember her. She was with an older blonde woman. Couldn't work them out, the older one was very possessive, almost motherly. There was a bit of an argument, I remember that. Some guy was chatting up the young one and the older one kicked off.'

'How did it end?'

'The older woman smashed her glass on the floor and the guy walked off. The two women hugged. It was over.' Realisation dawned. 'She's one of the victims?'

'Yeah.'

'Shit.'

'She was the last one to be killed.'

'The bastard that's doing it is cutting them up, right?'

'Yeah.' He put the print-out back in his pocket. 'You ever get much trouble, outside the club?'

The man shook his head. 'Not that I've ever seen, and I've been here two years. Mind you, there's safety in numbers.' He frowned. 'Do the cops think the killer found them here?'

'They're considering all options at the moment,' said Nightingale. 'But it seems unlikely they were taken from here because the bodies have been found all over London. But it's possible that the killer saw them here.'

'And followed them.' The man shook his head. 'He'd stick out like a sore thumb. Same as you do.' He tilted his head on one side. 'Unless he was a Goth too, I suppose.'

Nightingale took a drink of his lager. It wasn't something that he'd considered but it made sense. If the killers were Goths – or at least dressed like Goths – then that would explain why they had been able to get close to the victims.

'Is there a membership list, do you know?' he asked.

'Sure. It used to be a members' only club but these days non-members can just pay to get in.'

'So anyone can get in?'

Moore grinned. 'Well, you did, clearly.'

Nightingale laughed and raised his bottle in salute. 'Nice one,' he said. He looked around the crowd. 'Other than that woman kicking off, do you get many problems here of a night?'

'Almost never,' said Moore. 'They wear dark gear and scary make-up, but they're as sweet as pie. You hardly ever see anyone getting drunk, the drug use is mainly cannabis and ecstasy, and they're generally genuinely nice people. They're not confrontational, you know?'

Nightingale nodded. 'Passive.'

'You say that like it's a bad thing. I've dealt with hen parties where girls have gone for each other with their heels. And stag parties where the alcohol and testosterone gets everyone fired up. I've done security at football matches where people want to kill each other because of the team they support. Passive is good. But passive's the wrong word. They're easy-going. Maybe a bit insecure. Inward-looking, you know?'

'Yeah, I guess.'

'I tell you, I'd rather be stuck in a lift with a dozen Goths than a dozen football hooligans. Or a dozen bankers, come to that. Look around. They're listening to the music or they're chatting to each other. And it'll be like that until seven o'clock in the morning. Then they'll emerge blinking in the daylight and they'll go home.'

'It's a fair point,' said Nightingale. 'There's pretty much zero aggression.'

'That's why it's so fucked up that someone would target

them,' said Moore. 'They're not a threat. They're not evil, they're not in your face. Why would anyone want to kill them?'

Nightingale nodded. 'That's a very good question,' he said. He sipped his beer. It was an excellent question, in fact, and one that he couldn't answer.

He left the club at two o'clock in the morning, having given out more than twenty of his business cards but with no clearer idea of who might be killing Goths. Everyone he'd spoken to had been helpful and polite, and eager to help. He found several clubbers who remembered one or more of the victims, and he spoke to a guy who said he had bought Zoe and Abbie a few drinks two months earlier but couldn't remember much about their conversation. He hadn't met anyone who remembered seeing Daryl Heaton at the club.

As he left the queue was even longer than when he'd arrived. Jellybean nodded at Nightingale. 'Any luck?'

'Not really. But thanks.'

The doorman held out his hand. 'Give me that sheet, I'll copy it and hand it out. Maybe put your number it, yeah?'

'That'd be great,' said Nightingale. 'I appreciate it.' He took the sheet of paper from his pocket and gave it to him.

'We need to catch the bastard, that's for sure,' said Jellybean.

'Bastards, plural,' said Nightingale. 'We think there's more than one, working together.'

Jellybean grimaced. 'You wonder what the world's coming to,' he said. 'We're going to hell in a hand-basket.'

'You're not the first person to say that, and you won't be the last.'

'Just make sure the cops get the bastards, that's all.'

'I'll do my best,' said Nightingale. He took out his cigarettes and lit one as he went in search of a black cab.

17

Nightingale decided to drive down to Brighton, figuring that the Sunday morning traffic wouldn't be too heavy. The half marathon started at midday and Nightingale was there at the start to video Mr Drummond, who was most definitely not wearing a neck brace or using a crutch. He had a dark blue sweatband and a Cancer Research badge and was wearing an expensive pair of running shoes. His wife was with him offering moral support with far more enthusiasm then she'd shown when she was helping him in and out of their car when Nightingale last had them under surveillance.

He got several minutes' footage at the start, including some of Mr Drummond doing some very energetic warming up. Because of the way the route curved back on itself he got more footage at the halfway stage, with Mr Drummond grabbing a paper cup of water, drinking some, and pouring it over himself, and he was there at the finish to record Mr Drummond's very respectable one hour and fifty-three minute finish time, and to see him receiving his participatory medal. There was also some nice footage of Mr and Mrs Drummond walking hand in hand to their car, with not a crutch in sight.

Nightingale was driving back to London when his

mobile rang. The traffic was heavy so he let the call go through to voicemail and he waited until he had parked his MGB in his lock-up before taking his phone out of his raincoat pocket. He didn't recognise the mobile number that had called him. It was a girl. 'I'm calling for Jack Nightingale,' she said. 'Call me back when you get this.' Her accent was difficult to place. From the north, certainly, and the flat vowels suggested Yorkshire.

Nightingale pressed redial. 'This is Jack Nightingale,' he said when she answered.

'Hi. You were at The Crypt asking about the Goth Killers, right? You're a private eye?'

'That's right,' he said. 'I'm sorry, who are you?'

'My name's Caitlin. You were asking around about the Goths that were killed.'

'That's right.'

'I think I might be able to help you.'

'In what way?'

'There was a couple of strange guys at The Crypt a few weeks ago. They wanted me to go with them. And I think I saw them talking to one of the girls who died.'

'Did you tell the police this?'

'I don't want to get involved. At least I didn't. Now I'm starting to think that I should say something. Look, can I see you tonight?'

'I guess so,' said Nightingale. 'Where are you?'

'I can meet you in a pub,' she said. 'Do you know Garlic and Shots, in Frith Street, Soho?'

'I can find it.'

'I'll see you there at seven o'clock tonight,' she said. 'Basement bar.'

She ended the call before he could ask her how he'd

recognise her. He stared at his phone pensively. She hadn't asked him what he looked like, either. Which suggested that she already knew.

He pulled down the door to his lock-up and walked back to his flat, deep in thought. As always the Bayswater pavements were packed and he heard at least a dozen languages as he threaded through the crowds. The area was never quiet and there was always somewhere to eat or drink. There were hundreds of small hotels and several big ones close by, and thousands of rented rooms and studio flats favoured by students and migrant workers. He was so busy trying to decide whether to buy a bowl of duck noodles from the Chinese restaurant on the ground floor of his building or to go inside and make himself a bacon sandwich that he didn't see the plain-clothes police car waiting at the roadside in front of his building.

He looked around as he heard car doors slam and groaned, realising that middle-aged men in dark suits with their hands in the pockets of their long coats were never good news.

'Jack Nightingale?' growled the taller of the two.

Nightingale thought of coming up with a reply but he could see from their hard faces that they were as thrilled about the confrontation as he was so he just nodded. 'Yeah,' he sighed.

'Superintendent Chalmers wants a word.'

'Does Chalmers not know how to use a bloody phone?'

The detective shrugged. 'You'd have to ask him about that.'

'Warrant cards?' said Nightingale, just to be on the safe side, though there was no doubt that the two men were cops, and cops who had done their share of pounding the pavements.

The taller one was a DS Robert Waterman, his colleague DC Alex Shaw. Both were in their forties, wide-shouldered and square-chinned, relics of a bygone time before the Met lowered its standards of physique and fitness to allow in pretty much anybody. Nightingale nodded and the detectives put away their warrant cards.

DC Shaw stepped to the side and waved at the car, a black Vauxhall Vectra, the standard Met pool car. 'Your chariot awaits,' he said dourly.

'Any idea how long this is going to take?' asked Nightingale.

'Why, you got something important to do?' said DS Waterman.

'A date, as it happens,' said Nightingale.

'Lucky you.'

'So what do you think? Do you think we'll be done by seven?'

'How long's a piece of string?'

'See now, that's not very helpful, is it?' said Nightingale. The look that DC Shaw gave Nightingale left him in no doubt that the detective didn't care one way or the other. Nightingale sighed and headed for the rear door.

18

The car headed south across the Thames. DC Shaw was driving and DS Waterman had climbed into the back with Nightingale. Nightingale asked the detectives if he could smoke and when they didn't say anything he reached into the pocket of his raincoat and pulled out a pack of Marlboro. As he slid a cigarette between his lips DS Waterman put a hand on his knee and squeezed. 'You light that and I'll shove it so far up your arse that you'll be farting smoke rings,' he growled.

'Not a smoker then?' said Nightingale, putting the cigarette back into the pack. 'You should have said.'

The car drove through Clapham and Nightingale tensed as they turned into a road that he recognised. There were terraced houses on both sides, two storeys high with railings around basement steps. Ahead of them were two police cars nose to nose, blocking the road, their blue lights flashing but sirens off. In front of the cars was an ambulance and a SOCO van. A Scene Of Crime Officer was walking away from the van wearing a white paper suit and carrying a large metal case.

They pulled up behind the ambulance. DS Waterman gestured at the pavement. 'Out,' he said.

Nightingale got out of the car, a sick feeling in the pit

of his stomach. The driver wound down his window. 'The super wants him suited up,' he said.

The detective nodded and gestured at Nightingale. 'This way,' he said.

'What's going on?' asked Nightingale, but he said it for effect because he had a pretty good idea why they'd brought him to Clapham.

The detective ignored him. He walked between the two cars. There was another SOCO van parked in front of a house, which was being guarded by two burly policemen in fluorescent jackets.

A balding man in a white paper suit was rummaging around in a plastic trunk and he looked up as they approached. 'We need suits and boots,' said DS Waterman.

The SOCO grunted and leaned over a cardboard box. He pulled out two paper forensic suits in polythene bags and gave them to the detective. The detective handed one to Nightingale. 'Are you serious?' asked Nightingale.

'The guv wants you inside and we can't have you contaminating the crime scene,' said the detective sergeant. He took off his coat, folded it up and placed it on the floor of the van before ripping open the plastic bag and climbing into the paper suit. Nightingale followed his example.

As they zipped up their suits, the SOCO gave them latex gloves and paper covers for their shoes. Nightingale's mouth had gone dry – he had a pretty good idea that whatever had happened inside the house wouldn't be pretty.

The detective sergeant looked Nightingale up and down and nodded. 'You'll do,' he said.

'Will you at least tell me what's going on?' asked Nightingale, though he wasn't expecting an answer.

DS Waterman pointed at the front door. 'Superintendent Chalmers is inside, he'll fill you in.'

Nightingale nodded. He felt the nicotine craving kick in but he ignored it, knowing that there was no way that they would allow him to smoke. He leaned over and fished his mobile out of his pocket. 'Give me a minute,' he said. He tapped out a text message to Caitlin. 'Sorry, have to cancel tonight. Will call later.' He sent the message and put the phone back into his coat pocket, then followed the detective to the front door. The two fluorescent jackets moved apart to allow them in.

The hallway ran the full length of the house with purple doors leading off to the right and there was a flight of purple stairs leading up to the bedrooms. At the far end of the hallway was the kitchen. There was a SOCO with a camera photographing the body of a large black man in a blood-stained Puffa jacket, sprawled in front of the sink. Nightingale took a deep breath. His heart was pounding and he could feel sweat trickling down the small of his back.

DS Waterman walked along the hallway to the first door, his paper shoe covers swishing against the carpet. He pushed the door open wide to reveal a man in a forensic suit scribbling in a notebook. 'Where's the guv?' the detective asked him.

'Kitchen,' said the man.

Nightingale stood behind the detective and looked over his shoulder into the room. There were two other men standing in the room, wearing forensic suits. They were looking down at the body of another big black man lying spread-eagled by the window. The man's throat had been cut and blood had pooled around the body and soaked into the pale purple carpet.

There were three sofas around a coffee table that was littered with drug paraphernalia including several ornate bongs and a silver bowl filled with a white powder that could have been cocaine or heroin and a brass bowl piled high with yellowish crystals.

Lying across one of the sofas was a young black girl with waist-length dreadlocks. Her Bob Marley tank top was drenched in blood and her hands were covered in defensive wounds where she'd tried to fend off her killer. Her eyes were wide open, staring lifelessly up at the huge spherical white-paper lampshade hanging from the centre of the ceiling.

Nightingale shivered. DS Waterman turned on his heel and bumped into him. 'Keep out of my way, will you,' the detective growled. He walked along the hallway to the kitchen. Nightingale followed him.

Superintendent Chalmers was standing by a set of French windows that opened on to the lawn. He was staring out of the window and scowled when he saw Nightingale's reflection in the glass. 'Like the proverbial bad penny,' he said.

'To be fair, you did drag me here kicking and screaming,' said Nightingale.

Like the rest of the police and SOCO technicians, Chalmers was wearing a paper forensics suit and shoe covers. He turned to glare at Nightingale. Nightingale looked away and realised there was another body on the kitchen floor, a big guy in an LA Lakers shirt and baggy jeans. He was lying on his side, curled around a pool of congealed blood. There was a chrome pistol a few inches from his right hand.

Chalmers caught Nightingale staring at the gun. 'Makes

you wonder why he didn't pull the trigger,' said the superintendent.

Nightingale shrugged. 'Looks like his throat was cut from behind,' he said. 'He was probably heading for the hallway. Multiple attackers, obviously. Must have been at least two in the kitchen alone to take these two out.'

'Obviously,' said Chalmers, his voice loaded with sarcasm.

'Why am I here?' asked Nightingale.

'You don't know?'

Nightingale frowned. 'I haven't got time for games, Chalmers. I'm not in the job any more, remember?'

'This is no game, Nightingale. There's been a massacre here in case you hadn't noticed.'

'I had noticed, yes,' said Nightingale. 'I just don't see what it has to do with me. You wanted me to investigate dead Goths, not South London drug dealers.'

Chalmers frowned. 'How do you know they were drug dealers?'

Nightingale sneered at the superintendent. 'The clue was in the bowls in the sitting room,' he said. 'Industrial quantities of coke and crack.'

'Have you been here before?'

Nightingale faked surprise. 'Why would you think I'd been here before?'

'I'm always suspicious of people who answer a question with a question,' said Chalmers.

'Why's that?'

Chalmers pointed a warning finger at Nightingale's face. 'Don't push me, Nightingale.'

Nightingale held up his hands in surrender. 'Just tell me what you want and let me get the hell out of here,' he said.

Chalmers exhaled through pursed lips, then nodded at the hallway. 'Come with me,' he said. He took Nightingale up the stairs and along the hallway to a bathroom. The door was ajar and as they approached it there was a bright flash from inside, then another. Chalmers tapped on the door. 'Let the dog see the rabbit,' said Chalmers.

The door opened and a female SOCO holding a camera nodded at the superintendent. 'I'll be a while yet,' she said.

'Just give me a minute, will you?' said Chalmers, but his tone made it clear that it wasn't a request.

The SOCO nodded and squeezed past the two men. Nightingale moved to go into the bathroom but Chalmers put a restraining hand on his shoulder. 'When was the last time you saw Perry Smith?'

'What makes you think I know him?'

'Are you denying that you are acquainted with Mr Perry, drug-dealer of this parish?'

'Come on, Chalmers. Nicotine is my drug of choice, it always has been.'

'So answer my question and stop pissing around. Do you know Perry Smith?'

Nightingale stared at the superintendent, his mind racing. He did know Perry Smith but he couldn't see that anything good would come of admitting that to the super-intendent. 'No,' he said.

'You're sure about that?' The superintendent's grip tightened on Nightingale's shoulder.

Nightingale knew that having lied once, there was no going back. 'I'm sure,' he said. 'Look, what's this about, Chalmers? You can't possibly think I have anything to do with what's happened here.'

Chalmers raised one eyebrow. 'I can't? Perhaps you'd care to explain this then.'

He pushed the bathroom door open, giving Nightingale a clear view of the room. Perry Smith was sprawled in a whirlpool bath. His head had lolled back revealing a gaping wound in his throat. The blood had run down into his chest and turned the bathwater pink. And on the mirror, above the bath, were six words, written in blood. WE'RE COMING FOR YOU, JACK NIGHTINGALE.

19

Nightingale tossed the paper forensics suit into the back of the SOCO van and retrieved his raincoat. 'Can I smoke?' he asked Chalmers.

'You can burst into flames as far as I'm concerned,' said the superintendent. He leaned against the van and pulled off his paper shoe protectors.

As Nightingale retrieved his cigarettes, a middle-aged SOCO with receding hair and a goatee scowled at him. 'You can't smoke here,' he said.

'I'm outside,' said Nightingale, gesturing up at the overcast sky.

'Inside, outside, makes no difference,' said the technician. 'This van is my place of work so you can't smoke here.' He looked over at the superintendent and the policeman nodded.

'He's right,' said Chalmers.

Nightingale sighed and walked away from the van. Chalmers followed him. They stopped some twenty feet away from the SOCO van and Nightingale lit a cigarette.

'Who called it in? A neighbour?'

'There isn't much of a neighbourhood watch in this part of town,' said Chalmers. 'But we got a call from a pay-as-you-go mobile. The caller didn't leave a name.' He sighed. 'What aren't you telling me, Nightingale?'

Nightingale blew smoke before replying. 'You can't think that's anything to do with me,' he said.

'Your name's written on the mirror,' said Chalmers. 'I'd say that means you're involved. I'm going to ask you again, have you ever come across Perry Smith?'

'Not that I remember,' lied Nightingale.

'You're sure about that?'

Nightingale shrugged. 'I suppose our paths might have crossed when I was in the job, but nothing springs to mind. He's a drug dealer, right? Probably a turf war, don't you think?'

Chalmers smiled and shook his head. 'No, I don't think,' he said. 'Gang-bangers tend to use guns, not knives.'

Nightingale took a long pull on his cigarette and held the smoke deep in his lungs. Chalmers was right, of course. Drug dealers and gangsters didn't bother with knives. Knives were messy and meant getting up close and personal.

'That's what's so weird about this,' said Chalmers. 'Perry Smith and his crew aren't exactly low profile. Lots of bling, fast cars and loose women, and anyone who knows them would know they'd be armed to the hilt.'

'Including the cops,' said Nightingale.

Chalmers frowned. 'Your point being?'

Nightingale shrugged. 'Guns were banned years ago, but there are more than ever on the streets. If every man and his dog knew Smith's crew were carrying, why didn't the cops do something about it?'

'Send in CO19 and have a war on the streets of Clapham? You think that would solve anything?'

'It might get the guns off the street,' said Nightingale. 'I mean, how hard could it be? Owning a gun is a criminal offence punishable by up to ten years in prison. You know crews like Smith's carry guns, so arrest them and put them away. If every gang-banger with a gun got sent down for ten years, they'd soon get the message.'

The superintendent's eyes narrowed. 'You're very good at that, aren't you?'

'Good at what?'

'Changing the subject. I guess your negotiator training taught you that.'

Nightingale took another drag on his cigarette.

'That time we talked about the Goths. My men picked you up at a funeral.'

Nightingale nodded.

'Marcus Fairchild, right?'

'Sure, he was godfather to my assistant.'

'Ah yes, the lovely Miss McLean. How is she these days?'

Nightingale frowned, not sure what the superintendent was getting at. 'She's fine. She's staying with her parents this weekend.'

'How's she dealing with the death of her godfather?'

'It hit her pretty hard,' said Nightingale.

'Well, I say death, but of course I mean murder. Shot in the face and chest while sitting in the back of his limo.'

Nightingale blew smoke up at the sky and didn't say anything.

'I'm going to share some details of an ongoing investigation with you, Nightingale,' said Chalmers. 'It's against the rules, but then you were never a stickler for rules, were you?'

Nightingale blew smoke and studiously avoided eye contact with Chalmers.

'Here's the thing, Nightingale. The investigation is ongoing but one of the names in the frame for the murder of Marcus Fairchild was none other than Perry Smith.'

Nightingale could see that Chalmers was staring at him, gauging his reaction, and he fought to keep his face impassive.

'Cat got your tongue?' asked Chalmers.

'What do want me to say? I barely knew Fairchild.'

'You knew him well enough to go to his funeral.'

'I was there to support Jenny. She was pretty upset, obviously.'

'Obviously,' said Chalmers. 'But you can see where I'm going with this, can't you?'

Nightingale shook his head slowly. 'Not really, no.'

'It's about connections. Common threads. We have Marcus Fairchild shot in the back of his car. And we have Perry Smith and his crew butchered in their own home. And then we have you.'

'Me?'

'You knew Fairchild. And your name is written in blood above Perry Smith's corpse. I'm not a great believer in coincidences, Nightingale.'

'You think I killed half a dozen gang-bangers? Is that what you think?'

'Did you?'

Nightingale laughed out loud. 'Of course not.'

'Can you think of any reason why someone would go to the trouble of writing your name in blood at a crime scene?'

'Nothing springs to mind.'

'You don't seem worried.'

Nightingale shrugged. 'I'm a bit confused, truth be told.'

'Confused? If I'd been threatened like that I'd be a lot more than confused.'

'Being threatened goes with the job, it always has done.'

'Yeah, but you're not in the job, are you? And this isn't some drunk mouthing off, is it?'

Nightingale dropped what was left of his cigarette on to the ground and stepped on it.

'Doesn't seem like an empty threat, that's all I'm saying,' said Chalmers.

'I'll be vigilant,' said Nightingale.

'And you have no idea who it might be?'

Nightingale shook his head. 'I've made my fair share of enemies over the years, but that in there does seem a bit extreme, don't you think?'

'It seems to me that whoever killed Smith and his crew is threatening to come after you. And if I were you, I'd be a bit more worried than you actually are.'

'Like I said, I'll be vigilant.'

'I suppose I should be offering you police protection. I'd hate to be accused down the line of not doing enough to protect a member of the public.'

'I'll pass,' said Nightingale.

'I could put a uniform on your front door for a few days.'

'I'm sure Smith would have had some sort of security but it didn't do him any good.'

The superintendent nodded. 'Agreed, but at least I can say I offered and my offer was turned down.'

'Do you want it in writing?' asked Nightingale, his voice loaded with sarcasm.

'No need,' said Chalmers. 'You don't seem to be curious about the connection between Smith and Fairchild.'

'Why should I be?'

'You're a family friend, I thought you might have wanted to know who killed him.'

'Jenny's my friend. Marcus was barely an acquaintance.'

'And you wouldn't shed a tear over a dead lawyer?' Chalmers chuckled softly. 'Who would, right? Wasn't it Shakespeare who said "First kill all the lawyers"? Or Stalin? I can never remember.'

'Lawyers make enemies,' said Nightingale.

'Of course they do. But we can't find any connection between Smith and Fairchild. Except you. He didn't do much in the way of criminal work, and I certainly can't see him having a low-life like Smith for a client.'

'From what I heard, Marcus was shot by a pro. Guy on a motorbike, full face helmet.'

'That's pretty much it. The bike turned up a couple of days later, torched. No match from ballistics.'

'So how do you link Smith to it?'

'Fairchild was shot with a MAC-10, weapon of choice of gang-bangers like Perry. Plus we have intel from a CI. That's all I can tell you, and I shouldn't even be telling you that much.'

'Gossip from a confidential informant isn't a case, is it? Could be someone with an axe to grind, you've been around the block long enough to have learned that, surely.'

'One of Smith's soldiers was boasting about getting rid of a gun used to kill an old white lawyer. Our CI was within earshot. If we were being fed bullshit, there'd be a darn sight more of it.'

'That's not much, is it?'

'It was enough for us to put Smith and his crew under the microscope.' The superintendent gestured at the house behind them. 'But that bloodbath has put paid to that investigation, obviously.'

'A drug dealer shooting up a City lawyer seems a bit unlikely, doesn't it?'

'Who knows? Maybe they were in business together. It wouldn't be the first time a white middle-class professional has got into bed with a black drugs dealer.'

'What, you think Fairchild was bankrolling Smith?'

'Or buying drugs from him. We're exploring all avenues. If it was Smith behind the hit, he must have had a reason.' He shrugged. 'But with both men dead, I guess we'll never know.' He looked sideways at Nightingale. 'Unless there's something you want to share with me?'

'I'm as much in the dark as you are.'

'I didn't say I was in the dark, Nightingale,' said Chalmers. 'But if there's no other link between Fairchild and Smith, I'm drawn to the conclusion that you're the connection.'

'And if I am?'

'Let's cross that bridge when we get to it,' said Chalmers. He looked at his watch and then looked around. 'Where the hell is my driver?' he muttered.

'Any chance of a lift back to Bayswater?'

'I'm not going that way,' said Chalmers. 'Talk to the uniforms, tell them I said it was okay.'

'You're a prince among men,' said Nightingale.

Chalmers turned to look at him. 'Look, Nightingale, I

know when someone is being less than honest with me. I don't know what it is you're keeping from me, but this time you're playing with fire. What happened in there is as bad as anything I've seen in twenty-five years on the force. And that message on the mirror means that you could be next on their list. You watch your back, okay?'

'I intend to,' said Nightingale. The policeman's concern seemed genuine, which was surprising because Nightingale had never felt that the superintendent had had his best interests at heart.

'And what's happening with the Goths?'

'I'm on the case,' said Nightingale. 'I think I've found a connection. They all had tattoos, which isn't the norm for Goths. They might all have gone to the same tattooist. A shop in Camden. It's possible their paths had crossed there.'

'Give me the details, I'll get them checked out.'

'I've already spoken to them. They had a break-in and their records were stolen. The one guy who might be able to confirm that they all went there has gone walkabout.'

'Yeah, well, I'll get my people on it anyway.' He took out a small black notebook and a gold pen.

'The Ink Pit,' said Nightingale. 'It's run by two guys, Ricky Nail and Jezza Sampson.'

'Jezza?'

'Short for Jeremy, I guess.'

'Anything else?'

'I went to a Goth club last night. The Crypt, near the Angel. Showed the photographs around and left my card.'

'Any joy?'

Nightingale shook his head. 'The one thing I didn't find was anyone who remembered seeing Daryl Heaton.'

'So?'

'So I'm not sure he was actually a Goth. Seems to have been more of a biker.'

'He wore black.'

'So do cops.'

The superintendent's jaw tensed. 'This isn't a laughing matter, Nightingale.'

'I'm just saying, you're looking for Goth killers, but from what I've been told, Heaton wasn't a Goth. That's why I think the tattoo place is a better bet.'

Chalmers put away his notebook and pen. 'Keep at it, Nightingale. Nose to the grindstone, I need a name in the frame for those killings and soon.'

'I'm on it,' said Nightingale.

A black Jaguar parked some way down the road flashed its lights and Chalmers waved back. 'Why the hell did he park all the way down there?' muttered the super-intendent. He walked over to the police tape, ducked under it and headed for the car, his coat flapping behind him. Nightingale lit another cigarette as he watched the superintendent climb into the back of the Jaguar. Chalmers was right, of course. Nightingale did know Perry Smith. He knew him and had done business with him. But there was no way that Nightingale could ever admit that, not without opening up a very messy can of worms.

20

Nightingale climbed out of the police patrol car that had parked a short distance from his flat in Inverness Terrace. 'Thanks, guys, I really appreciate it,' he said.

The driver, a uniformed sergeant with greying hair, winked up at him. 'No problem, Jack. Good to see you again.'

'Cheers, Barry, love to the wife.' He closed the door and patted the roof of the patrol car.

The sergeant waved and drove off. Nightingale pulled his keys out of his pocket and fumbled for the one that opened the main door. As he was slotting the key into the lock a large shadow fell across the door. He flinched and twisted around, his hands flying up in front of his face to protect himself. A large figure was looming over him. Nightingale staggered back and his shoulders slammed into the door.

The man raised his hands. 'Hey, Bird-man, chill. It's me.'

Nightingale sighed as he recognised the man. 'Bloody hell, T-Bone, you gave me the fright of my life.' He shook his head and patted his chest. 'You nearly gave me a heart attack.'

'You live here?' asked T-Bone, nodding at the door.

'Home sweet home,' said Nightingale.

'Can we go inside?'

'That was my plan before you crept up on me,' said Nightingale. 'Next time, shout out or something, will you?'

'I had to wait for Five-0 to leave.'

Realisation dawned and Nightingale nodded thoughtfully. 'You were outside the house?'

'Yeah. And was there when they brought you in. Why were you there, Bird-man?'

'You didn't go inside?'

The big man shook his head.

Nightingale gestured at the door. 'Best we talk inside, T-Bone.'

'No argument here.'

Nightingale unlocked the door and took T-Bone upstairs. He unlocked the door to his flat and showed T-Bone inside before taking off his raincoat. 'You want a drink?' he asked T-Bone, who was looking around the small flat with a look of disdain on his face.

'You live here?'

'Nah, it's a safe house. My main place is a mansion in St John's Wood.' He grinned. 'Of course I live here.'

'It's a bit small, innit?'

'I live on my own, T-Bone, I don't need a big place. Now do you want a drink or not?' He went into the kitchen and took a bottle of Corona from the fridge.

'Got any wine?' asked T-Bone, taking off his Puffa jacket to reveal a black Versace T-shirt that appeared to have been sprayed across his massive chest. T-Bone's forearms were thicker than Nightingale's thighs and his six-pack was clearly visible through the thin material.

'Wine?'

'What, a black man can't enjoy wine?' said T-Bone, dropping down on to the one sofa. There was a sharp cracking sound and Nightingale half-expected the sofa to disintegrate under the weight, but it held firm.

'Just didn't have you down as a wine drinker, that's all,' said Nightingale. 'Red or white?'

'Red's cool,' said T-Bone.

'That's a problem because I've only got white,' said Nightingale, opening the fridge.

'So why did you ask?'

'I was trying to be a good host,' said Nightingale.

'Offering a man a drink you don't have doesn't make you a good host, Bird-man.'

Nightingale showed him the one bottle of wine he had in his fridge. 'My assistant gave it to me so it's probably a decent one.'

T-Bone looked at the label and nodded. 'Nice bottle of Chardonnay,' he said. 'Your assistant knows her wine.'

Nightingale rooted around in a drawer and pulled out a corkscrew. He opened the bottle, poured some into a glass and gave it to T-Bone. He put the bottle down on the coffee table and took a chair from his dining table and reversed it so that he could rest his arms on the back of it as he sat down opposite his guest.

T-Bone raised the glass in salute. 'Cheers, Bird-man.'

Nightingale clinked his bottle against T-Bone's glass. 'You called three nines, right?'

T-Bone frowned. 'How do you know?'

'If you'd have been inside the house you'd be dead. I'm guessing that you followed me here from Clapham. Which means that you must have been waiting outside the house. The cops were acting on a nine nine nine call from a throwaway mobile.' He gestured at T-Bone with the bottle. 'Elementary, dear Watson.'

'Yeah, well the big question is what the fuck you were doing there.'

'I was summoned. Didn't you see them bring me in? I was one step away from being cuffed.'

'Looked to me like you were helping them with their enquiries. And you seemed very pally with that detective. What is he, a CI?'

'Superintendent. Chalmers is his name, making my life misery is his game.'

'And he wanted your input because?'

Nightingale sipped his beer, playing for time. He wasn't planning on lying to T-Bone but there were things Nightingale needed to know and he didn't want the man clamming up. 'You didn't go inside the house?'

T-Bone shook his head. 'I saw them leave and figured I'd best not get involved with what had gone down. Smith's dead, yeah?'

Nightingale nodded. 'Yeah. I'm sorry.'

T-Bone shrugged his massive shoulders. 'Our line of work, not many get to collect a pension.' He looked at Nightingale with narrowed eyes. 'They're all dead?'

'I'm told seven guys and two girls. What did you see, T-Bone?'

T-Bone took a deep breath. He blinked several times and then took another breath, steadying himself. 'When I parked I could see that there was no security on the door. That's our golden rule – there's always someone there, usually two. I knew something was wrong but didn't know what so I moved the car down the street and waited.

I called Perry but he didn't answer and he always takes my calls no matter what so I was pretty sure the shit had hit the fan. I figured maybe gang-bangers but they wouldn't normally attack a base, drive-bys are more their thing.'

'That's when you called it in?'

T-Bone shook his head, drained his glass and refilled it. 'I wanted to have an idea of what was what before I rang the Feds,' he said. 'Just in case I was wrong, you know?'

Nightingale nodded. 'Yeah, I know. Perry wouldn't have been best pleased if he'd been upstairs shagging and CO19 had gone in with guns blazing.'

'Ain't that the truth,' said T-Bone. He took another swig from his glass and then held it up. 'This is one fine wine,' he said. 'Your assistant, you said?'

'Yeah, her dad's got a cellar full of the good stuff. So who came out, T-Bone?'

'White guys,' said T-Bone. 'At first I thought maybe they were Drugs Squad but there were no uniforms and they got into unmarked cars. A Lexus and a BMW SUV. And a white van. I didn't see no guns but they were carrying small bags. Like they'd just been to the gym.'

'Did you get to see their faces?'

'They had on hoodies.'

'How many?'

'Eight men. And two women.'

'Women?'

'Girls. Looked like hookers. Short skirts and their tits hanging out.'

'The sort that Perry liked?'

T-Bone nodded. 'Yeah, his spec. One blonde and one brunette. You think they were the bait?'

'Sounds like it. The girls got inside and did what they had to do to get the others inside.'

'So why didn't anyone hear the shots?' asked T-Bone.

'They didn't use guns.'

T-Bone frowned and rubbed the back of his neck. 'Now how the hell can that be true?'

'Perry was stabbed,' said Nightingale. 'They all were.'

'But they had an arsenal in there.'

'I'm guessing that Perry didn't see it coming. None of them did.'

T-Bone drained his glass and refilled it. He'd already worked his way through half the bottle. 'You haven't told me why you were there, Bird-man.'

Nightingale finished his beer then went through to the kitchen to get another.

'Why do I get the feeling you're avoiding the question?' called T-Bone.

Nightingale took his beer back to the sitting room. He stood with his back to the window. 'They wrote my name on the mirror in Perry's bathroom.'

T-Bone screwed up his face as he looked up at him. 'Now why the hell would they do that?'

'It was a threat. They said they were coming for me next.'

'And they wrote that on the bathroom mirror?'

'Yes, they did. In blood.'

T-Bone frowned and shook his head. 'That makes no sense. No sense at all.'

'You're telling me.'

'Is this about you, Bird-man?'

'I think it's about Marcus Fairchild.'

'That old lawyer that Perry took care of?'

'Yeah. The cops got a tip that Perry's crew were involved.'

'Damn right he was involved. Once you told him that Fairchild was a paedophile and a child-killer it was all I could do to stop him pulling the trigger himself.' His face clouded as he realised what Nightingale had said. 'Someone grassed us up?'

'The cops have a CI, someone on your crew or close to it. Whoever the CI is he told the cops that one of your guys got rid of the gun.'

T-Bone nodded thoughtfully. 'You can't trust anyone these days.'

'Tell me about it,' said Nightingale.

'So what are you saying?'

'It sure as hell wasn't a gang hit. I doubt it was a robbery because they would have used guns and not knives. It all felt very personal.'

'Revenge?'

Nightingale nodded. 'It was well planned and executed. Using the girls to get in and then killing everyone before they had a chance to fire a shot. Then getting clean away.'

'Not quite clean away,' said T-Bone. He stuck his hand into his pocket and pulled out a smartphone. He tapped on the screen and showed it to Nightingale. 'I got the numbers of the Lexus and the white van. Thought you might be able to trace them.' T-Bone had photographed the two vehicles as they drove away.

'You don't want to give the numbers to the cops?'

'You get me the names and I'll take care of it,' said

T-Bone. 'Besides, if it was revenge for that lawyer, you'd wonder how they knew it was Perry what done it.'

'The cops gave the information to the killers? Is that what you think?'

'Why not? Grassing works both ways. Give me your number and I'll send you the pics.'

Nightingale gave T-Bone the number and T-Bone sent the pictures. Nightingale's phone beeped twice as the messages arrived. 'What about you, T-Bone? What are you going to do?'

'I'm going to do to them what they did to Perry.' He raised his glass in salute. 'And some.'

'I meant about Perry's organisation. Who takes over?'

'Who do you think, Bird-man?'

'You, right?'

'I don't see anyone else ready to take up the reins, do you? We've plenty of foot soldiers and our supply lines are still in place. Business-wise, we won't miss a beat. Not unless some of our rivals decide to try and muscle in. But I'll make sure that doesn't happen. I've already made a few calls.'

'Sounds like you know what you're doing.'

'I'm not a virgin at this, Bird-man,' said T-Bone. He drained his glass and got to his feet. 'I'm going to love you and leave you,' he said. 'Mountains to climb, rivers to cross and all that jazz.' He grabbed Nightingale's free hand and bumped shoulders with him. 'You be careful, hear?'

'Can you do me a favour on that front?'

'A gun?'

'You read my mind. Something small and concealable.'

'I'll get you sorted,' promised T-Bone as he pulled on his Puffa jacket. 'I'll send someone round.'

'Let me know how much I owe you.'

'Fuck that, Bird-man. It's on the house. And get me those names, soon as you can.'

21

As soon as T-Bone had left, Nightingale phoned Robbie Hoyle, his former colleague on the Met. 'Where are you, mate?' he asked.

'In front of the TV with my lovely wife,' said Robbie.

'I need a favour,' said Nightingale.

'Of course you do, that's the only reason you call me.' Nightingale heard a muffled voice and then Robbie laughed. 'My darling wife asks if you'd like to come to dinner on Saturday.'

'Love to,' said Nightingale.

'And she said you should bring Jenny.'

'Tell her that I'm happy enough to ask her but she's wasting her time if she's planning on matchmaking.'

'I'm with Anna on this – Jenny's lovely.'

'No arguments there, but I don't want to spoil a perfectly good working environment.'

'You can always hire another assistant.'

Nightingale laughed. 'Not on the money I pay,' he said. 'Seriously, I'll ask her. And you know how much I love Anna's cooking. But this favour, it can't really wait. What shift are you on tomorrow?'

'I'm in at ten.'

'Can I buy you a coffee at nine thirty? That place on the corner, close to the factory.'

Factory was slang for the police station, in Robbie's case Lavender Hill in South London.

'Coffee and a chocolate muffin.' Nightingale heard a muffled comment from Anna and Robbie laughed. 'Anna says no to the muffin.'

'She's got your best interests at heart. See you at nine thirty.'

22

Nightingale woke up to the sound of his intercom buzzing. He grabbed a bathrobe and padded over to it and picked up the receiver. 'Delivery for Jack Nightingale,' said a voice.

Half asleep, Nightingale pressed the button to open the door downstairs and immediately regretted it. He had no idea who it was and images of the carnage at the Clapham house flashed through his mind. He cursed under his breath, ran into the kitchen and rifled through the drawers until he found a large yellow-handled carving knife. He hurried back to the front door and stood with his eye to the peephole, the knife clutched in his right hand. He was panting heavily and he took a deep breath and held it, trying to calm himself down. He realised his phone was on the bedside table and he cursed under his breath. He considered rushing to get it but then decided it was more important to see who the visitor was. If it was the men who'd killed Perry Smith then the locked door would hold them long enough for him to get to the bedroom and phone for the police. Though considering London response times he might be better off going out of the kitchen window and down the drainpipe to the rear of the flats.

He heard footsteps on the stairs and a figure appeared, its face shrouded in a hoodie that gave the appearance of a monk. Then the man lifted his head as he pressed the doorbell and Nightingale caught a glimpse of a young black teenager with acne-scarred skin. He couldn't have been more than fourteen and he looked left and right before pressing the bell. Even though he was expecting it, the sound made Nightingale jump. He shoved the knife into the drawer of the hall table, unlocked the security chain and opened the door. The teenager eyed Nightingale suspiciously. 'You the Bird-man?' he asked.

'Nightingale. Yeah.'

The teenager reached inside his hoodie and pulled out a yellow padded envelope, which he thrust at Nightingale. 'T-Bone says you're to have this.'

Nightingale took it. It was heavy.

'T-Bone says it's untraceable but he doesn't want to see it again, no matter what you do with it.'

'Understood.'

'And he says he wants the names. As soon as.'

'Tell T-Bone I'm on the case.' He hefted the package. 'And tell him thanks for this.'

The teenager nodded then hurried back down the stairs. Nightingale closed the door, put on the security chain, and carried the package through into the kitchen. He switched on the kettle and then opened the package. Inside was a matte black Glock 27 and two clips filled with rounds. He checked the weapon and smelled it. If it had ever been fired it had been scrupulously cleaned. He picked up one of the clips and ejected half a dozen rounds. They were all in as-new condition. He slotted them back into place. He immediately felt a lot safer with the gun in the flat, especially knowing that the men who had killed Perry Smith and his crew favoured knives.

He padded through to his bedroom, knelt down by the side of the bed and pulled out his old Metropolitan Police kitbag. The black nylon was covered with dust and he took it through to the bathroom and wiped it down with a damp flannel before unzipping it. Inside was a stab-proof jacket, knee and elbow protectors, a couple of T-shirts and a collapsible baton. Under the jacket was a nylon shoulder holster and a leather holster that could be clipped to a belt. He zipped up the bag, shoved it back under the bed and took the holsters to the kitchen. The kettle had boiled so he put them down next to the gun and made himself a coffee.

He sat down and tried the holsters for size. The Glock 27 fitted them both perfectly. The shoulder holster was the easiest to use and there was less chance of the gun getting caught in his clothing. But it was also the most likely to be spotted. If he was wearing a regular jacket it only had to open a few inches to reveal the holstered weapon. And it would only take one concerned member of the public to call the cops and he'd find himself staring down the wrong end of a half a dozen CO19 carbines.

The belt holster would keep the weapon concealed in the small of his back and away from prying eyes, but reaching for it was awkward and there was always the chance that it would get snagged on his shirt or jacket.

He slotted in a clip but didn't put a round in the chamber. The Glock's in-built safety trigger meant that it was almost impossible to fire the weapon by accident but he doubted that he'd need the fraction of a second it would take to slot a round home before firing.

He flinched as the alarm clock went off in his bedroom. He had half an hour to get ready before heading to his meeting with Robbie close to Lavender Hill police station so he gulped down his coffee and headed to the bathroom.

23

Nightingale was sitting at a corner table with two coffees and two chocolate muffins in front of him when Robbie walked in. The detective laughed when he saw the muffins. 'Anna will have your guts for garters,' he said. He dropped down on to the seat opposite Nightingale. 'So to what do I owe the pleasure?'

Nightingale leaned across the table and lowered his voice. 'Can you check out two cars for me?'

Robbie looked pained. 'Jack, you know those days are long gone. Anyone caught accessing the PNC without just cause is out on his ear. You know that, Jack.'

'I know that you always give me this speech whenever I ask.'

'If I lose my job, who looks after Anna and the kids?'

'I wouldn't ask if it wasn't important,' said Nightingale. 'And you know the drill: put them through at the same time as you're doing others. Or better still, sit down at a terminal where someone has forgotten to log off.'

'It's a sackable offence, don't you get that?' He picked up one of the muffins and bit into it before sighing with pleasure. 'Anna's cutting down my carbs,' he said.

'Just so long as she doesn't cut off your nuts.'

Robbie laughed and took a sip off his coffee. 'What's the story?'

'Do you really want to know?'

'Don't be a prick, Jack. If I'm going to put my job on the line for you, the least you can do is to tell me why.'

Nightingale reached into his inside pocket and took out a folded piece of paper. 'There are two numbers there – a white van and a BMW SUV. Did you hear about the killings here yesterday?'

'Station was buzzing with it.'

'You involved?'

Robbie shook his head. 'Bloodbath by the sound of it. Group of gang-bangers, right? Operation Trident are on it so it's black on black, they think.'

'Yeah, well, they're wrong,' said Nightingale. 'The killers were white.'

'Says who?'

Nightingale put the piece of paper down in front of his friend. 'Says the guy who gave me those numbers.'

'Hell's bells, Jack. A witness?'

'He's a gang-banger, there's no way he's going to talk to the cops.'

Robbie picked up the piece of paper and looked at the two registration numbers. 'This witness, he saw the killers.'

'He saw a group of men leaving the house. He was close enough to see the vehicles but not close enough to see their faces.'

'And what's your interest?'

Nightingale grimaced. 'Seriously, Robbie, the less you know, the better.'

Robbie shook his head. 'No bloody way,' he said. 'You're

asking me to run a PNC check on two vehicles tied in to a mass murder. If anyone else discovers that those vehicles were involved then they could easily spot that I'd been giving them the once over.'

'Which is why you need to cover your tracks.'

'And that's why I need you to stop pissing about and tell me everything.'

Nightingale sipped his coffee while Robbie broke off a piece of muffin. 'The killers wrote some crap on a bathroom mirror about me being next. Chalmers was on the case so he hauled me in. I said I knew nothing, which is true. But afterwards the witness came forward. He's an old contact of mine. He was outside and he saw the killers leave. Or at least he saw half a dozen men and a couple of girls. They got into those vehicles and drove off. My contact called the cops and waited for them to get there.'

'And he won't go public because he's a gang-banger?'

'You know what they're like, Robbie. A grass is the lowest form of pondlife in their world.'

'So what's your interest? You get the names of the owners of the vehicles, and then what?'

Nightingale took another sip of his coffee. That was the big question, of course. And if Nightingale answered it honestly then Robbie would probably throw the piece of paper in his face and storm out. And he'd be right to be angry, too, there was no getting away from that. Nightingale was going to give the names to T-Bone and T-Bone would do what he had to do. And that would probably involve guns and a lot of blood. He put down his mug and flashed Robbie his most sincere smile. 'One step at a time,' he said. 'I want to know who wrote my name on the bathroom mirror.'

'Why don't you just give the information to Chalmers? You don't have to tell him where you got it from.'

Nightingale shook his head. 'He already thinks I'm up to my eyes in it. If I give him the numbers he'll be sure I'm involved and then he'll make my life really difficult. I just need to know who I'm up against.' He sat back in his chair and felt the Glock press against his spine.

'Then send it in anonymously.'

'Robbie, mate, just do me this one favour, will you?'

Robbie laughed but the sound came out like a harsh bark. 'It's never one favour though, is it, Jack? It's non-bloody-stop. And it's always one way.' He waved the piece of paper in Nightingale's face. 'It'd be nice if every now and again you gave me something that might help my career,' he said.

'Most of my stuff is divorce or helping confirm alibis,' said Nightingale. 'This is one of a kind—'

Robbie put up his hand to cut Nightingale short. 'I'm just saying, this is always a one-way thing with you and it would be nice if you'd give me the occasional tip off, that's all.'

Nightingale put his hand on his chest. 'I swear, the next murder case I get, I'll run everything by you. But you wouldn't want this one, Robbie. It's messy and no matter how it plays out, Chalmers would know anything you had could only have come from me and that would do you more harm than good.'

'That's true enough,' agreed Robbie. He slotted the last piece of muffin into his mouth and washed it down with coffee. 'Okay, here's what I'll do. I've a couple of ongoing investigations that involve a lot of PNC checks. We've a CSO on attachment so I'll slip these into his file.

But I'm not handing anything over to you on paper. I'll take snaps on a pay-as-you-go phone and send them to you.'

'You devious bugger.'

'It has to be that way, Jack. They can follow any paper trail and this way it could have come from anyone. But you need to forget that you asked me.'

Nightingale put his hand over his heart. 'Cross my heart.'

'And if you get asked who gave you the information . . .' He left the sentence unfinished.

'They'll have to pull my fingernails out with pliers.'

'Yeah, but even then, your lips stay sealed.'

Nightingale nodded. 'Scout's honour.'

'You never were a scout.'

'No, but I take their oath seriously.' He picked up his coffee mug and raised it in salute. 'You're a scholar and a gentleman.'

'No, I'm a twat for letting you twist me around your little finger. But you owe me, Jack. And I'm going to want paying back. Get me something that'll raise my profile. I don't want to be a sergeant forever.'

24

Robbie left the coffee shop first, off to start his shift at Lavender Hill. Nightingale nursed his coffee. He remembered the sheet of paper that the receptionist at the Ink Pit had given him and he took it out and unfolded it. Ricky Nail's girlfriend lived less than half a mile from where he was sitting. He took out his mobile phone and called Nail's number. It was the sixth time he had called and yet again it went straight through to voicemail. He had left a message the first time, and the second, and sent a text, so he cut the connection and then phoned Jenny on her mobile.

'How did it go yesterday?' she asked.

'Brilliant,' he said. 'He finished in under two hours, which is good going.'

'Video?'

'Loads of it,' he said. 'I'm on my way in but I'm going to swing by the home of the girlfriend of that tattooist. Can you hold the fort?'

'Consider it held,' said Jenny.

Nightingale ended the call, finished his coffee and headed out of the coffee shop. It took him just ten minutes to walk to Suw's place. She lived in a stucco-clad terraced house that had been converted into flats. Her flat was in the basement so Nightingale pushed open a gate in the railings and carefully went down the concrete steps. There were a couple of conifers in wooden tubs either side of the front door. He pressed the bell and after a few seconds he heard footsteps and the door was opened by a woman in her late twenties wearing a red top and a short black skirt. She had several piercings in her ears and eyebrows and a tattoo of a rose on her left leg, close to her ankle.

'Suw?' he said.

She frowned. 'Yes?'

'I don't suppose Rusty's here, is he?'

'Rusty?'

'Ricky? Ricky Nail?'

'Why would that bastard be here?'

'I thought you were his girlfriend.'

'One of several, as it turns out,' she said. 'Does he owe you money?'

'Actually I'm with the police,' he said, conscious as always that he was deliberately stretching the truth but that he wasn't exactly telling a lie.

'Good, I hope you catch him and throw away the key.'

'You seem pretty upset,' said Nightingale.

'Do I? I wonder why.' She put a hand up to her head and looked up theatrically. 'Oh, wait, now I remember. It's because he was shagging anything that moved behind my back.'

'I'm sorry.'

'Not half as sorry as I am,' said Suw. 'He made a right fool out of me, he did. Why are men such bastards?'

'I think we're hard-wired that way,' said Nightingale.

She screwed up her face as if she didn't understand what he meant, and then she grinned. 'Yeah, that'd be right. Anyway, if you want to catch up with him you'd best look for Stella or whoever his new bitch is.'

'Stella? Stella Walsh?'

'I don't know,' she said. She frowned at him. 'Why, you know her?'

'Maybe,' he said. 'How did you meet her?'

She shook her head. 'I never met the bitch. She was some Goth girl that he'd tattooed. She was just a kid. I found texts from her and some pictures on his phone.'

'Pictures?'

'Sexts, they call them, right? Sex texts. Flashing her breasts, she was. And it wasn't his regular phone. He used an iPhone but this was a Samsung that I found in the pocket of his jeans. I threw him out there and then. Haven't heard from him since.'

'When was that?'

'Three weeks ago, give or take.'

Nightingale reached into his pocket for the print-out of the five Goths but then remembered that he'd given it to the bouncer at the Crypt. 'Look, Suw, can I show you a picture of Stella Walsh, see if it's the same Stella that sent the texts to Rusty? It's important.'

She nodded. 'Okay.' She opened the door. 'You'd better come in.'

She led him down a cramped hallway to a sitting room that was surprisingly light considering that it was underground. The walls were painted white and there was a skylight to the right of a Victorian fireplace that had also been given a coat of white paint. The sofa was white and there were white rugs on the bare floorboards that had been polished and varnished.

'Do you want a coffee?' she asked.

He didn't, but he intuited that making it would make her feel more relaxed. 'I'd love one,' he said. She went off to the kitchen and he phoned Jenny. 'It's me again.'

'The fort's being held,' she said. 'You don't need to worry.'

'I'm not worried,' he said. 'Can you do me a favour and send a photograph of Stella Walsh to my phone?'

'Your wish is my command, oh master.' She ended the call and thirty seconds later his phone beeped.

When Suw returned with two mugs of coffee he showed her the photograph and she nodded. 'That's her,' she said. 'Though in the texts she sent Rusty she had her tits out. I mean look at her. How old is she? Sixteen? He said she was eighteen but she doesn't look it.'

'No, she was eighteen. Just turned.' He put his phone away. She sat down on the sofa and Nightingale dropped down on to a wicker chair with a tasselled cushion.

'Was?'

Nightingale nodded. 'Yeah, she was killed a few weeks ago.'

Suw's hands flew up to her mouth. 'Oh my God,' she said. 'Killed? Like murdered, you mean?'

'You've heard about the Goth Killers, right? In the papers and on TV?'

'Sure.' Her eyes widened. 'Oh my God,' she said again.

'She was one of the victims. The first, in fact.'

Suw sat back and hugged her knees up to her chest. 'Oh my God,' she repeated.

'Was he actually going out with her?' asked Nightingale.

'He said no but he was a compulsive liar. After I'd thrown him out two of my girlfriends told me that he'd hit on them. He was a dog.'

'Better off without him,' said Nightingale.

'Exactly,' she said.

'So she was a client.'

'Just a client, is what he said, but that was before he realised I'd seen the texts. And that I knew he had an extra phone.' She leaned over and picked up her coffee mug. 'Look, I'm sorry she's dead and all but she had no right to go messing with my man.'

'In her defence, I'm guessing that Rusty didn't tell her that he already had a girlfriend.' He sipped his coffee. 'You haven't tried to call him or been around to his place?'

'Why the hell would I? We're done. Finished. Over.'

'I've been calling his mobile but it goes straight through to voicemail.'

'He's not a great one for answering his phone. Or maybe he just doesn't answer his iPhone but takes calls from his whores on his Samsung.'

'At the tattoo parlour they said he'd been talking about going to some band thing in the US?'

'The Warped Tour. Yeah. He'd said we might go but nothing came of it. It's an indie concert tour, lots of great bands, and this year there's half a dozen that he likes so we talked about it, yeah.'

'Could he have gone on his own?'

'More likely he's taken one of his whores with him,' she said.

She stood up. 'There's something I need to give you,' she said. She left the room and returned a few minutes later with a cardboard box. She dropped it on the coffee table with a dull thud. 'You can take this crap with you,' she said. 'And if you find him, tell him I've already moved on.'

'Have you?'

She forced a smile. 'No, not yet. But don't bloody well tell him that. Tell him I've got a new boyfriend and he can go screw himself.' Tears welled up in her eyes. 'Bastard,' she whispered.

25

Jenny looked up as Nightingale walked into the office carrying the cardboard box. 'Been shopping?' she asked brightly.

'A gift from Rusty Nail's ex-girlfriend,' he said, placing the box on her desk. 'He's had a bust-up with her and that's the stuff he left in her flat. And here's something big – Rusty had a thing with Stella Walsh.'

'That's why you wanted me to send the picture?'

Nightingale nodded. 'You know what a sext is?'

'Of course. Oh, she was sexting Rusty?'

'Yes she was. And his girlfriend caught him and threw him out. Three weeks ago.'

'Not long before Stella was killed.' She pushed her chair away from her desk. 'Do you think Rusty killed her?'

Nightingale sat down on the edge of her desk. 'I didn't until you said that. Why would he kill one of his customers? And he was a bit Gothy himself.'

'I'm not sure that Gothy is a word, actually.'

Nightingale wrinkled his nose. 'It's a thought, though, isn't it? If he was the killer it would account for the fact that he's gone missing, too.'

'You should tell Chalmers.'

'I will, I will.'

'Now, Jack.'

'I thought I might go around and ring his doorbell.'

'You've phoned, right?'

'Sure, but his ex says he doesn't answer the phone much.'

Jenny grinned mischievously. 'You could send him a sext.'

'I think it'd probably work better if you did it. He is apparently one for the ladies.'

'Well, I've told you what I think. You need to pass this on to Chalmers and get back to working on our cases. We make our money from divorce and insurance work, not by playing detective for the Met. Speaking of which – where's the video from yesterday?'

Nightingale reached into the cardboard box and pulled out his video camera. 'All there, start, refreshments midway and the finish, with some footage of him skipping to his car.'

'Excellent,' said Jenny. 'I'll get that off to the bus company today. Mr Drummond is in for a nasty surprise. He's expecting his cheque today but he'll be getting a visit from the cops instead.'

Nightingale slid off the desk. 'I'll be at Rusty Nail's place if you need me.' He gestured at the box. 'Can you go through that and see if there's anything of interest. There are a few notebooks and thumb-drives. Most of the CDs seem to be music but there might be video that's of interest.'

'Don't you think you should take this with you, seeing as how it's his property?'

'Let's see if I can find him first. And I'd like to know

a bit more about him, just in case he's the link between all the victims.'

'You're playing at being a cop again,' she said, wagging her finger at him. 'If you're not careful it'll end in tears.'

26

Ricky Nail lived in Lanark Road in Maida Vale, in a block of six terraced houses that had been knocked together and converted into flats. There were two entrances, one on the left for flats numbered one to eight and a matching one on the right for flats nine to sixteen. Nail lived in number fifteen. There was a bank of eight bells to the side of the door, and a speakerphone. Nightingale pressed the bell for number fifteen, then when there was no answer he pressed it again.

Underneath the speakerphone was a metal plate on which was engraved the fact that the caretaker was in flat number nine and that deliveries could be left there. Nightingale pressed the button and after a few seconds a man answered. Nightingale explained who he was and the man said he'd be there in a few minutes.

The caretaker was in his sixties, balding and wearing a tweed jacket over a pair of overalls. He was overweight and the effort of walking up from the basement flat had beaded his brow with sweat. 'You're a cop, you said?'

'I'm with the cops,' said Nightingale. 'I'm not getting an answer from Mr Nail's flat and I wanted to go up and knock on his door.'

'So who are you exactly?'

Nightingale took out his wallet and gave the caretaker one of his business cards. The man took a pair of reading glasses from a pocket on the front of his overalls and perched them on the end of his nose before scrutinising the card.

'Ah. A private detective,' he said, emphasising the 'private'.

'I'm helping the police with a case and I really need to know if Mr Nail is home.'

'You tried the bell?'

Nightingale resisted the urge to say something sarcastic. 'Yes, I did,' he said. 'But Mr Nail has a habit of not answering his phone so I'm thinking that maybe he also ignores the doorbell.'

Nightingale caught the caretaker looking at the money in his wallet. He took out a twenty-pound note and offered it to him. 'For your trouble,' he said.

The caretaker scratched his chin. 'To be honest, it's a lot of trouble. And you're not a cop.'

Nightingale nodded. 'Fair enough,' he said. He took out a second twenty-pound note and handed over the two of them.

The caretaker grinned and pocketed the money. He pulled out a key chain and unlocked the door. He walked slowly up the stairs to the top floor, breathing heavily. When he reached the top he stood with his hand on the banister, taking deep breaths.

'Are you okay?' asked Nightingale.

'I've been a bit off colour the last few days,' he said. 'My wife says I need to lose a few pounds. What do you think?'

Nightingale thought his wife was probably right, except

kilos would be better and a dozen or so would be closer to the mark. 'I'm not a big fan of dieting,' he said.

The caretaker laughed and patted his ample stomach. 'You and me both.'

Nightingale leaned over and pressed the doorbell. A buzzer sounded from somewhere inside the flat. 'How big are they, these flats?' he asked.

'The ones on the top floor are one-bedroom,' he said. 'There are some two bedrooms on the floors below, and they're one bedrooms in the basement.'

'Do you see much of Mr Nail?'

'He's the one with the tattoos, right? Once a month, maybe. Seems to be one for the ladies.'

Nightingale smiled. 'Yeah, I've heard that.' He pressed the doorbell again.

'Doesn't look as if he's in,' said the caretaker.

Nightingale knelt down and pushed the brass letterbox open. 'Mr Nail, are you in?' he called, then the stench hit him and he rocked back on his heels and let the letterbox snap back into place.

He stood up gasping for breath.

'What's wrong?' asked the caretaker. He bent down close to the letterbox and stared at it.

'You really don't want to get a whiff of that,' said Nightingale. He stood up and took a deep breath to clear his lungs.

The caretaker flipped open the letterbox, peered through, then almost immediately started to gag. He pushed himself up and retched several times, though thankfully nothing came up. 'Jesus, Mary and Joseph,' he gasped.

'I did warn you,' said Nightingale.

'That's disgusting.'

'That's death,' said Nightingale. 'That's what flesh smells like when it rots.'

The caretaker's stomach heaved again and he bent over, but despite retching several times he didn't actually throw up. He put a hand against the wall to steady himself. 'It always smells like that?'

Nightingale nodded. 'Always. Men. Women. Children. Death is an equal opportunity employer.'

'How come you know so much about it?'

'Like I said, I was a cop,' said Nightingale. 'Who gets called first when a body is discovered? The police. Murder, suicide, natural causes, it's almost always a cop who's first on the scene. You don't walk a beat for more than a few weeks before you come across a body. I probably averaged three or four a year.'

'You think that's Mr Nail?'

'I guess so, but we won't know until we open the door.'

'I don't have a key,' said the caretaker.

'That's okay,' said Nightingale. 'This is a job for the police. The real police.'

'I'm not going in there,' said the caretaker, heading down the stairs. 'Not for love nor money. I'll be in my flat if they need me.'

27

The street had been cordoned off with blue and white tape by the two officers who had arrived in a patrol car just minutes after Nightingale had phoned Chalmers. An armed response vehicle had arrived and two officers had gone into the building and were waiting outside the top floor flat. Shortly after the ARV had arrived, two detectives had arrived in a black Vectra closely followed by the SOCO van. The two detectives had put on forensic suits and gone upstairs. Nightingale had offered to go with them but they told him to wait for the superintendent. It was only when Superintendent Chalmers climbed out of his black Jaguar that Nightingale remembered he had a loaded Glock pistol in a holster in the small of his back. He lit a cigarette and was blowing smoke when Chalmers strode up. He was wearing a black overcoat that looked like cashmere over a dark suit that was probably Savile Row. 'You'd better not be wasting my time, Nightingale,' said the superintendent.

'I'm not. There's a body in there.'

'Fine. But just so you know, if we get in there and there's bloody writing on the bathroom mirror, your goose is cooked.'

'That's hardly fair,' said Nightingale.

'Fair or not fair, that's the way it's going to be. Now put out that cigarette and we'll get suited up.'

They went over to the SOCO van and changed into white forensic suits and shoe covers, then pulled on blue latex gloves. Chalmers looked around for a hanger for his coat and when he couldn't find one he took it over to his Jaguar and carefully laid it on the back seat.

'Right, come on,' Chalmers growled at Nightingale. 'What floor?'

'Top floor. Flat fifteen.'

A uniformed cop in a fluorescent jacket held the door open for them and Nightingale followed the superintendent up the stairs. 'Tell me again who we think this is,' said Chalmers.

'The flat belongs to Ricky Nail. He's the owner of that tattoo place I told you about in Camden. The Ink Pit.'

'Yeah, we called but he wasn't there.'

'I told you that, remember?'

'Yeah, well, just because you tell me something doesn't mean it's necessarily so,' said the superintendent.

'I'm fairly certain Nail worked on at least some of the victims,' said Nightingale. 'And he was having a thing with Stella Walsh.'

Chalmers froze, mid-step. He turned to look down at Nightingale. 'What?' he said.

'She was sexting him.'

'What the hell are you talking about?'

'Sexting. Sex texting. She was sending him sex texts. Pictures.'

'How long have you known about this?'

'I literally found out this morning. Then I came here.'

Chalmers pointed a gloved finger at Nightingale's face.

'I've already warned you about this,' he said. 'As soon as you find something out, you tell me.'

Nightingale put his hand on his chest. 'Hand on heart, swear to God, I left the ex-girlfriend's house an hour or so ago at most, and came here. Rang the bell, knocked on the door, smelled the smell, and called you.' Nightingale decided against telling Chalmers about the box of Nail's belongings that he'd dropped off at the office.

Chalmers lowered his hand but continued to glare at Nightingale. 'What sort of texts?'

'I haven't seen them. Pictures, I'm told. He had a spare phone which I assume was a pay-as-you-go and Stella sent him topless pictures.'

'I can't believe I'm hearing this for the first time,' said Chalmers.

'Better late than never.'

Chalmers scowled at Nightingale then headed up the stairs again. Four officers were waiting, two in regular uniforms and stab vests and two in forensic suits and shoe covers. One of the uniforms was holding a black steel tube with a steel pad at one end, a handle at the other and another handle in the middle. Known as the enforcer, it weighed sixteen kilos but in the hands of an expert it could exert close to three tonnes of pressure, more than enough to open most doors.

'There's no key?' asked Chalmers.

Nightingale shook his head. 'There's a caretaker but he doesn't have one, no.'

Chalmers nodded at the officer holding the enforcer. 'You have my authorisation to gain entry,' he said. He took a tube of Vicks VapoRub from his pocket and dabbed some under his nose before offering the tube to Nightingale.

The officer swung the enforcer back and then slammed it into the door, just below the lock. The wood splintered and the door tilted inwards. Nightingale was dabbing the mentholated cream under his nose when the officer swung the battering ram a second time. The door crashed inwards. The other uniformed officer gasped and then twisted around and vomited down the stairs. The two officers both gasped and turned their faces away.

Even with the mentholated cream under his nose the stench was enough to make Nightingale gag. Chalmers smiled at his discomfort and made his way past the broken door. There were bluebottles buzzing around the ceiling, another sign if it were needed that there was a body on the premises.

Chalmers walked slowly down a white hallway, his shoe covers brushing against a pale green carpet. The first door on the left led into a sitting room but it took only a brief look to see the room was empty.

The next door was on the right and it was closed. Chalmers opened it. It was the bathroom. He took a step back, a look of horror on his face. 'You're not going to believe this, Nightingale,' he said.

Nightingale's heart began to pound and he hurried down the hallway. He pushed past Chalmers and stepped into the bathroom. There was a bath, a cramped shower, a washbasin and a toilet. Everything was clean as could be expected in a flat occupied by a single guy. He jumped as a hand fell on his shoulder. 'Had you going,' chuckled the superintendent.

Chalmers continued down the hallway. The buzzing of the flies was louder, and even with the mentholated ointment under their noses the smell was getting stronger.

Chalmers looked into the bedroom. Nightingale peered over his shoulder. There was a double bed with a leopard-skin print duvet and a large mirror on the wall behind it. A dozen shirts on hangers had been thrown on to the bed. The buzzing was insistent now. A large fly lazily buzzed by Nightingale's ear and he swatted it away.

The two other officers in forensic suits had entered the flat and were standing by the bathroom door.

Chalmers stepped into the room. Nightingale followed him. There was an iPhone on the bedside table. The buzzing was louder to their left and they turned to look at a built-in wardrobe with mirrored sliding doors. The left hand door had been pulled to the side and there was a body hanging from the rail inside the wardrobe. 'There we go,' said Chalmers.

The body was that of a man, but the fact that it was swarming with flies and the skin had turned black and blue made it hard to make out his features. He was wearing a black T-shirt and around his ankles were a pair of Batman boxer shorts. Nightingale took a step closer, trying to breathe through his mouth, and saw that there was a leather belt around the man's neck, looped around the clothes rail. The man was on his knees, his head slumped forward, held in place by the belt around his neck.

Death was never pretty, but the longer a body was left to decompose, the uglier it got. Nightingale knew if he touched the flesh it would be soft. Bodies tended to go stiff about three hours after death – rigor mortis – but within a day they started to relax again.

At the moment of death the body's individual cells begin to die, broken down by scavenging bacteria.

Neurones died within minutes, skin cells could survive for up to a week. Within minutes of the heart stopping pumping, the blood would begin to settle at the lowest points of the body, in this case the man's legs, from his knees down to his bare feet.

The bacteria in the gut would then multiply rapidly and start to break down the tissues around them. As the body decomposed, hydrogen sulphide and methane and half a dozen other foul-smelling gases were released, creating the distinctive odour produced by rotting flesh.

The base of the wardrobe was coated in a thick, treacly green fluid, another by-product of putrefaction. Flies loved putrefied flesh and would smell it from half a mile away, finding any way into the flat to feed. Then they'd lay their eggs, up to three hundred at a time, close to the food supply, and in any skin openings they could find, the mouth, the eyes, the nose, and in any open wounds. Maggots would hatch within a day and immediately start to suck up the putrefied liquids. Then they would move up the body, burrowing into the flesh, little marvels of nature, able to eat and breathe at the same time.

Over the first three or four days the flesh would change into the consistency of cottage cheese, then after a week it would start to discolour, starting at the abdomen and moving outwards. The skin would blacken and the veins would become visible and the whole body would puff out, bloated by the gases inside.

'How long do you think?' asked Chalmers.

'Two weeks,' said Nightingale. 'Maybe three. The abdomen is well bloated so the internal gas is pretty much at maximum pressure. Central heating's off so it's not been too warm. A couple of the fingernails have fallen off, that usually happens at three weeks or so, right?'

Chalmers nodded. 'So he's probably not our killer.'

'That's what you were thinking?'

'Hoping rather than thinking,' said Chalmers. 'If he was the common point of contact and he'd killed them and killed himself in remorse, well, it would make my life a lot easier.'

'So you think this was a sex game gone wrong?'

'It happens,' said Chalmers. 'It happens a lot.' He leaned through the door and called down the hall to the overalled detectives. 'One of you phone the coroner's office and arrange for the body to be taken to the mortuary. We'll need a full forensic post-mortem. One of you needs to stay with the body at all times.'

'Nail had girls queuing up to sleep with him,' said Nightingale when Chalmers turned back into the room.

'I've no doubt. Which suggests he had a high sex drive, which is what leads to sex games like this.'

Nightingale exhaled through pursed lips.

'What?' said Chalmers.

'It just feels wrong.'

'Not to me,' said the superintendent.

'It could be a set up.'

'What, someone gets in, fakes this and leaves. Because?'

'Because they want the cops to think that it's exactly what you think it is.'

'Now you're just confusing me, Nightingale.'

'It's starting to look as if Nail was the link between the five Goths. He might even have had a relationship with Stella Walsh. You don't think that it's a coincidence that he ends up dead, too?'

'Nail is hanging up in a wardrobe with his pants around his knees. The Goths were hacked to death with knives.'

'True enough,' said Nightingale. He could see that Chalmers had already made his mind up. Rusty Nail had killed himself, either accidently or deliberately.

28

Nightingale left Chalmers staring at the decomposing body and went back along the hallway to the sitting room. It was about twelve by twelve feet with a large window overlooking the street. There were wooden blinds on the window, slanted so that he could look down on to the street below. A blue saloon had arrived and a middle-aged man in a grey suit was climbing out. Probably the doctor come to confirm the death. He heard a noise behind him and turned to see the SOCO, a large black case in one hand and a camera in the other. 'Straight down on the left,' said Nightingale. 'The bedroom.'

The SOCO headed to the bedroom. There was no television in the room but there was an expensive printer on a desk behind the door. There had once been a fireplace in the wall to the right of the window but it had been bricked up and papered over. There was a bookcase to the left of the chimneybreast and Nightingale ran his eyes along the shelves. There were horror and sci-fi novels and a lot of books on graphic design. One shelf was devoted to books about tattooing and he pulled one out and flicked through it. Some of the designs were huge, intricate works of art that covered a whole back or a leg.

'You're not here officially, Nightingale, don't go touching anything,' Chalmers said.

Nightingale put the book back. 'The doc's on his way up.'

'That was quick.'

'Are you going to write this off as a suicide?'

'Accidental death or death by misadventure,' said Chalmers. 'I don't think he meant to kill himself. You weren't the world's best cop but even you must have learned that people don't use auto-asphyxiation as a way of ending it all. And if it was suicide, he'd have probably left a note. No, he was just having a bit of fun and he let the noose tighten just a bit too much and a bit too long.' He shrugged. 'It happens.'

'No computer,' said Nightingale, nodding at the desk. 'No TV either.'

'Yeah, but there didn't seem to have ever been a TV in here, but there's a printer on the desk and a space that suggests that there used to be a laptop there.'

'Interesting,' he said. 'But we're clearly not looking at a robbery.' He pointed at the coffee table. There was a wallet next to a pile of tattooing magazines. Chalmers picked it up and showed Nightingale a wad of notes and three debit cards. 'If they were thieving, why take a laptop and not the wallet? And his iPhone is in the bedroom. What sort of housebreaker doesn't take an iPhone?'

'Exactly,' said Nightingale.

Chalmers took out a driving licence and scrutinised it, then showed it to Nightingale. 'Definitely our man in the wardrobe,' he said. He slid the driving licence back into the wallet and tossed it on to the table. He scowled at Nightingale. 'What do you mean by that? "Exactly"?'

'You think it's a coincidence. Fine. But I don't think it is. He didn't strangle himself, he was killed. By the same people who killed the Goths. They weren't here to rob, obviously, but they took his laptop. Why? Because they wanted whatever was on it. His client list maybe. I told you they had a break-in at the shop.'

'I checked that. There was a lot of stuff stolen. Computer, DVD, pretty much anything that wasn't nailed down.'

'Who robs a tattoo store, Chalmers? Seriously?'

'Drug addicts who aren't thinking too clearly,' said Chalmers. 'But you can sell an iPhone and a computer and a DVD player no matter where you stole it from.'

'And what if it wasn't? What if someone wanted the Ink Pit's client list? And what if having stolen the shop's computer they realised Nail had another client list on his laptop.' He gestured at the door. 'Maybe they came here three weeks ago and killed Nail and took his laptop and on it were the names of his clients.'

Chalmers frowned. 'That's one hell of a conspiracy theory.'

'Well, what do you have? If you write Nail's death off as misadventure, that doesn't get you any closer to catching the killers of the five Goths.'

'I need evidence, Nightingale, not half-arsed theories.'

'Find the computer,' said Nightingale. 'Or talk to the staff in the Ink Pit again. See if there's CCTV near the shop.'

'All that'll do is confirm that all five victims went to the shop.'

'And that Ricky Nail worked on them. And if Nail is the common factor and if Nail was murdered, then there could be forensics here that leads us to the killers.'

Chalmers sighed and rubbed the back of his neck. 'Feels like clutching at straws to me.'

'What else have you got?'

The superintendent didn't answer. He turned and walked out of the sitting room, still rubbing the back of his neck.

29

Nightingale was biting into a bacon sandwich as he watched the evening news when his phone beeped to let him know he'd received a message. It beeped a second time a few seconds later. He put down his sandwich and reached for the phone. He didn't recognise the number. There were two attachments, both photographs of computer print-outs. One contained the PNC details of the owner of the white van that had been outside Perry Smith's, the other identified the owner of the BMW SUV. Nightingale started to text back his thanks but stopped as he realised Robbie would probably already have ditched the SIM card. He took another bite from his sandwich before fetching a pen and paper from the kitchen.

The owner of the white van was a Billy McDowell. No criminal convictions but a plethora of parking tickets, speeding fines and a licence that was always a few points away from being suspended. McDowell was a plumber, married with two children, one of whom had a conviction for possession of marijuana in the days when the police bothered to prosecute.

The BMW's owner was Tony Barnett, unemployed and with a string of convictions for violence including a six-month sentence for assault and three years for GBH. He was single and lived in Croydon, South London. One obvious question for Mr Barnett was how he managed to run a two-year-old BMW on benefits.

Nightingale finished his coffee and then phoned T-Bone. 'You got news for me, Bird-man?' he asked before Nightingale had even had chance to identify himself.

'I have indeed,' said Nightingale. 'We need to meet.'

30

There were half a dozen five-a-side football matches going on in a line of outdoor pitches, each team trying to outdo the others in aggression and volume. Sweaty shaved heads glistened under the floodlights and it seemed that every other player sported at least one tattoo. There were more players than spectators and most of those watching seemed to be wives and girlfriends who given the choice would have preferred a quiet night in.

Nightingale saw T-Bone's black Porsche SUV at the far end of the car park and he drove up next to it. He climbed out, walked over to the Porsche and got into the front passenger seat. Rap music was blaring through the car's sound system and T-Bone turned down the volume. He was wearing impenetrable Oakleys, a tight mesh T-shirt that showed off his bulging biceps, and blue Versace jeans.

'I wouldn't have had you down as a soccer fan,' said Nightingale as he slammed the door shut.

T-Bone grinned. 'Two of my nephews are playing. I'm doing a favour for my sister.' He gestured over at Nightingale's MGB. 'I can't believe you drive around in that piece of shit,' said T-Bone.

'It's a classic,' said Nightingale.

'It's a rust bucket, and I bet it leaks in the rain.' T-Bone patted the steering wheel of the Porsche. 'You should get yourself one of these. German engineering. Vorsprung durch Technik.'

'That's Audi, isn't it?'

'Porsche, Audi, BMW, the Germans build good cars,' said T-Bone.

'The Brits used to,' said Nightingale. 'Anyway, I'm not here to talk up the British automotive industry.'

'You've got the names?'

'That's why I'm here.'

T-Bone held out a gloved hand. 'I need to come with you,' said Nightingale.

'What?'

'I've got the names. But before you do what you've got to do, I want to talk to them.'

'No way,' said T-Bone.

'That's not a request, T-Bone. It's a condition. If you want the names, I get to go with you.'

T-Bone looked at Nightingale over the top of his shades. 'Let me ask you a question, Bird-man. What's to stop me just taking those numbers off you?'

'Nothing,' said Nightingale. 'You could just lie to me. But I know you won't. I trust you.'

T-Bone pushed the glasses higher up his nose. 'What possible reason would you have to get in on the act?'

'What they wrote on the mirror. I need to know why I'm on their shit list.'

'These names? They gangsters?'

Nightingale shook his head. 'One's a plumber with a wife and kids. The other's on the dole but the fact that he has a BMW suggests he's got irons in the fire. Few convictions for violence but no sign of him being connected.'

'I'll be careful, then,' said T-Bone. He flashed Nightingale a smile. 'No drugs connections?'

'None on the system and these days the PNC is pretty accurate. They might be flying below the radar but I doubt it.'

'So if it wasn't a turf war, why did they do what they did?'

Nightingale shrugged. 'No idea, T-Bone. Now what's your game plan?'

T-Bone smiled thinly. 'This ain't no game, trust me on that. We're gonna talk to the two names you've got and get them to roll over on the others.'

'Then?'

T-Bone frowned. He leaned towards Nightingale and began patting his chest with his right hand. 'You think I'm wired?' asked Nightingale indignantly.

'Once a cop, always a cop,' said T-Bone, running his hand around Nightingale's sternum.

'I'm the one doing all the law-breaking at the moment,' said Nightingale. 'I got you these names off the PNC and I'm carrying the gun you gave me. That's worth ten years right there.'

'Not if you're working with the Feds to set me up.'

'Now you're just being silly,' said Nightingale. 'Perry and his crew are dead, why would the cops want to set you up on a conspiracy to murder charge? They're after the killers, they don't have time to be pissing around.'

T-Bone took his hand off Nightingale's chest. 'You can understand me getting jittery, right?'

'Yeah. Jittery is always how I feel when a group of nutters with knives put me on their to-do list.'

'You think they're nutters?'

'Wrong word,' said Nightingale. 'They went to a lot of trouble to do what they did, so they must have had a good reason.' He fished his cigarettes out of his pocket. 'Okay if I smoke?'

T-Bone nodded. 'But I want you blowing smoke out of the window and not up my arse.'

'T-Bone, mate, I am most definitely not blowing smoke up your arse.' He opened the window and lit a cigarette then offered the pack to T-Bone. T-Bone shook his head and Nightingale put the pack away. 'So do we have a deal?' he asked.

'You want to be there when we kill them? Is that what you want?'

'Hell, no,' said Nightingale. 'That's the last thing I want. In fact, I'd be happier if you just beat the crap out of them and handed them over to the cops.'

'Yeah, well, I can tell you right now that's not going to happen. Not after they did what they did. They're dead men walking, all of them. And that includes the sluts they used to get into the house.'

Nightingale blew smoke out the window and didn't say anything. He knew there was nothing he could say to T-Bone that would persuade the man to change his mind.

'Give me the names,' said T-Bone, holding out his massive hand and clicking his fingers.

'You'll let me be there when you question them?'

'I'll call you.'

Nightingale took the piece of paper with the names

from his pocket and gave it to T-Bone. 'Don't forget, yeah.'

'It's in my diary, Bird-man.'

Nightingale opened the door, climbed out of the Porsche and walked over to his MGB.

31

Jenny was sitting at her desk watching a video of a young man being tattooed when Nightingale walked into the office on Tuesday morning. He leant over her shoulder. 'What's that?' he said.

'That's Rusty Nail hard at work,' she said. 'There are a dozen CDs in that box you gave me. Looks like he videoed a lot of his work. For fun or for insurance purposes, I'm not sure which.'

'Well, he doesn't look like that now, I can tell you that much,' said Nightingale. He hung up his coat and went into his office to put the Glock in the bottom drawer of his desk. He hadn't told Jenny he was carrying a gun, and didn't intend to.

'What do you mean?' she asked.

Nightingale went back to her office, dropped into a chair and explained what had happened the previous day.

'You need to give all this stuff to Chalmers,' she said when he'd finished. 'It's evidence.'

'I got it from Nail's ex, it's not as if it was in his flat.'

'He's dead and that box contains his personal effects. Chalmers will hit the roof if he finds out you've got it.'

'To be honest, I don't think Chalmers will give a toss,'

said Nightingale. 'He thinks that Nail killed himself. Either accidentally or intentionally.'

'How he died isn't really the point, is it?' She pointed at the cardboard box, which was on the floor at the side of her desk. 'That's his personal stuff. You were supposed to give it to him.'

'And now he's dead so it makes no difference to him, does it?'

'This playing detective is going to get you into trouble, Jack.'

'Playing detective? I am a detective.'

'You're a private detective. And this is a police case.'

'A case I was asked to help with.'

'Help being the operative word,' said Jenny. 'Hiding evidence isn't helping, is it?'

'I'm hardly hiding it,' said Nightingale. He sighed. 'Okay, I take your point. I'll take it to Chalmers tomorrow.'

'Why not today?'

'Let's just look at the video, okay? Let's see if we can find Nail working on any of the Goths that died. At least then we'll be taking something useful to Chalmers.'

She nodded reluctantly. 'Okay, but first thing tomorrow.'

'Deal,' he said.

He leaned forward and looked at her screen. Rusty Nail was tattooing a leaping tiger on the arm of a man in his twenties. Rock music was playing in the background. Every now and again the man would take a swig from a bottle of cider. 'Is that allowed, drinking while you're being tattooed?' he said.

'I think it's up to the individual tattooist,' said Jenny.

Nightingale rubbed his chin. 'There's no CCTV in the shop. He must have used his own camera.' Realisation dawned and he sat back in his chair. 'Nail did a lot of late-night stuff, I bet he videoed it so that he wouldn't have problems down the line.'

'What sort of problems?'

'His partner was telling me that they always discussed a tattoo with the customer to make sure everyone was happy before they started work, but that Nail was always trying to push the envelope. That's why he worked late at night.' He gestured at the screen. 'I'm guessing that letting the punters drink meant they'd be more amenable to experimentation. By videoing what he was doing, they couldn't turn around later and say that he'd forced them into it.'

'What do you mean by experimentation?'

'Jezza didn't say.' He gestured at the tiger. 'That looks pretty standard.'

'There are lots of designs in the notebooks in the box,' she said.

Nightingale went over to the box and picked it up. 'I'll have a look,' he said. 'How many videos are there?'

'This is my second CD and there are fifty or so on each of them. Each file is from ten minutes up to a couple of hours, depending on the complexity of the tattoo. I'm not watching them all the way through, just checking their faces.'

Nightingale took the box through to his office and sat down. There were half a dozen notebooks and two ring binders and he placed them on his desk. 'What about a coffee?' he shouted.

'Lovely,' said Jenny.

'I meant would you make me one?'

'How about we have another race?'

'Pretty please?'

He heard Jenny sigh and then get up from her desk. He picked up one of the notebooks and slowly turned the pages. They were ideas for tattoos, some just sketches but many were much more detailed. Ricky Nail was clearly a talented artist. There were glorious animals – lions, tigers, fish – and mythical creatures such as gargoyles, mermaids and dragons. Some of the drawings were in colour, but most were black and white.

There were pages of different typefaces where Nail would play around with the structure of letters, and he had drawn several hundred words in Arabic, Chinese and Hindi and other languages he didn't recognise.

Jenny came in with a mug of coffee and put it on his desk. 'He was talented, wasn't he?' said Jenny. 'There's some really good stuff in there.'

Nightingale grinned. 'Are you thinking of getting a tattoo?'

She nodded at the notebook. 'If it was a good one, artistic, and had some meaning, then maybe. I almost got a seagull when I was at university.'

'A seagull?'

'I read a book called *Jonathan Livingston Seagull*, written by Richard Bach. I think everyone in my year read it. It's about a seagull learning how to fly.'

'Sounds riveting.'

'You can be such a Philistine, Jack. It's about striving for perfection, in whatever you do. A couple of my friends had seagull tattoos and I very nearly got one.'

'What changed your mind?'

'I don't know. It's the fact that they're permanent,

you know? Okay, I know they can be lasered off, but you know what I mean.'

'Where would you have it, if you'd got one?'

'I don't know. My ankle maybe. Or my hip. But it would have been a small one. I can't understand women who go big on tattoos. Men okay, they can look good on a ripped body, but a woman just looks . . .'

'Cheap?'

'I was going to say damaged,' she said.

She picked up one of the ring binders and flicked through it. It contained photographs of finished tattoos. The name of the customer and the date was in the bottom right-hand corner of each of the pictures. One of them was a huge tattoo of two carp, nose to tail, which took up the whole of a man's back. She showed it to Nightingale. 'That's impressive,' said Nightingale.

'That must have taken days to do,' she said. 'The colours are amazing.' The carp were a reddish orange and they had bright blue eyes and were swimming through plants of various shades of green.

'It certainly puts mine to shame,' said Nightingale.

Jenny's eyes widened in surprise. 'You've got a tattoo?'

'I was young, and drunk,' said Nightingale. 'What can I say?'

'Where is it?'

'You don't need to know,' said Nightingale.

'Okay, what is it?'

'Jenny, a tattoo is very personal thing,' said Nightingale.

He leaned over to pick up his coffee mug but she beat him to it and held it just out of his reach. 'Fair trade,' she said.

'Oh, come on,' Nightingale protested. 'I was a kid.'

'Eighteen?'

'Nineteen. And I'd been drinking. There were three of us and the deal was that other two decided on the tattoo that the other one got.'

Jenny giggled. 'That's a recipe for disaster if ever I heard one,' she said. She waved the mug in front of him. 'Come on, I want details.'

'You know this entire interview contravenes the Police And Criminal Evidence Act,' said Nightingale. 'You're not allowed to interrogate someone like this.'

'I'm not a cop,' she said. 'And neither are you. Now where is this tattoo and more importantly, what is it?'

Nightingale sighed. 'It's the pink panther. Wearing a top hat and carrying a cane.'

Jenny sniggered and put her hand over her mouth. 'No,' she said.

'Yes.'

'And where is it?'

'My backside.'

'No way!'

'Why would I lie about something like that?'

Jenny put the mug down on the desk again. She motioned with her fingers. 'Come on, give.'

'Give?'

'I want to see it.'

'You think I'm going to drop my pants in the office?'

'I think you know if you don't I'm never going to shut up about it,' she said, folding her arms. 'So you might as well get it over with now.'

'Are you serious?'

'I'm using my serious voice, can't you tell?'

Nightingale groaned, stood up and turned so that he

had his back to her. He undid his trousers and pushed them down to his knees, then pulled down his boxer shorts on the right side. The tattoo was about three inches high, a grinning Pink Panther tipping his top hat as he leant on his cane. Jenny's laughter echoed around the office. 'That is priceless,' she said. 'Absolutely priceless.'

32

Nightingale walked slowly up the stairs. 'Jenny?' he called. 'Are you there?' There was no reply. 'Come on, stop pissing around, the front door was open.' There was a flash of light behind him and he flinched, then realised it was just a car driving by Jenny's mews house. He stopped and listened, wondering if she was in the shower, but other than the sound of the receding car the night was quiet. 'Jenny?' Nightingale took another step, then another, his heart pounding.

He took another step. And another. Then he was walking towards her bedroom door, his Hush Puppies squeaking softly on the bare wooden floorboards. The door to the bedroom – like the front door – was ajar. A pale yellow light seeped through the gap. Nightingale reached it and stretched out a trembling hand. He pushed the door open and his breath caught in his throat as he saw the body lying on the blood-stained sheets. Jenny's body. She was lying on her back, her arms outstretched, her lifeless eyes staring at the ceiling. She had been gutted from her neck down to her crotch, the skin folded back and her entrails pulled out and piled next to her. The sheets glistened wetly and blood was dripping down on to the floor with a soft plopping sound. Nightingale's stomach lurched and he tasted bile at the back of his throat. He swallowed, fighting the urge to vomit. His whole body began to tremble as he stared at the butchered corpse.

He turned to look at the mirror above her dressing table. Someone had written a message in bloody capital letters. WE ARE COMING FOR YOU, JACK NIGHTINGALE. Nightingale stared at the words in horror. His reflection stared back, his mouth open, his eyes wide and fearful, his skin sickly white.

The bedside phone began to ring. Nightingale looked at it fearfully, knowing with a dreadful certainty that the call was for him.

He took a step towards the phone, his shaking arm outstretched. The ringing seemed to be getting louder and louder and the handset was vibrating as if it had taken on a life of its own. He took another step forward, certain now that the call was for him.

'Answer the phone, Jack.' Nightingale jumped as if he had been stung. He turned and stared down at Jenny. Her blood-smeared face had turned towards him and he could see his own reflection in her lifeless eyes. Jenny's mouth opened again and this time she screamed at the top of her voice. 'ANSWER THE PHONE, JACK!'

Nightingale woke up, gasping for breath. His face was bathed in sweat and he felt light-headed as if he'd been holding his breath for several minutes. His mobile was ringing on the bedside table and he groped for it. 'Bird-man?' It was T-Bone.

'Yeah,' said Nightingale.

'You okay? You're panting like a dog in heat.'

'I'm fine. Bad dream.'

'Yeah? Well, we all get those. The names you gave me, I've got one of them with me now. You still want a word with him because if you do the clock is ticking?'

Nightingale sat up and ran a hand through his unkempt hair. 'Damn right I do.'

'Then get your arse over here. And quickly.'

'Where?'

'I'll send you the address. Don't use that piece of shit MGB, it'll attract too much attention. Take a cab to the address I give you and keep an eye out for Kipper.'

'Kipper?'

'The lad who gave you the piece. He'll bring you to us.'

Before Nightingale could say anything else, the line went dead. He rolled out of bed and was pulling on his trousers when his phone beeped to let him know he'd received a text message. He finished dressing, grabbed the phone and headed downstairs.

33

Nightingale walked around to Queensway and flagged down a black cab. It was two o'clock in the morning but the pavements were busy and half the shops and restaurants were still open. The cab headed south, crossed over the Thames and dropped him in Streatham High Road in front of a bakery. Nightingale paid the driver, asked for a receipt, and then looked around as the cab drove away. Someone whistled from behind him and he saw a black youth in a hoodie sitting on a BMX bike fifty feet away. Nightingale was pretty sure it was Kipper, but the hood covered most of his face. The youth nodded at Nightingale then flipped his bike around in the opposite direction.

Nightingale walked after him, his hands in the pockets of his raincoat. Kipper reared the bike up on its back wheel, turned a full three hundred and sixty degrees, then pedalled down a side road. 'Show off,' muttered Nightingale.

A police van drove by and three uniforms stared at Nightingale impassively through dirt-streaked windows. Nightingale turned into the side street. Kipper was waiting for him, holding a lamppost to steady himself. As soon as Nightingale stepped around the corner, Kipper sped off.

Nightingale cursed under his breath. He figured the song and dance was to make sure he wasn't being followed and while he understood T-Bone's nervousness, he still resented being treated with suspicion. Nightingale figured that he'd already done enough to prove himself by giving the names to T-Bone. He took out his pack of Marlboro and lit one as he walked down the street.

When he reached the end of the street, Kipper pulled a tight circle then bobbed up and down, first on the rear wheel, then on the front, back and forth like a demented jack in the box.

'Yeah, very clever,' muttered Nightingale to himself. He blew smoke and took a quick look over his shoulder. A second youth had appeared behind him. Like Kipper he was wearing a hoodie and was riding a BMX. Under any other circumstances he'd have been wary of a mugging, but he knew they were there to take him to T-Bone. Kipper started pedalling again, but slowly enough for Nightingale to keep up with him. The second youth kept pace with them as they headed west.

Kipper turned into an alley that looked like a dead-end. There was a single light high up on a wall but it barely illuminated the ground. Something black and furry scurried by Nightingale's feet but he couldn't tell if it was a small cat or a large rat.

Kipper reached a wooden door and he banged on it with the flat of his hand, then waved for Nightingale to join him. The door opened outwards. It was a fire door and a West Indian in a black Puffa jacket kept his hand on the metal release mechanism as he stared deadpan at Nightingale. 'In, but lose the cigarette,' he said.

Nightingale dropped the cigarette on the ground and stood on it, then went inside as Kipper pedalled off back the way they had come.

The man in the Puffa jacket pulled the door closed. They were standing at the foot of a short flight of concrete stairs. The man squeezed by Nightingale and went up the stairs. Nightingale followed him. He pushed through another door into a corridor with walls made of concrete blocks. Overhead were fluorescent lights. At the end of the corridor was a set of double metal doors. The man pushed the doors open and held one so that Nightingale could enter the room. It was a commercial kitchen with stainless-steel ranges, a walk-in fridge and racks of pots, pans and plates.

In the middle of the kitchen there was a man in his thirties, naked and tied to a chair. Blood was trickling from between his lips.

On the metal counter next to him was a selection of stainless steel knives, cleavers and kitchen shears. And there was a Glock, similar to the one Nightingale had clipped to his belt.

T-Bone was standing by the fridge, drinking from a bottle of milk. He was wearing a dark blue tracksuit and white Nikes and was naked from the waist up. His chest and forearms were glistening with sweat as he wiped his mouth with the back of his arm. There were two other men in the room, both black, one tall and thin with his head shaved, the other shorter with a weightlifter's physique – massive forearms, a barrel-like chest, a tiny waist and bowed legs. They were both wearing tracksuit bottoms and were bare-chested. The tall man was holding a pair of bloody pliers.

T-Bone gestured at the naked man. 'This is Tony Barnett, the owner of the BMW SUV,' said T-Bone.

'Vorsprung durch Technik,' said Nightingale.

'He's helping us with our enquiries,' said T-Bone. The man tossed the pliers on to the metal table next to three teeth that had obviously been pulled from Barnett's mouth.

'Good to know,' said Nightingale. 'What's he told you so far?'

'Basically that I can go fuck myself and that he wants to fuck my mother.'

'Nice,' said Nightingale.

'Pain doesn't seem to worry him much.'

'Fuck you!' shouted the man in the chair.

'But it's early yet. By the time we've taken off a few toes, he'll probably feel a bit different. Then we'll start on his fingers.'

Nightingale walked around Barnett. There was a tattoo on his left shoulder. It wasn't ink, it was as if the design had been burned into the flesh. There was a goat's skull and where the mouth should have been was an insignia, like a seven-pointed star that had been squashed into an irregular shape. Nightingale recognised the insignia – it was the symbol of the Order of Nine Angles.

'Where did you get that done?' asked Nightingale.

'What?'

'The tattoo on your back.'

'That's no tattoo, fuckwit.'

'Did you get it done in Camden?' asked Nightingale, walking to stand in front of him.

Barnett frowned. 'Camden?'

'Did you get it done in Camden. The Ink Pit.'

Barnett laughed but then his laugh turned into a series of coughs that racked his entire body. 'You think that was done by a human hand?' he sneered. He spat on the floor. 'You've no idea what's going on, have you?'

'So tell me,' said Nightingale. 'Who gave you the tattoo?'

'A demon,' said Barnett. 'A demon from hell.'

'Which one?' asked Nightingale.

'Which one?' repeated T-Bone. He sneered at Nightingale. 'You're as crazy as he is.'

Barnett stared at Nightingale, his eyes wide and manic. 'Proserpine,' he said. 'That's her name. And she's one mean bitch, I can tell you that much.'

'Proserpine gave you the tattoo?'

'Who the hell is Proserpine?' asked T-Bone.

Nightingale held up his hand. 'Give me a minute,' he said. 'This is important.'

He bent down and put his mouth close to the man's ear. 'Why did you write what you did on the mirror?' he asked.

'Fuck off.'

'Did you write it?'

'I didn't write anything on the mirror. What mirror anyway?' He cleared his throat and spat bloody phlegm on to the floor.

'Upstairs. In Perry Smith's bathroom.'

'I didn't even go upstairs. I was in the kitchen.' He coughed and spat again.

'Who was upstairs?'

Barnett shook his head. 'I don't know. It was bedlam in the house.'

'No, it was well planned. They had guns and you had knives so you must have known what you were doing.'

'We had guns,' said Barnett. 'Of course we had guns.'

'But you didn't use them?' said T-Bone.

'We used them, we just didn't fire them,' said Barnett. 'We had them outgunned, so we got them to drop theirs—'

'Then you gutted them in cold blood?' said T-Bone. 'What sort of scum are you?' He stepped forward and slapped Barnett across the face, the blow echoing off the walls like a pistol shot.

Barnett glared at him. 'What sort of scum am I? The sort of scum that's going to come for you. And the rest of your crew. And we're going to keep coming for you until you're all dead.'

'Yeah, well, I assume that's the royal "we" because you ain't gonna be coming after anyone,' said T-Bone.

'You think I care?' said Barnett. 'Kill me and I take my place on Satan's left side and I'll be back, but when I come back I'll be a thousand times stronger. So stop talking and do it, do it now!'

T-Bone looked at Nightingale. 'What the hell's he talking about?'

'They're devil worshippers,' said Nightingale. 'Satanists.' He stared at Barnett. 'Where did you get the tattoo from?' he asked.

'Go fuck yourself,' said Barnett.

'It's the only tattoo on your body so it must be important.'

Barnett shook his head but said nothing. Nightingale took out his phone, walked behind the chair and took a photograph of the tattoo.

'Bird-man, what are you doing?' asked T-Bone.

'It's important.'

'Not to me it ain't,' said T-Bone. 'Why do you care

what he's got tattooed on him? This is not the time to be discussing body art. Seriously.'

'It's special, this tattoo. It's something to do with the organisation they belong to. The Order of Nine Angles. That symbol is their logo, but I've never seen it with a horned goat before.' He walked around to stand in front of Barnett. 'That's right, isn't it? You're in the Order of Nine Angles?'

'Fuck off,' snarled Barnett. He kept his head down, staring at the floor. Blood was dribbling down his chin and his nostrils flared with each breath he took.

'Let me work on him a while longer,' said T-Bone.

'I'm not sure how much good that will do,' said Nightingale. There was a bottle of water on the bar. Nightingale picked it up, unscrewed the top and held it to Barnett's mouth. The man drank greedily and gulped down half the bottle. Nightingale took it away, leaving Barnett gasping for breath. 'He's going to continue hurting you, you realise that?' said Nightingale.

'Pain doesn't frighten me. And neither does dying. So do your worst and fuck off.'

'Dying doesn't scare you because your place in Hell is guaranteed, right? You've done a deal and you walk in under your own steam.'

Barnett's eyes narrowed. 'Who the fuck are you?' he asked.

'Nightingale. Jack Nightingale.'

Barnett's upper lip curled back in a sneer. 'You're Jack Nightingale?' He laughed harshly. 'You're on our to-do list. You're as good as dead.'

'Why?'

'You know why? Same reason that Smith got what was

coming to him. You killed one of ours. So we kill you and yours.' He lifted his chin contemptuously. 'You're a dead man walking, Nightingale.'

'At least he's walking,' said T-Bone. He picked up the pliers. 'Whereas you ain't gonna be walking anywhere.'

Barnett sneered at him. 'You're a dead man walking, too,' he said. He looked back at Nightingale. 'We've got a list, Nightingale. A list of your family, your friends, and everyone you care about. Everyone on that list is as good as dead.'

'Say's who?' said Nightingale. 'Who's giving you orders? Proserpine?'

'Your pretty assistant, Jenny. Your friend Robbie, the cop. Your relatives. They're all dead, Nightingale. And so are you.'

'I'm gonna shut this bastard up here and now,' said T-Bone, pushing Nightingale out of the way.

T-Bone raised the pliers and stepped forward, but Nightingale moved quickly and blocked his way. 'That's what he wants, T-Bone,' said Nightingale, holding T-Bone's wrist with both hands.

'And that's what he's gonna get,' said T-Bone. 'Now let go of me, Bird-man, or I'll forget that we're friends.'

'Give me a minute,' said Nightingale. 'Just one minute, okay?'

Barnett turned his head and stared at T-Bone with dead eyes. 'You're a dead man walking, too,' he said. 'And your sister, Jaynee. And your mother, and her little dog. Might even have a bit of fun with your sister before we kill her. What is she, eleven?'

T-Bone bellowed like an angry bull. He grabbed at the gun on the counter, pointed it at Barnett's chest and pulled the trigger. The bullet slammed into Barnett's chest and his whole body stiffened. There was a grin of triumph on the man's face; T-Bone saw it and pulled the trigger again and again until he had emptied the clip and Nightingale's ears were ringing from the explosions in the confined space. Only when the last shot had been fired did Barnett's head slump down on his chest.

34

'He wanted you to shoot him,' said Nightingale. T-Bone's men were wrapping Barnett's bullet-riddled body in a sheet of polythene.

'Fool got what he wanted then,' said T-Bone. He tossed the Glock back on to the counter.

'We needed to talk to him,' said Nightingale. 'There were questions that needed answering.'

'I was done talking,' said T-Bone. 'And he wasn't telling us anything. You heard what he said about my sister. And my mother.'

'Yeah, and your mother's little dog. He was just saying that to rile you up, and it worked.'

'Yeah, I was riled,' said T-Bone. 'And the fool's dead. Talking about it ain't gonna make it unhappen.' He tucked the gun into the back of his belt. 'Who the hell is this Proserpine, and why are you so interested in that damn tattoo?'

'It's complicated.'

'Yeah, well, I'm no simpleton. You need to start talking, Bird-man, before I tie you to that chair and start working on your teeth. And you can start with that tattoo. That ain't no run-of-the-mill ink. That's a brand. That's been done with fire.'

Nightingale took out his cigarettes and lit one, playing for time while he got his thoughts in order. T-Bone deserved to know the truth, the problem was that the truth was pretty much unbelievable.

'The tattoo or whatever you want to call it uses the logo of the Order of Nine Angles,' he said eventually. 'That's the seven-pointed star thing that's superimposed on the horned goat.'

'And that's some black magic voodoo shit, is it?'

'Satanism,' said Nightingale. 'Devil worship. They believe in human sacrifice and serving the Devil.'

'So he's got something wrong in the head, is that what you're saying? He believes in ghosts and vampires and things that go bump in the night?'

Nightingale shook his head. 'Barnett wasn't mad. Psychopathic, maybe. But he knows what he's doing. So do the rest of them. They sacrifice children in the belief that it will get them power.'

T-Bone gestured at the corpse, which was now completely wrapped in polythene. The men were winding silver duct tape around it, turning it into a metallic mummy. 'He killed kids?'

'They all do. That's part of being in the Order.'

'And that lawyer, Marcus Fairchild, he was part of it?'

Nightingale nodded. 'Very much so.'

'I don't seem to remember you telling Perry that. All you said was that Fairchild was a paedophile.'

'He was. No question. He was a child-molester and a rapist.'

'You just neglected to mention the fact that he was also a member of a group of nutters who believe killing kids makes them powerful.' T-Bone pointed a finger at

Nightingale. 'You were playing fast and loose with the truth, Bird-man, and because of you Perry and a lot of good men died.'

'I didn't know this would happen. How could I have known?'

'That's not the point. The point is that Perry should have been given the opportunity to make his own call.'

'What's done is done, T-Bone.'

'No use crying over spilt blood, is that what you're saying?'

'T-Bone, I'm sorry it happened. I had no idea that they'd kill Perry and his crew. But what's done is done and what we need to do now is to stop it going any further. And to be honest that would have been a lot easier if you hadn't blown our only source to Kingdom Come.'

'He wasn't telling us anything. And I feel a lot better for shooting the fool.'

'He was starting to open up. Handled right, he might have given us more.'

T-Bone shook his head. 'He knew he was going to die. And the pain didn't seem to worry him.'

'What about the other name I gave you? The plumber?'

'Still looking for him. He wasn't at home. This Satanism stuff is bullshit, right? Like voodoo and haunted houses.'

'They believe in it, T-Bone, and that's what matters.'

'And they believe in the Devil?'

'In the Devil and devils. And demons. Guys like Barnett, they believe when they die they go to serve Satan in Hell.'

'That's like the al-Qaeda bombers thinking that they're gonna get seventy-two virgins taking care of them in the afterlife?'

'Pretty much,' said Nightingale.

'And that tattoo, it's a sign of their commitment?'

'That's what it looks like.'

T-Bone nodded thoughtfully. 'And who's this Proserpine he talked about?'

'One of the demons.'

'A female,' he said.

Nightingale nodded. 'They can be male or female.'

T-Bone's eyes narrowed. 'You believe in that shit, Bird-man?'

Nightingale took a long pull on his cigarette as he returned T-Bone's gaze. He had no choice other than to lie to the man because the alternative was to explain why he believed and if he started down that road there was no way of knowing how it would end. 'Do I look stupid?' he said. Answering a question with a question meant that at least he wasn't telling a deliberate lie. 'So where do we go from here?'

'I've got guys waiting for white van man to appear. Soon as he does, we'll play show and tell with him. You want in?'

'I'm not sure I'd get anything out of it,' said Nightingale. Nightingale was being less than honest – the simple fact was that he didn't want to be dragged into another murder scene. One was more than enough. He pointed with his cigarette at the body on the floor, which was now swathed in duct tape. 'What about him?'

'He'll never be found, don't worry about that,' said T-Bone. 'It's not the first body I've disposed of.'

'I'm sure it isn't,' said Nightingale. 'But if you're leaving the rounds in him, you'll need to be careful with the gun.'

T-Bone laughed out loud. 'I'm not a virgin at this,

Bird-man,' he said. 'Don't you go worrying your pretty little head about the corpse or the gun.' His face hardened. 'Speaking of guns, you're still carrying?'

Nightingale nodded. He'd finished his cigarette so he stubbed it out on the sole of his shoe and slipped the butt into his raincoat pocket. 'Yeah.'

'Where?'

'Small of my back.'

'That a police issue holster?'

'Bought it myself when I was with CO19.'

T-Bone nodded his approval. 'It does the job,' he said. 'You'd never know.'

'That's the idea.'

35

Nightingale went home intending to catch a few hours' sleep but he slept through his alarm and didn't wake up until eleven. He picked up coffees and croissants at Costa Coffee before hurrying to his office.

'You look terrible,' said Jenny as he handed her a coffee and croissant.

'Thanks,' he said. 'Bit of a rough night.'

She had paused one of Nail's videos on the screen. 'Well, the good news is that I've found Daryl Heaton at the Ink Pit.'

'Are you serious?'

She clicked the mouse and the video started moving again. Nail was working on a large tattoo on the man's hip. Nail wiped the tattoo with a cloth, then sat back and stretched.

Nightingale held up his hand. 'Can you freeze it there?'

'Sure.' She clicked her mouse and the picture froze.

Nightingale peered at the screen. Half the tattoo was hidden by Nail's hand and the tattoo gun but he could make out two twisted horns and the top of a skull. 'That's a goat, right?'

'Looks like it, yes.'

'And you're sure this is Daryl Heaton?'

'You get a good view of his face when he lies down,' said Jenny. 'It's definitely him. Why?'

'I've seen that tattoo before.' He took his phone out of his pocket and opened his picture gallery. He showed her the picture he'd taken of Barnett's shoulder.

'Where did you get that from?' she asked.

'I'll explain later,' he said. 'It's the same design, right?' He took the phone off her and put it into his pocket.

'Looks like it,' she said. She clicked the mouse and the video started moving again. They both watched as Nail worked on Heaton, slowly and methodically adding to the design.

'It's pretty ugly.'

'Yeah. What about the others?'

Jenny wrinkled her nose. 'Not yet but I've plenty more footage to look at.'

Nightingale hung up his raincoat and took his coffee and croissant through to his office. He sat down at his desk and slid the Glock into the bottom drawer before gathering up Nail's notebooks. He had given them a cursory glance but he needed to check every drawing now that he knew what he was looking for.

36

It took almost an hour for Nightingale to find them. They were in the third notepad, a dozen or so drawings of the goat skull and the logo of the Order of Nine Angles. He cursed under his breath as he flicked through the pages. The first few were rough sketches as if Nail wasn't sure how the goat should look, and two of the pages were filled with sketches of the logo, the strange seven-pointed star. Again Nail had taken several stabs at it, each one slightly different. Then he'd amalgamated the two, the goat's skull and the logo, and done half a dozen versions until he'd found one that he was happy with. The final one was similar to the one in the video. Nightingale took out his phone and compared the photograph of the brand on Barnett's back to the final drawing. It was a perfect match.

Jenny made a whooping sound from her office. 'Bingo!' she shouted.

Nightingale pushed himself up out of his chair. 'Gabriel Patterson!' she called. 'He's just taken his shirt off.'

Nightingale hurried through to her office. Jenny clicked her mouse and leaned back so that he could get a better look at the screen.

Patterson was sitting bare-chested on Nail's reclining chair. He had Maori tattoos on his upper arms and as he turned over and lay down on the chair they could see several others on his back. A large bat, a hideous skull with a worm crawling out of an eye socket, and a burning cross.

'They're pretty gruesome,' said Jenny. 'And he seemed like such a nice guy before he took off his shirt.'

'He only had them done where they couldn't be seen when he was wearing a shirt,' said Nightingale. 'You can see why. Who'd employ someone if they knew they had that skull thing tattooed on them?'

'As opposed to someone with a top-hatted Pink Panther on their arse?' said Jenny. 'What's the rule about cops with tattoos, anyway?'

'No one ever saw mine, and I'm starting to regret that I let you see it,' said Nightingale. 'You can't have tattoos above the collar line or on the hands. They have to be covered at all times when you're on duty. And they mustn't be violent or intimidating or offensive to any religion or belief.'

'So the Pink Panther is cool?'

'He's positively frosty,' said Nightingale. 'Now can you jump ahead and see what design Nail did on Gabe.'

Jenny clicked on the mouse and fast-forwarded. Nail sketched a design on Patterson's back in triple time and then reached for his tattoo gun. He alternated between using the gun and dabbing with a cloth in a series of jerky movements. Even on fast-forward, Nightingale could see that the design was a match to the tattoo that Nail had done on Heaton. Jenny turned to look at him, her eyes wide. She had obviously had the same thought.

'What are the odds?' she said. 'Two victims with the same tattoo? The tattoo is the link?'

Nightingale held up a hand. 'Let's not jump to conclusions,' he said. On the screen, Nail continued to fast-forward on the design, inking in the curly horns. 'We need to see if he did the others, too.'

'What is it?' said Jenny, pointing at the screen. 'That's a goat's skull, obviously, but what's that thing below it? A pentangle?'

Nightingale shook his head. 'No, a pentangle has five points. That's got seven.'

'So what is it?'

Nightingale didn't say anything. He took out his cigarettes, playing for time.

'And how come you have that picture on your phone? You know what the tattoo is, don't you?' Nightingale stood up and headed to his office. 'Jack?' she called after him. 'Jack, what's going on?'

She stood up to follow him but her phone rang.

Nightingale flopped down at his desk, lit a cigarette and picked up one of the ring binders. He was flicking through the photographs when Jenny appeared at his door, ashen-faced. 'It's Chalmers for you,' she said.

'Tell him to sod off, I've had enough of him this week.'

Jenny shook her head and Nightingale realised she was close to tears. 'What is it?'

'Line two,' she said. 'You need to talk to him. It's about Robbie.'

37

Robbie Hoyle's house was a neat semi-detached in Raynes Park. Anna's black VW Golf was in the driveway and the Jaguar that Chalmers used was parked behind it. The driver was at the wheel, reading a newspaper.

As Nightingale climbed out of his MGB, he recognised a uniformed inspector striding purposefully towards the house. 'Colin!' he shouted.

The inspector turned and looked at Nightingale. Nightingale had worked with Colin Duggan when he was on the job, though they had lost touch since Nightingale had left. He was short and balding and his uniform always looked as if it was a size too big for him. Duggan nodded. 'Jack.'

'This is . . .' Nightingale shrugged, not sure what to say.

'Yeah,' said Duggan. 'A bloody hit and run.' He looked up at the sky. 'I hate this. I never know what to say.'

'It's not about saying anything. It's about being there.'

'Yeah, I know.'

'I told him,' said Nightingale. 'I told him to be careful about crossing the road.'

'He wasn't a kid, Jack.'

'They're looking for the car?'

'It was a van,' said Duggan. 'A white van. Witnesses saw it speeding away but no one got a look at the registration number. We're checking all CCTV in the area but you know how many white vans there are in London.'

38

Anna's mother opened the door. Her eyes were red from crying but she smiled when she saw Nightingale. 'Jack,' she said. 'Thank you for coming.'

'I'm so sorry, Louise,' said Nightingale, stepping forward and hugging her. 'How's Anna?'

'Not good,' she said.

'Where are the girls?' asked Nightingale. Robbie and Anna had three young daughters.

'Sarah's still at school, the twins are asleep upstairs. Angela's here, she's looking after them.' Angela was Anna's sister. She held the door open for them. 'Please come in.'

Nightingale and Duggan stepped into the hallway. Nightingale introduced Duggan and she shook his hand. 'I'm sorry for your loss,' said Duggan.

They went through to the sitting room. Anna was sitting on the sofa in between her mother-in-law and her brother, Dave. Dave was a forklift truck driver and had obviously rushed over from work, still wearing his overalls.

Anna's chestnut hair was clipped up at the back and her face was flushed. At first she stared at Nightingale with unseeing eyes, then she recognised him and stood up. She was unsteady and Nightingale moved forward and held her. She buried her face in his chest. He held her and felt her start to sob. 'I'm so sorry,' he whispered.

She continued to sob and Nightingale felt tears prick his own eyes. Over the top of Anna's head he saw a line of photographs on a mahogany sideboard. The largest, in the middle, was a gilt-framed wedding picture, taken almost ten years earlier when Robbie and Nightingale had both been beat bobbies. On either side of the big picture were framed photographs of the girls. One of the pictures was of the oldest, Sarah, smiling proudly in her school uniform. Nightingale blinked away tears. He couldn't imagine how little Sarah would take the news that she was never going to see her father again.

'I keep thinking this is a dream,' sobbed Anna.

'I'm sorry, Anna.' He closed his eyes, knowing how futile the words were. There was nothing that he could say that would help her, or make either of them feel better. Robbie was gone and they were going to have to deal with that, one way or another.

'Do you need someone to get Sarah from school?'

'My sister's going to pick her up. How am I going to tell her, Jack? What do I say?'

He held her for several minutes and then the doorbell rang and Louise showed in Robbie's brother, Paul. Paul was ashen-faced and he strode over to Anna. Anna turned and hugged him and they both began to cry.

Nightingale moved away. Robbie had been his best friend and he loved Anna like a sister, but he wasn't family.

Someone had opened a couple of bottles of whisky and placed them and several dozen glasses on a table by the French windows that led out to the back garden.

Chalmers was there, pouring himself a Scotch. He nodded at Nightingale and poured him a glass.

'What happened?' Nightingale asked Chalmers.

'I can't add much to what I said on the phone,' said the superintendent. 'It happened at about ten o'clock this morning. Robbie was heading to work, he was crossing the road and a white van slammed into him. No tyre marks so he didn't brake, just kept on going. Carried Robbie twenty feet or so and then he went under. The body's a mess.' He took a deep breath. 'There are some evil bastards in the world, that's for sure.'

'No argument here,' said Nightingale.

'We've got two witnesses who saw it happen. They said they thought Robbie was on his mobile. Neither of the witnesses got the registration number but we'll get the bastard, eventually. There'll be CCTV somewhere and there'll be damage to the van. Robbie was bleeding so there'll be blood and tissue on it and once we get the bastard he'll be going down for a long time.'

Nightingale nodded but didn't say anything. The silence was awkward but eventually Nightingale's phone rang. He apologised to Chalmers and went out into the garden to take the call. It was Caitlin. 'You never got back to me, Mr Nightingale,' she said.

'Caitlin, yes, I'm sorry, I've had a lot on my plate.'

'Do you want to talk to me or not?'

Nightingale looked through the window into the sitting room. Anna had put her head in her hands and was sobbing. 'Yes, of course.'

'Tonight then. Same time, same place. Okay?'

'I can't tonight.'

'Are you messing me around, Mr Nightingale? Maybe you don't want the information I have.'

She sounded as if she was about to hang up on him so he spoke quickly. 'It's not that, Caitlin. A good friend of mine died today.'

There was a short pause. 'I'm sorry to hear that,' she said eventually.

'That's okay,' he said. 'But I'm with the family now and it's going to be a while before I can get away.'

'Tomorrow then?'

'Yes. Tomorrow should be okay.'

'So tomorrow. Same place I told you about before. Garlic and Shots, in Frith Street, Soho.'

'Seven o'clock?'

'Seven o'clock, basement bar,' she said, and ended the call.

39

Nightingale had his feet up on his desk and was flicking through one of Ricky Nail's notebooks when Superintendent Chalmers burst into his office. 'What aren't you telling me, Nightingale?' he snapped.

'What do you mean?'

Jenny appeared behind the policeman, clearly flustered. 'Jack, I'm sorry, he just—'

'It's okay, Jenny,' said Nightingale, swinging his feet off his desk. 'The superintendent isn't one for the social niceties.'

Jenny went back to her office. Chalmers stood in front of Nightingale's desk, pointing his finger at Nightingale's face. 'You've got some cheek, going to Anna's house the way you did yesterday. I don't know what you think you're playing at, but if you're not careful it's going to backfire, big time.'

'You're going to have to be more specific, Chalmers.'

'I'd rather you called me Superintendent Chalmers, to be honest.'

'Yeah? Well, to be honest I'm not in the job any more. So I'll call you whatever I want. Now what's your problem? And what do you mean about me going to Anna's house?'

Chalmers stared at him for several seconds, then held out his hand and clicked his fingers impatiently. 'I want your phone,' he said.

Nightingale pushed the telephone on his desk towards the policeman. 'Be my guest.'

'Your mobile phone.' He clicked his fingers again.

'Why?'

'Because I want to see it.'

'It's a bog-standard BlackBerry, nothing special.'

'Don't screw around, Nightingale. Give me your phone.'

'Not without a reason.' He took out his cigarettes and lit one.

'You know it's an offence to smoke in a place of work?'

'Yeah, punishable with a fifty-pound fine reduced to thirty pounds if paid immediately.' Nightingale took out his wallet, pulled out three ten-pound notes, and tossed them at the policeman. 'Help yourself.' The notes fluttered across the desk and on to the floor.

'If you've got nothing to hide, you've no reason for not letting me see your phone.'

'And if you've got a good reason for looking at my phone, you'll get a warrant.' He blew smoke up at the ceiling and grinned at the superintendent. 'I can play this game all day,' he said.

'I can get a warrant, that's not a problem.'

'On what basis?'

'On the basis that I believe your phone has information pertinent to an ongoing investigation.'

'Bullshit,' said Nightingale. 'What's going on, Chalmers?'

'You're refusing to give me your phone?'

'Damn right I am,' said Nightingale.

Chalmers took a deep breath as he stared at Nightingale

as if he hoped he could persuade him to change his mind by force of will alone. Then he shook his head as if he had realised he was wasting his time. 'You're a prick, Nightingale.'

'I thought we were on the same side,' said Nightingale. 'I've been helping you with the Goths thing, haven't I?'

'Not really, no,' said Chalmers. 'It's not as if you've cracked the case, is it?'

'I think I'm getting somewhere,' said Nightingale.

'With help from Robbie Hoyle?' said Chalmers.

Nightingale froze, his cigarette a few inches from his lips. He realised instantly that Chalmers had seen his reaction. He forced a smile. 'What makes you say that?' he said, trying to keep his voice level. Chalmers wasn't the smartest of coppers but he had more than enough experience to spot when someone was under pressure.

'Are you denying that Sergeant Hoyle was providing you with information?'

'And if he was, what would be the problem with that? You gave me the case, remember?'

'That would depend on the nature of the information he was giving you,' said Chalmers. He held out his hand again. 'The easiest way to resolve this is for you just to hand over your phone.'

Nightingale shook his head. 'That's not going to happen. Why don't you tell me what you think you know?'

Chalmers took back his hand and glared sullenly at Nightingale. 'All right, Nightingale. I'll put my cards on the table. Two mobile phones were found among Sergeant Hoyle's personal effects. The phone that he used for work and personal use, and a pay-as-you-go mobile. The latter was missing its SIM card.'

Nightingale said nothing and concentrated on keeping his hand steady as he smoked his cigarette.

'No comment, Nightingale?'

'I'm waiting to see where you're going with this.'

'Where I'm going with this? I think you know exactly where I'm going. As I said, the SIM card was missing but the phone's memory was intact and we found that he had sent two text messages to your number.'

'Is that right?'

Chalmers clenched his jaw and glared at Nightingale.

'If you know he sent me texts, why do you need my phone?' He waved at a chair. 'And sit down, you're making me nervous looming over me like that.'

Chalmers pulled up a chair, unbuttoned his cashmere overcoat, and sat down. 'Here's the problem we have. For whatever reason, Sergeant Hoyle deleted the content of the messages from his phone's memory. So we know they were sent, we just don't know what he sent.'

Nightingale shrugged. 'I'm not sure I remember getting any texts from Robbie, certainly not from a strange phone.' He looked the policeman in the eyes as he spoke, trying to give as much authority to the lie as he could.

'Which is why I'd like a look at your phone.'

'The thing is, I delete pretty much all the messages I get. Security.'

'Security?' Chalmers repeated.

'I wouldn't want confidential information falling into the wrong hands, would I? And street muggings are on the rise, haven't you heard?'

'So you can't recall receiving texts from Sergeant Hoyle on Monday?'

Nightingale shrugged. 'Sorry.'

'Sorry doesn't cut it, Nightingale. My cards are on the table so I might as well go all in. Sergeant Hoyle might have thrown away his SIM card and deleted the messages, and you might well have done the same, but they'll still be sitting on the phone company's servers and once the paperwork's done I'll know exactly what it was he sent you. So if there's anything in those texts that you don't want me to know about, you're wasting your time.'

Nightingale held smoke deep in his lungs. He knew Chalmers was right. It would take a day or two at most but then the superintendent would have copies of the texts that Robbie had sent him. He groaned and swung his feet off the desk. He pulled open the top drawer and took out a bottle of malt whisky and two glasses. He put them on the desk, poured himself a decent measure, and showed the bottle to Chalmers. Chalmers scowled and then nodded. 'Fuck it, go on. It'll get the taste of smoke out of my mouth.' Nightingale poured whisky for the superintendent and handed over the glass. 'Thought you only drank that fancy Mexican beer,' he said.

'The whisky's for special occasions,' said Nightingale. He raised his glass in salute before drinking. Chalmers did the same. Nightingale's mind was racing. Once Chalmers had copies of Robbie's texts, he would know about the two vehicles and the two owners, Billy McDowell and Tony Barnett. Barnett was dead and hopefully buried, so Chalmers wouldn't get anywhere there. But so far as he knew Billy McDowell was still out and about. Nightingale was going to have to come up with a plausible explanation for Robbie passing him the information and one that wouldn't lead Chalmers to T-Bone. Nightingale looked down at the bottom drawer. It was still open and he could see the Glock there, sitting on top of its holster. He leant down and pushed the drawer closed.

Robbie had been breaking the rules by giving him information from the PNC, but if Nightingale could persuade Chalmers that it had been in connection with the Goths case then he might let the matter drop.

Chalmers put down his glass. Nightingale topped it up, and refilled his own. 'Look, yes, Robbie gave me some intel, but I don't want Anna having problems because of it.'

'What do you mean?' asked Chalmers.

'You know what they're like now about access to the PNC. I wouldn't want her having problems with Robbie's pension and stuff. She's got enough on her plate with the three kids, I can't have her worrying about money. Robbie was just helping me out.'

'What case?'

'The Goths, of course. I needed a couple of vehicles checking and I asked Robbie to run the registration numbers.'

'Why ask him? Why not come to me?'

Nightingale shrugged. 'I called your office but you weren't in.'

'Did you try my mobile?'

'I made one call, you weren't in, then I was talking to Robbie about something else and I gave him the numbers. That's all you'll find in those text messages – the PNC details of the two vehicles and their owners.'

Chalmers took a sip of his whisky. 'And what was special about these vehicles?'

Nightingale fought to keep his hand steady and he put his glass down on the desk. He flicked ash into the crystal ashtray by his computer. 'Someone I'd spoken to had said they'd seen them outside the home of one of the Goths.'

'Which one?'

Nightingale frowned. 'Which one?' he repeated, not understanding the question.

'Which Goth?'

Nightingale frowned. 'I'm not sure. I'd have to check my notes.'

Chalmers waved his hand over the desk. 'Then check.'

Nightingale made a pretence of looking for his notebook on his desk, then he shrugged. 'I might not even have made a note.'

'But you must have made a note of the registration numbers. You don't have a photographic memory, do you?'

Nightingale frowned. 'Yeah, you're right. I must have, mustn't I? Let me see if I can find my notebook.' He stood up and then hesitated. It wouldn't be a smart move to leave Chalmers alone in his office, not when there was a loaded Glock in the bottom drawer of his desk. He sat down again. 'Hey, Jenny!' he called.

Jenny appeared at the open door. 'Coffee?' she asked.

'My notebook,' he said. 'It should be in my coat by the door.' He looked at Chalmers and nodded at the whisky. 'Do you want a coffee to go with that?'

'No, the whisky's fine,' said Chalmers.

'Just the notebook, kid,' said Nightingale. He stubbed out the remains of his cigarette in the ashtray and refilled his glass. He went to pour more whisky for Chalmers but the detective shook his head and moved his glass away.

Jenny reappeared with Nightingale's notepad. She stood between Chalmers and his desk as she gave it to him. 'Are you okay?' she mouthed.

Nightingale flashed her a thumbs-up. She turned to look at the policeman. 'You sure I can't get you a coffee, Superintendent Chalmers?'

'I'm fine,' he said.

Jenny gave Nightingale a final look of concern and then left, though she kept the door ajar. Nightingale flicked through his notebook. He knew the more he lied, the more likely it was that Chalmers would trip him up. He had to keep the untruths to a minimum, but Chalmers was an experienced copper and knew that the best interrogators piled question upon question. It was like building a house on weak foundations – if you continued to pile lie upon lie eventually the whole edifice would collapse under its own weight. Nightingale needed to keep the story simple, but he had to keep T-Bone and Perry Smith out of it.

'Stella Walsh, the first girl who was killed.' he said, looking up from the book.

'Somebody saw the two vehicles at her house?'

Nightingale nodded.

'At the same time?'

That was a good question, of course. 'No,' said Nightingale. 'On different occasions.'

'And the same witness told you about the two vehicles?'

'That's right.'

'And wrote down the registration numbers?'

Nightingale felt his stomach tighten as he stared at the notepad. Another good question. T-Bone had a vested interest in the vehicles but why would a neighbour go to the bother of writing down registration numbers? 'They were in the local neighbourhood watch.'

'They?'

'The woman who wrote down the numbers. A pensioner, she spends a lot of time looking out of her window. She'd seen the vehicles parked out in front of the Walsh house on several occasions.' Nightingale immediately regretted giving out too much information. The less he said the better, because every lie was a fact that could be checked.

'Did this pensioner see the occupants of the vehicles, or see them interact with Stella Walsh?'

Nightingale shook his head. 'She just got the numbers.'

'So nothing suspicious?'

'Not that she mentioned.'

Chalmers frowned. 'She must have written down a lot of numbers then? Every time a strange car parked in her road she'd write it down, is that what you're saying?'

Nightingale swallowed. His mouth had gone bone dry so he took a quick drink of whisky. 'She only gave me these two numbers. I suppose because the drivers were sitting in the car, watching the house.'

'Ah, so there was something suspicious? Something that made these vehicles stick out.'

Nightingale could feel himself being painted into a corner, but there was nothing he could do. That was the trouble with lying, once you started you had to keep on adding to the lies – either that or admit that you weren't telling the truth in the first place. 'She just said the two vehicles had been outside the house, she didn't say why she'd written the numbers down.'

'And what was the name of this witness?'

Nightingale made a show of flicking through his note-book. 'You know, I don't think I wrote it down. I wasn't planning on going back. Like I said, she didn't see anything, just the vehicles.'

'And the vehicles were what?' asked Chalmers.

'An SUV and a van.'

Chalmers held out his hand. 'Let me see what Sergeant Hoyle gave you?'

'I told you, I deleted the texts.'

'But you wrote the information down, right?'

Nightingale nodded. 'Sure. Yes.' He flicked through to a blank page and then copied down the names, addresses and vehicle details that Robbie had given him. He tore out the sheet and gave it to the super-intendent.

'And this is all that Sergeant Hoyle gave you? When we get the records from the phone company, there are going to be no nasty surprises? Because if there are, I'll have your guts for garters.'

'That's all, swear to God.' Nightingale closed his note-book and took another drink of whisky.

Chalmers studied the piece of paper that Nightingale had given him. His eyes narrowed. 'This Billy McDowell, he drives a white van it says here.'

'The plumber? Yeah. A white Transit.'

'Sergeant Hoyle was killed by a white van.'

Nightingale tried to look unconcerned. He shrugged carelessly. 'There are thousands of white vans in London,' he said.

Chalmers held up the sheet. 'You don't think it's a coincidence that you asked Sergeant Hoyle to check up on a white van and it's a white van that runs him over?'

'If it had been a yellow Rolls-Royce then maybe, but a white van?' He took another drink of whisky. 'You're saying you think the hit-and-run wasn't an accident?'

'I'm not saying anything, Nightingale,' said Chalmers. He folded up the piece of paper, took a small black notebook from his jacket pocket and slipped the paper between its pages. 'But as I told you yesterday there were no tyre marks at the scene which suggests that the vehicle didn't brake.' He put the notebook into his pocket and stood up. 'Are you sure there's nothing else that you want to share with me?'

Nightingale looked up at the superintendent. He had a hollow feeling in the pit of his stomach. Chalmers clearly wasn't satisfied and would probably make a point of checking all the houses near where Stella Walsh lived, looking for an elderly woman in the Neighbourhood Watch who collected car numbers. If that did happen and if Chalmers came back to him, Nightingale's fallback position would be that he had been confused about the victim and that the witness had been outside another house, but even that would only be playing for time. The best way of getting Chalmers off his back would be to give him something else to concentrate on.

'I'm making progress on the Goths case,' he said.

Chalmers cocked his head on one side. 'You don't say.'

'Two of the victims had the same tattoo.'

Chalmers frowned. 'How would you know that, the bodies were all butchered to buggery?' He sat down.

'I managed to get some video from the Ink Pit.'

'There was no CCTV in the shop.'

'It was a video that Ricky Nail made. Anyway we've found two of the victims with the same tattoo so far.

Daryl Heaton and Gabe Patterson. The tattoo was based on a horned goat.'

'A horned goat?'

'A Satanic thing. A goat with big curly horns. And superimposed on it is a logo of a devil-worshipping group. The Order of Nine Angles.'

'And why are you only telling me this now?'

'I've only just confirmed it. I knew they went to the Ink Pit. But I've only just found out that they had the same tattoo.'

'We've spoken to the staff at the Ink Pit and got as many client names as we could. We've been working our way through it.'

'Looking for serial killers?'

'Looking for anyone with a history of violence, or who can't account for their whereabouts at the times of the murders.' He tilted his head to one side. 'Don't take the piss, Nightingale. It's basic police work, that's how we catch ninety per cent of criminals. We're working on the assumption that the victims met the killer at the tattoo parlour.'

'It could be more complicated than that.' Nightingale reached for his cigarettes and lit one. 'I think it's the tattoo that they have in common. That's why they died. The Order of Nine Angles are a group of Satanists, I think they're the ones who killed your Goths.'

Chalmers took a deep breath as he glared across at Nightingale. 'I've half a mind to arrest you for hindering an investigation,' he said.

'Chalmers, I'm the one helping you here.'

'Except that this is the first you've told me about any of this. Didn't I make it clear to you that the moment you had any information you were to give it to me? Immediately?'

'I had to wait until I had something concrete,' said Nightingale. 'I'd just be wasting your time if I ran every scrap of intel by you. It's only come together in the last day or two.'

'You should have told me straight away, as soon as you walked through the door.'

'You didn't give me a chance, you started on about the text messages and this is the first chance I've had to open my mouth.'

Chalmers rubbed his chin as he stared at Nightingale. 'I'm assuming you have a theory,' he said eventually.

Nightingale unscrewed the top off the bottle of whisky and refilled the two glasses. 'I do,' he said. 'But you'll think I'm crazy.'

'Nightingale, that ship has already sailed,' said Chalmers.

40

Nightingale flicked ash into the ashtray and swung his feet up on to the desk. 'The Order of Nine Angles was formed sometime in the Swinging Sixties,' he said. 'They were originally an ad-hoc group of pagans and white witches based in Herefordshire and Shropshire, but they moved over to black magic and Satanism. They operate in small cells, a bit like the IRA used to, with very little in the way of connections between the various groups. These days they're everywhere, right across Europe and the United States and they're spreading fast in Russia. The Order is linked with some pretty nasty far-right groups, but they're not political.'

'Then what the hell are they?' asked Chalmers.

'They're devil worshippers. They believe by serving devils they get power on earth and even more power in the afterlife.'

'Now you're losing me, Nightingale,' said Chalmers. 'You don't seriously believe this crap, do you?'

'It doesn't matter what I believe or don't believe,' said Nightingale. 'What matters is what *they* believe. A lot of so-called black magic practitioners do it for fun, for a bit of a laugh, and because there's a fair bit of free sex involved. You'll find older men pretending to be Satanists and telling impressionable young girls that sex is part of the process. The Order is different. They believe they have to prove themselves. So they carry out human sacrifices, they kill children, and they do whatever is asked of them by the ones they serve.' .

'The Devil?'

'Devils, plural,' said Nightingale. 'Satanist is a catch-all term, they don't just serve Satan. They serve a whole range of devils and demons.' He sipped his whisky. 'The members of the Order see us normal people as sheep. "Mundanes", they call us. And they see nothing wrong with sacrificing a Mundane for their beliefs. The opposite, in fact. They see it as culling, getting rid of worthless parts of the population.'

Chalmers looked at Nightingale scornfully. 'Are you telling me that a group of Satanists have been carrying out human sacrifices since the sixties and no one is aware of it?'

'A lot of people are aware of it, it's just that it's not spoken about in public. Every year people go missing and are never heard of again. A fair number of them are children. These people are experts at what they do, Chalmers. The bodies are never found, and more often than not they sacrifice people who won't be missed.'

Chalmers shook his head. 'I'm not buying this.'

'I'm not selling it,' said Nightingale. 'I'm just telling you how it is. Kids do go missing every year and unless they're pretty and blonde generally the media doesn't pay much attention. And the Order have members in the media, the cops, the government. They're like the Masons, they're everywhere, and they help each other.'

'Oh, come on, now you're in the realms of conspiracy theories.'

'Really? What about Jimmy Savile? He got away with systematic child abuse for decades. You think that wasn't covered up? And at a high level, too. The man was given a knighthood and a papal knighthood. And we all know how close to the cops he was.'

'So now you're saying that Jimmy Savile was in this Order?'

'No one knows who's in it,' said Nightingale. 'Like I said, the whole Order is made up of individual cells. Communication between the cells is kept to a minimum, but they do help each other and they work together when needed. What I'm saying is that the reason you don't hear about them is because they have members in very high places.' He raised his glass to the superintendent. 'For all I know, you could be a member.'

The superintendent's eyes hardened. 'That's not funny, Nightingale.'

'None of this is funny. You were suggesting that the idea of a bunch of child-killing Satanists was a figment of my imagination. I'm telling you that they exist and that they're good at covering their tracks.'

Chalmers rubbed the back of his neck, then turned his head from side to side.

'Problems with your neck?' asked Nightingale.

'Slipped discs,' said Chalmers. 'Too much tension, coupled with too much time sitting at a desk.'

'You should walk more,' said Nightingale.

'Have you any idea how much paperwork I have to deal with?' said Chalmers. 'And how many meetings I have to sit in on?' He sighed mournfully. 'Okay, so let's suppose that I buy the idea of child-killing Satanists. How do they tie in with the five murder victims? Were they members, is that what you're saying?'

'Members of the Order do sometimes have tattoos, but not always. There's no point in having a secret society if every member has the logo tattooed on his body. And I've found no evidence that any of the five were members. They don't fit the profile, either.'

'Profile?'

'Most of the members of the Order are male and middle-aged. And they join for money and power, remember. None of the five victims was either rich or powerful.'

'But two of them had the same tattoo. A winged goat and the logo.'

'A horned goat,' corrected Nightingale.

'Have you got a picture?'

Nightingale nodded. 'Jenny?' he shouted.

Jenny appeared at the doorway again. 'You know that phone thing on your desk works as an intercom,' she said.

'I can never get it to work,' said Nightingale. 'Can you get print-outs of the goat tattoo that Daryl and Gabe had done.'

'I hear and obey,' she said, and disappeared back into his office. Nightingale shrugged apologetically. 'Can't get the staff these days,' he said.

Chalmers chuckled. 'You should see what we have to deal with in the way of civilian staff,' he said. 'Half of them can barely read and write.' He took another sip of whisky. 'So, what about the tattooist? Nail? How is he involved?'

'I don't know for sure,' said Nightingale. 'But if he

didn't have the tattoo, maybe that's why his body wasn't mutilated.'

'You're assuming he was murdered,' said Chalmers. 'We still have it down as a sex game gone wrong. Or a suicide.'

'I'm more inclined to think he was murdered by the same people who killed the Goths.'

'Hunches don't count for anything, Nightingale. You know that. Now, could Nail have been a member of this group? Is that possible?'

'I can't answer that,' said Nightingale. 'It's not as if they keep a mailing list.'

'The cell thing?'

'That's why they do it. Even if you tracked down one member, you'd only be able to find out who was in his cell.'

Chalmers nodded. 'Okay, so we have five Goths, two with the same tattoo. A tattoo that somehow symbolises a group of Satanic child-killers. The Goths are butchered, presumably to hide the fact that they had this tattoo. And the man who gave them the tattoos is also dead. I guess the question is: were they killed because of the tattoo?'

'It looks like it,' said Nightingale.

'There you go with your hunches again,' said Chalmers.

'I'm wondering if Nail saw this design somewhere. And he decided to do it as a tattoo. He put the tattoo on a few of his clients and the Order found out. They killed him to get his client list and tracked down the Goths and butchered them to destroy the tattoo so that no one would see it.' He saw the look of disbelief on the superintendent's face and shrugged. 'It's just a theory.'

Chalmers sighed. 'Okay, so what we need to find out

is whether or not any of the shop's clients had the tattoo but haven't been killed.'

'Agreed,' said Nightingale. 'You need to check every client. Though there's a problem.'

'Why am I not surprised?'

'Nail did a lot of clients late at night, off the books. I think those names were on the computer in his flat. The missing computer. And the one stolen from the shop.'

Chalmers nodded. 'We're talking to the Internet server Nail uses and there's a good chance we can get a back up copy of his files and the shop files too but that's taking time.'

Jenny reappeared in the doorway, holding a couple of print-outs. She handed them to Chalmers. Nightingale smiled and winked and she went back to her desk.

'Why would anyone want this tattooed on their skin?' asked Chalmers. He looked up from the print-outs. 'My daughter wants a tattoo. A bloody dolphin on her ankle. I've told her over my dead body.'

'How old is she?'

'Fifteen.'

'Problem solved: they can't get it done until they're eighteen.'

'The age isn't the point,' said Chalmers. 'The point is that she wants to mutilate her body.'

'I'm not sure a cute dolphin counts as mutilation,' said Nightingale.

'Doesn't matter what it is, tattoos mean trouble. Especially on a woman. We've got guys in the job with tattoos, most of them ex-army, but when a woman has a tattoo . . .'

'A tramp stamp.'

'Exactly. Kids, huh?' He sipped his whisky. 'Is it possible that all five of the dead Goths had this tattoo?'

'That's what we're checking now. We've a lot of CCTV footage to get through. What about Nail? Did you see a tattoo like that on him?'

'I haven't seen the body. But it's in the care of the coroner so I'll get it checked.' He folded up the print-outs and slipped them into his pocket before standing up. 'Next time you get any information on this case, you let me know straight away.'

'Sure. Not a problem.'

'I'm serious, Nightingale. You should have told me about these Satanists before.' He patted his jacket pocket. 'And this tattoo is important, you should have got that to me earlier.'

'I just wanted to get all my ducks in a row. I would have called you today.'

Chalmers stared at Nightingale for several seconds, then turned away without saying anything. Nightingale put the whisky bottle away as he heard Chalmers say goodbye to Jenny and leave.

As he straightened up, Jenny came back into his office. 'Everything okay?' she asked brightly.

'Swings and roundabouts,' he said. 'He's giving me grief about the Goth case.'

'Yeah, I thought it best not to mention that you stole Rusty Nail's belongings.'

'Borrowed,' said Nightingale.

'I heard him asking you about Robbie.'

'Robbie gave me some PNC stuff – Chalmers isn't happy.'

'Is it a problem?'

Nightingale stood up. 'Hopefully not,' he said. 'I've got to go out for a bit.'

'Anything I can do?'

Nightingale shook his head. 'I've got to do this myself,' he said. He went over to the window and peered down into the street below. Chalmers was climbing into the back of his black Jaguar. He watched it drive away. There was a small chance that Chalmers would get so distracted with the Nine Angles tattoo that he might forget about the registration numbers that Robbie had checked for him. But somehow Nightingale doubted it. He was going to have to get into damage limitation mode, and quickly.

41

Nightingale found a working phone box a short walk from his office and slotted in a fifty pence coin before tapping out T-Bone's number. The phone rang out but he didn't answer and eventually it went through to voicemail. 'Hey, it's me,' said Nightingale. He didn't want to leave his name and hoped that T-Bone would recognise his voice. 'I'll call back in two minutes, pick up, yeah?' He ended the call, waited for two minutes and slotted in another coin. The second call also went through to voicemail and Nightingale cursed under his breath. 'Okay, I need to talk to you ASAP. But don't call my mobile, call the office. I'm in the book. And don't use your mobile. And don't use your name, just say you're a friend. It's important. Obviously.' Nightingale replaced the receiver, picked up two coffees and a chocolate muffin from Costa Coffee and took them back to the office.

'That was quick,' said Jenny as he walked in through the door.

'Sorry about the cloak and dagger, I needed to call someone and didn't want to use my phone.' He put one of the coffees and the muffin in front of her.

'It's about the Goth case?'

Nightingale nodded. 'Yeah, I've a contact I need to talk

to and he's a bit shady. With Chalmers on my case I'm going to have to be careful.' He gestured at her phone. 'So if someone claiming to be my friend calls, put him through.'

T-Bone called fifteen minutes later. 'What's the problem?' he asked.

'We need to talk, face to face,' said Nightingale. 'Where are you?'

'Out and about,' said T-Bone. 'North of the river.'

'The sooner the better,' said Nightingale. 'This is important.'

'You're in South Kensington, right?'

'Not stalking me, are you?'

'I made a few basic enquiries, Bird-man. You wouldn't expect me to do anything less. Take a walk up to Hyde Park in about half an hour. There's a coffee place by the lake in the middle.'

'The Serpentine? Yeah, I know it. I'll be there.' T-Bone had already ended the call.

42

T-Bone was already sitting at a table overlooking the Serpentine when Nightingale arrived. He was sitting alone with two coffees in front of him, but at a neighbouring table were two large black men wearing matching Puffa jackets and Oakleys and two black teenagers in hoodies on BMXs watched from the path that wound around the water. T-Bone looked at Nightingale impassively as he sat down. 'Thought you'd take your coffee same as you choose your friends – black and strong,' said T-Bone. His face broke into a grin. 'Then I thought you'd probably have milk in it, yeah?'

'So long as it's got caffeine in it, I'll not be complaining,' said Nightingale. He looked around. Most of the other tables were taken up by Asian and Arab tourists. 'Sorry about this, but I needed to see you and quickly.' He leaned closer to T-Bone and lowered his voice. 'The cops know about Barnett and McDowell.'

'How come? I only told you.'

Nightingale could see his reflection in the lenses of T-Bone's sunglasses. And even he could see how fake his smile looked. 'They know I got the names off the Police National Computer.'

'But that's all they know, right?'

'They don't know the numbers came from you, that's for sure.'

'Because the only person who knows that is you, right?'

Nightingale sat back and picked up his coffee.

'You hear what I'm saying, Bird-man?'

'T-Bone, this isn't down to me. The cop who gave me the information was killed. He was a friend of mine, doing me a favour. He sent me the info on the cars from a pay-as-you-go mobile and the cops have it. So they know about the vehicles.'

'And what did you tell this cop friend?'

'Nothing. Just that I wanted the numbers run through the PNC.'

'So there's no big deal, then?'

'The problem is that I lied and if they dig they'll find out that I lied.'

'Just say you forgot. People forget all the time.'

Nightingale nodded. 'Yeah, I can do that. But it'd be a lot easier if the white van was out of the picture.'

'I'm working on that,' said T-Bone.

'If there's anything you can do to speed it up, it'd be a help,' said Nightingale. 'The cop who was helping me, Robbie, he died in a hit and run. And they think it was a white van.'

T-Bone's jaw tensed. 'What are you saying, Bird-man? This McDowell guy killed a cop?'

'Maybe. But it means the cops are looking and looking hard. And if they pull him in and find a link to the killings at Perry's house, then it all gets very murky.'

'Damn right it does.' T-Bone's right hand had bunched into a tight fist but he flexed it in and out and placed it palm down on the table. 'How the hell did this happen, Bird-man? I gave you those numbers in confidence.'

'I didn't broadcast the fact, T-Bone, give me some credit. But the only way to get the names and addresses of the owners was to go through the PNC and for that I needed a cop. It was just bad luck.'

'A hit and run?'

'At the moment they're treating it as a hit and run. But if they find the van and it turns out that it was the van that he ran through the PNC, they'll haul me in for sure. The problem I have is that I said I got the numbers off a nosey little old lady who lived opposite a murder victim. That story won't hold up for long.'

'Like I said, just say you forgot.'

'Then they'll think about charging me with obstruction or worse.'

'But that'll be your problem, not mine.'

'It might become your problem if they pull McDowell in and he talks about what happened to Perry.'

T-Bone shrugged. 'Don't see how. But you're preaching to the converted, Bird-man, I don't want the cops getting to McDowell before me.'

'So you'll pull out all the stops?'

'We already know where he is. He's at home with his family, we were waiting for him to be on his own before we took him.'

'Yeah, well, you might want to rethink that. The cops won't wait long. What about the van?'

T-Bone shook his head. 'No sign of it. But if it's been involved in a hit and run, that's no surprise.' He sipped his coffee. 'Here's what I don't get, Bird-man. I gave those numbers to you. You gave them to your pal Robbie.

But within hours, the owner of one of those numbers kills him. How can that be?'

'That's a good question.'

T-Bone took off his sunglasses and fixed Nightingale with brown eyes that were so dark that they were almost black. 'Have a stab at answering it, Bird-man.'

'I didn't tell anyone else, T-Bone. I swear.'

'I believe you. And I'm guessing that your friend didn't broadcast it, either. So what are we saying? It's a coincidence? Your friend was just in the wrong place at the wrong time? He steps out into the street and just happens to get run over by one of the guys he's checking out?'

'That's unlikely.'

'You're telling me. But what's the alternative?'

'I don't know,' said Nightingale. 'But I could take a guess and say that the Satanists have their own people inside the Met.'

'Well, give the man a cigar. Seems to me that's exactly what's happened, Bird-man. Somehow they found out that your friend was asking about them. Maybe they had access to the PNC. When they found out what he was up to, they killed him. We grabbed the Barnett guy and while we were dealing with him, McDowell ran down your mate.'

Nightingale nodded. 'That sounds about right.'

'You're the connection here, Bird-man. You do see that, right? You get Perry to take out Marcus Fairchild but you skip over the fact that he's a child-killing Satanist. The Satanists kill Perry and most of his crew. You get a mate to check up on two of the Satanists and he ends up dead.' He stared at Nightingale and his hands tensed into fists again.

'I had no idea this would happen, T-Bone.'

'That might well be true, but that's not the point. The point is you used Perry, and he's dead. And you used your pal, and now he's dead.' He gestured at the two men sitting at the neighbouring table. 'Now wherever I go, I have to watch my back.' He took a deep breath and unclenched his fists. 'Is there anything else you need to tell me, Bird-man? Anything at all?'

'You know as much as I do,' said Nightingale.

'Nothing else is going to come out of the woodwork?'

'Not that I know of.'

'Nothing about Perry's bathroom that I should know about?' said T-Bone, his voice a low growl.

Nightingale felt his breath catch in his throat. There could be only one reason T-Bone would ask – he already knew what had been written on the bathroom mirror. He took a sip of coffee as his mind raced. 'There was a message, written on Perry's mirror,' said Nightingale. 'It was about me. That's why the cops took me there.'

'What did this message say?' asked T-Bone.

Nightingale knew without a shadow of a doubt that T-Bone knew exactly what had been written on the mirror. 'It said I would be next, that they would be coming for me.'

T-Bone nodded slowly. 'So this is all about you, isn't it?'

'I guess so.'

'You need to think about that, Bird-man,' said T-Bone. 'I've got the resources to take care of myself and my family. Have you?'

Nightingale couldn't answer. It was a simple enough question, but if the Order of Nine Angles were after him, was there anything he could do to stop them? T-Bone got to his feet. His huge bulk blocked out the sun and Nightingale felt a sudden chill run down his spine.

'I'm assuming you want to talk to this McDowell after we take him?' said T-Bone.

Nightingale nodded. 'Please.'

'But once we've done that, we have to part company, you and I. Do you understand?'

'I understand, T-Bone.'

'You're bad news, Bird-man. Seriously bad news.'

T-Bone walked away, followed by his two bodyguards. Ahead of him rode the two hooded teenagers on their BMX bikes.

43

Nightingale was late getting to Garlic and Shots. He'd taken the Tube and the trains were delayed by a suicide at Oxford Circus. The announcements didn't say suicide, of course, they referred to it as an incident. It would only be a couple of days later that the details would make their way into the paper – a banker who had been defrauding his company and whose wife had revealed all to the police as part of a very nasty divorce. The man was about to lose everything – his wife, his children, his job, his money, his freedom. Nightingale didn't know any of that as he sat in the train between stations with the rest of the frustrated passengers; all he knew was that time was ticking by.

He was ten minutes late when he eventually got to Frith Street and it took him another five minutes to find the bar. It was small and nondescript, as if it was trying to avoid customers. He eventually found it and opened the door into an equally bland bar and restaurant area. A strong smell of garlic made him almost gag. It was more than a smell; it felt as if he was in a garlic fog that was seeping into his skin and clothing. He smiled at a waitress in a black T-shirt and jeans with half of her head shaved, the hair on the other half hanging down in thick braids. 'Downstairs bar?' he said.

She pointed towards the rear of the bar. There was a hallway that opened on to an outside seating area and a rickety staircase that led down to the basement. Nightingale carefully made his way down. There was a horned skull of a steer fixed to the ceiling and he ducked as he passed under it. Loud, thumping music assaulted his ears and the smell of garlic seemed even stronger as he descended. The basement was painted black and most of what light there was came from candles shoved into empty Jack Daniels bottles on a handful of small tables. The only customers were two Japanese girls sitting in a corner taking pictures of themselves on their mobile phones. In the opposite corner, in a glass case, was a life-size replica of Frankenstein's monster. At a small bar counter to his left a big man with a face that appeared to have been thumped a few times looked at him with bored disinterest. Hanging behind him were a shrunken head and a rubber bat and a photograph of a manic Jack Nicholson from *The Shining*. Nightingale flashed the man a smile but he was studiously ignored. Nightingale looked at his watch. It was twenty past seven.

On the far side of the bar was an archway and he walked through it into a tiny brick-lined vault where a small girl in a short black dress, black boots with a dozen steel piercings in her eyebrows and ears was sitting at the one long wooden table. 'Caitlin?' he said.

'Mr Nightingale?' She had a multi-coloured Mohawk that made it look as if she had a parrot perched on her head.

'Call me Jack,' he said. He shook her hand and hers

was dwarfed by his. He sat down opposite her. 'I'm sorry about cancelling last time,' he said.

'No problem,' she said. 'Better late than never.' The music was so loud that she had to lean towards him and raise her voice. She was wearing a sweet perfume that smelled vaguely familiar. 'What do you want to drink?' she asked.

'Corona.'

She frowned. 'Corona?'

'It's a beer. Mexican.'

She laughed. 'This place serves shots,' she said. 'They'll take you out and shoot you if you order anything else. The clue's in the name. Garlic and shots.'

'I'd prefer a Corona. Or any beer. I saw beer in the bar back there.'

'Beer is for wimps,' she said. She stood up. 'Here you drink shots.' She said went over to the bar. She really was tiny, even in her high-heeled boots. He doubted if she was more than five feet tall though the Mohawk added a couple of inches. She returned two minutes later with four shot glasses on a small tray.

'Really, I'm not a huge fan of shots,' said Nightingale.

'Well, I am,' she said. She picked up one glass and handed another to Nightingale. There was a red liquid in the glass that looked disturbingly like fresh blood with a bulb of garlic floating in it. 'You're kidding me,' he said. 'What is this?'

'It's called a Bloodshot,' she said. 'Vodka, tomato juice, garlic, chilli, spices. All good stuff. Now stop being such a girl.' She clinked her glass against his 'Down in one,' she said, and drank it. Nightingale smiled tightly and did the same. He shuddered. It was like drinking pure garlic with a fiery kick.

'Good, yeah?' she said, grinning.

'I guess it's an acquired taste,' said Nightingale, putting down his glass. He gasped as the burning liquid reached his stomach. It felt as if a fire was burning in his chest. 'How old are you?'

'Why do you ask?' she said, leaning across so that her mouth was just inches from his ear. He smelled her heady perfume again. And garlic.

'Because you look like a kid. And kids shouldn't be knocking back shots.'

She put down another glass in front of him. 'Knock that back and I'll tell you.'

'Caitlin, really—'

'Don't be a girl, Jack.' She raised her glass and waited for him to do the same. He groaned, picked up his glass and downed it in one. She did the same. Nightingale gasped. If anything the second shot had an even mightier kick.

Caitlin grinned at his discomfort. 'I'm twenty-two, Jack,' she said. She put her hand up and ran her finger-nails down his cheek, then sat back laughing as he flinched. 'We need another drink,' she said. 'To celebrate the fact I'm legal.'

'Can I at least see a drinks menu?'

She grinned and flounced over to the bar, returning with a menu that was a list of a hundred and one different shots. There was no beer. 'See anything you like?' she asked. Nightingale shook his head. 'More Bloodshots, then,' she said, and went back to the bar. She came with two more glasses and made him drink his down in one.

'Caitlin, much as I can see the attraction of this place,

I'm not great in confined spaces and I really need a cigarette. Can we go upstairs?'

'You're a smoker?'

'Oh yes, I'm a smoker.'

She grinned. 'Finally, we have something in common,' she said. 'Come on.' They went back up the staircase and out on to a cramped terrace at the back of the building. There were space heaters but the night wasn't too cold and they hadn't been switched on. They sat down on a bench. The waitress with the half-shaved head walked over and stood looking down at them, her face a blank mask. 'Two Bloodshots,' said Caitlin. The only sign that the waitress had heard her was that she turned around and went back into the bar.

Nightingale took out his cigarettes and offered the pack to her. Caitlin took one and Nightingale lit it for her and then lit one for himself. 'Okay, you said you had something to tell me about the five Goths who died.'

'That was some heavy shit, right?' said Caitlin.

'Very heavy.' Nightingale put a hand up to his head. He felt a little dizzy and tried to remember how many shots he had. Three? Only three?

'Are you okay?'

'A bit tired,' he said. 'I've had a rough few days and I'm not getting much sleep.'

'I hardly sleep at all,' she said. 'I'm a night owl.' She laughed. 'That's funny. I'm a night owl. And you're a nightingale.'

'You said you had some information for me.'

She nodded enthusiastically. 'There was a photographer, at the Crypt. I saw him talking to Stella Walsh, the first girl who was killed.'

'When was this?'

'A couple of months ago.'

Nightingale frowned. 'You knew Stella?'

'No. But I recognised her when I saw her picture. The photographer was going around saying that he was doing a portfolio of Goths.'

'Did he have a camera?'

Caitlin frowned. 'No. I didn't see one.'

'So how did you know he was a photographer?'

She rolled his eyes. 'Because he spoke to me and gave me his card.'

'Have you got it?'

'Sure.' She picked up her bag, black leather with chrome studs, and rooted through it. She pulled out a purse in the shape of a bat and unzipped it. She looked into it and wrinkled her nose. 'Must be back at my place.'

'Was there something off about this guy?'

'Why do you say that?'

'Because you obviously remembered him, and you remembered him talking to Stella Walsh. Or do you remember everybody?'

Their drinks arrived. Nightingale took out his wallet but Caitlin waved it away. 'I paid already,' she said. The waitress put the shots on the table and walked away without saying a word.

'They're not very friendly here,' said Nightingale.

'That's why people come. For the shots, the music, and the attitude.' She picked up one of the glasses. 'Down in one.'

Nightingale sighed and downed the drink. He was sweating so he took off his raincoat.

'I saw him with Luke Aitken, too.'

Nightingale rubbed his face with his hand and his palm came away wet. 'Who?'

'Luke Aitken.'

Nightingale was sure he'd heard the name before. 'Luke Aitken?' he repeated.

'Another of the Goths who was killed. About a week after he was talking to Stella I saw him talking to Luke.'

'You knew Luke?'

'Sure, he was a regular at the Crypt. The photographer was very interested in Luke.' She shrugged. 'Maybe he was gay.'

Nightingale was finding it difficult to concentrate. 'Luke?'

She looked up and sighed. 'I know Luke was gay. Obviously Luke was gay. Luke was like the gayest person you could meet. I mean the photographer, I thought he might be gay.'

'And he spoke to . . .' Nightingale frowned. He was having trouble concentrating. 'Stella. He spoke to Stella as well?'

Caitlin nodded. 'And one of the other Goths. Gabe something or other. I saw his picture on the TV.'

'You knew Gabe?'

'To say hello to, sure. He was a regular at the Crypt.'

Nightingale leaned towards her. He knew he had something important to say to her but the thought kept slipping away. The more he concentrated, the less he seemed able to focus.

'Jack, are you okay?' asked Caitlin. She put her tiny hand on his. 'Maybe we should get out of here.'

44

C aitlin peered up at the building. 'This is it,' she said. She groped in her bag and pulled out a set of keys. 'Soon be home.'

Nightingale ran a hand through his hair and looked up and down the deserted street. 'Where are we?' he said. He didn't remember getting into a cab but he didn't remember walking there either.

'My place,' said Caitlin. She slotted the key into the lock. 'I don't normally do this,' she said.

'What? Lock your door?'

She laughed but there was an uncertain edge to the sound, as if she was faking it. Nightingale rubbed his face with his hand. He felt so tired. He shook his head, trying to clear it. Something was wrong. He wasn't a regular drinker of shots but he was no stranger to the effects of alcohol and there was no way that he could have become drunk so quickly.

'Take strange men back to my place, that's what I meant.'

'I'm not that strange. Honestly.'

She reached up and stroked his cheek. 'You're quite cute.'

'I do my best,' said Nightingale. He shook his head.

She must have put something in his drink, he realised. The thought that she had drugged him was surprisingly funny, and he found himself giggling.

'Let's get you inside,' she said.

'Sounds like a plan.' He knew that the sensible thing to do was to push her away and run down the street, but his legs felt rooted to the pavement.

She unlocked the door and pushed it open. He followed her inside as she switched on the light. 'Watch the stairs,' she said. 'There are holes in the carpets, be careful you don't trip.' He followed her upstairs, bumping against the wall every second step. Her flat was on the second floor and by the time he reached it she was already opening the door. 'Home sweet home,' she said.

She held the door open and he walked in. It was quite a large room with a window overlooking the rear of the building. There was a double bed and a small sofa, and a circular dining table with four chairs. The door closed behind him. There was a doorway to the left that opened into a small kitchen, and another door that must have been to the bathroom. Nightingale shook his head, trying to concentrate. There were no personal belongings in the room, he realised. No posters. No photographs. No cuddly toys. No books. The bed didn't look as if it had ever been slept in.

There was a mirror on the wall opposite the front door. Nightingale's vision had gone blurry so he blinked to clear his eyes and then he saw Caitlin in the mirror, standing behind him. She had her arm raised and he realised she was about to slam something against the back of his head. He twisted around but he was too slow to avoid the blow completely and whatever it was grazed the side of his head, stunning him. He slumped to his knees, his head spinning, then went down on all fours. As he looked up he saw the bathroom door open. A man in dark clothing appeared, holding a machete. Behind him was another man. He had what looked like a cleaver in his hand.

Nightingale shook his head again and took a deep breath. Caitlin said something to the men and one of them laughed. Nightingale fumbled his right hand under his coat and groped for the Glock. His fingers found the butt of the weapon and he pulled it out. He rocked back on his heels as he brought the gun up. He brought his left hand up to pull back the slide and heard the click-clack of a round being chambered.

The first man, tall with receding hair, snarled and stepped forward, the machete raised above his head. Nightingale fired once and the bullet caught the man just below the chin. He froze, then blood spouted from the neck wound and less than a second later blood frothed from between his lips.

Nightingale swung the gun around. The second man had pulled up, his cleaver at waist height. His eyes darted from Nightingale to Receding Hair. Receding Hair slumped to his knees as blood trickled down his shirt and on to the floor. His eyes had already gone dull and lifeless. The second man's eyes flicked back to Nightingale and the Glock that was now centred on his chest. Nightingale had no choice other than to stay on his back with the gun pointing between his knees. 'Your call,' he said quietly.

The man growled, raised his cleaver and sprang forward. Nightingale tightened his trigger finger and shot the man in the chest, just above the heart. The man took another step then the strength went from his legs and he collapsed, his mouth working soundlessly. Nightingale rolled over, pushed himself up from the floor.

Caitlin bent down and picked up Receding Hair's machete. She held it up and glared at Nightingale. He kept the Glock centred on her chest.

'Put it down, Caitlin,' he said. 'It's over.'

The second man's legs twitched and then went still.

'Put it down,' Nightingale repeated. 'I will shoot you.'

She shook her head fiercely. 'You won't.' She swished the machete from side to side. There was a manic look in her eyes as if she was staring through him rather than looking at him.

'Why are you doing this?' said Nightingale, his finger tight on the trigger, ready to react the moment she moved towards him.

She tried to smile but it turned into a snarl. 'You wouldn't understand,' she said. 'We serve Lucifer and providing we do his bidding without question we walk into Hell and sit on his left side.'

'Put it down, Caitlin. We can walk out of here. I can get you help.'

'I don't need help,' she sneered. 'I have my place in Hades.'

'And because of that you kill innocents in this world?'

'I serve my Master and will do so until I die.'

'You don't have to die, Caitlin,' he said.

She smiled. Her eyes seemed to be burning redly and her nostrils flared as her chest rose and fell. 'Yes, I do,' she said. She held out the machete and Nightingale's finger tightened on the trigger.

'Caitlin, drop the—'

Before he could finish she had switched her grip on the machete so the blade was upright. She grinned in triumph, then looked up at the ceiling and shouted at the top of her voice. 'My Lord, I am coming!' She placed the edge of the blade against her neck and in one smooth movement sliced her throat open from ear to ear. Blood washed down her shirt and she continued to stare at Nightingale for several seconds before the machete fell from her fingers and rattled on the floor.

Nightingale stared at her in horror, his eyes stinging from the cordite in the air. He was still pointing the gun at her chest, but his trigger finger had relaxed.

Caitlin was still smiling, even though several pints of blood had gushed from the gaping wound in her throat. He couldn't work out why she was still standing.

She opened her mouth and there was a gurgling sound like water disappearing down a drain. 'We're coming for you, Jack Nightingale,' she said, then she fell backwards and hit the floor so hard the television shuddered.

Nightingale's heart was pounding as if it was threatening to jump out of his chest. He shook his head, trying to clear his thoughts. The adrenaline coursing through his system was helping to sober him up. He stared at the gun in his hand. Then at the three bodies on the floor. Two shots. And Caitlin's screams. If anyone had phoned the police he only had a few minutes. If he stayed, he was in big trouble. The police would find him with a gun and two men shot dead and while he might well find a jury would believe he had acted in self defence he'd still have to explain why he had the Glock in the first place.

He took a deep breath, trying to focus his thoughts. If the police were on their way, he had to act fast. And even if they weren't, he still needed to be out of the flat as quickly as possible. His mind raced. What had he touched? Nothing. Caitlin had let him into the flat. She had unlocked the doors and opened them for him. He'd touched nothing so there were no surfaces to wipe down.

He tucked the Glock back into its holster then went over to the machete she'd dropped and picked it up. He carried it over to the kitchen area and pulled off a piece of paper kitchen roll. He used it to wipe the handle clean, then took it over to Receding Hair. He knelt down and placed the handle in Receding Hair's right hand, pressing it hard. He stood up. So Receding Hair had cut Caitlin's throat. Her blood was on the machete, the machete was in his hand.

The positions of the bodies weren't great. He was going to have to make it look as if Caitlin had shot the two men as they were heading towards her.

He bent over and pulled Receding Hair's legs so they pointed towards Caitlin. Then he did the same with the second man. There was something familiar about both men and suddenly he realised what it was. They had been helping to carry Marcus Fairchild's coffin.

He stood up and listened for a few seconds. No sirens. He walked over to Caitlin. Blood was pooling around her but there was none gushing from the throat. Her heart had stopped.

He closed his eyes and forced himself to concentrate. He needed to paint a picture that the police would believe. He was less unsteady on his feet now and the fog that had enveloped his mind was gradually dissipating. He opened his eyes, pulled out his Glock and wiped the butt with the piece of kitchen towel, then put it in Caitlin's right hand. The scenario would make sense. Two men with knives attacking a young girl. She has a gun and shoots them both but not before one of them had slashed her throat. There were a lot of holes in the story, not the least being how a young girl had a Glock in her possession, but it was better than the truth. The problem was SOCO would do a gunshot residue test on her hands and at the moment they were clean. He held her hand around the gun and forced her first finger on to the three triggers – the Glock's patented safety mechanism that prevented the gun from being fired accidentally. He aimed at the wall behind the two bodies. The investigating officers might be prepared to believe two lucky shots but only if there was at least one that had gone wide. Two would be better, he realised. Two shots followed by a pause and then two more, just in case there were neighbours counting. It would look as if she had shot twice and missed, then shot twice again and killed them. Sometime between the first shots and the second, Crew Cut managed to cut her throat.

Nightingale squeezed her finger against the triggers, keeping a tight grip on her dead hands. The first bullet hit the wall above the door, then he moved her hand to the right and fired again, this time at the wall above the television set. He let her arm fall to the floor then stood up. He took a quick look around then walked around her body, taking care not to get any blood on his Hush Puppies, then used the paper towel to open the door and let himself out. He stood in the hallway, which was in darkness, listening carefully. He didn't hear anything so he tiptoed down the stairs, taking care not to touch the walls or the bannister. He used the paper towel to open the door to the street. He took a deep breath before stepping out, half expecting to find himself staring down the barrels of an armed response unit, but the street was deserted. He kept his head down as he walked away.

45

Nightingale took deep breaths as he walked. He was still a little fuzzy but his head was getting clearer by the minute. He looked around, struggling to get his bearings, then realised that he wasn't far from Oxford Street. He walked past Tottenham Court Road Tube station and went down Oxford Circus station instead, figuring that if the police did start checking CCTV they'd only check the nearest station. He went down to the westbound platform. He felt exhausted but didn't want to risk taking a taxi home in case the driver remembered him. He kept his head down as he waited on the platform, though there were so many passengers he doubted that he would be identified even if the CCTV footage was examined.

The train arrived and it was busy but not packed and he managed to squeeze into a seat between a man with a large briefcase perched on his knees and a woman who kept muttering to herself. Nightingale folded his arms and kept his head down, wishing he had a hat. He got off at Bayswater and hurried back to his flat. As soon as he had let himself in, he switched on the kettle in the kitchen and went through to the bathroom and stripped off all his clothes. He put everything into the bath. As he took off his jeans he almost fell, staggering to the side and banging into the washbasin. He bent down and splashed cold water on his face. Caitlin had put something in his drink, he was sure of that, almost certainly GHB.

He tried to check the back of his head in the mirror but no matter how he twisted he couldn't get a decent look. He pressed his hand against the spot where he'd been hit but there didn't appear to be any blood, which he took as a good sign. If he hadn't spotted Caitlin in the mirror about to bash in his skull it would have been a lot worse.

He went back through to the kitchen and made himself two mugs of strong coffee, pouring a lot of milk into one to cool it down so he could drink it straight away. He picked up two black garbage bags and went back to the bathroom. He was reluctant to throw away a perfectly good pair of Hush Puppies, but he knew he had no choice. Even a good cleaning wouldn't remove the gunshot residue trapped in the sole or lace holes, and even the tiniest speck of blood would tie him to the killings. He put them in one of the bags and put his raincoat in another. Dry cleaning would get rid of any gunshot residue, but he could also leave the coat at the dry cleaner's for several weeks, out of harm's way.

He carried the rest of the clothes through to the kitchen and put them in the washing machine on the longest and hottest cycle, then drank his second mug of coffee.

He took a bottle of bleach from the cupboard under the sink and went back in the bathroom. He turned on the bath taps and poured in a good slug of bleach. When the tub was half full he sat in the water and washed himself carefully and methodically, then he used a plastic nailbrush to clean under his nails. When he'd finished he turned off the taps and pulled the plug, then stood up and rinsed himself under the shower. He shampooed his hair twice and then used conditioner and then rinsed himself a final time before stepping out of the bath and putting on a bathrobe.

His head was starting to clear and he made himself another cup of black coffee and took it through to his sitting room. He switched on the television, dropped down on the sofa and swung his feet up on to the coffee table. He now had a throbbing headache. He remembered he had a bottle of paracetamol in his bathroom cabinet so he went to get it and washed down two tablets with his coffee.

There was a football match on Sky TV but it was nothing more than wallpaper to Nightingale. He stared at the screen as he went through everything that had happened. No one had seen him going into the flat with Caitlin. No one had seen him leave. If the police had been called they would be inside the flat now. The scene-setting he'd done might fool them for a while, but the angle of the cut in Caitlin's neck was a worry. And there was no good reason why a young Goth girl would be carrying a Glock. If Nightingale was really lucky then the cops would assume Receding Hair and Crew Cut were the Goth killers and they had taken Caitlin to the flat to kill her. But if he was that lucky, he ought to go out and buy a couple of lottery tickets.

If the cops did start to look for someone else, the Glock would hopefully be a dead end. T-Bone had been positive the gun was untraceable. Nightingale was sure he'd left no trace of himself in the flat. And when he'd finished cleaning his clothes and disposing of his shoes, there'd be no trace evidence linking him to the killings.

46

Nightingale opened his eyes and groaned. It took him a few seconds before he realised where he was – lying on his sofa. He sat up and ran his hands through his hair. His head was aching, either from the drug that Caitlin had slipped him or from the bang on his head. He staggered over to his kitchen and drank from the cold tap, then pulled a bottle of malt whisky from a cupboard and poured himself a decent measure. He took the glass and the bottle back to the sofa. The television was on but he had muted the sound.

On the wall was a photograph of him and Robbie Hoyle on the day they'd graduated from Hendon Police College, both looking proud in the spotless new uniforms. Nightingale forced a smile and raised his glass. 'I'm going to miss you, Robbie,' he said. He drank. He could still taste garlic at the back of his mouth.

Next to the graduation photograph was a framed photograph of Nightingale with his father and uncle in front of the Old Trafford stadium. Nightingale's father – his adoptive father – had been a lifelong Manchester United fan, and so was his brother, Nightingale's uncle Tommy. He stared at the photograph, remembering the day that it had been taken.

His father was long dead, killed in a car crash with Nightingale's adoptive mother. It had been an accident, that was what the coroner had said, anyway. The man driving the petrol tanker that had crushed the Nightingales' car swore that he hadn't seen the red traffic lights and hadn't seen their car. He hadn't been drinking and he tested negative for drugs and his tachometer showed that he'd only been driving for four hours before the accident. William and Irene had simply been in the wrong place at the wrong time.

He raised his glass to the photograph of his uncle Tommy. 'At least you're still around,' he said. He drank some whisky and wiped his mouth with the back of his hand. As soon as the words had left the mouth he felt a sudden chill and his stomach lurched as he remembered what Tony Barnett has said, shortly before T-Bone had shot him. 'We've got a list, Nightingale. A list of your family, your friends, and everyone you care about. Everyone on that list is as good as dead.'

It had been two months since he had last spoken to his uncle and to his aunty Linda. He looked at his watch. It was three o'clock in the morning and while his aunt and uncle were usually in bed by ten they wouldn't be up and about for a couple of hours. He knew he should wait until the morning but the feeling of dread was growing by the minute. He reached for the phone and called their landline. The phone rang out, unanswered. He redialled and he let it ring longer this time, but still nobody answered. His aunt and uncle didn't have an answer machine and while they both had mobile phones they only had them in case of emergencies and rarely used them. He tried anyway. Both mobiles went straight through to the answering services but Nightingale didn't bother leaving a message.

For a moment he considered getting into his car and driving straight up to Manchester but he figured that the whisky and the drug that Caitlin had given him didn't make that a practical proposition so he drank two more glasses of whisky before falling into a dreamless sleep on the sofa, fully dressed.

47

Nightingale left his flat at eight o'clock in the morning after he'd showered, shaved and changed into clean jeans and a denim shirt. He phoned his uncle before he showered, and after, and again one last time before he left the flat. The calls went unanswered. He didn't make himself a coffee or breakfast, just headed downstairs and around the corner to Queensway, carrying the black bag and his raincoat. He dropped the black bag in a litterbin close to Queensway Tube station and then walked to the dry cleaner's that he had been using for the past three years. It was run by an Iraqi family who had fled Iraq during the nineties after one of Saddam Hussein's sons had taken a fancy to their daughter. Mrs Naghdi was behind the counter as usual, and she gave Nightingale a beaming smile when he walked in with his raincoat over his arm. 'How are you, Mr Nightingale?' she asked. She was in her fifties, a striking woman with olive skin and large brown eyes and a figure that always made Nightingale think about what a lucky man her husband was.

'Busy as always, Mrs Naghdi,' he said. He dropped the coat on the counter. 'Can you dry-clean this for me?'

'Of course,' she said. 'But first check pockets, Mr Nightingale. Always check pockets.'

Nightingale did as he was told. In one of the pockets he found the piece of paper that the receptionist at the Ink Pit had given him.

'See,' said Mrs Naghdi. 'Always check pockets.' She took the coat from him and printed out two receipts. She clipped one to his coat and gave him the other. 'I see you wear this coat long time but you never clean before,' she said.

'When will it be ready, Mrs Naghdi?' He slipped the piece of paper into his trouser pocket.

'Thursday evening.' She handed him the receipt. 'It says so on receipt.'

'And if I should lose the receipt, would it be a problem?'

'You never lose your receipt, Mr Nightingale. I know you how many years?'

'More than I can remember,' laughed Nightingale. 'But if lose my receipt, I can still get my coat?'

'Of course,' she said. 'I always remember you and your coat. No receipt, no problem.'

'You're a sweetheart, Mrs Naghdi,' said Nightingale. He left the shop and as he walked he screwed up the receipt and tossed it into a litterbin. He bought himself a coffee from Costa Coffee and then headed into a mobile phone shop. He bought a cheap Samsung phone and a pay-as-you-go SIM card with ten pounds' credit. The salesman set the phone up for him and Nightingale called T-Bone as he walked along Queensway. The call went straight through to voicemail, which meant he'd either turned his phone off or was making a call. 'T-Bone, this is Bird-man. I need another thing from you, same as last time. Soon as you can. This number is okay.' He ended the call and slipped the phone back into his jacket pocket and then went off in search of a shoe shop that would sell him a new pair of Hush Puppies.

48

Nightingale phoned Jenny from a service station an hour's drive from Manchester. 'I won't be in today,' he said.

'Helping out with Anna?'

'Sort of.'

'Please give her my best and tell her if there's anything she needs.'

'Her family's rallied round,' said Nightingale.

'Have they found the driver?'

'Not yet,' he said. 'Look, kid, why don't you call it a day and head off for the weekend?'

'It's ten o'clock in the morning, Jack.'

'I know, but there's nothing pressing. Why don't you take the CDs down to your parents, you can watch them there just as easily as in the office. And you can have all calls diverted to your mobile.'

'Are you sure?'

'Sure I'm sure. I won't be back today and tomorrow's Saturday.'

'Okay. I'll do that, thanks.'

'And say hi to your mum and dad.'

There was a short pause. 'Jack, are you okay?'

'I'm fine.'

'You sound a bit tense, that's all.'

'I'm still coming to terms with what happened to Robbie,' he said.

'I know how you feel,' she said. 'I still miss Uncle Marcus so much.'

Nightingale's jaw tensed. 'Sure,' he said. 'Anyway, you lock up and I'll see you on Monday.'

He ended the call, then phoned his uncle's number. It was the tenth time he'd called and as before it rang out, unanswered. He went into the service station and bought himself a coffee before continuing the drive north.

49

Nightingale found a parking space for his MGB across the road from his uncle and aunt's tidy three-bedroom semi-detached house in Altrincham, South Manchester. It was eleven o'clock in the morning. Their car, a black Renault Megane, was parked in the driveway. Nightingale wasn't sure if that was a good sign or not. He locked up the car, walked across the road making sure he looked both ways and opened the garden gate. His aunt and uncle spent hours working on the garden, tending its large rhododendron bushes, mowing the lawn and, for all he knew, polishing the twee stone wishing well and the bearded gnome with its fishing rod and line. He looked around for their cat, a black and white monster by the name of Walter, but there was no sign of it.

Nightingale rang the doorbell and said a silent prayer. The one thing he wanted in the world just then was to hear his aunt's slippers rubbing against the carpet and for the door to open and for him to see her smiling face. He pressed the bell again, longer this time. His heart was racing and his mouth had gone dry. His aunt and uncle were early risers, always had been. Part of him wanted to walk back to his car and drive away, but he knew he had no choice. He had to follow this through to the end, no matter what.

He walked around the side of the house and pushed open the wooden gate that led to his uncle Tommy's vegetable patch and prize-winning rose garden. He walked slowly towards the kitchen door and gingerly knocked on it. There was no answer. He didn't bother knocking again. He was sure now that neither his aunt nor his uncle would be opening the door. He walked across the lawn to his uncle's shed, opened the door and pulled a spade from the pile of garden tools next to the lawn mower. He walked slowly over to the kitchen window and used it to smash the window and knock the glass out of the frame before tossing the spade aside and climbing through on to the counter by the sink.

He clambered down and stood for a few seconds, listening intently, but all he could hear was the dull metallic clicking of the grandfather clock in the hallway. Uncle Tommy wound it once a week, every Sunday evening before he went to bed. Nightingale moved on tiptoe across the kitchen, then realised how ridiculous it was to be creeping around.

He found his aunt in the sitting room, her unseeing eyes staring up at the ceiling, the dark bruises on her neck proof that she had been strangled, the blood on her fingernails evidence that she had tried to defend herself. She was wearing her nightdress, which meant that she had been killed early in the morning or late at night. A forensic expert would know for sure by checking the temperature of the liver, but it didn't make any difference to Nightingale because all that mattered was that Aunty Linda was dead.

He backed away from the body and went slowly upstairs, fighting to keep breathing slowly and evenly. He already knew all that he needed to know and part of him, the sane part, the logical part, was screaming at him to turn around and leave the house and get as far away from it as possible. But the other part, the part that was always getting him into trouble, was telling him that he had to see for himself what was upstairs. He had to see Uncle Tommy with his own eyes, even though he knew with every fibre of his being that he was dead.

The body was in the bathroom. In the bath, to be specific. Under water. His eyes too were open wide, staring lifelessly up at the single shaded light hanging from the ceiling. The tiled floor was still wet from where his struggles had sent water cascading over the side of the bath. He was wearing his pyjamas and the trapped air in the wet fabric made him look twice his true size. One foot, the left one, was jammed over the cold tap, and his right leg was trapped under his left. Water was dripping slowly from the hot tap making soft, regular plopping sounds.

Nightingale closed his eyes and put his hands over his face. 'I'm sorry, Uncle Tommy,' he whispered. 'I'm so, so sorry.' It was his fault that his aunt and uncle were dead, of that Nightingale was sure. If proof were needed it was written across the mirror above the sink in what appeared to be lipstick. Seven words. WE ARE COMING FOR YOU, JACK NIGHTINGALE.

50

Nightingale spent ten minutes in the bathroom, cleaning the message off the mirror with bleach and then washing it down with water. He wore a pair of yellow Marigold gloves that he'd found in the cupboard under the kitchen sink as he worked. When he'd finished he went downstairs and unlocked the back door before wiping his fingerprints off the handle of the spade and returning it to the garden shed. He wiped all the surfaces of the shed that he'd touched, and the kitchen door and the garden gate. When he left he took the gloves with him.

He drove back to London on autopilot, barely aware of his speed or the traffic around him. He had hoped that Tony Barnett had been lying, that the threats he'd made were those of a man who knew he was going to die and who wanted to lash out at his tormentors. But now he knew the truth: the Order of Nine Angles were after him and they would keep coming after him until he and everyone he cared about was dead. The Order had members all over the world, rich and powerful men with the resources to get away with murder.

When he reached London he drove to Camden. He left his MGB in a multi-storey car park a short walk from

Camden Lock market. The Wicca Woman shop was tucked away in a side street between a store selling hand-knitted sweaters and socks and another specialising in exotic bongs and T-shirts promoting cannabis use. Nightingale pushed open the door and a small bell tinkled somewhere above his head. Alice Steadman was unpacking a cardboard box, taking out small packages of incense sticks and arranging them in a glass display case. She smiled when she saw him. 'Mr Nightingale, this is a nice surprise,' she said. She was in her late sixties, a tiny pixie of a woman. Her grey hair was tied back in a ponytail and her skin was wrinkled but she had the greenest eyes that Nightingale had ever seen, eyes that burned with a fierce intensity. She was dressed all in black, a long tunic with silver buttons over skin-tight leggings and black ankle boots with tassels on the side. Around her waist was a black braided belt from which hung dozens of silver moons and stars. 'What brings you to my little shop?'

'I need your help, Mrs Steadman.'

'Do you now?' she said. She smiled brightly. 'How about we start with a nice cup of tea?' There was a beaded curtain behind the counter and Mrs Steadman pulled it back. 'Alana, be a sweetie and mind the shop for a while, will you?'

There was a clatter of footsteps on wooden stairs and a pretty blonde girl with her hair in pigtails appeared. She was wearing a black T-shirt that seemed to have been hacked with a razor blade and a black leather miniskirt. She was a good six inches taller than Mrs Steadman and had long nails that she'd painted blood red. Mrs Steadman took Nightingale through into the back room where a gas fire was burning. She waved

Nightingale over to a circular wooden table above which was a brightly coloured Tiffany lampshade. She switched on a kettle on top of a pale green refrigerator. 'You still take milk and sugar?'

'I do indeed,' said Nightingale, pulling out a chair and sitting down. Mrs Steadman spooned PG Tips into a brown ceramic teapot. 'I need your help, Mrs Steadman.'

'Yes, my dear, you said. What appears to be the problem?'

Nightingale pointed at the chair next to him. 'Please, sit down, will you?' Mrs Steadman did as he asked. 'I'm in trouble, Mrs Steadman. The Order of Nine Angles are after me. They want me dead. They've killed my aunt and uncle and my friend Robbie and they're not going to stop until they've killed me.'

'They are a nasty bunch of people, that's true,' she said.

'I have to stop them before they go any further. Can you help me?'

'They are angry at you because you helped kill one of their own, Marcus Fairchild.' It was a statement, not a question.

'How did you know that?'

'There isn't much that escapes me,' she said. 'You must have known that when you caused harm to Marcus Fairchild there would be repercussions?'

'I guess I didn't think that far ahead,' he said.

'You assumed that they wouldn't find out? You thought you had covered your tracks?'

'I suppose so, yes.'

'And you were wrong.'

'Clearly.'

'And now you are paying the price.'

'Yes.'

The kettle finished boiling and switched itself off. Mrs Steadman smiled and got up to make the tea. She carried the teapot to the table on a tray with two blue and white striped mugs and a matching milk jug and sugar bowl. She sat down and poured tea for him, then added milk and sugar.

'Mrs Steadman, can you help me?'

She looked at him over the top of her spectacles, which were perched on the end of her nose. 'Who exactly do you think I am, Mr Nightingale?'

'You're Mrs Steadman.'

She smiled. 'Perhaps I should rephrase the question,' she said. 'What do you think I am?'

Nightingale could feel his nicotine craving kicking in but he knew Mrs Steadman didn't approve of smoking. 'You're an angel,' he said.

'And what do you think an angel is?'

Nightingale screwed up his face as he considered the question. 'I don't know,' he admitted eventually. 'I guess angels do good. They help people.'

She shook her head. 'I'm afraid it's not as simple as that,' she said.

'I know you don't have haloes or even wings and you don't sit on clouds playing harps but . . .' He shrugged. 'You're with the forces of good.'

'There's that word again,' she said. 'Good.'

'But you are, right? There's good and there's evil. And you're on the side of good. Or have I got this wrong?'

Mrs Steadman sipped her tea. 'It's about order, not about good or evil,' she said. 'Angels are there to maintain order. To make sure things happen as they should.' She put down her mug. 'If angels made good things happen, don't you think there would be less evil in the world? Children get sick and die. Innocents are murdered. Nuns are raped. Don't you think angels would prevent that if they could?'

Nightingale was lost for words. He just sat back in his chair and waited to see what she would say next.

'Angels aren't policemen, Mr Nightingale. Angels don't go around stopping bad people doing bad things. We're more like judges. But we only interfere if the order of things is threatened from outside.'

'Outside?'

'Change can only come from outside and when it does come, we may act. But we don't act because something evil is happening. We act because the order of things is threatened.'

'Are you saying there's nothing you can do?'

She smiled thinly. 'No, I'm saying there's nothing I *will* do. It's not my place to interfere. What happens, happens. If it's meant to happen, it will.'

'Because it's God's will?'

'Because it's the order of things, Mr Nightingale.'

'So if I'm meant to die, I'll die?'

'You all die, Mr Nightingale. That's how it is for you. You are born, you live, you die, and your souls move on. We angels are here to make sure order is maintained during that process.'

'So I have no free will, is that what you're saying?'

'What I'm saying is that angels cannot interfere. Not unless the order is threatened.'

Nightingale sat back in his chair. 'Mrs Steadman, I really need your help.'

'I know you do. I'm sorry.'

'Even though the Order of Nine Angles are killing everyone I care about, and they've already tried to kill me, there's nothing you can do?'

'It's not my place to interfere, Mr Nightingale.' She clasped her hands together on the table. 'But I shall watch what happens with interest.'

51

Nightingale left his MGB in the rooftop car park at the Whiteleys shopping centre in Queensway. On the way back to his flat he found himself constantly looking over his shoulder. He let himself in, locked the door and then made himself a coffee before phoning Jenny. 'Where are you?' he asked.

'Driving to my parents as we speak,' she said. 'Is everything okay?'

Everything wasn't okay, thought Nightingale. Everything was as far from okay as it could possibly be. 'Sure,' he lied. 'Just be careful.'

'What do you mean?'

'I mean drive carefully,' he said. 'There are a lot of idiots on the road.'

'You shouldn't be on your own, Jack,' she said. 'Why don't you come down to my parents, too? There's always a spare room for you, you know that.'

'I've got a lot on,' he said.

'You need to be with someone,' she said. 'I know how much Robbie meant to you.'

'I'll be okay.'

'You shouldn't be alone at a time like this.'

'I won't be,' he said. 'I'm going to see someone this afternoon.'

'Well, don't drink too much. Alcohol won't help.'

Nightingale laughed. 'I know,' he said.

He phoned T-Bone and the call went straight through to voicemail. 'You need to get back to me right now,' he said. 'This is urgent, T-Bone. And keep your back to the wall. Call me.'

He ended the call and paced around his sitting room. He wanted a drink but now was not the right time for alcohol. For what he had to do he needed to be totally sober and focused. He needed help and he knew of only one person who could provide it. Proserpine.

52

Nightingale straightened up, put his hands on his hips and surveyed his work. He'd spent the best part of an hour scrubbing the floor of his lock-up and it was probably now clean enough to eat off. He'd left his MGB in the Whiteleys car park and told Jenny that he'd be busy all afternoon. He placed his bucket and scrubbing brush next to the wall furthest from the metal door, took a final look around and then headed back to his flat.

He showered twice using a fresh bar of coal tar soap and used a brand-new nailbrush to clean under his finger and toenails. He shampooed his hair twice and then rinsed it for the best part of ten minutes before drying himself with a new towel. He put on clothes that had all been dry-cleaned and a new pair of Adidas trainers that he'd bought the previous day. He'd put everything he needed in two black bags in the kitchen and he collected them and walked back to the lock-up, his hair still damp. He let himself in, switched on the light and pulled the shutter down. He emptied his pockets and put his wallet, watch, cigarettes and lighter next to the bucket. He knew that to take anything that wasn't scrupulously clean into the protective circle would weaken it and put his life – and his soul – at risk.

He opened the two black bags and carefully placed the contents on to the concrete floor. From a small box he took a piece of white chalk and used it to carefully draw a circle about six feet in diameter then he used a small branch that he'd ripped from a birch tree on Hampstead Heath that morning to gently brush around the outline of the circle. That done he put the branch back into one of the bags and used the chalk to draw a pentagram inside the circle, making sure two of the five points faced north. Finally he drew a triangle around the circle with the apex pointing north and wrote the letters MI, CH and AEL at the three points of the triangle, spelling out the name of Michael, the Archangel.

He stood up and checked that everything was exactly as it should be, then he picked up a small bottle of consecrated salt water, removed the glass stopper and carefully sprinkled water around the circle. He took five large white church candles and placed them at the five points of the pentagram, then used his lighter to light them one at a time in a clockwise direction.

His heart was starting to race and he stood for a minute taking deep breaths to calm himself down before picking up a Ziploc bag containing a mixture of herbs. He moved clockwise around the circle sprinkling the herbs over the candle flames. Once he had done all five he poured the remainder of the herbs into a lead crucible. He set it down on the floor in the middle of the protective circle and used his fingers to mould the herbs into a neat cone before igniting it with his lighter.

The herbs crackled and the air was filled with fumes that stung his eyes and made them water. He stood up, coughing and spluttering, and pulled a piece of paper from his back pocket. He had carefully written down the Latin incantation that had to be said perfectly if the spell was to work.

He took a final look around the circle to check that he hadn't forgotten anything, then slowly and carefully he read out the words on the paper, raising his voice until by the time he reached the end he was shouting. '*Bagahi laca bacabe!*'

The fumes from the burning herbs began to spin around him as if he was at the centre of a miniature tornado. There was a strong smell of burning, as if an electric circuit had blown, and the floor was vibrating beneath his feet. The acrid fog swirled around him, faster and faster, and it was already so thick that he couldn't see the walls or ceiling of the lock-up. The single fluorescent light above his head was just a dull patch of whiteness in the fog. Suddenly lightning flashed and he flinched, but he stood his ground, knowing that it would be all over if he stepped out of the protective circle.

Lightning flashed again and there was a deafening crack of thunder that left his ears ringing. Nightingale's eyes streamed with tears. He shoved the paper back into his pocket and wiped his eyes with the back of his hands. He was finding it hard to breathe; it was as if his lungs were filled with acid and every movement of his chest made him wince. He forced himself to breathe tidally, taking the minimum amount of foul air into his pain-racked lungs.

There were two flashes of lightning that were virtually instantaneous and then time folded in on itself and there were a dozen or so quick flashes as if a paparazzo's flash gun had gone off and then she was there, standing in a space between the tip of the north-facing point of the triangle and the edge of the circle.

53

Nightingale's eyes were watering from the fumes of the burning herbs and he blinked away the tears. His heart was racing but he knew he had nothing to fear. According to the spell, Proserpine had to stay where she was until he released her. And providing he stayed within the protective circle, she could do nothing to harm him. That was the theory, anyway.

She was wearing a long leather coat, open at the front, with large lapels that flapped in the swirling fog. The lapels were dotted with silver symbols – an ankh, an upside-down cross, a pentagram, and various others that made no sense so him. Her jet-black hair was longer than the last time he'd seen her, and cut with a fringe that almost obscured her eyes. Her lipstick was as black as her hair and her face was deathly white, as pure and untainted as porcelain.

Under her coat she wore a cropped black T-shirt that revealed a navel pierced with a small silver crucifix. The navel always confused Nightingale because Proserpine was a demon from the bowels of hell, which meant that she didn't have a mother, which meant no umbilical cord.

'It's a fashion statement,' said Proserpine.

'Did you just read my mind?'

'You were staring,' she said. In her right hand she was holding a steel chain leash attached to the collar of her black and white collie. The dog was staring at Nightingale with a look that said it would like nothing more than to leap into the pentagram and rip him apart but Nightingale knew the protective circle would prevent it from doing that. Hopefully. Proserpine jerked the chain and the dog sat down obediently, its eyes still fixed on Nightingale.

'I've told you before, Nightingale, I can't abide being summoned.' Her eyes were black pools of emptiness and though her voice was dull and flat it still echoed off the garage walls.

'It's important,' he said.

'Not to me, it's not.' She pointed down at the pentagram. 'You can summon a demon if you wish to make a deal; we are not to be called just because you have a question you want answering. That's what Google is for.'

'Things are happening to me and I need to know if you're behind it.'

She laughed and the ceiling vibrated, sending a shower of dust down through the swirling fog. 'You're not the centre of my universe, Nightingale. You think too highly of yourself.'

'People around me are dying,' he said. 'And I'm getting messages saying that I'm next.'

'Life is hard, Nightingale. Deal with it.'

'If it's you, then tell me to my face. And tell me why. Is it because I won back my soul? Are you playing some sort of sick game with me?'

'You think I'd waste my time playing games?'

'I think that people who answer a question with a question often have something to hide.'

Proserpine threw back her head and roared with laughter. The entire lock-up vibrated and Nightingale almost lost his balance. The sound was deafening and he put up his hands to block out the sound. The dog got to its feet and began barking.

Proserpine stopped laughing and jerked the dog's chain to quieten it. 'Hush, baby,' she said. The dog sat obediently but continued to stare at Nightingale with undisguised hatred.

'I'm normally good with dogs,' he said.

'And not so good with people,' said Proserpine.

'My friend Robbie died two days ago,' said Nightingale. 'It was a hit and run. And from the sound of it, the van was involved in the murders of a group of South London drug dealers that I'd been involved with.'

'You should be more careful of the company you keep.'

Nightingale ignored her. 'Whoever killed the drug dealers wrote a message on the mirror. In blood. Saying that they were coming for me.'

Proserpine shrugged. 'I'm not a big fan of messages on mirrors,' she said.

'So it's not you?'

'If it was, Nightingale, if I did want to make your life a misery, what would you do about it?'

'Ask you to stop.'

'And you think that would work?'

'Look, if it's not you, who is it?'

Proserpine shook her head. 'It doesn't work like that, Nightingale. I'm not the phone-a-friend option to be used whenever you're in trouble.'

'I have to offer you a deal before you'll tell me anything, is that it?'

She sneered at him and shook her head scornfully. 'The only thing I want is your soul, Nightingale. And I know you'll never risk that again.'

'I thought we had a – I don't know – a special relationship? After what we've been through.'

'Then you thought wrong, Nightingale. I barely give you a moment's thought. Now are we done?'

'What if I say please?'

'What?'

'Pretty please. I need your help.'

'That's the best you've got?'

'It's all I've got. My back's up against a wall here. You're my only chance at . . .' He couldn't find the words to finish the sentence.

'What do you think is happening here, Nightingale?'

'To me?' He threw up his hands in frustration. 'Everyone close to me is dying. Robbie, my aunt, my uncle. It looks as if they're not going to stop until everyone I care about is dead. And then they'll finish me off.'

'And you think it's me doing it?'

'It's the Order of Nine Angles who are doing the killing, but someone has to have wound them up. They have a hotline to you and yours, right?'

She wrinkled her nose. 'Are you asking or telling?'

'They're devil worshippers. You're a devil. I need to know, Proserpine, did you set them on me?'

'You don't think that you've done enough to piss them off on your own?'

Nightingale folded his arms. 'Yes, I got Perry Smith to shoot Marcus Fairchild. But there's no way anyone could have known that.'

'What, criminals don't grass each other up? What planet are you living on?'

'No one knows that I knew Fairchild's dirty little secret.'

'Perry Smith knew. At least he knew that Fairchild was a child-killer. You neglected to tell him that he was also a Satanist, and a very powerful one at that.'

'Proserpine, is it you winding them up? Did you set the Order on me?'

She stared at him and he felt her eyes pulling him towards her. His right foot twitched and moved towards her as if it had a life of its own. The dog growled menacingly and she flicked its chain.

'Has someone accused me?'

'What if they have?'

She smiled slyly. 'Now who's the one answering a question with a question?'

'I just want a straight answer to a simple question. My life is falling apart and I want to know why.'

'And you thought I'd be able to point you in the right direction?'

'Sounds stupid, right?' Nightingale coughed. The herbs were still smouldering in the crucible, adding to the thick fog that swirled around them. 'One of the killers had a tattoo, the logo of the Order superimposed on a horned goat's head.'

'Sounds lovely. Why do I care?'

'He says that you gave it to him.'

'Did he, now? That's interesting.'

'Do you do that? Do you tattoo your followers?'

'I prefer to think of it as a brand,' said Proserpine.

'Did you brand him?'

Proserpine smiled thinly. 'Despite what you seem to think, I'm not psychic,' she said. 'Who are we talking about?'

'Barnett. Tony Barnett.'

She shook her head. 'The name doesn't ring a bell. Sorry.'

54

The fog was still swirling around them but Nightingale's eyes had stopped watering. 'You're just screwing with me, aren't you?'

'Maybe.'

'If it's you screwing with me, at least have the balls to tell me to my face.'

'Why should I? What do I have to gain by telling you anything?'

'My gratitude?'

Proserpine threw back her head and laughed again. The walls and ceiling throbbed as if they had a life of their own and another shower of dust fell from the ceiling.

Nightingale waited until Proserpine stopped laughing. 'You understand what's happening to me, don't you?' he asked.

'You thought you could change the past? How naive are you?'

'Are you saying that there's nothing I can do? That everything I've done has been a waste of time?'

'Nightingale, I had your soul in the palm of my hand. Your father, your real father, traded it to me for riches and power. You got your soul back by giving me something I wanted even more. That was a fair trade, I have no problem with that. But that wasn't enough for you, was it? You wanted to save that little girl so you did a deal with Lucifuge Rofocale and basically screwed him over. You died to save the innocent and that meant your soul was out of play.' She nodded slowly. 'It was a clever move, Nightingale. But you can't have expected Lucifuge Rofocale to have been happy about what you did.'

'I didn't plan it that way,' said Nightingale. 'I just wanted to save Sophie.'

'That might be true, but you made Lucifuge Rofocale look foolish and he'll never forgive you for that.'

'Are you saying that Lucifuge Rofocale is behind this?'

'I wouldn't put it past him. I'll tell you this much, Nightingale. If Lucifuge Rofocale is on your case, you're done for.'

Nightingale swallowed but his throat was so dry that he almost gagged. 'To be honest, it doesn't matter who's behind it, does it?' He held up his hand. 'That's rhetorical.'

'I figured that out for myself,' said Proserpine.

'If it is Lucifuge Rofocale then I'm screwed. If it's the Order of Nine Angles acting on their own then I'm still screwed because there's nothing I can do to stop them.'

'There's a lot of them, and they're pretty fanatical,' agreed Proserpine. 'You should be more careful about who you choose to piss off.'

'Pretty much the only hope I had was that it was you and I could appeal to your better nature,' said Nightingale.

Proserpine grinned and shook her head. 'You're a very funny man.'

'I'm not trying to be,' he said. His eyes were watering and he brushed the tears away with his right hand.

'Don't tell me you're crying,' she said quietly.

'It's the fumes,' hissed Nightingale. 'I can barely breathe in here.' He folded his arms again. 'I can only see one way out of this. One way that I can stop the killing.'

Proserpine raised a single eyebrow. 'Pray tell.'

'If I wasn't here, there'd be no point to the killings. If I wasn't around . . .'

'You think you can hide from them?' said Proserpine. 'The Order has people all over the world. Rich and powerful people, too. Heavy hitters. They're in most of the world's governments, police forces and intelligence organisations. That's what the Order does. You give your loyalty to the Order and in return you get your heart's desire.'

'And you sell your soul? Is that what happens? The members of the Order have all done deals?'

'Not necessarily,' said Proserpine. 'The Order has a power of its own, and a network of connections and favours on a par with the Masons.'

'They're devil worshippers.' It was a statement, not a question.

'Oh yes.'

'And they sacrifice children?'

'They sacrifice a lot of things,' she said. 'They're at the cutting edge of Satanism with direct lines to Lucifuge Rofocale among others.'

'What about you? Do you deal with them?'

Proserpine chuckled. 'That would be telling,' she said. 'But you can't run from them. Or at least you can't run for long.'

'I wasn't planning on running,' said Nightingale. 'I was planning on ending it. Killing myself.'

The dog growled softly and looked up at his mistress. She smiled at him. 'We won't be long,' she said. 'We're almost done here.'

'You heard what I said?' said Nightingale.

'I heard.'

'That would work, right? All this is about terrorising me. If I was dead, there'd be no point.'

'Your logic sounds irrefutable.'

'So here's my question,' said Nightingale. 'If I kill myself, do I go straight to Hell?'

'Without passing Go and without collecting two hundred pounds?'

'Well, do I?'

Proserpine's eyes narrowed. 'What is it you want, Nightingale? You want me to tell you if killing yourself is a good idea or not?'

'I want to know what the rules are? Do suicides burn in Hell, like the church says?'

'Like the Catholic Church says,' she corrected him. 'Let me say this: you don't want to be using the Catholics as the sole arbiter of Heaven and Hell. They have their own axes to grind.'

'So not all suicides go to Hell?'

'There are worse things than taking your own life,' said Proserpine. 'Have you put this question to your friend Mrs Steadman?'

'She wasn't very helpful,' admitted Nightingale.

'And you're surprised at that? Have you learnt nothing?'

'What do you mean?'

She shook her head sadly. 'You don't understand, do

you? Mrs Steadman and I are the same. We don't play favourites, we're not here to offer you a helping hand. We observe and we maintain order. Yes, I'm one of the Fallen and she isn't, but other than that we are the same.'

'You're an angel?'

'I'm a fallen angel.' She lowered her eyes and fluttered her long eyelashes. 'I've been a bad, bad girl.' She began to laugh and the walls shook again. 'If you're looking to Mrs Steadman for help, you're looking in the wrong place.'

'But you can help me, is that what you mean?'

'Are you ready to sell your soul? Because that's the only thing of valuc you have.'

'If I do that, you'll put a stop to this?'

'Are you ready to deal, Nightingale? Are you ready to offer me your soul?'

Nightingale stared at her for several seconds and then slowly shook his head. 'I'll find another way,' he said.

'Well, good luck with that,' she said. 'Are we done?'

Nightingale nodded. 'Yes, we're done.' He spoke the Latin words that ended the spell, there was an ear-splitting crack, space folded in on itself and she and the dog were gone. The strength suddenly drained from Nightingale's legs and he fell to his knees. He felt something wet trickle over his lips and he touched them with his hand. The fingers came away glistening with blood and he realised his nose was bleeding. He tried to get up but felt as weak as a kitten and he had to put both hands on the concrete floor to steady himself. The swirling fog began to disperse and he found it easier to breathe. Gradually his strength returned and he staggered to his feet. He pulled open the door to the lock-up and walked unsteadily into the sunlight. He wiped his nose with the back of his hand and then took out his cigarettes and lit one. As he blew smoke up at the sky the irony that he was replacing one foul atmosphere with another wasn't lost on him, but the nicotine craving overruled any sense of embarrassment.

55

Nightingale phoned Jenny as he walked back to Whiteleys shopping centre. She told him she was already at her parents' house and they were heading out to walk the dogs. 'Have you got a number for Eddie Morris?' Nightingale asked.

'The housebreaker?'

'Alleged housebreaker,' said Nightingale. 'He's never been convicted.'

'Only because you keep helping him get off,' said Jenny.

'Horses for courses,' said Nightingale. 'Eddie breaks into places and I keep him out of prison. It's the nicest bit of osmosis you'll find.'

'I think you mean symbiosis,' said Jenny. 'What do you need Eddie for?'

'Best you don't know,' he said.

'You want him to break into somewhere, that's the only reason you ever call Eddie.'

Nightingale grinned. 'Allegedly.'

'So Eddie is the friend you're going to be hanging out with? I'm not sure that's a good idea.'

'You worry too much.'

'I'll text you the number,' she said.

'Can you do something else for me? I need a number

for a guy called Joshua Wainwright. He's an American billionaire but keeps a low profile. I'm hoping you can Google or whatever it is you do and get me a number.'

'I'll see what I can do,' she said.

'He's from Texas, I think. Black and youngish. Thirty, maybe. Flies around in his own personal Gulfstream jet.'

'Nice work if you can get it,' she said. Nightingale ended the call and two minutes later his phone buzzed to let him know the promised text had arrived. It was Eddie's number, along with a promise that she would get back to him about Wainwright. He phoned Eddie and was relieved when he answered on the third ring. 'I need a favour,' said Nightingale.

'I guessed that,' said Eddie. 'Let's face it, that's pretty much the only time I hear from you.'

'So that's a yes, is it?'

Eddie laughed. 'No problem,' he said. 'Spot of breaking and entering, I suppose?'

'Just entering, I doubt that any breaking will be involved.'

'Where and when?'

'The where is Surrey. I'll meet you in a village called Hamdale. The house is about six miles from there so you can follow me in your car from there.'

'You're still driving that piece of crap, are you?'

'My classic MGB, you mean? Yes.'

'So you'll be easy to spot, then. You'll be the guy standing by the repair truck.'

'Soon as you can, Eddie.'

'Anything I should know about the place?'

'It's empty. Not overlooked. No burglar alarm. I just need you to get me inside.'

'And what's the name of this place?'

'Gosling Manor,' said Nightingale. 'I'll see you in Hamdale's main street.'

As he ended the call his phone buzzed gain. It was a text from Jenny with Joshua Wainwright's number. He sent her a text back. YOU'RE A STAR.

She replied almost instantly. I KNOW.

56

Nightingale drove slowly down the narrow country road. He took a quick look in his driving mirror to check that Eddie Morris was still behind him in his Jaguar. The road behind him was clear but as he braked the Jaguar came into view and Eddie flashed his headlights. Morris had got to Hamdale first and had been waiting when Nightingale pulled up in his MGB. As the two men had driven out of the village the sky had darkened and there were flecks of rain on Nightingale's windscreen. He flicked the wiper switch and the wipers groaned into life. He checked the driving mirror again and this time the Jaguar was close enough for him to make out the features of the man behind the wheel. Eddie was in his late twenties but looked almost a decade younger, with an acne-spotted forehead and spiky gelled blond hair. Eddie had a mobile phone pressed to his ear and was nodding animatedly.

Something flashed across Nightingale's vision and he stamped on the brake pedal as he realised a tractor was pulling out in front of him. The MGB's wheels shuddered and he swung the steering wheel to the left. The tractor accelerated away and the MGB's front bumper missed its back wheels by inches before the car skidded to a halt inches from a five-bar fence and stalled. Nightingale cursed, his heart racing.

The Jaguar pulled up behind him and Eddie beeped the horn. Nightingale wound down his window and waved before restarting the MGB and heading off down the road.

The rain grew heavier as he drove by a field of cabbages. There was a high stone wall to his left and he slowed, knowing that he was approaching the main entrance. Ahead of him he saw a large circular metal mirror attached to a tree and he indicated a left turn. He pulled up in front of black metal gates and a sign that said GOSLING MANOR, leaving room for Eddie to park next to him.

As the Jaguar drew up alongside the MGB, Nightingale reached over and pulled a pair of bolt-cutters from under the passenger seat. As he climbed out of the car, Eddie wound down his window. 'Looks like you don't need me,' he said, nodding at the bolt-cutters.

'This is the easy part,' said Nightingale. There was a thick chain linking the two gates and a brass padlock. He used the cutters to cut the hasp of the padlock and unravelled the chain before pushing the gates open. On the other side of the gates a narrow paved road curved to the right through thick woodland.

He waved Eddie to drive on to the house and then got back into the MGB and put the chain and the bolt cutters under the passenger seat. He restarted the engine and followed Eddie. The paved road merged into a parking area large enough to park several dozen vehicles, and in the middle stood a massive stone fountain. There was no water in the fountain, the centrepiece of which was a weathered stone mermaid surrounded by dolphins and fish. By the time Nightingale had parked next to the fountain, Eddie was already out of his Jaguar, looking up at the roof with his hands on his hips. The rain had stopped but there were still heavy grey rain clouds overhead. The house was built of local stone with upper facades of weathered bricks two stories high, topped by a tiled roof almost the same colour as the bricks and with four towering chimney stacks. The walls were covered with a thick layer of ivy that had been growing for decades, with some of the vines as thick as a man's wrist. The main entrance was shrouded in ivy around a massive oak door that gleamed in the sunlight.

Nightingale took a torch from the glove compartment and joined Eddie. Together they looked up at the house. 'How much lead do you think is up there?' Eddie asked.

'Don't even think about it, Eddie,' said Nightingale.

'Who owns it?" asked Eddie. 'Must be worth what, three million? Four?'

Nightingale feigned disinterest. 'Not sure,' he said.

'Like you said, no alarm,' said Eddie. 'Plenty of CCTV though.' He nodded at a camera covering the front door, and another up by one of the chimneys that covered the main driveway. 'In fact it looks like we're on *Candid Camera* already.'

'There are cameras inside as well but there's no need to worry about them. There's no external feed. Just a hard drive and I can wipe that.'

Eddie looked across at Nightingale. 'You seem to know a lot about the place.'

'Mate, I just need you to get me inside without causing any damage.' He took out his cigarettes and lit one, before gesturing at the door. 'Front or back?'

'It's not as if we're overlooked, is it?' said Eddie. He reached into his bomber jacket and took out a small leather case. He unzipped it to reveal a dozen metal picks of varying shapes and sizes. 'And just to be sure – there's no rotting corpse in there?'

'Not that I know of,' said Nightingale. 'Cross my heart and hope to die.'

As Eddie jogged up the stone steps to the front door, Nightingale blew smoke up at the roof. Next to the main building was a single brick block with four garage doors, painted white to match the house's window frame. There was a conservatory that looked as if it had been added as an afterthought, and a wing beyond the conservatory that was at right angles to the main building.

Eddie bent over the lock, his head cocked to one side as he worked on it. He hummed to himself, then Nightingale heard the lock click. There was a second lock, close to the door handle, and that one opened in less than a minute. Eddie stepped back, grinning. 'Easy, peasy,' he said, slotting the picks back into the case.

'You're a star, Eddie,' said Nightingale.

Eddie pushed open the door. 'You're sure there's no alarm?'

'Positive,' said Nightingale.

Eddie stepped into the wood-panelled hallway, his shoes squeaking on the marble floor. He looked up at a massive chandelier hanging from the ceiling. 'That's worth a pretty penny,' he said.

'Don't even think about it, Eddie,' said Nightingale. He flicked the light switch by the door but nothing happened.

'Power must be off,' said Eddie. He walked across the hallway and pushed open an oak door. It opened into a large room with a vaulted ceiling and a huge white marble fireplace. Along one wall was a line of windows that looked over ornamental gardens with bushes that had been trained into the shapes of exotic animals. Eddie pointed at what looked like a giraffe. 'Someone with too much time on their hands,' he said.

'Eddie, it's time for you to push off,' said Nightingale.

He looked out of the window. The sky was darkening as the sun dipped down below the horizon.

'There's a letter for you here, Jack,' said Eddie, reaching for an envelope on the mantelpiece.

'Put it back,' said Nightingale.

'It's addressed to you,' said Eddie.

'Eddie, will you just do as you're told,' said Nightingale. 'Put the bloody thing back where you found it.' He watched Eddie walk back to the mantelpiece and replace the envelope. Nightingale took out his wallet and gave Eddie a handful of fifty-pound notes.

Eddie grinned as he took the money. 'Always a pleasure doing business with you,' he said.

'Now listen to me, Eddie, and listen good,' said Nightingale. 'Get back in your car and drive away from here. Don't ever come back. And you need to forget you ever knew me.'

Eddie's forehead creased into a frown. 'Are you serious?'

'As cancer, Eddie.'

'Are you in trouble?'

'Nothing you can help me with.'

'I know people, Jack.'

'Yeah, I know people too, Eddie. But I have to handle this myself. And you need to put a lot of distance between us. Get rid of your phone. Get a new phone and new SIM card. Don't ever call me again. Don't ever tell anyone that you know me. If anyone ever asks you about me, you know nothing.'

'Who's going to be asking about you?'

'Are you listening to me? It doesn't matter who asks. You don't know me.' He dropped what was left of his cigarette on the floor and stamped it out. 'I'm bad news, Eddie. The worst possible news. Now get the hell out of here and don't look back.'

Eddie opened his mouth to protest but Nightingale pointed a warning finger at his face. 'Just piss off,' he said.

'There's no need to be a prick about it,' said Eddie. He turned on his heel and walked out of the room. Nightingale took his cigarettes out of his pocket and lit one. He was holding the smoke deep in his lungs when he heard Eddie drive off in his Jaguar.

57

Nightingale walked back into the main hall and blew smoke as he stared at the panelled wall. He stepped forward, reached out with his left hand and gripped a section of carving. He pulled it and the panel swung open smoothly. There was a light switch just inside the doorway and Nightingale clicked it on. Nothing happened. He switched on his torch, seized a brass banister with his left hand and slowly went down the wooden stairs. The basement ran the length of one of the wings of the house. The walls were lined with book-filled shelves and down the middle of the space were two lines of display cases. At the bottom of the stairs were two large red leather Chesterfield sofas either side of a coffee table piled high with books, and a huge desk that was covered in newspapers. There was an antique globe that was almost four feet high and a massive oak table with more than a dozen candles on it. Molten wax had dripped from the candles down the legs of the table and pooled on the floor.

Despite the cigarette in his hand, Nightingale wrinkled his nose at the bitter, acrid smell that pervaded the basement. His stomach lurched and for a moment he tasted bile at the back of his mouth and came close to throwing up. He swallowed and grimaced. He walked past a display case filled with skulls, then by a cabinet filled with knives, some of which were spotted with what appeared to be dried blood. The next display case was full of crystal balls, and the one after that was full of what seemed to be shrunken heads, leathery fist-sized lumps with straggly hair and pig-like noses.

He found a trunk full of black candles and took out a dozen, spacing them around the basement and lighting them. The flickering flames cast strange shadows on all the surfaces, moving like living things.

There were half a dozen LCD screens on the wall in two banks of three. In front of the screens was a black wooden desk with a straight-backed chair. There was a large stainless-steel console dotted with labelled buttons on the desk. Nightingale sat down and lit a cigarette and studied the console. There was no sign of the power being on and no matter what he did the screens stayed blank so it looked as if the cameras weren't recording.

He stood up and walked back along the bookshelves. Most of the books were leather-bound and clearly very old. It took him the best part of an hour to find the three volumes that he was looking for and he took them over to the coffee table by the stairs before flopping down on one of the sofas. He took out his mobile phone and tapped out the US number that Jenny had given him. It was just after nine so he figured it was early afternoon in the United States.

The woman who answered had a no-nonsense clipped tone that suggested he was wasting her valuable time by just calling her. 'Joshua Wainwright's office. This is Elizabeth speaking.'

'Hello, Elizabeth. Is Joshua there?'

'Who's calling?' she asked.

'My name's Jack Nightingale.'

'Does he know you, Mr Nightingale?' she asked, though her tone suggested that she knew the answer already.

'Not in this life, no,' said Nightingale, immediately regretting the flippancy. 'No. But it is important.'

'Can you tell me what it is in connection with?'

'It's personal,' he said.

'I'm sorry, Mr Wainwright doesn't have personal conversations with people he doesn't know,' said the woman, briskly. 'Thank you for calling.' She ended the call.

Nightingale grinned, lit a cigarette and swung his feet up on to the coffee table before redialling.

'Joshua Wainwright's office. This is Elizabeth speaking.'

Nightingale blew smoke up at the ceiling. 'Elizabeth, this is Jack Nightingale again. I think we might have got off on the wrong foot just then. I have something that Joshua wants. Could you just please give him a message and I'm sure he'll get back to me.'

'Mr Wainwright is a very busy man,' she said.

'I understand that, Elizabeth. But what I have, he wants, big-time. So please just take a message. Tell him I have a copy of *The Formicarius*, first edition, printed in 1475. Written by Johannes Nider, but of course he'll know that. And it has the special cover, he'll know what I mean by that. Also tell him that I have three books by Aleister Crowley. *Magick Book 4*, *Liber Al Vel Legis*, and his personal diary. So that's four books in all.'

'Are you a dealer, Mr Nightingale?'

'No, but I have those four titles for him.' Nightingale gave her his mobile number and cut the connection. He stared up at a damp patch in the ceiling above his head as he blew smoke up at one of the fluorescent lights. He was just about to finish his cigarette when his mobile rang. He stubbed out the cigarette and took the call.

'Jack Nightingale?'

'Joshua, thanks for calling me back.'

'Boy, you'd better not be pulling my chain or I'll be madder than a bobcat caught in a piss fire.' Wainwright had the laconic drawl of an elderly Texas rancher but Nightingale knew that the man on the other end of the line was barely into his thirties.

'I've no idea what that means, Joshua, but this is no hoax. I've got the four books for you, on the table next to me.'

'Name your price,' said Wainwright. 'I'm serious, just tell me what you want.'

'Where are you?' asked Nightingale.

'The good old US of A,' said Wainwright. 'Where are you?'

'England,' said Nightingale. 'I need a sit-down with you and you're the one with the private plane so when can you get here?'

'I'm on my way,' said Wainwright. 'I usually fly into Stansted. The private aviation terminal.'

'I know,' said Nightingale. 'What time?'

'I'll call you en route to confirm, but probably first thing in the morning. And you take care of those books, you hear?'

'I'll guard them with my life, Joshua, you can count on that.'

58

Nightingale snapped awake when his mobile phone buzzed to let him know he'd received a text message. It was from Wainwright, telling him that the plane would be touching down at 9.15. Nightingale yawned. He'd stayed late at Gosling Manor and hadn't got back to his flat until the early hours. He rolled out of bed, shaved and showered and pulled on a white shirt, a blue tie and a dark blue suit before heading down to his MGB.

He arrived at the private aviation terminal at Stansted just after nine and he was parking the car when Joshua Wainwright's sleek Gulfstream jet swept down on to the runway like a bird of prey. Nightingale stood by the side of his MGB and smoked a cigarette as the jet turned off the runway and taxied over to the terminal.

As the door opened and the stairs folded out of the plane, Nightingale ground what was left of his cigarette into the Tarmac before pulling open the boot and taking out a Tesco carrier bag containing the four books from the basement of Gosling Manor. He walked over to the plane just as a pretty blonde stewardess in a tight black skirt and crisp white shirt came down the stairs. She flashed him a professional smile. 'Mr Nightingale?'

'That's me,' said Nightingale.

'Would you show me some identification, please?'

Nightingale pulled out his wallet and handed her his driving licence. She studied it, compared the picture to his face, then smiled and gave it back to him. 'Follow me, please, Mr Nightingale.'

She headed back up the stairs and Nightingale went after her, getting a good look at a pair of legs that were possibly the best he'd ever seen.

Joshua Wainwright was wearing tight blue jeans, a red cowboy shirt, a pair of gleaming cowboy boots with silver tips on the toes, and a New York Yankees baseball cap. He was sprawled in a white leather armchair with his feet up on a matching footstool. He stood up to shake hands with Nightingale. He was tall, just over six feet, and looked like a young Denzel Washington. 'You're not what I expected, Jack,' he said in his lazy Texan drawl. 'Most of the booksellers I meet are grey-haired and smell of dust.'

'I'm not a bookseller, I'm a private eye,' said Nightingale. He held up the carrier bag. 'But I know you want these.'

Wainwright looked surprised. 'You've got them with you?'

'Of course,' said Nightingale. 'That's why I'm here.'

'I assumed you were going to talk up the price before you handed over the merchandise,' said Wainwright, taking the bag from him and sitting back down. 'To be honest I figured you were working a con. The books you mentioned, they're not in general circulation.' He pulled one of the books from the bag and his mouth opened in surprise. It was *The Formicarius*.

'This isn't about money,' said Nightingale, sitting down opposite the American.

Wainwright held up the book he was holding. 'Do you have any idea how much this is worth?'

'Two million euros,' said Nightingale.

Wainwright nodded, impressed.

'Can I smoke?' asked Nightingale.

'Go ahead,' said Wainwright. 'I'm a cigar man myself.'

'Yeah. I know.' Nightingale lit a cigarette as Wainwright slowly turned the pages of the book.

'This is amazing.' Wainwright looked up and his eyes were burning with a fierce intensity. 'Where did you get this?'

'It belonged to my father. He was a collector.'

'And you father was . . .?'

'He's dead now. And I'm his sole heir. And I need money.'

'Well, you've got it,' said Wainwright. 'I'll buy this from you, no questions asked. Money in the bank or cash in your hand.'

He put down the book and picked up a smaller one. His eyes widened. 'Now this one I really didn't believe you had,' he whispered. He held it up. 'You know what it is, right?'

Nightingale blew smoke and nodded. 'Aleister Crowley's personal diary.'

'So you know the significance of this book?'

'I know Aleister Crowley was one of the most powerful Satanists who ever lived,' said Nightingale. 'And I also know while that diary might well be priceless, I can never sell it to you.'

Wainwright grinned and nodded. 'You know about the curse?'

'It's not a problem. You can have it, as a gift.'

'You're a very generous man, Jack.'

'With the diary, I don't think I have a choice. From what I've heard, on the two occasions it was sold, both the buyer and the seller died shortly afterwards.'

Wainwright flicked through the handwritten diary. 'This really is priceless,' he said. 'I can't believe I have it in my hands.' He sat back and clasped it to his chest. 'I don't know what to say to you, Jack. I am stunned. Literally stunned. You have come from nowhere and given me my heart's desire.'

'That's good to hear, Joshua.'

'And I'm assuming that you want something in return.'

Nightingale smiled thinly. 'I need help, Joshua. I'm in a real mess and I'm looking for a way out.'

'You wanna tell me about it?'

'That's why I'm here.'

59

As Nightingale spoke, Wainwright lit a large cigar and by the time Nightingale had finished he'd smoked it down to the last couple of inches. He flicked ash into a large crystal ashtray on the table by the side of his chair. 'That's one hell of a story,' said the American.

'It's the truth,' said Nightingale.

'I'm sure it is.' He stubbed out what was left of his cigar and steepled his fingers under his chin. 'I had a feeling that we'd met before,' he said. 'A tickle at the back of my neck.'

Nightingale grinned. 'That's how I knew what books you wanted.'

'You did a deal with Lucifuge Rofocale and you went back?'

'It sounds crazy, right?'

'Not crazy. But a deal like that . . .' He shook his head. 'I've never heard of that being attempted. I need a drink.' He pressed a button in the arm of his chair and the blonde stewardess appeared with an eager-to-please-smile. 'Get me a whisky on the rocks, honey,' he said. Nightingale couldn't tell if it was her name or a term of endearment. 'What do you want, Jack?'

'A whisky's fine.'

'Two whiskies, honey. Glenlivet. He looked at Nightingale. 'Glenlivet's okay?'

'In my experience, any malt beginning with a G or an M can't be faulted,' said Nightingale. 'No ice in mine though, thanks,' he said to the stewardess. She smiled and walked away.

'That conversation. We had that last time,' said Nightingale.

'Which one?'

'About Glenlivet.'

Wainwright took off his baseball cap and ran a hand through his hair. 'So this is what, an alternate universe?'

'I think it's the same universe, it's just changed. But in a small way.'

Wainwright put his cap back on. 'But the girl she saved is now alive. That's no small thing.'

'There's a few people who died who are alive now. But that's the problem, Joshua. Everything that happened the first time is starting to happen again. I thought I'd changed things, but it looks as if all I did was to postpone it. Robbie died and then he was alive and now he's dead again. My uncle and aunt. They died and then they weren't dead and now they are. I tried putting off going to Gosling Manor because I thought that was the key to all this and look what's happened.'

'There are more books in the basement?'

'A whole library. I'm hoping that the answer lies somewhere in that basement, Joshua. There has to be a book there that can help me.'

'You have a plan?'

'The beginnings of one.' He gestured at the four books he'd given the American. 'I can get you more. Not too many because I need the library to be pretty much intact, but if you give me any other titles you want I'll see if I can find them.'

'And in return?'

'I need your help.'

'Anything I can do, I'll do it.' The stewardess returned with their drinks. Wainwright raised his glass and clinked it against Nightingale's. 'Now tell me about this plan.'

Nightingale sipped his whisky. 'I'm going to have to kill myself, Joshua. That's the only thing that will stop them.'

60

Nightingale drove from the airport to Gosling Manor. On the way he stopped off at a service station to fill up his tank and he bought half a dozen sandwiches, two cans of Coke, two of Red Bull and a coffee. He reached the house at just after midday and while it was bright and sunny outside, the house was cold and damp. He took his purchases down into the basement, using his torch until he had relit the candles. He took another bundle of candles from the trunk and lined them up close to the bookshelves before lighting them.

He stood and looked at the books. The shelves ran the full length of the basement and Nightingale did a quick calculation in his head. He decided there were close to one and a half thousand books. Many of them leather-bound and dusty and the writing on the spines had faded on many of them. He would have to take out each book to examine it. Assuming it took ten seconds to remove a book, look at it and replace it, it was going to take about four hours to check them all. There didn't seem to be any cataloguing and they weren't in any order that he could fathom so he didn't appear to have any choice other than to start at the top left-hand corner and work his way methodically through them.

It was an hour before he found the first book on Wainwright's list. It was a book written by a German Satanist, printed on hand-made paper that had turned beige with age. Nightingale flicked through it but it was written in German and he could make no sense of it. There were several diagrams scattered throughout the text, mainly designs of magic circles. Nightingale put the book in a cardboard box. He found the second book some thirty minutes later, a book on black magic written by a follower of Aleister Crowley. In the following hour he found another six books that were on Wainwright's wanted list.

Nightingale had been in the basement for almost three hours when he finally found the book that he needed. It was written by a former French priest, Joseph-Antoine Boullan, in the eighteen hundreds. According to Wainwright, Boullan was the most famous Satanist of the 19th century and at one point had claimed to be the reincarnation of St John the Baptist. He had written several books detailing Satanic rituals, but the very few that hadn't been destroyed were in the hands of private collectors.

Nightingale took the book over to the sitting area at the bottom of the stairs and dropped down on to one of the sofas. He sipped a can of Red Bull and ate a ham and cheese sandwich as he studied the book. It was handwritten, in French. Nightingale's French was very basic – he'd studied it at school but rarely used it – but Wainwright had written down the name of the ritual he was looking for and he found it in the index.

He flicked through the book to the chapter. It was fairly long, almost a dozen pages. There was a list of what he would need, then a diagram of the circle that had to be drawn, then two pages of what was obviously the Latin incantation that had to be spoken. His schoolboy French kept failing him and he realised he was going to need help with the translation. He stood up, switched on his torch and blew out all the candles one by one.

61

While he was driving back to London, Nightingale's mobile buzzed to let him know he'd received a text message. He pulled over at the side of the road and took out the phone. It was T-Bone. 'WE NEED TO MEET. TONIGHT. OK?'

Nightingale sent an SMS back. 'SURE. WHERE AND WHEN?'

A second text arrived. An address in Lewisham. And the words 'NOW. OK?'

Nightingale replied. 'ON MY WAY. BE THERE IN TWO HOURS'. He restarted the car and continued to drive to London. His first thought was to drive to Lewisham but the more he thought about it the more the texts worried him. T-Bone had used his regular mobile and not a throwaway. And in the past he'd always phoned and not sent texts. Nightingale drove to Beckenham and parked close to the station before flagging down a black cab and giving the driver the name of the road in Lewisham.

The sky was darkening and the streetlamps were coming on as they turned into the road. 'What number do you want, guv?' asked the driver.

'Just drive down the road slowly, then hang a left,' said Nightingale. He settled back in his seat and put his hand up to shield his face. The street was deserted. The pavements were empty. That worried Nightingale because in the early evening there was usually someone around.

'Left, yeah?' said the driver.

'Yeah, left and left again,' said Nightingale.

The taxi prowled back down the road parallel to the one they had been on. They went past a grey police van with half a dozen officers in the back. The lights were off but all the officers had riot gear on. Nightingale cursed under his breath.

'Do me a favour, hang a left at the end and then second left. Okay?'

'Sure, mate. It's your money. You lost?'

Nightingale forced a laugh. 'All these roads look the bloody same.'

The taxi made the two turns and they drove slowly parallel to the road where he was supposed to be meeting T-Bone. There was a black Jaguar parked on the left hand side. The interior light was on and the driver was reading a copy of the *Evening Standard*. Nightingale recognised the man. It was the man who usually drove Chalmers around.

When they reached the end of the street, Nightingale leaned forward. 'Tell you what, take me back to Beckenham,' he said.

'No problem, mate,' said the driver. 'Don't feel bad about it, sometimes I get lost around here.'

Nightingale took out his phone and sent a text message to T-Bone's phone. 'STUCK IN TRAFFIC BUT ON MY WAY'.

62

Nightingale had the taxi drop him close to Beckenham station and walked to his car. He lit a cigarette and then called Chalmers. It was clear from the superintendent's angry tone that he realised Nightingale was on to him. 'Where are you, Nightingale?' he said.

'Well, I'm not coming to see you, Chalmers, that's for sure,' said Nightingale. 'Did you think I'd fall for your silly little trap?'

Chalmers cursed under his breath and Nightingale smiled to himself.

'You need to come in and talk to us, Nightingale,' said the superintendent. 'We can sort this out.'

'Sort what out?'

'Let's talk about it face to face.'

'No, Chalmers, let's talk about it on the phone. Or I'm hanging up.'

'You're in trouble, Nightingale. Up to your neck in it. So if you've got an explanation you need to give it up now before it gets any worse.'

'What's happened, Chalmers? Why are you sending me texts on T-Bone's phone?'

'He's dead,' said Chalmers, flatly.

The news hit Nightingale like a blow to the solar

plexus, even though he'd been expecting it. 'How?' he asked.

'His throat was cut. And there was a note, on the bathroom mirror. Written in his blood. No prizes for guessing what it said.'

'You don't think I did it, surely?'

'You're stupid, but you're not stupid enough leave your own name at a murder scene,' said the superintendent. 'But you do appear to have been stupid enough to have left voicemail messages on a gangster's phone.'

Nightingale swallowed but didn't say anything.

'I don't have the exact words to hand, but it went something along the lines of you telling him that you needed something from him, same as the last time. So what were you buying from a gangster, Nightingale?'

'Alleged gangster.'

'Nothing alleged about T-Bone Williams, I can assure you of that. His record might not be as long as my arm but it's certainly longer than your dick.'

'Nice,' said Nightingale. 'Do you kiss your wife with that mouth?'

'I'm reaching the end of my patience, Nightingale. You're either buying drugs or weapons off him, now which is it? And just what is your connection to Perry Smith and T-Bone? How come their killers are throwing your name around?'

'I don't know.'

'Like hell you don't,' said Chalmers. 'And there's something else you should be aware of.'

'I'm listening.'

'We had three deaths in Soho on Thursday night. Two men and a Goth girl. And the men had tattoos that matched the design you gave me. More like brands than tattoos. But the same design, as near as damn it.'

'So?'

'So what the hell is going on, Nightingale? You obviously know more than you're letting on.'

'I've already told you what I know. You need to find out if anyone else who went to the Ink Pit ended up with that goat's head tattoo. If they did, they need protecting.'

'And the killers are in this Satanic group, the Order of Nine Angles?'

'I know it sound crazy, but yes.'

'And why is this Order of Nine Angles after you?'

'I don't know,' lied Nightingale.

'And that's where I don't believe you.'

'What do you want me to say, Chalmers?'

'I want the truth. Those registration numbers that you had Robbie Hoyle check out for you. You said some pensioner in Neighbourhood Watch gave them to you. You did say that, right? That's what you told me.'

'I guess so.'

'And now you're going all vague on me. You said some old woman saw the vehicles outside Stella Walsh's house. You said she was in the Neighbourhood Watch.'

Nightingale said nothing.

'And there you go being all coy again.'

'Get to the point, Chalmers.'

'I think you know what the point is. We've canvassed the area and there is no little old lady in the Neighbourhood Watch. So where did you get the numbers from? The numbers that you gave Robbie Hoyle.'

Nightingale stayed silent.

'It's the way you don't answer that tells me you're

involved in this, Nightingale. You get the registration numbers of two cars that you claim were in front of Stella Walsh's house. And within hours of Robbie Hoyle checking on those numbers for you, he gets mown down by a white van. Coincidentally one of the vehicles you asked him to check on was a white van. You and I both know that's not a coincidence. You worked with Robbie Hoyle and now he's dead. You owe him the truth, if nothing else.'

'You're right,' he said.

'Then come in and we'll do this properly.'

'I can't. Not just now.'

'You don't have any choice, Nightingale. We'll bring you in whether you like it or not.'

'I need time, Chalmers. Just a day or two.'

'Why?'

'I've got things to do,' said Nightingale.

'Then at least tell me what's going on. You owe that to Robbie Hoyle. If nothing else.'

Nightingale took a deep breath and exhaled slowly. 'How about this? I'll tell you what I know, but you have to do something for me.'

'What?'

'My assistant. Jenny McLean. She's staying with her parents, James and Melissa McLean. They've got a big pile in Norfolk. Edmund House. I need you to protect her.'

'You know how stretched the Met is these days,' said Chalmers.

'That's the deal, Chalmers. I'll tell you what I know and you protect Jenny.'

'She's in danger?'

'Yes.'

'Tell me what you know.'

'I need your word,' said Nightingale.

'You have it.'

Nightingale sighed. 'The guys who killed the Goths are the same people who killed Perry Smith and T-Bone. They're in the Order of Nine Angles. I think that most of the members have a brand, that goat's head thing.'

'You've told me that already.'

'I think that Ricky Nail saw the tattoo and started putting it on a few of his clients. The Order found out, tracked them down and killed them. They killed Nail, too.'

'And how do the deaths of Perry Smith and T-Bone fit into this?'

'Perry Smith killed Marcus Fairchild, and Marcus Fairchild was in the Order.'

'And why did Perry Smith do that?' asked Chalmers.

Nightingale took another deep breath. He could tell the truth or he could lie. But he was tired of lying. And lying wouldn't help him anyway. 'Because I told him that Marcus Fairchild was a child-killer and a paedophile.'

Chalmers went quiet for several seconds before speaking. 'Nightingale, you do not have to say anything, but it may harm your defence if you do not mention when questioned something which you later rely on—'

'Are you serious, Chalmers?' interrupted Nightingale. 'You're giving me the caution? I know what my rights are.'

'You realise what you're saying? You were involved in a conspiracy to commit murder.'

'I told Perry what Fairchild was. And I wanted Perry to kill Fairchild. I didn't know the Order would find out and that they would start to kill everyone involved. That's why I'm telling you, Chalmers. You need to track down the members of the Order. And you can start by looking for the owner of the white van, Billy McDowell. I'm pretty sure he's the one who killed Robbie and probably T-Bone too if T-Bone didn't get him first. You need to take a close look at Marcus Fairchild as well. Those guys with the dead Goth in Soho, I'm fairly sure they were pallbearers at Fairchild's funeral. I don't know their names but they were in the Order, the fact they had the goat's head brand proves that.'

'You're telling me you were there? In the flat?'

Nightingale took a deep breath. There was no point in hiding anything from Chalmers. 'Yes, damn it, I was there. They were trying to kill me.'

'And you shot them, right?'

'That doesn't matter, Chalmers. What matters is that you catch these bastards and stop them killing.'

'I'll decide what matters, Nightingale. We didn't think that slip of a girl could have taken out two grown men. So the Glock, that was yours?'

'You're not listening to me, are you? They were trying to kill me. The girl drugged me and took me back to the flat where they were waiting for me with a machete and a cleaver. Chances are they're the ones who butchered your Goths. That's how they were able to get close to them, they had their own Goth as bait.'

'You need to come in and make a full statement, Nightingale.'

'There's something I need to do first,' said Nightingale. 'But you need to get moving. Phone records, search their places, you need to find out who they were working with.'

'Where are you?'

'It doesn't matter where I am. Are you listening to me? They're your Goth killers. You've cracked the case and all the glory is yours. But you need to protect Jenny McLean until you have them all in custody. You promised, remember?'

'I remember. Now you listen—'

Nightingale ended the call and switched his phone off. He turned the ignition key and the MGB coughed but didn't start. He tried again and the engine turned over once and then stalled. 'Third time lucky,' Nightingale muttered to himself. 'Pretty please.' He turned the key and this time the engine kicked into life.

He knew he couldn't go back to his flat. Chalmers almost certainly had it staked out already and if he didn't there'd be men on the way as soon as their call had ended. Nightingale had to stay out of Bayswater. In fact he'd be better off staying out of the Met's jurisdiction completely until he had done what he had to do. He wasn't happy about spending the night at Gosling Manor but he didn't seem to have any choice.

63

Nightingale stopped at a pub about ten miles from Gosling Manor. He'd only eaten a couple of sandwiches during the day so he ordered a steak pie and chips to go with his bottle of Corona. He sat at a corner table and took out his book, notepad and pen. As he waited for his food he went through the chapter again, noting down the words and phrases that he didn't understand. Then he wrote down a list of everything that he would need. It was a long list, and several of the words that he couldn't translate were on it.

The landlady brought over his food and a selection of condiments. He tucked in and continued to make notes as he ate. When he'd finished he ordered a second Corona, switched on his phone and called Jenny.

'I've been calling you but your phone was off,' she said.

'I know. Sorry.'

'Your friend Superintendent Chalmers has been on to me and he's sending a car around to sit outside the house. Something about the Goth investigation taking a nasty turn. What's going on, Jack?'

Nightingale felt a surge of relief wash over him. At least Chalmers had kept his word. 'It's probably nothing,' he lied. 'But I think the killers know I've been working on the case so just to be on the safe side he's decided on a bit of police protection.'

'What about you?'

'I'm a big boy, Jenny, I can take care of myself.'

'How serious is this, Jack? I know how stretched the police are. They don't normally have the resources for twenty-four-hour-a-day guards.'

'It won't be long,' said Nightingale. 'Chalmers has a good lead on who they are, once they're caught it'll be over. You just enjoy the rest of your weekend. Now, are you sitting comfortably?'

'Am I what?'

'I need some help. How's your French?'

'Better than my Japanese but not quite as good as my German. Didn't you ever read my CV?'

'Can I run some French words and phrases by you?'

'Sure.'

Nightingale picked up his pen and ran through the queries he had in his notebook. Jenny answered quickly and authoritatively and he realised she was pretty much fluent in the language.

'What's this about?' she asked when they'd finished.

'It's a spell,' he said. 'An incantation.'

'Are you serious?'

'Yeah, some defrocked French priest wrote a book and I'm trying to get a handle on what it's about.'

'Why?'

'It's a long story. I'll explain later. And thanks for your help. You're a lifesaver.' Nightingale smiled to himself. At least that much was true. 'Jenny?'

'Yes?'

He took a deep breath and let it out slowly, wondering

exactly what he could and couldn't say to her. 'I don't appreciate you enough.'

'I've been saying that for years,' she said.

'I mean I don't tell you how much I appreciate you. I'd be lost without you.'

'Why, thank you, Jack. That's good to hear. Are you sure you don't want to come down? Mum and Dad have a lovely group of people here and we're shooting tomorrow.'

'Shooting?'

'Pheasant.'

'I hate loud noises, you know that.'

She laughed. 'I'm serious. I don't like you being on your own, not at the moment anyway.'

'I'll be fine,' he said.

'Well, I'll see you on Monday.'

'You can count on it.' He looked down at his notepad. 'Jenny . . .?'

'Yes?'

'Take care.' He ended the call. There was so much more that he wanted to say to her, but he knew he had to finish it there. He'd never talk to her again but at least his last words to her showed how much he cared.

64

Nightingale spent Saturday night sleeping fitfully on one of the sofas in the basement surrounded by flickering candles. He woke at dawn and showered in one of the upstairs bedrooms before getting to work. The list of what he needed ran to some two dozen items and he found most of what he needed in the cupboards and display cabinets in the basement. There were bottles of herbs and potions, animal parts stored in earthenware jars and glass bottles, and candles of every size and colour. He worked methodically from one end of the basement to the other, stopping only to snack on the remaining sandwiches he'd bought at the service station the previous day, washed down with a can of warm Coke.

When he'd finished he was still missing a number of items so he drove to Woking shopping centre, close to Junction 11 on the M25. He got there just after midday and spent an hour shopping, visiting Debenhams, Boots, a Robert Dyas hardware store, and several clothing stores.

The moment he walked out of the centre with his purchases, he stopped to light a cigarette. As he put the lighter away he heard a soft growling sound to his left and he flinched.

'Easy, boy,' said Proserpine. She was sitting cross-legged

with her back to the wall. Her dog sat next to her, panting, with its long tongue lolling from the side of its mouth. In front of her was a piece of cardboard on which was written in felt tip – 'NEED MONEY FOR FOOD'. Below the word 'FOOD' was a carelessly drawn smiley face.

'Hey, Proserpine,' he said.

She grinned up at him. 'You know smoking's bad for you?'

'The jury's still out on that,' he said. He took a long pull on his cigarette.

'You don't worry about cancer?'

Nightingale blew smoke up at the clouds. 'Sure. More than I worry about global warming but less than I worry about losing my hair.'

'Your hair?'

'I'd hate to go bald.' He wrinkled his nose. 'I know, vanity. What can I say?'

'Cancer's not funny,' she said.

'It can be.'

'Seriously?'

Nightingale smiled. 'A guy goes to see his doctor. The doctor says I've got some good news and some bad news. The guy asks for the bad news. The doctor tells him he's got lung cancer and just three months to live. The guy asks for the good news. The doctor tells him that he's sleeping with the hot receptionist outside.' Nightingale shrugged. 'Maybe you're right.'

'What's in the bags?'

'A few things I'm going to need later.'

'I know what you're planning to do, Nightingale.'

'Well, aren't you the smarty pants?'

The dog growled menacingly and Proserpine stroked

its head. 'It's okay, baby, it's just his way,' she whispered and the dog twisted around and licked her cheek.

'Can I ask you a question?' asked Nightingale.

'Sure, but not maths. I was never good at maths.'

'It's not maths,' said Nightingale. 'It's about the way you keep popping up. If I want to see you I have to go through a whole song and dance. A clean room, a pentangle, incantations, herbs, candles.'

'You set the scene, yes.'

'I summon you. And when I summon you you're stuck between the star and the circle until I'm finished.'

'What's your point, Nightingale?'

'My point is that when I want to see you, I have to do a whole dog and pony show. But you, you just appear.'

'There are times when I want to talk to you. Like now.'

'That's what I don't get. You're a demon from Hell. You sit at the side of Satan. Why do you keep bothering me?'

'I need to talk to you. And I'd rather do that face to face. Texting is so impersonal, don't you think?'

'You have a mobile?'

She smiled. 'I was being sarcastic.'

'You could do that astral plane thing, where you speak to me in my dreams.'

'But then you'd never be sure if it was really me, would you?' She nodded at his cigarette. 'Got a spare one of those?'

Nightingale took out his pack of Marlboro, flicked it open and held it out to her. As she reached for it he pulled it back, a reflex action. When he was standing in a pentagram he had to avoid touching her because that would break the protective circle. She smiled at his discomfort and he held out the pack again. There was no protective circle so touching her would make no difference. She slid out a cigarette and put it between her lips. Nightingale took out his lighter but before he could offer it to her she shook her head and the end of the cigarette burst into flame. She took a long drag on it and then blew smoke towards him. 'It's quite a clever idea, what you're planning.'

He smiled. 'I'll take that as a compliment.'

'And you think it'll work?'

'I'm going to give it a go.'

She blew smoke up at the sky. 'You could just do a deal with me.'

'My soul?'

She looked at him with her cold, black eyes. 'What else? The car you drive is a pile of shit and that's pretty much the only physical asset you have. Of course your soul.'

'And then what?'

'Then everything will be all right.'

'Except you'll have my soul.' His flicked away what was left of his cigarette and it spun through the air in a shower of sparks.

Proserpine smiled. 'It's either that or everyone close to you dies.' She ran her hand down the dog's flank and it quivered with pleasure. 'It's your call.'

'Are you behind this?'

'Behind what?' she asked, her face a picture of innocence.

'Everything that's being happening to me.'

'You already asked me that, Nightingale. Remember?' She blew smoke at him and for a brief moment it formed a snake that reared back as if about to strike him, then just as quickly it dispersed in the wind. She laughed. 'Scaredy cat,' she said contemptuously.

Nightingale shrugged. 'Maybe you were lying.'

'Why would I lie?'

Nightingale didn't reply.

'I'm serious, Nightingale. Why would I bother lying to you?'

'Because you want my soul. You want me to do a deal.'

She tickled the dog behind the ear with her left hand and it panted happily. 'I'm not the one you need to worry about.'

'Who then?'

'You make enemies easily, Nightingale. You seem to attract them. Like flies to shit.'

'Lucifuge Rofocale?'

She smiled up at him. 'I couldn't possibly comment,' she said.

'What I'm planning, will it work?'

Proserpine laughed softly. 'Wouldn't you like to know?' She stubbed out the cigarette on the cardboard sign and flicked it into the gutter.

'That's why I'm asking. Can I fix this or am I wasting my time?'

'Are you asking me if there is such a thing as free will?'

'I guess so.'

'Then of course there is. Every day you get to make choices. You chose to stop and talk with me. You could just have easily walked by and said nothing, right?'

Nightingale fished out his cigarettes again. 'Again?' she said. 'You've only just put one out.'

'I like to smoke,' said Nightingale. But he put the packet away.

'How many do you get through in a day?'

'A couple of packs. It depends.'

'You see, your smoking is a choice, too,' said Proserpine.

'My nicotine addiction begs to differ,' said Nightingale.

'So what are you asking? If there is anything you can do to change things? Can you make a difference?'

'I thought I had changed things,' said Nightingale. 'But then Robbie died. And my aunt and uncle died. So maybe nothing I do makes any difference.' He looked up at the clouds above and sighed. 'You told me once that you saw time differently to me.'

'I see everything differently,' she said.

'You come and you go,' he said. 'Time moves on for me but for you . . .' He rubbed the back of his neck. 'I didn't really understand what you were saying.'

'I didn't expect you to,' she said. She smiled sweetly up at him. 'Trying to explain the universe to you would be like discussing nuclear physics with an earthworm.'

'Thanks,' he said.

'You're welcome.'

'What I do remember is that you said you were sometimes here and sometimes you weren't. You moved in and out of this reality.'

'What passes for your reality,' she said. 'Yes, that's pretty much true.'

'And you said that for you, time doesn't really pass. You don't see time in terms of seconds and minutes and hours.'

She grinned. 'See, you were listening.'

'So if that's true, is everything fixed? If the past, present and future are all there for you to see, is there nothing I can do to change it?'

'Now, Nightingale, if you knew the answer to that, wouldn't it take the fun out of life?'

'I don't understand why you won't answer the question.'

'Because it's not a question that can be answered. It's like me asking you what the colour blue sounds like.'

'You're being evasive, and I don't understand why.'

Her eyes narrowed. 'Let's say I told you that what you were planning is doomed to failure. What would you do?'

'Are you saying it won't work?'

'I'm speaking hypothetically.'

Nightingale nodded thoughtfully. 'I'd still have to try.'

'Because you don't believe me?'

'Because I have to do something.'

'Which demonstrates free will. Even if you knew you were wasting your time, you'd still do it.'

Nightingale shook his head. 'Maybe I'll do it because that's what I'm meant to do.'

Proserpine smiled slyly. 'Then don't do it.'

Nightingale pointed his finger at her. 'Is that why you're here? To stop me doing it?'

'It's your call, Nightingale. Your decision.'

'Do you know what I'm going to do? Do you really? Or are you just messing with my mind?'

'Now that would be telling.'

'And you know whether it'll work or not?'

She smiled but didn't say anything.

Nightingale exhaled through pursed lips. 'My head hurts.'

Proserpine lowered her voice to a soft whisper. 'I know how you could prove that you have free will.'

'How?'

She pointed behind him at a six-storey building. 'There's a metal fire escape running up the back of that building,' she said. 'It'll take you up to the roof.'

Nightingale frowned. 'And?'

'And you could go up there and jump off. Free will. That would prove once and for all that you had it.'

Nightingale chuckled. 'That's like the old witch ducking. Duck a suspected witch and if she drowns she isn't a witch, if she doesn't drown then she is.'

Proserpine grinned. 'They were fun days, that's for sure,' she said.

'There is no way I can prove it one way or another, is there?'

'I'm not sure why it matters so much. Does a battery chicken have free will? Its future is pretty much pre-ordained from the moment it hatches.'

'That's how you see us? Battery chickens?'

Proserpine laughed and the pavement vibrated beneath Nightingale's feet. He moved his left foot back to steady himself but the shaking stopped as abruptly as it had started. 'Don't overthink it, Nightingale,' she said. 'But I'll tell you something, for old time's sake.' She paused to make sure she had his full attention. 'If you do go ahead, don't forget the meat.'

'The meat?'

'The meat,' she repeated.

Nightingale jumped at the sound of smashing glass and a car alarm bursting into life. He turned just in time to see a man in a hoodie running away from a BMW, clutching something to his chest. The BMW's lights were flashing as the alarm continued to blare. The sound of the man's trainers slapping against the Tarmac faded into the distance. When Nightingale turned back, Proserpine and the dog had gone but the cardboard sign was rustling in the wind. Nightingale bent down to pick it up. As his fingers touched the cardboard it burst into flames and Nightingale pulled his hand back. He smiled as he straightened up. 'I've seen David Blaine do that trick, it's no biggie,' he muttered, before heading towards his car with his carrier bags.

65

Nightingale needed petrol. A lot of petrol. He went to four different filling stations, each of them at least twenty miles away from Gosling Manor. At each filling station he parked his MGB away from the CCTV cameras and kept his head down as he filled a red plastic can with fuel. Each can held five litres and each time he paid in cash.

When he got back to Gosling Manor he carried the cans inside, two at a time, then took in the carrier bags. He had already decided that the best place to do it would be the massive sitting room where Eddie Morris had found the letter on the mantelpiece. He left the cans in the hallway and took the carrier bags into the living room, then went downstairs and fetched his notepad and the original book.

He had already found a large green plastic water barrel in a greenhouse at the back of the mansion and had hosed it clean before setting it up in the middle of the sitting room. The book called for a barrel but didn't specify what it should be made of. Nightingale stood and looked around as he held his notepad, checking that he had everything he needed.

He realised the bolt-cutters he'd used to cut the chain

at the main gate were back in the MGB and he went out to get them. Without the bolt-cutters there'd be no meat. And he needed the meat.

He brought up two dozen candles from the basement. Six orange, six red, six yellow and six blue. The book was very specific about where the candles had to be placed. He positioned then carefully, lit them and drew the curtains. It was time.

66

The first thing Nightingale had to do was to draw a magic circle around the plastic barrel. It was very different from the one he used when he summoned Proserpine. This was composed of three equilateral triangles one on top of each other so they formed a nine-pointed star. It had to be drawn with yellow chalk and then Nightingale had to use a silver needle to pierce his thumb and drip blood on to all nine of the points.

In between the nine points there were nine individual marks, like runes, and he carefully copied each one from the diagram in the book. They were complex and it took him the best part of an hour to complete.

Nine brass bowls had to be placed around the barrel, each containing a specific amount of a specific mineral. There was common salt, potassium chloride, calcium carbonate, sodium hydroxide, ammonium nitrate, and other compounds, all of which had been down in the basement. Nightingale had used an electric scale to weigh out the chemicals and carried them carefully up to the sitting room.

Once the bowls were in place he went through to the kitchen where he already had two three-litre water jugs ready. He filled them from the tap, took them back into the sitting room and poured them into the barrel. He had to make twenty-five trips before the barrel was full.

Nightingale slipped off his Hush Puppies and socks, then took off his jeans and shirt and put them in a neat pile by the door. He stripped off his boxer shorts and walked back naked into the middle of the room with the book.

They say you can't put a value on a human life, but the human body is a different matter. The elements that make up the average eighty-kilogram body cost about a hundred pounds, give or take. Most of that value comes from two elements – potassium and sodium – but together they make up less than half of one per cent of the total mass of a body. Some three-quarters of the human body is made up of oxygen and hydrogen, combined together to make water. And another eighteen kilograms of the average body comes from nitrogen. Take away the water and nitrogen and you're left with a small pile of chemicals that wouldn't fill a bucket, mainly carbon, calcium and phosphorus.

The smartest scientist on the planet couldn't combine the elements to make life – but according to the book, a magician could. The elements themselves were easy enough to come by, and the book contained the incantation that would make the magic happen.

Nightingale began to repeat the words in the book, and one by one he tipped the contents of the bowls into the water. As he continued to read, the horror of what he had to do gradually hit home. Proserpine had been right, of course. Chemicals and magic alone wouldn't produce the desired result. To do what had to be done, he would need meat.

67

Nightingale poured the contents of the last of the nine bowls into the barrel. He walked slowly over to the mantelpiece and put down the book, then picked up the bolt-cutters. He clicked them open and shut. He had already decided what part of his body to use. The middle toe on his left foot. He had decided that it was the part of his body that he could most do without.

He unscrewed the top off a bottle of whisky and took a mouthful. He swallowed and felt the warmth spread across his chest before he took a second mouthful. He put the bottle on the floor and slid the shears of the bolt-cutter either side of the toe. He took a deep breath. He knew he had to do it once and do it with conviction. It would hurt but the pain wouldn't last forever. He took a deep breath. He looked down at his foot, then turned his head away and closed his eyes. Better not to look. He took another deep breath. He wanted another slug of whisky but he knew it was his subconscious playing for time. He had to do it, and do it now. His hands were trembling on the handles of the bolt-cutters and he steeled himself. He roared and at the same time he slammed the handles of the bolt-cutters together. The shears sliced through skin and flesh and bone and then clicked together and pain lanced up from his foot to his hip. His roar of defiance merged into a scream of pain as he dropped the shears. He fell back and sat down heavily, blood pouring from the stump of his middle toe. He grabbed for the whisky bottle and gulped some down, then groped into the Boots carrier bag and pulled out a bottle of TCP. He poured a good measure of the antiseptic over his injured foot and screamed again, then took another mouthful of whisky.

He fell back and lay on the bare floorboards, gasping for breath, his foot throbbing as if it was about to explode. He groped for the Boots bag and pulled out a bandage and a dressing. He sat up, unwrapped the dressing and pressed it gingerly over the end of his foot before wrapping the bandage around it. He tied off the bandage and forced himself to his feet, taking all his weight on his right leg. He picked up the notebook but almost passed out and had to take several deep breaths to clear his head. His foot was throbbing now, but the pain was bearable.

He bent down and picked up the severed toe and then hopped awkwardly back to his position near the barrel. He had two more paragraphs to read in Latin. He cleared his throat and said the words, enunciating them slowly and clearly. As he got to the end of the final passage, he tossed the toe into the barrel. The contents began to steam and bubble and a foul ammonia-like stench filled the air. Plumes of greenish smoke curled up out of the barrel and wound their way up to the ceiling. Lightning flashed inside the room and Nightingale tasted something metallic at the back of his throat.

He felt a wind tugging at his hair, as if the barrel had become a vacuum and was sucking the air in the room towards it. The bubbling intensified and then something emerged from the steaming liquid. Something brown. Hair. As Nightingale's eyes widened a neck emerged, and then shoulders.

Nightingale reached into the Robert Dyas carrier bag, took out the hammer it contained, and hefted it in his hand.

The creature continued to emerge. Its back was to Nightingale, the spine clearly defined and glistening in the candlelight.

Nightingale took a step forward. It was nothing, he kept telling himself. It was his creation. He'd made it. From chemicals. It was alive but it wasn't really alive.

The creature was upright now, holding its arms above its head as it stretched as if it had just woken up. There was a small mole on the left shoulder, a perfect match for one that Nightingale had. It was an irregular shape – like a miniature Cyprus – and five years earlier Nightingale had gone to see his GP for reassurance that it wasn't skin cancer. The GP had told him not to worry about it and was far more concerned about Nightingale's smoking habit.

Nightingale stepped forward again, raising the hammer. The creature made a moaning sound as if unsure how to speak. It made it easier to think of it as 'the creature', Nightingale realised. And it was easier not to have to look it in the eyes.

He took another step forward. The creature began to turn as if it had heard Nightingale's feet on the floorboards. Nightingale brought the hammer crashing down on the creature's head with a sickening crunch. It fell forward and the barrel went with it, water cascading over the floor. Nightingale hopped forward, bent down and lashed out with the hammer again. The skull splintered and blood splashed across the wet floor. The creature shuddered, then went still.

Nightingale pulled the barrel away from the body and rolled it into the corner of the room. There was a large towel in a Debenhams carrier bag and he used it to pat the body dry. Then he dressed it in the clothes he'd been wearing. He had to keep rolling the body over to pull the boxer shorts up, and had to do the same again with the jeans. The socks were easier but the polo shirt was even harder. He tried not to look at the face but he kept finding himself staring into the dead eyes of his doppelganger. The last thing he put on were the Hush Puppies he'd recently bought, taking care to make sure the laces were tied correctly. Nightingale's wallet and keys were in the jeans. He took off his watch and put it on the corpse's left wrist before taking the brand new clothes he'd bought at the shopping centre. He put on new Levi's, a black pullover and Nike trainers.

Finally he switched on his mobile phone and placed it on the mantelpiece. Within seconds it would log on to the nearest antenna providing yet more proof that Nightingale was in the house. He took a look at his left wrist and then smiled ruefully as he realised he wasn't wearing a watch. It didn't matter. Whatever the time was, it was time to go.

68

Nightingale opened the boot of the MGB, took two of the cans of petrol out and carried them down into the basement. He switched on his torch and one by one blew out the black candles. When the last one had been extinguished he slopped petrol over the CCTV consoles, then walked over to the stairs, sloshing petrol left and right. He walked up the stairs backwards, spilling the last of the fuel on the staircase, then propped open the secret panel with one of the cans.

He took the cardboard box of books outside and placed them on the steps, then retrieved the remaining two cans of petrol from the car and went back into the house. He emptied one of the cans around the body in the sitting room, then sloshed the contents of the final can around the hallway. The air was thick with fumes and he felt light-headed. He stood at the door and took a box of matches from his pocket. He stepped out, took a final look inside, then lit a match and tossed it into the hallway. The petrol ignited with a loud whoosh as Nightingale picked up the box of books and walked away.

He took a last regretful look at the MGB parked by the mermaid fountain. He was going to miss the car but it had to stay at the house as yet another indication that it was Jack Nightingale's corpse inside.

He limped away, holding the cardboard box of books to his chest. Behind him windows shattered in the heat and he heard the crackling of wood burning. The flames cast shadows in front of him that writhed like living things. He didn't look back. It took him almost five minutes to reach the main gate by which time the house was fully ablaze.

There was a black stretch Mercedes limousine parked at the side of the road with its lights off. Nightingale pulled open the rear door and cigar smoke billowed out. 'How did it go?' drawled Wainwright from inside.

'As well as can be expected,' said Nightingale. He climbed into the back, handed the box to the American, and pulled the door shut.

The chauffeur, a red-haired woman in a grey suit, started the engine.

Wainwright flicked through the books as the car pulled away from the kerb. 'You've done me proud, Jack,' he said.

'I've put the Boullan book in there too.'

The American grinned. 'Cool. You never know when a doppelganger might come in useful.'

Nightingale twisted around for one last look at Gosling Manor, now a ball of orange and red from which curled a huge plume of thick black smoke.

'Best you don't look back, Jack,' said Wainwright. 'From this moment on, Jack Nightingale ceases to exist.'

Nightingale turned around. Wainwright was right. Jack Nightingale was dead. For ever. There was no point in looking back. Though he wasn't quite sure what he had to look forward to.

69

Superintendent Chalmers slotted a piece of chewing gum into his mouth and studied the burned corpse laid out on the stainless-steel table. 'So what do you think?' he asked the coroner.

Leslie MacDiarmid shrugged. 'Definitely dead,' she growled.

Chalmers sighed. 'What I need to know,' said Chalmers patiently, 'is if this is the body of Jack Nightingale?'

MacDiarmid flicked a sheet of paper over and stared at the sheet under it. 'No question,' she said. 'We fast-tracked the DNA analysis and compared it with the sample you gave us. There's no doubt.'

'And cause of death?'

MacDiarmid wrinkled her nose. 'The fire was the actual cause. There was smoke and fire damage to his lungs so he was alive when the fire started. But he was in no state to get out. Someone had clubbed him over the back of the head with the proverbial blunt instrument.'

'Any thoughts as to what that might have been?' asked Chalmers.

'A hammer, possibly. Something circular and metallic, anyway. Three distinctive blows. Two at the back of the head and one more on the top.'

'So someone hit him twice and then again on the top of his head as he went down?'

'I would say so, yes,' said MacDiarmid.

'And the fire? The body was found in a burned building and the arson investigator thinks that the fire started in the room where the body was found.'

'And they found the accelerator, of course?'

'Petrol, they said.'

MacDiarmid nodded. 'It was poured over him, no question. Someone wanted to make sure he burned. I'm guessing that they didn't want anyone to know who he was.'

'But there's no doubt?'

'There's no mistake with DNA,' said MacDiarmid. 'Back in the day when we needed fingerprints and dental records then a good fire might well make identification impossible, but these days you'd have to reduce a body to ash and a petrol-based fire isn't going to do that. You'd need a crematorium furnace for that.' She looked over at him and raised her eyebrows. 'Was he one of yours?'

'Used to be,' said Chalmers. 'He left the force a few years ago. He's a private detective now.' He forced a smile and corrected himself. 'Was a private detective.'

'I'm sorry,' said MacDiarmid. 'Do you have any suspects?'

Chalmers shook his head. 'Place was burnt to the ground so there's not much evidence to go on. But we're working through his client list.'

The doors to the post-mortem room opened and a young man in a blue suit mimed holding a phone to his ear. 'Call for you, Leslie,' he said.

MacDiarmid patted Chalmers on the shoulder. 'I have to take this, it's about a suicide we had last night.'

As she left, Chalmers stared down at the burned corpse chewing thoughtfully. Eventually he sighed and shook his head, almost sadly. 'Well, Jack, I always said you'd burn in Hell. Looks like I wasn't far off the mark.' He took out his mobile phone and called his number two, an inspector who had being assigned to his unit just three weeks earlier. The inspector answered quickly, he was still at the eager-to-please stage. 'Simon, we've got a murder. That corpse in Gosling Manor was Nightingale and his head had been bashed in before the place was torched. Get me a room sorted and arrange HOLMES support.' Chalmers was fairly sure the Met's computerised investigation program had been called the Home Office Large Major Enquiry System for no other reason that it would have echoes of the legendary fictional detective, but there was no doubt that it had simplified the gathering of intelligence. 'And get on to his secretary, a girl called Jenny McLean. We need his full client list, going back a year. And arrange for her to come in for an interview later this afternoon.'

Chalmers ended the call, put away his phone and walked out of the room. The door to MacDiarmid's office was open and as he walked by he saw the coroner put down her phone. 'Are you off, Superintendent?' she called.

Chalmers nodded. 'I've got a murder enquiry to kick into gear,' he said.

'Good luck with that,' she said.

'No witnesses, no CCTV footage, and if I know Jack Nightingale we'll find dozens of possible motives, so I'm going to need some luck, that's for sure.'

'Well, at least you knew who the corpse was,' she said. 'If you hadn't given me that DNA sample to cross check with, we'd never have identified him. His DNA wasn't on any of the databases.'

'You'd have got a match through his dental records eventually,' said the superintendent.

The coroner shook her head. 'We'd have been waiting forever for that,' she said.

Chalmers frowned. 'What do you mean?'

'By the look of it Mr Nightingale never went near a dentist his whole life. Perfect teeth. Not a single filling.'

70

Jenny McLean stood at the graveside, tears running down her face as she listened to the vicar say whatever it was that vicars said as coffins were lowered into the ground. Ashes to ashes, dust to dust, maybe. Jenny's parents stood either side of her staring sombre-faced at the grave. Jenny was holding a red rose, Nightingale realised. There were two dozen or so people gathered in the churchyard. Superintendent Chalmers was there, and so was Colin Duggan. There were another half-dozen policemen, all guys that Nightingale had worked with, back in the day. Eddie Morris was standing some distance away from the grave, clearly keeping well away from the cops who were there.

Nightingale couldn't help but notice that there were far fewer people than there had been at Marcus Fairchild's funeral. He was sitting in the back of the black stretch Mercedes with Joshua Wainwright. The American was smoking one of his huge cigars. He nodded with his chin at Jenny who was dabbing at her eyes with a handkerchief. 'Who's the blonde?'

'My assistant, Jenny McLean.' .

'I'm guessing the relationship was more than professional, judging by the tears.'

'Not in this life,' said Nightingale. 'I just wish there was some way that I could . . .'

Wainwright silenced Nightingale by pointing a finger at his face. 'Don't even think it,' he said. 'The moment, the instant, the Order of Nine Angles even suspects that you're not dead then the killing will start again. Everyone you know, everyone you care about, will die. But more than that, Jack. If they think that Jenny or any of your friends knows where you are they'll torture them for whatever information they have. You have to stay dead. For ever.'

Nightingale nodded. 'I know.'

'For ever, Jack,' said Wainwright, punctuating his words with jabs of his cigar. 'There's no statute of limitations on this. No happy ending. No reunions. No postcards from somewhere sunny. You're dead to them all.'

'I get it, Joshua.'

Wainwright nodded. 'I hope so because I'm one of your friends and I do not want the Order on my back. I can afford the best protection there is but even that . . .' He left the sentence unfinished and looked at his watch. 'Wheels up in thirty minutes,' he said. 'We need to go.'

Nightingale took a deep breath and took a last look at Jenny. As he watched, she tossed the red rose into the grave and turned to bury her face in her father's chest. 'Okay,' he said. He looked across at Wainwright. 'Where are we going, exactly?'

'Does it matter?' asked the American.

'I guess not,' said Nightingale.

In the best books, the ending often comes as a shock.
Not just because of that one last twist in the tale,
but because you have been so absorbed in their world,
that coming back to the harsh light of reality is a jolt.

If that describes you now, then perhaps you should track down
some new leads, and find new suspense in other worlds.

Join us at www.hodder.co.uk, or follow us on
Twitter @hodderbooks, and you can tap in to a
community of fellow thrill-seekers.

Whether you want to find out more about this book,
or a particular author, watch trailers and interviews, have
the chance to win early limited editions, or simply browse
our expert readers' selection of the very best books,
we think you'll find what you're looking for.

And if you don't, that's the place to tell us what's missing.

We love what we do, and we'd love you to be part of it.

www.hodder.co.uk

 @hodderbooks

HodderBooks

HodderBooks